XAVIER'S LEGACY

A TALE OF BOATS, GIRLS, GREED AND EXTREME PERVERSION

BOOK 5 IN THE FIREBIRD SERIES

IAN DOLBY

DISCLAIMER:

This is a work of fiction. While names, characters, businesses, events and incidents are the products of the author's warped imagination, places and locales are as correct as possible, but are used in an entirely fictitious manner. Some characters are a composite of several personalities the author has encountered in his travels across Australia as such richness of true-life character could not be ignored. However, any resemblance to actual persons, living or dead, or actual events is unintended, accidental and purely coincidental.

The opinions expressed by the various characters in this story are deemed appropriate for their role and should not be assumed to be those of the author. I ride bikes and embrace the right to freedom of the open road on two wheels for everybody.

Published in Australia by Silverbird Publishing

First published in Australia 2021

Copyright © Ian Dolby 2021

Cover design, typesetting: WorkingType (www.workingtype.com.au)

The right of Ian Dolby to be identified as the Author of the Work has been asserted in accordance with the Copyright, Designs and Patents Act 1988.

Dolby, Ian

Xavier's Legacy — Book 5 of the Firebird Series

ISBN: 978-0-6487179-2-8.

pp390

ABOUT THE AUTHOR

I was born and raised on the Gold Coast, Queensland where my extended family always had boats. My love of sailing came from this background and developed through a series of racing catamarans that in turn led to the purchase of an old 47-foot wooden, engine-less, monohull yacht that had been built in Ireland in 1905 and had taken part in the Dunkirk evacuation. I lived on this boat at a marina in Rushcutters Bay, Sydney Harbour for several years and my engine-free adventures on this wonderful old boat may one day appear in writing.

The love of flying dragged me away from the boating scene, and after 38 years of glider, aeroplane and helicopter flying, I have retired to live in country New South Wales with my partner, who is my Chief Editor, and our two cats. While my writing has evolved from a part-time hobby to become a full-time occupation, it is no less enjoyable while the story lines keep coming to mind.

*Thank you Jenny, for the brainstorming sessions
when the plot grew foggy*

*Thank you Wayne and Lyn for
your invaluable input as beta readers*

*Welcome to the Krazy kitten,
whose carefree antics are a joy to behold*

And always The Bandit...never forgotten.

CONTENTS

CHAPTER 1

I'm Harry Stevens, an Australian ex-SAS Major, and together with my lovely lady, Sandy Thomson, who is a Queensland Police Inspector, my two cats Jasper and Krazy and our two cheerful and competent crew members, Alex and Bree, we were happily leaving Indonesian territorial waters heading for Darwin, Australia.

An additional temporary crew member was a very attractive lady by the name of Dell Petrie, who was a reformed bad guy officially being held by me and Sandy in Protective Custody. She had provided a lot of information about the shadowy figures behind the recent operations in Western Australia and Indonesia, which were intended to overthrow the entire system of democratic Australian Government, as well as assassinate the Prime Minister.

In reality, Dell was more than happy to stay aboard *Firebird*, since she knew that back in Australia, some very nasty and vindictive individuals were anxious to get their grubby little paws on her for being a whistle-blower. Her ex-employers were the crooked administrators of the United Trade Union Superannuation Funds, and they had placed her as the personal assistant to another particularly bad guy, Terry Xavier Johnson. Mr Johnson, who preferred to be called Mr Xavier, formerly ran the dodgy and unprincipled organisation, Stainless Associates, and was now very deceased, courtesy of a quartet of hungry Komodo dragons.

I was happy to have the extra crew and now the spectre of Xavier's presence had been terminally removed, Dell was bright and cheerful, in addition to being very pleasant to look at.

A welcome easterly breeze hastened our departure from the

picturesque waters and islands of the Indonesian Archipelago, where we'd spent the past few weeks having more adventures than we neither needed nor wanted. However, because we seem to be a permanent trouble magnet, that's what happens. We had come to Indonesia with two tasks to complete; the first of which was pure payback to eliminate a pair of serious bad guys, Terry Williams and his partner Paula Henderson, a monstrously evil bitch. They were responsible for setting up a home-grown eco-terrorist mob who tried to destroy the Australian oil and gas industry as part of the grand plan to overturn the Australian Government.

Our second task in Indonesia was to assist our friends, Dr Roger Jacobs and RN Jill Zellman, find an island in the western part of the Indonesian Archipelago. They'd been on a sailing holiday and heard about the place from a woman they'd rescued from a native canoe when she was near death from dehydration. While coming out of her delirium, she told a rambling tale of a bush which grew on an island and the green paste made from it by the islanders, that had almost magical healing properties, as well as being a very powerful aphrodisiac. They would have ignored her delirious tale, if it were not for the stash of small, green cosmetic jars the girl, Anna, had in a small backpack.

As a trial, Jill had applied some of the green goo to an infected coral graze that refused to heal and both were stunned when, 24-hours later, not only was the infection gone, but the deep cuts had largely healed!

That demonstration had been more than sufficient to get Dr Roger's medical instincts on full alert, but they were unable to afford a proper search for the island. Therefore, to raise funds, he and Jill had joined the fledgling EarthCare organisation as their 24/7 medical team since the job paid an outrageous salary.

This was the island we'd searched for and finally found, but not without numerous encounters with pirates.

It was with a distinct sense of relief, that we all relished the lively movement as our nautical home, my 60-foot sailing catamaran *Firebird*, responded in appropriate fashion to open waters at last, seeming to be happy to be carrying us back to familiar territory. Well, almost, but I'll get to that in due course!

Although the wind was hustling us along at a steady fifteen to sixteen knots, the long and sleek AB100 Italian super-cruiser *Seeker*, owned and crewed by my dear friends Corrine Johns and Dave Robson, was maintaining an effortless position 50-metres off our stern quarter, idling along on just one of its two massive diesels to conserve fuel. The third engine, a compact and light gas turbine jobbie which could churn out a huge 5,600 horsepower, was rarely used since it tended to be a bit thirsty compared to the superb V-16 MTU diesels.

The shedding of tension was almost palpable as the sea miles slid smoothly past. Although we'd succeeded admirably in our quest to lay our own particular form of justice on two of the lowest forms of life in the known world, it hadn't happened without leaving a few mental scars.

Despite knowing we were able to stop peering over our shoulders for once, we were unable to relax completely. The presence of the delectable Dell, was a continuing reminder of the festering legacy, left by the late and very unlamented Xavier Johnson, and continued to haunt us. Indications were that the final little sideline in Johnson's operations involved what might be a rare and precious gem smuggling pipeline, with Xavier's house on Lord Howe Island being one end of the pipe feeding into Australia.

Consequently, my employers, the Australian Commonwealth Police and several other semi-nameless agencies, had directed we take ourselves to, and spend our hard-earned work-break, on the lovely and intriguing Lord Howe Island. All expenses paid, of course! Not only is the island a piece of Australian territory, but is classed as part of the state of New South Wales with the postcode of 2898, and lies 600 kilometres east of the mainland town of Port Macquarie.

Although we normally travelled in company with *Seeker*, the plan we had worked out was we would part company with them once we reached international waters. The main reason was the presence of the Australian Prime Minister aboard *Seeker*. Also aboard was a genuine and very substantial pirate's treasure gained through just one of our recent adventures, where Corrine, our resident assassin and explosives expert, got to actually blow up an entire island!

Before we had left the sheltered waters of Timor, there had been some swapping of passengers between the two boats to suit destinations. We kept a minimum crew, five in total, for our travel to Lord Howe Island in comfort and with a degree of safety. The other item of equipment we grabbed off *Seeker*, was the very clever and capable UAV or Unmanned Aerial Vehicle, *Dragonfly*. It was a fully autonomous, hybrid, Vertical Take Off & Landing UAV, with 8-hour endurance, full-colour, electro-optical UHD camera with 25x zoom and auto-track functions, plus a full IR camera with real-time stabilised HD video links, two-way HD satellite feed and stealth characteristics. It could be launched and retrieved from either *Seeker or Firebird*. My lovely lady, Sandy, was the principal operator of the device and if you'd asked me why I wanted it included in our stock of handy surveillance tools, I probably couldn't have given a straight answer. Nevertheless, its small coffin-like travel case was carefully stowed right forward in the bow cabin, just ahead of our master cabin and lashed down tightly.

The plan was for *Seeker* to press on ahead at best speed to Darwin, where most of her passengers would leave to head south. Dave and Corrine would then refuel and head off, again at best speed, to her home port on the Gold Coast where the treasure would be assessed, valued and placed at auction. The planned carve-up of the proceeds with the crew, would ensure that everyone, regardless of whatever part they played in the operations against the pirates, would receive well over a million dollars each. It was something I considered to be a fair return for some of the very hazardous encounters we had endured during our time in the vast and beautiful Archipelago which comprises Indonesia.

As the principals in the operation, as well as funding the entire trip, Sandy, Corrine, Dave and myself, hung onto a bunch of other treasure, and were rewarded with many millions each, so we weren't exactly wondering when our next pay cheque was coming in!

When we officially crossed the line which marked Indonesia's extended territorial claim, *Seeker* let off a series of blasts on her huge triple brass airhorns before smoothly accelerating away; the bass thunder of her twin MTU V16 diesels echoing across the sparkling sea, until it slowly faded in the distance along with their foaming, white wake.

I think we all felt a slight sense of loss as *Seeker* disappeared over the horizon. Friendships formed after a period of such high stress and violence, are a lot different to those formed normally. They are far more intense and while it was a common enough sensation with military personnel in a war zone, it is only rarely experienced in normal civilian life.

Still, life goes on and both crews had jobs to do, although ours promised to be the more challenging and hazardous, which is why I was glad to have the very large and capable Alex Chetty in the crew for our trip to Lord Howe Island.

With George the autopilot doing the steering, we were having lunch seated around the cockpit table, while Sandy regaled us with facts and figures on Lord Howe Island.

'It says here there are less than 400 permanent residents on the Island, and the number of visitors is strictly controlled to a maximum of 400 at any given time.'

'Maybe that's why crime is virtually non-existent,' I commented, 'although I'm sure there's a copper on the Island.'

'Yeah, there is,' Sandy said absently, 'it's normally just a Senior Constable for a three-year term and the NSW boys consider it to be the best posting in the State.'

We had all the information about Xavier's connection with the island that Dell could provide, due to her visit to the island with him.

Interest in the quiet little backwater, nestled in the sunny South

Pacific Ocean, had been sparked by her report of strange things and happenings at Xavier's house on the island. Like the two heavies guarding the house; the mysterious locked room containing a big safe which Xavier wouldn't allow Dell to enter; fishermen banging on the back door in the middle of the night and half-overheard conversations about drop-offs and pick-ups.

Our cruising routine didn't change with the departure of *Seeker*; the sea was just emptier without the sleek, royal-blue presence idling off our port or starboard quarter all the time. The chart plotter informed me that at the current rate of progress, we would lob at the marina at Stokes Hill Wharf, Darwin harbour at 18:00 tomorrow, Tuesday. Being a bit too close to last light for comfortable mooring in a strange place, I decided to speed up a bit from tomorrow morning on, with the aim of arriving around 16:00 at the latest.

When consulted, the all-knowing chart plotter agreed an increase to 17 knots from 09:00 tomorrow would meet the objective.

Since there were five of us to stand night watches, we were able to mix and match personnel so we all got a decent amount of sleep. I paired with Dell at first to teach her as quickly as possible, and found she was a quick learner with a natural feel for boats.

My ulterior motive, apart from enjoying being with her and finding her attractive, was to gently pump her for more information about the men behind the abortive coup. They were the ones who originally employed her to spy on Xavier, so she naturally had been supplied with a lot of information about him and his dealings. But I soon found there wasn't much additional info she could add about either of them; Xavier or Lord Howe Island.

So I knocked off the official line of questioning and spent the rest of the watch finding out more about Dell, the person. I have never apologised to anyone for my strong interest in ladies because I had decided when I was medically and honourably discharged from the Defence Force, for injuries received on the job, that I wouldn't seek refuge from PTSD in a bottle like too many of my mates. Chasing pretty ladies seemed like a no-brainer alternative to alcohol and drugs and helped me keep my wits about me.

I was very fortunate in having Sandy as my permanent lady, and had discovered she was almost as much of a deviate as I was. Regardless, we got on very well and were very comfortable with each other. Even without being in the close quarters of a relatively small boat, Sandy knew I was interested in Dell and she shared that interest.

Our other two crew, Alex Chetty, a former South African mercenary and Brianna Welsh, had been enlisted in the military arm of the former EarthCare movement, but as that organisation began unravelling in a most violent fashion, they both elected to join our tiny squad of opposition and had both proved their capability and loyalty many times over.

It also wasn't all that long ago they both decided to share a bed, and that most unlikely relationship seemed to be working out very well for them both. In the past Alex had demonstrated a capacity for extraordinary violence and brutality, but to see him being so careful and gentle with Bree was a revelation. It was also slightly odd that the usual effect of lowered moral standards which being on a boat away from land has upon most persons, hadn't so far affected Alex or Bree.

To the best of my knowledge, Bree hadn't even taken her top off in front of any other crew, despite it being almost the standard dress code for the ladies in the tropics. They also refrained from participating in the semi-regular, alcohol-induced, skinny-dipping sessions which seem to develop with very little encouragement.

I was pleased to report that Dell had shown she was more than happy to join in with all such happenings!

TUESDAY

We were still chatting happily when the sun was compelled to heave its bulk above the horizon in the usual breathtakingly beautiful display of colour and majesty. That was close enough to the end of our watch and apparently was the time when my two cats, Jasper and Krazy, decided they needed to be fed immediately, despite the bowl of dry food always down for them to graze on.

Like Alex and Bree, the two cats were a study in contrast. Krazy was a pure black female DSH, with a liberal dose of silver flecks scattered throughout her coat and had decidedly short legs and tail. She had been presented to Jasper as a companion by two lovely ladies at the conclusion of our first adventure and she still looked like a kitten. Jasper, on the other hand, was supposed to be an F5 version of the crossing of an Indonesian jungle cat with a Chausie domestic cat. Something or someone got things terribly wrong, since Jasper looked nothing like a Chausie, and everything like a pure black jungle cat, to the extent where the locals on Herba Island surreptitiously set up small shrines to him and referred to him as a demi-god.

He'd been presented to me as a large, black kitten by a Korean cook on a cargo-ship. I'd been told at the time he was a very special cat who had certain special abilities, but thankfully, and despite his heritage and 25 kgs of long lean body, Jasper had retained all the quiet and affectionate characteristics of a normal domestic cat. Until such times as he perceived someone or something was threatening anybody under his protection. That's when affectionate pussy turned jungle wildcat!

With five or six kills and a number of severe mauling's of designated bad guys to his credit, he was a force multiplier I was very glad to have on my side. The intimidation factor of his glare and growl was often enough to subdue a bad guy from pushing the point.

At his other behaviour extreme, one persistent image was of Jasper on a beach near Lakes Entrance, Victoria, giving a small girl a ride on his back while her little brother hung onto his long, muscular tail and was dragged squealing with delight through the sand.

He had also proved many times since, he had other very special abilities; not the least of which was the ability to understand quite comprehensive instructions. His reply was usually a loud 'Huff' sound which indicated that he understood.

His other, rather mystical ability, was being able to communicate soundlessly at a higher level with almost any other creature. The growing list so far, had included seals, a giant crocodile and two Orcas. He had also demonstrated an ability to heal wounds with his saliva; something a medical crew was unable to explain. I only discovered that little trick after I'd been shot in the shoulder during an altercation with bad guys off the Western Australian coast. Jasper allowed a Navy medic to bind the wound, but then scared the hell out of everyone by clamping his jaws lightly over my shoulder and flooding the bandage with saliva. Within seconds, the pain had disappeared, and a degree of movement was restored, allowing me to welcome Corrine back to the 'mother' ship.

Now, however, he was just like his little companion cat, Krazy, both making a nuisance of themselves to ensure that pussy feeding was the highest priority. To keep the peace, I went and fed them, while Dell went below to wake Sandy for the first daylight watch.

With the beasts subdued, I put the kettle on for tea for three, but when the two girls were still a no-show when it was poured, I diplomatically took mine out to the cockpit, grinning to myself.

It actually wasn't very long before Dell appeared first, looking a bit ruffled up, then Sandy with a smirk on her face.

I couldn't pass up a bit of bum patting as they collected their steaming mugs and joined me in the cockpit. Dell seemed to be a bit flushed when they sat, but I refrained from comment. Instead, I mentioned I'd be starting the second engine shortly to make the extra speed we needed to get into Darwin by late afternoon in daylight.

The Stokes Hill Wharf precinct was utterly dominated by the gigantic white shape of the 137,000 tonnes, 311-metre-long, *Voyager of the Seas*, lying at the next wharf where we needed to enter the small harbour. *Firebird's* tall carbon mast, 22 metres above the water, looked like it barely reached the main deck level of this colossal boat, whose sharply-raked bow very nearly over hung the narrow entrance between the two wharves.

The remainder of the run through the day had been both uneventful and suitably relaxing. Our pre-arrival call to the Harbour Master had also alerted Customs, who were waiting for us when we tied up at Fisherman's Wharf to refuel.

The Indonesian certificates for the cats had proved to be a godsend with the Quarantine Officers, and it was accepted they hadn't been off the boat or mingling with other animals. I noticed the refueller checking his flowmeter several times as we filled all tanks to the brim, even though we hadn't used all that much on the run down.

We then re-located to Stokes Hill Wharf to pick up a mooring for the night. Once secured to our mooring, having safely slipped under the towering white cliff of *Voyager's* bow, everyone was keen to get ashore on Australian soil once more, so we crammed into the dinghy and hit the bar for a while, then lined up for a meal in the excellent restaurant.

There were a few other visiting yachties in the bar, including two couples in a 44-foot Antares catamaran. It was a happy evening and we all got a bit pissy since there was no need to stand night watch, although I gave Jasper full roaming rights for the night with instructions that anybody approaching wouldn't be a friend and to come and wake me. Otherwise, he was free to bite any strange body who made it aboard.

I had just completed my nightly harbour security check and on returning to our cabin, I found Dell there chatting with Sandy who was already sitting up in bed, the sheet lying across her lap and her top half very attractively bare. Dell was in her sleeping outfit; a men's size T-shirt with a large photo of a black kitten on the front, the image only a little bit distorted by her chest. The T-shirt and a pair of panties was all she had on and she was sitting with her back to the forward bulkhead, her knees up across Sandy's legs

In my mind, I flashed to similar scenes which had been repeated several times before this, although I didn't know if the pair of scheming little darlings had arranged something or if Dell was just having a friendly pre-bed chat.

Regardless of the display of female flesh in front of me, I was tired and needed a good sleep before we headed east in the morning, so I slipped out of my going-ashore clothes, hung them up neatly, then crawled up the bed to where I could slide under the sheet.

It's probably the only downside to having elevated queen beds on a cat; the crawl up from the foot to the head is less than elegant, although Sandy always seemed to get away with it. On this occasion, I felt the full force of Dell's attention, which produced the expected growth in my nether regions by the time I had regained the dubious safety of the sheet.

'Bloody hell, Harry!' Sandy remarked with a grin. 'Careful you don't kneel on that thing. It could be painful!'

Dell managed to suppress her giggles reasonably well. Sandy didn't even try, which set Dell off again until the pair were rolling round clutching at aching sides or each other and gasping for breath.

'Oh, c'mon you two. It wasn't that funny! Was it?' It must have been something I said, but they went into hysterics again and as so often happens, laughter turned to a high degree of lust and they cuddled for a while, trading the odd kiss or three. That, as to be expected, turned into a fairly heavy groping, fondling session which saw Dell divested of her T-shirt and panties. At that point, I gave up trying to read, turned my bedside light out and closed my eyes, attempting to ignore the variety of interesting and very stimulating sounds coming from the other side of the bed.

Sometime in the wee small hours, I woke and as usual, let my senses reach out for anything that sounded different, or smelled different or if there was any movement to the boat that could indicate a problem, but there was nothing out of line, so I concentrated my senses closer in to what had wakened me in the first place.

There was a definite feeling of deja vu, as I was lying on my left side, with a firm and bare female bum parked against my lower belly and its owner's head sharing my pillow. The mass of long, silky hair suggested it wasn't Sandy come to say, 'Hi!' In fact, by lifting my head slightly, I could see my lovely lady fast asleep over the far side of the bed, snoring softly.

Even though Dell wasn't snoring, she still played the part of being asleep, so I thought that if I did nothing, she would go back to sleep, but no matter how hard I tried to concentrate on other things, my almost non-existent erection had other thoughts. Within a minute, Dell was being poked in the back and as I had no room to retreat, parking it somewhere much more pleasant was the only other option.

With that achieved, Dell stirred with a satisfied sound and proceeded to make the most of it.

WEDNESDAY

Apart from the obvious ones, there were no more disturbances that night and I awoke in the pre-dawn stillness to take a quick look around. Careful not to disturb the sleeping ladies, I slowly stood up on the bed so my upper body protruded from the full-sized overhead hatch. Scanning around I saw the anchorage was quiet, with the giant steel, white whale called the *'Voyager of the Seas'* still tied up at the outer wharf.

As I was about to slide back down, I felt a small hand tugging on my dangling bits by way of suggestion, I guess. I'd hoped we could actually depart about now, but figured a delay of 30-minutes or so wouldn't hurt, and as expected, it certainly didn't hurt!

When I finally managed to make the bathroom, I washed quickly, then started the engines to let them warm up, before feeding the kitties and putting the kettle on. Alex was close behind me and together we checked the boat over, dropped the mooring line and we were officially separated from Darwin.

There was no breeze at all, so it was just motoring until we came abeam the Tiwi Islands, where we picked up a fitful northerly which at least filled the sails and increased boat speed enough to allow the shut-down of the engines. Bree, whose cooking talent just seemed to get better every day, whipped up a number of tasty snacks for brunch.

My two ladies were in no hurry to drag themselves out of bed, so when Bree asked where Dell was, I replied, 'Last time I was down there, she was chatting with Sandy, but she shouldn't be long.'

'No rush. It was just something I wanted to ask her, but it can wait until she comes back up. Not important by any means.'

I think it was hunger that finally drove the ladies up to be social again and I was glad to see they were looking rested, since we were in for a long trip. I had decided that a fuel conservation mode would apply for the rest of the voyage, the same as we had used coming over to the west several months ago as well as much of our movement around the Indonesian Archipelago.

This was based on a minimum speed of fourteen knots; a speed we could maintain in zero wind conditions by using both engines, but if some breeze was blowing, then we could shut down one or both engines. The 14-knot minimum made route and leg planning much simpler to the extent I calculated we could reach Yeppoon on the Queensland coast, before we needed to refuel. A skipper we talked to last night in the bar, gave the Keppel Bay Marina adjacent to the Rosslyn Bay Resort a big rap for having all facilities necessary for visiting yachties, as well as super-friendly staff.

So, as we settled into a routine, the crew had to adjust to the increased watch workload caused by having fewer warm bodies available.

The pussies probably suffered the most by not having shore-time to run around, particularly on beaches which they loved, so I promised them we'd break the journey several times for all of us to get ashore and enjoy a beach or three. The ever-present threat of crocodiles meant we had to be extra careful.

I knew we were into the start of the cyclone season, since we'd been experiencing monsoonal storms whilst in Indonesian waters, so it was with a sense of unease that I noted the first of a series of warnings from the Australian Bureau of Meteorology about a low pressure system expected to form just north-west of the Gulf of Carpentaria over the next six to eight hours. It was also expected to move westwards across the top of the Northern Territory as it deepened.

The breeze, while slow to kick in, started to come from the south-west which meant we were able to kill the engines and raise all sail, making a very good pace to the east.

Over a lovely morning tea of hot scones, jam and cream whipped up by Bree, I made the crew aware of the potential weather threat and laid out our options.

'We could turn around and head back to Darwin, but then we'd have to find ourselves a narrow creek which wasn't already full of boats also trying to find shelter. Sometimes it's more dangerous being in company of other boats since there's always some dickhead who forgets to tie something down properly.'

'That doesn't sound like much of an option Commander,' Alex

stated in his deep voice with the pleasing South African accent. 'May we presume you have a better alternative?'

Alex was a huge bear of a man, not given to say much, but with a fine mind and was an excellent sailor, but from the day he joined our band of merry trouble-magnets, he always addressed me as 'Commander' and Corrine as 'Major', the rank she had held in the now defunct EarthCare Army.

He patently adored Bree, who in turn was developing a new level of self-esteem as her confidence grew. Her share of prize-money from our various encounters with bad guys in Indonesia probably helped. Being a millionairess tends to do that!

I smiled reassuringly at Alex, 'Hopefully, yes. There's no real prediction at the moment where this low will move once it deepens, so although it's relatively stationery now, in that position they usually move west.'

'But is it wise to be heading toward it?' he asked with raised eyebrows.

I nodded, 'I understand your concern, but since it's only just starting to form, they usually don't become a nuisance for a couple of days. If this breeze holds, we could easily be past it before it even becomes a cyclone, especially if it does move west as expected. We'll sort of sail right past it on opposite courses.'

Our lovely new bed partner, Dell, weighed into the discussion with, 'OK. But what if it doesn't obligingly move and just sits there? We don't want to sail into it, do we? In which case, where do we go for safety now we're away from Darwin?'

'We simply go to ground,' I said, 'which means we find ourselves a narrow creek, with low trees either side we can tie all our mooring ropes onto and make like a spider in his web. Then we wait it out. There's no point in trying to stay at sea when there's a lot of good places to hole up close by. It'll be noisy for 24 hours, but with all the anchors, chain and heavy ropes we have, sheltering in a narrow creek without tall trees nearby, is recommended as an excellent option. As opposed to being in open water, that is.

The other good place is in shallow water, like on a sandbank, where the anchor chains are almost horizontal giving the anchors maximum grip and the waves are low in height.

She nodded thoughtfully, but seemed satisfied with the answer.

'So that's it, folks. We run east as fast as we can. That way, we either clear the storm, or if it looks like we won't, then we duck into the nearest creek system, make like a spider and break out the ear-plugs.'

The crew looked happy with the fact we had a plan and it was a simple one. As the girls cleared away the licked-clean evidence of morning tea, I said to Alex, 'If it looks like we are going to cop a hiding from this thing, I want to strip the sails off the forestay and the inner forestay to reduce windage. I've got a funny feeling about this low. It doesn't look like much so far, but something isn't right. Jasper feels it too; he hasn't settled down all morning.'

Right on cue, my beautiful black cat popped his head up to Alex for a reassuring scratch, a plaintive 'merowl' his only comment on the situation. As Alex obediently provided the scratch, he said, 'My mother taught me never to ignore those little warnings, Commander. It was her belief we all get them, but very few are still sensitive and sensible enough to act on them.'

I considered his words and hoped, for once, the voices had it wrong. A short time later, I walked for'rard with Alex and went over the procedure to safely remove the fore triangle sails in a hurry without wrecking the rigging.

Our progress east was pleasingly rapid and Dell experienced the delights of steering a big cat at high speed under strong wind conditions. That was a momentary diversion from the task of almost constantly monitoring of the development of the low, which oddly, didn't seem to be doing very much at all.

Unbeknown to us, the apparent inactivity was caused by an event which would have a profound effect on us and many other boating folks in Northern Territory waters. Above us in a geostationary high Earth orbit, a relatively new GOES-R high-definition weather satellite was quietly and reliably going about its business of looking at the surface of Earth and sending a stream of data back to be interpreted by the massive computers of the USA's NOAA.

The tiny chunk of metallic rock, smaller than a child's marble, had been travelling through space for millions, if not billions of years, and was on a path which would take it just past the pretty blue planet. It would have made its visit completely un-noticed by the inhabitants of the blue world below, except for the large, white, cylindrical object with arrays of solar panels splayed out like palm tree fronds which sat squarely on its curving path.

Had an observer been close and looking at the right spot on the curving, white hull, he or she would have seen a small black spot appear. Closer inspection would show that the black spot was a small hole about 10 millimetres in diameter, but this inspection would be rather pointless since the satellite had long since vomited its internals out either end of the body and the other side was left a twisted mess of composite fibres and metal. Only the side facing the impact strike was left intact and almost undamaged.

The demise of the GOES-R was signalled by a soft alarm and a sudden blank screen in a control room in the faraway US of A. It was still a significant time before the duty operator, a young man with hormones raging through his system, noticed the problem; he was desperately trying to impress the pretty female data analyst sufficiently so she'd go out with him.

So even when he did get to checking his flock of satellites, his only action was to turn the alarm off, before resuming his relentless attack on the girl's resistance. But to his dismay, she was more interested in the blank data screen than in copping another earful of bullshit from this nerd.

'How come there's no data at all coming back?' she asked. 'Even just the basic housekeeping data should be flowing. It's on a separate circuit to the camera and sensor data.'

The operator tried to divert her attention from the screen to himself, but he might as well have been trying to divert the flow of the mighty Murray River.

'Who are you going to call?' she asked. 'And if you say 'Ghost-busters' I'll hit you with that stupid keyboard you wear around your neck!'

Grumpily, he picked up the internal phone and savagely punched a number before delivering a report which would slowly filter up and down the chain of command and out to all users of the data.

In a separate report to users of its on-line services, the Australian Bureau of Meteorology stated there were an unusually large number of data errors in the information received from the constellation of dedicated world-wide weather satellites, which would delay some weather reporting and they hoped that full system accuracy would soon return to normal.

The significance of this was that the weather satellite concerned, was situated over northern Australia at the time. This wasn't appreciated by the BOM, except to note that its data stream had either cut off or wasn't being updated for some reason.

The end result of this series of cascading errors would be called 'Murphy's Day' in the BOM history from then on, particularly since it led me and many others, to conclude the low wasn't developing at all!.

An oil-rig supply boat, en-route from the Timor Sea to Cairns for an overhaul, radioed that they were experiencing Force 10 storm conditions with wind gusts hitting 70 knots, which is hurricane force. That first-hand report was carelessly mis-labelled as merely being an unusually violent monsoonal thunderstorm and disregarded as not significant in the wider picture.

For most land-based weather-watchers, the misinterpretation of the data was an inconvenience, but for us, it was a different story since we were blithely sailing straight at a very rapidly developing, violent cyclone, quite unaware until we got to within radar range!

CHAPTER 3

Strangely, weather conditions were beautiful as we rounded the tip of Croker Island and laid a straight course ESE for the famous 'Hole in the Wall' channel which separates Raragala and Guluwuru Islands, and in turn, forms part of the Cape Wessel chain of islands poking like a long, skinny finger towards West Papua.

We were having lunch and I was telling the crew about the 'Hole-in-the-Wall' and my plan to find a safe, sandy beach where we could give *Firebird* a quick bottom scrub.

'There's what looks like a lovely little bay just on the southern side of the west entrance to the channel and it should do for the scrub-up.'

'What about crocodiles, dear one?' asked Sandy. 'Aren't we still right in the middle of their territory?'

'Yep. We sure are, but there aren't any mangroves or other type of vegetation growing close to the water to provide nests, so I reckon we'll be safe if we keep a croc watch at all times. Other boats have reported safe swimming in the area, so I think we should be fine. We won't be there until late tonight, but the charts are good and the approaches straightforward, so if safe, we'll go straight into one of the little bays and anchor for the rest of the night. Dell and I will take the first night watch to cover the approach and I might even get my head down for a while this arvo for a bit of a rest.'

Alex spoke up, 'Bree and I will be happy to do the afternoon watch, Commander, so that should work out well.'

'Thanks Alex. Almost too easy, but keep a good lookout for any weather developing from the east. I'm still uneasy about that low and Jasper is even more unsettled than he was earlier.'

The big man nodded, 'I'll do that Commander, and perhaps we should set the radar out to maximum range and put it into weather mode?'

'Yeah. Good idea. I'll set it up before I go below.'

Dell was still hand steering as the breeze had stayed fresh, but curiously, I noticed it had backed around to come from the southwest and had in fact increased somewhat.

I said to Alex, 'How about taking a 20% reef in the main and maybe furl the Code Zero altogether?'

He grinned, having seen the way that Dell was wrestling with the wheel when an occasional stronger gust caused *Firebird* to heel further to port and made the wake hiss out behind us. 'Yes. Very good idea. We'll get onto that now if you set up the radar.'

'Done. I'm off then,' I announced, pleased Sandy indicated that she'd be down as soon as she had cleared away the lunch debris. I couldn't think of a better way to relax on a breezy afternoon than with my favourite lovely lady, and Sandy looked like she was just as keen.

As I passed the chart table, I paused to turn the radar on to continuous operation, alarms set and in weather mode which would pick up very small traces of rain at a greater distance than if left in the normal ship-scan mode. A quick slash, scrub the fangs and into bed, my mind automatically cataloguing the sound of the hulls through the water and the wind through the rigging.

Sandy wasn't long and looked lovely as she dropped the small amount of clothing she had on, before wriggling her way up and into the bed, cuddling up against me. We left the hatch over our heads open for ventilation since there was very little spray coming across the decks with the wind where it was.

Sandy knew I was thinking about the conditions and also about the night landfall and forcibly dragged my attention back to the here and now with very satisfying results. We were at the stage of slowly drifting off to sleep in that delightfully relaxed, post-coital state, when there was a knock at the door and Bree stuck her head around the edge, her sun-bleached hair tousled by the wind and said apologetically, 'I'm sorry to disturb you Harry, but Alex is concerned about the weather. It looks a bit dirty up ahead. Jasper isn't happy with it either.'

It was Jasper's concern for the conditions, more than anything else, which really got me moving, and I was back awake in a moment and flung the sheet back without considering modesty.

'On my way, thanks Bree.'

She grinned at my nakedness before backing out of the cabin as I hastily hauled on a pair of shorts, then headed for the bathroom before going topside.

When I walked out into the cockpit, everything looked good, bathed in the afternoon sunshine, although the wind was up a lot and appeared to have backed some more, so it was now coming from the south.

Alex was hand-steering and looked relieved to see me. He said nothing, except point ahead of us, so I turned to look and saw the problem immediately! A huge wall of purple-black cloud stretched from the northern horizon right around to the southern horizon to overhead, and without a doubt, was blacker and more menacing than any storm I'd ever seen before.

I ducked back into the saloon and checked the radar. Bad, scary move!

The upper half of it's screen was mostly filled with a huge, dark-red mass, a colour that denotes the heaviest rainfall and one I'd never seen in such a large area before. The closest edge was still 10 miles away and only moving west at 4 knots, so I returned to the cockpit in some haste.

'Head for the coast as soon as I get the sails furled,' I directed Alex, as I started the engines. 'The mess ahead is that festering low-pressure system that's somehow turned into a cyclone without letting anybody know!'

I used the electric winch to furl the main, after easing off the halyard and as soon as it was furled, I used the roller furling to douse the inner jib which was the only foresail still up. As soon as Alex saw the sails were under control, he powered the engines up to full and turned right.

'Hold a heading of 180° for now, please Alex. I'll work out exactly where we need to go as soon as I get the sails tidied up.'

'I'll put Bree on the wheel, Commander. She can steer 180° while I help you strip the two headsails off and tidy up the main. We need to tie the main halyard down as well and cover the slot in the boom.'

He was a good man to work with and we made relatively short work of a difficult job, bundling the Code 0 headsail and the inner staysail into two bulky sausages each. Normally, I would wash each sail carefully in fresh water before stowing it below, but we had no time to do anything except run hard for the coast and shelter, so they were just bundled as is, into the big forward deck locker which we latched down tight.

We were about 40 miles offshore so at top engine-driven speed of 16 knots, we would take about 2.5 hours to reach the coast. According to the chart, the safest place to drive into at speed was an un-named inlet just east of Wangularni Bay which was, in turn, inshore from Goulburn Island. Under the circumstances, I didn't think the traditional owners of the land would object if we borrowed some sheltered water up one of their narrow creeks for a while.

So, it became a real race between the evil-looking purple-black wall of cloud implacably advancing west, and the safety of the sheltered shore. The high-level shelf of cloud was expanding much more rapidly westwards, although incongruously, in the far west, the sun still shone brightly from a narrowing band of clear blue sky. Unusually, and perhaps because the low had developed so incredibly quickly, there wasn't the trademark long, deep swell that normally precedes a cyclone or hurricane.

Instead, the seas were fairly flat with only an insane frothing white chop of wind-driven waves less than a metre in height. These did little to hinder our progress, although we were pushing into the very strong wind that hit 65 knots in gusts and was due to the clockwise circulation typical of a cyclone in the southern hemisphere. With the engines at full-power, we could do no more, so I asked the ladies to pack all loose items away in secure lockers and to bring all electronic devices to the saloon to be placed in electrically insulated boxes called Faraday cages, otherwise known as a microwave oven, which would protect them from a direct lightning strike on the boat.

We were reminded of that particular hazard by the nearly-continuous display of stabbing forks of blue-white discharges being flung at the uncaring sea just ahead of the advancing wall of cloud. Our course was almost at 90° to the cloud line, so the distance between it and us was shrinking all the time.

When we had prepared all that we could, I decided to call Greg to let him know we would be holed up for a day or two and might even have our comms disabled temporarily.

'Gidday Harry. I was wondering when I'd hear from you again. How's the pleasure cruise going? Imagine being ordered to go to Lord Howe Island and to pose as a bunch of wealthy degenerates! Some people really do fall on their feet.'

'Actually, Greg. This is one time when we all would cheerfully trade places with you. We're running for cover, and just about 5 miles from the cloud wall of a very nasty little cyclone that some dickhead in the BOM forgot to tell anybody about!'

'What cyclone? There's no cyclone. I was just in with Bob, looking at the forecast and he was saying what a great trip you must be having. Maybe you're just seeing a local thunderstorm.'

'Well, I'd love to think that it was just a thunderstorm mate, although there's plenty of lightning. But I can assure you this is just a bit more than a thunderstorm. In fact, I called to let you know we may even be off air for a few days, depending on how well we get ourselves into cover before this cyclone-we're-not-supposed-to-be-having chews our arse off! Also I wanted to ask you to place an immediate call to the BOM to let them know there is a small but very intense cyclone currently centered somewhere just west of Cape Wessel and moving west at 5 knots. The pressure with us, roughly 60 miles from the centre, is 970 hPa and falling. If you can pass that info, I'd be much obliged, as it might save some other silly bugger like us sailing straight into the bloody thing.

Don't they know that these things are a hazard to navigation? Oh yeah. One last thing. They might want to let Darwin know as well. People up here are a bit touchy about things that go huff and puff in the middle of the night! Anyway, gotta go! I'll call you when I can. Cheers, Mate.'

I hung up on his startled prattling as the truth finally sank in, but I had more important things to do before we got our ears blown off, than reassuringly hold Greg's hand!

When I'd stowed the SatPhone safely in the oven, I checked the chart plotter to see we had less than 5 miles to run to make the mouth of the inlet which showed good water, well inside the narrowing waterway. According to the chart, it looked like our best bet was a creek system which was to the right side of the inlet and not too far in from the mouth. A meandering creek had a smaller creek feeding in from the right bank which seemed to be ideal, as it certainly looked narrow enough to allow easy tying off to the low-set mangroves, as well as shallow water for the best scope for the three anchors.

As we closed the coast, I had Alex prepare the lightweight stern anchor, that although it was tempered aluminium, was of the same superior Australian design which would keep us secure. It had 50 metres of 12mm chain attached, then 200 metres of 2-inch diameter braided rope with a Dyneema® core.

With the cloud wall just two miles away, we shot into the mouth of the inlet at full speed, not daring to slow down, and with the forward-looking sonar showing we still had good water, we stayed to the right of the main channel and following a hard right turn, spotted the creek mouth a few hundred metres up from the bend. It looked to be just about right; wide enough so we didn't have to worry about being stranded on the trees when the storm surge subsided.

I'd had Alex tip the stern anchor over just as we entered the creek and to feed out line until there was just 50 metres left aboard.

When I felt the tug of the stern anchor biting in, I dropped both bow anchors and backed down to get some decent length of chain out, as Alex winched in the slack. Held securely at those three points, we launched the RIB to allow us to quickly attach our best mooring lines as high up the thick trunks of several mangrove trees as possible to allow for the storm surge water rise. Just ten minutes of frantic activity saw us suspended between three anchors and four heavy lines to mangrove trees.

Alex and I also laid out two bright orange circular fenders attached with light lines to the trees where the main mooring lines were attached.

'There will probably be very severe flooding from heavy rain,' I told the crew, raising my voice over the noise of the wind which was starting to scream through the rigging, 'as well as a storm surge brought on by this very low pressure. So when this whole area goes under, we will have to be careful we stay centred in the creek. Those marker buoys we put out will help, but if we get pushed off the creek line, we'll settle back into the mangroves instead of the water, which won't do *Firebird* much good at all!

We may have to slacken the lines at some point, but that's a small price to pay for being safe.'

It was the last easy briefing I made as the cyclonic cloud wall and associated winds abruptly struck. My own design, masthead-mounted, stress-gauge wind speed indicator, jumped from 45 knots to 75, then 85 knots in seconds as the force on just the carbon mast heeled *Firebird* to more than 20° before she eased back to a more comfortable 5° heel. The wisdom of choosing a place without tall trees to batter us with torn-off limbs was quickly apparent as the boat heaved mightily in the violent gusts, the hollow carbon mast making a deep, mournful droning which lifted in pitch with the gusts.

With the wind came the storms, preceded by their sizzling blue arcs which lit the cabin into stark, blue-white relief far beyond daylight levels, and the crashing blasts of thunder shook the whole boat and drove the pussies into hiding. Then the rains came!

I'd been through some good storms before, but they were nothing compared to this monster! The rain approached with a hissing roar which built quickly until it was pounding on the cabin top with a continuous thunder, as though several large jet engines were being run just outside. That roar masked all other sounds, including the wind and the thunder! Speech was virtually impossible, so we took to writing each other notes.

Visibility outside was severely compromised, both by the cyclone sealing off any chance of sunlight seeping through and the sheer amount of water falling. It was so intense we could barely see the guard rails, only half a metre away from the windows, with a powerful torch. After thirty minutes of this, I checked the cleats where we'd attached the mooring lines and thought that they looked tight, so I prepared to go outside to check and ease the line tension if necessary.

'*Don't be silly, Harry!*' my lovely lady wrote on her pad. '*You can't work in that!*'

By way of answer, I went aft in the starboard hull, through our bathroom, toilet and laundry to where I could access some of the stern lockers from inside. Returning to the saloon after a few minutes rummaging through accumulated junk, I proudly displayed a Gath lightweight surfing helmet with a fixed face-shield and a wetsuit, complete with gloves and booties.

Sandy pointed at Alex, but I mimed that he was too big for the wetsuits I had, so she grabbed the one I had and shooed me back down below to get another one. I took all that to mean that she was going to help me and I didn't object, as she's a strong and very capable lady. By the time I got back, she had already wriggled into the outfit that looked a lot better clinging to her than it did to me.

I quickly dropped my clothes where I was and pulled my suit on, figuring that Dell already knew me too well and Bree had copped an eyeful earlier. On my pad I wrote, '*We have to loosen all mooring lines an equal amount so we stay in the creek. Let out about two metres on each.*'

Sandy gave me a thumbs up, so we ventured outside, the crew slamming the saloon door behind us with indecent haste!

Once clear of the cockpit roof, it was like stepping under a waterfall as the weight of water falling was a physical presence pushing down on our bodies, although the little, lightweight helmets were marvellous. With next to no insulation, the rain noise was alarmingly loud, but we soon ignored that as we shuffled carefully along the side decks to get to each cleat.

The mooring lines were just becoming tight, so we didn't waste time letting the two metres out on each. Then, after a quick check of the anchor chains, we scuttled back to the shelter of the cockpit like a pair of drowning rats. There was no point in dumping water all over the saloon, so we stripped off completely under the cockpit roof and slipped inside through the smallest door opening we could, heading down below to dry off and dress.

Returning to the saloon, we found that Bree, bless her little cotton socks, had brewed up steaming mugs of tea for us with a slug of dark rum liqueur that transformed the humble tea into a fortifying brew I called NQ tea. I'd heard from a visitor that a very similar concoction was a staple in the western parts of Austria, although I was happy to call this particular recipe my own! A large platter of toasted sandwiches went down just as easily.

CHAPTER 4

THURSDAY, CYCLONE SHELTER – ARNHEM COAST

Outside, rain still thundered down and the wind still howled through the rigging, keeping the mast moaning, but we were safe and warm. As the hours ticked along with no let-up in conditions, the favourite board games of Scrabble and Monopoly were broken out. Cheating was not only expected in these games, but was assessed for subtlety and inventiveness with points being added to players scores. For safety, I wanted to keep at least two on watch all night, so crew drifted off at intervals when they felt sufficiently tired to sleep through the cacophony outside.

By 00:30 the rain was easing, the barometer rising slightly from the abysmal depths it had plummeted to and the wind had dropped around 20 knots on average. The radar was able to penetrate the lighter rain a bit better and showed the heaviest mass of moisture moving westwards and well off to the north-west from us. By 03:00, the rain had eased to what could be classed as light, so I turned on the big LED spotlights which could fry eyeballs at one kilometre, and made a 360° scan of our surroundings. Although expected, it was still a bizarre sight to see we were sitting in the middle of a vast expanse of water, complete with small breaking waves! There was no land showing at all between us and the open sea, and that prompted me to make a weird decision.

'We're going to move camp,' I announced and it was only Alex who appreciated the reasoning behind the idea.

'That's crazy!' Dell exclaimed. 'I mean, we can't see where the real creek is and the trees start, so how do we get out of here safely?'

I smiled at her trepidation, 'I'm concerned that despite our precautions, if we're out of position even a few metres when the water level drops, we may get parked in the mangroves, instead of beside them. So I'd rather move now while water covers everything.'

She smiled back, 'OK. But you obviously have a plan?'

'Yeah, I do. We watch the chart plotter and the 3D forward-looking sonar very carefully, since between them they will still show where the channel is. We back up until we're in that larger creek behind us, then drive east-south-east until the plotter says we're in the main inlet. Once there, we drop the main bow anchor, the really big jobbie, and let the wind and all the flood water run past us until the inlet level has dropped and the wind has subsided a bit more.'

'Won't it be rough back out in the ocean?'

'Yeah, it will, but we're not going out there just yet. It's 03:30 now, so we should be anchored in the inlet channel by 04:00 or so. We'll stay there the rest of today and tonight until things settle down, but we'll still stop at the Hole-in-the-Wall to do that bottom scrub. Until then, relax, do some fishing or whatever takes your fancy.'

She gave a cheeky grin at that last remark, but Alex and I were too involved with making the move before the water subsided, to indulge in any more discussion.

The re-location plan actually worked out much as expected with only a few chopped green leaves tossed up in our wake to suggest the water levels were dropping fast as we carefully felt our way out of our refuge to the main inlet. Our main anchor got good holding immediately, even with the strong outflow as the huge amount of rain found its way back to the sea from whence it came.

I set both the radar and chart plotter anchor alarms to be sure we'd know about any anchor dragging and decided to return to bed when Alex offered to stay on watch. Sandy joined me, but we were tired from the stressful night and fell asleep in each other's arms almost immediately.

I awoke alone in the bed when it was nearly midday, and imme-diately stood up on the bed with my upper half out of the hatch to check our situation. There was still a solid cover of high-level cloud, but the wind was down to normal levels. The same couldn't be said for the water levels, which were still very high with an amazing amount of water flowing rapidly past us, carrying any amount of tree parts and other flotsam. Naturally, the water colour had changed from the usual dull, muddy green to that of a dirty light-brown.

I was busting for a pee and a feed, in that order, so padded aft to perform the first function, before grabbing a pair of shorts and a T-shirt from the washing basket so I could decently go up top and take care of the second requirement.

I found Sandy and Dell, deep in lively, amicable conversation, and it was Dell who offered to make me some scrambled eggs for brunch, because they'd already eaten.

'What's the plan for the rest of the day, Oh Great Lord and Master?' Sandy asked with a cheeky grin.

I grinned back. 'We stay here until tomorrow morning so everything has had time to settle down. I need to check the BOM website to see what the cyclone is doing. We wouldn't want the fool thing to head back this way. Then tomorrow, we head for the Wessel Peninsula and a bottom scrub. Today is just relaxing, although I have a bit of work to do on the boat, but that won't take long, so you two can do what you want.'

I looked around, seeing just Dell in the galley, 'I presume if Alex and Bree are sleeping, we shouldn't do anything too noisy and going ashore doesn't look too inviting.'

Sandy shook her head, scanning the huge expanse of mangrove tree tops just showing above the slowly lowering water levels. 'No, it doesn't look too inviting, so I'm quite happy to stay here and relax. Camping on the trampolines would be good, seeing as there's a decent breeze. It's too hot and humid down below without the air-con running and maybe the bar will open early.'

'I'll be in that,' Dell added, parking a plate of steaming scrambled eggs on toast in front of me. 'Sounds like a great way to waste an afternoon.'

Sandy smiled at her, 'I'm glad you think so. It'll be a nice way to celebrate our survival of the storm.'

When Dell giggled in return, I had my suspicions about their plans for the afternoon, but as they usually turn out to be a lot of harmless fun, I ignored them and kept on eating, figuring I might just need the carbs. With brunch disposed of and everything cleaned up and put away, I carefully checked the anchor.

It was under a fair bit of strain, since the outflow hadn't diminished to any noticeable extent, so I left it to keep on working as it was designed. There hadn't been any evidence of dragging, so once again, the Aussie design was proving itself to be highly effective and reliable.

Overhead, the high-level cloud was still in place, although a few patches of blue sky were present far to the east. I logged onto the BOM website and discovered why we were nearly cleaned up by an un-announced cyclone. The satellite story was feasible and as they had already moved another one to cover our area, forecasts were back on-line.

The cyclone was still very compact and had belted the Tiwi Islands and had done a lot of damage to Darwin, before moving out to sea where it was intensifying to a Category 4, while it decided where or who to go bash up next.

Some flying debris had scored a section of the starboard coachouse roof beside the inboard handrail and also the hardtop over the cockpit, so I wanted to sand the damaged areas back, apply some bog, then paint the repair to stop water entry. I got the necessary bits together and got stuck into the small jobs.

As I worked, I heard the ladies rattling around below, first in the galley, then forward in our cabin. The odd giggle floated up to me, but I was content they were happy and getting on so well. I had nearly finished the coachouse repair when they came up and eased past me, heading for the bow. They carried cushions and towels which were spread out on the starboard trampoline. I carried on working and soon had the coachouse looking as though nothing had happened to it, then moved aft to the hardtop. I quickly noticed the ladies had stripped down to just panties and that made sense in the heat and crushing humidity, although the stiff breeze helped to keep sweating bodies relatively cool.

I was getting hot myself, then heard a call from the foredeck, 'Keep going Harry, but when you've finished tarting up the boat, how about making a bucket of Pina Coladas, you lovely man?'

They sounded half-pissed already which might have been what they were doing earlier when all the giggling started. So I dutifully finished the job, stowed my gear and put together the ingredients for a bucket of PCs and if I was a little heavy-handed with the rum, well...too bad! Bucket in one hand and three glasses in the other, I carefully balanced my way forward to a slightly debauched welcome from the two lovely ladies who looked very desirable covered in a fine layer of sweat and nothing else.

The thick cloud cover kept the sun off us, but the heat and humidity were ferocious and a swim would have been a treat, but we weren't going to chance the presence of crocodiles scavenging for game washed down by the flood waters. That only left having some more chilled PC and it was really good, smooth and bitey. The first two hardly touched the sides of my throat and by the time number three was sliding down a little more slowly, the heavy dose of alcohol was kicking in and the girls were getting the giggles; yet again!

It was about then that Alex and Bree wandered up to see what all the fun was about. Both were rather more modest than we three, but Bree did have on a very brief bikini and Alex showed some moral daring by stripping down to bikini jocks that managed to look slightly odd on his huge frame! Nevertheless, they both joined in the fun mood and did their best to catch up to our intake of the dynamite Pina Coladas, to the extent I had to make an emergency re-supply run to the galley for more.

All in all, it was a funny and fun afternoon which slowly drew down to a dull sky for the evening. Unfortunately, it also meant that most of the local mosquito population had heard about the fresh meat available and they arrived in droning squadrons. Yes, these mozzies were so big, they droned rather than whined and their sting was proportionally more savage, so we beat a very hasty retreat to the safety of the saloon, where I fired up the generator and kicked in the air-con. I figured we'd earned a cool, restful night and planned to leave it running all night. The generator only kicked in when needed to supplement the batteries, so we weren't burning much fuel.

FRIDAY, HEADING EAST

Next morning saw *Firebird* being hustled out of the sheltering inlet with almost indecent haste because the flood waters were still running hard. Naturally, there was a lot of mud stirred up by the flood and this was carried well out to sea by every small creek or river we passed, so the effect was like passing a series of brown tongues poking out seawards, with clear water in-between.

The distance to the luxury of our next overnight anchorage was 167 nautical miles which would be about 12 hours at 14 knots. Since there was only a light southerly breeze blowing, I left one engine running so we could maintain our usual cruise speed and get to the Hole-in-the-Wall before dark.

CHAPTER 5

At the same time as we were enjoying the peaceful run across the top of the Northern Territory, the opposite was happening in a modest three-bedroom house on Lord Howe Island.

The sound of a rock-hard fist hitting another person in a soft tissue area is usually a sickening smack, but some warped personalities get off on inflicting pain on others. In particular, inflicting pain on persons who can't or simply won't fight back.

The stream of foul curses which accompanied the all-too regular beatings don't need repeating, nor is there any need to dwell on the escalating level of injury being inflicted on the hapless subject of the attack.

The woman was tall and lean, an attractive mane of white-blonde hair framing her very pretty face and with a swimmer's physique, she was broad-shouldered and narrow-waisted. The charming smile that was nearly always present, was very much absent as she braced herself for the rest of the onslaught and the standard but highly unpleasant finale.

Without any alcohol in his system, her husband, Senior Constable Darryl Fitzgibbon, was a very pleasant and engaging sort of man, equally at ease with a group of men or women.

It was only when he'd had more than three drinks, he became in progression, morose, low-esteemed and apologetic, then violently belligerent!

He was very careful to hit her where the bruises could be easily covered by clothing, and he left her face alone, something she was grateful for, but it was precious little to be thankful for.

As the island's only law enforcement officer and a highly respected member of the community, Darryl was in a position where he was almost immune from censure. If his mouse of a wife ever mustered the courage to try to draw attention to her injuries, there was no one else in a position of authority for her to refer to. Oddly enough, he actually regretted the regular beatings which he administered, classifying them as a necessary stepping-stone to the second phase of those sessions. That phase, the climax to the beatings, was what he had no remorse for in the slightest and looked forward to them with a voracious hunger which had his heart pounding, his blood pressure sky-high and gave him a raging erection which seemed to last for hours.

As he delivered a final few punches to his wife's cringing body, he felt the familiar and very welcome blood lust rising like an evening mist, except this one wasn't quiet and peaceful, but blood red and violent; it threatened to turn him into a raging animal. Kelly, his long-suffering wife wouldn't hesitate to call him a raging animal as she mentally braced herself for the coming round of brutality. One part of her mind clinically assessed his actions and noted there was a progressive change where he had more and more difficulty reaching the 'red mist' phase, although she was able to speed up the whole process, and save some punches as well, if she begged him not to go any further.

The more desperate she sounded, the quicker he'd reach the dreaded climax although to get there he first had to rip her clothes off, as violently as possible, so she quickly learned to wear very flimsy pants and tops with no underclothes at all, to reduce the amount of damage inflicted.

This ritual baring of her body was cause for him to froth at the mouth, grunt incoherently, then rape her. That part had become a lot easier, since she'd learned to recognise the signs of one of his 'episodes' coming on and would discretely apply some lubricant in advance. The bit she really hated and that was potentially lethal, was in order to orgasm, Darryl had to choke her with his huge, hard hands until her eyes bulged and she started to lose consciousness. At that moment, he'd release the pressure, she'd draw in an agonising breath and he'd climax explosively.

Generally, she'd be too distracted trying to get her breathing back under control to notice the considerable discomfort lower down.

Afterwards, he'd be overcome with remorse and be incredibly tender and caring; for all of ten minutes!

One day, she idly speculated what would happen if his routine of building up to the climax stage were to be interrupted. The images her fertile mind produced were sufficient to give anyone else nightmares, being akin to the transformation scenes by 'The Incredible Hulk'.

On this occasion, he seemed to be having trouble reaching his climax, and took her much closer to the brink of unconsciousness before he was able to release the raging flood of his pent-up lust! She took so long to regain her breath, he was long gone before she recognised her surroundings again.

That occasion also became the final straw, and hardened her resolve to finally do something about this despicable man! As per his normal routine, he stayed away from the marital bed for the night, affording Kelly some time to relax and plan just what she could do about her situation. She was awake most of the night, her mind churning over possibilities and rejecting them, one after the other, until there was just one left.

No one outside of her family knew she was the younger sister of Australia's current Prime Minister, Andy Friar, although Darryl had to be told when they married. Even before he had entered politics, she had promised herself she would stand on her own and not be running to big brother to have her hand held every five minutes!

Her present situation seemed serious enough for her to ignore the promise to herself, and when she was certain Darryl was at work, she called a number she'd kept tucked away.

After following an identification protocol which had been established when she was given the number, a quiet female voice come on the line.

'This is Alice Lawson. How may I help you?'

'Hi Alice. This is Kelly Fitzgibbon. We haven't spoken before, but I'd like to get a message to my big brother if you don't mind.'

'Certainly Kelly. It'll will be a pleasure. What's the message?'

'Ask Andy to call me within the next hour, please. Does his schedule permit those times?'

'I can let you speak to him very soon if you care to hang on.'

'No. Circumstances dictate it'd be best if he calls me on a private line, please Alice.'

'Very well. Then expect his call within five minutes. Good to talk to you Kelly. I hope we can do it again soon. Bye now.'

Kelly replaced the handset back in its rest very gingerly as if afraid to wake the hungry tiger as she contemplated the course of action she was about to undertake.

In fact, it was barely three minutes when the phone rang and Andy's laughing voice and sunny personality flooded from the speaker.

'Gidday little Sis. What's happening on your island paradise?'

Kelly's dispassionate resolve immediately cracked and in a flood of tears, told Andy everything, including the fact that the physical abuse had been going on for many years. She also mentioned the attacks were increasing in frequency and there were several occasions when he had come home with a fair amount of blood and what looked suspiciously like semen on his shirt and pants. As the island virtually had no crime, his explanation of subduing a fight had little to recommend it.

By the end of her recital, her tears had stopped and she was able to quickly answer the stream of questions her tale of terror had generated. Finally the Q & A session stopped.

'OK, Sis. I've got the picture and it looks crappy! My first response is to send a team of the biggest ACP coppers we've got to sort this prick

out, but that isn't a very PM'ish thing to do. My alternative is to say that I have some friends heading your way in a big catamaran. They're on a separate matter, but I'll ask them to call you when they arrive.

The man is Harry Stevens and his boat is Firebird. *He just might be the one to sort this mess out without making too much fuss about it!'*

'How long until he gets here?'

'Better allow about a week, although he may be able to speed things up if it's really urgent.'

'No. No. That's OK. I think I should be right for at least two weeks after this one; I hope.'

After promising to contact his friend on the boat immediately, they severed the connection. Andy made a fairly brief phone call to a very long number which had no area or country code, then returned to the combination of farcical theatre and a live firing range which was question-time in the House. Kelly just hoped like all hell this Harry somebody was as good as her big bro seemed to think he was.

FIREBIRD, SATURDAY

'Gidday Andy. Good to hear from you. What's it like back minding the store?'

.... 'A favour? Yeah, we do them all the time, especially for old friends. Oh, OK. I didn't know you had one and what a co-incidence she's on Lord Howe!

.... 'Ouch! That's a nasty one all right. So, he's a NSW copper then?'

.... 'So how far do you want us to go?

.... 'Just checking, Andy. I need to be sure, mate. Anyway, Dell might know a bit more, having been there.'

.... No problem. It'll be low profile and no significant names will be mentioned.'

.... 'Sure thing. We can be there in about five days if that'll help. I'll call Kelly in a couple of days when we have a more precise ETA. You'll get reports as things happen.'

.... 'You're welcome Andy. We'll talk soon. Bye for now and take care, mate.'

We were in the process of picking our way carefully through the sand shoals and strong currents between the islands of Stevens and Burgunngura, and were just an hour out from our overnight anchorage when I took the strange call from Andy Friar asking for help for his little sister. I made a bunch of calculations and measurements before I went to tell the crew about the new plan.

'So that's where we stand,' I finished my briefing. 'We still need the bottom clean, so that happens tomorrow. The sleep-in is cancelled, so we get to go overboard as soon as we can see clearly all around and the croc patrol is comfortable there aren't any bities lurking about. If we're quick with the scrub-up, we can just catch the slack water for the run through the canal, but if we are even just a few minutes late, we'll be caught by the start of the rip tide flow against us and that won't be fun!'

'We're going to have to be very careful dealing with a deranged NSW copper,' Sandy said. 'I won't have any jurisdiction without being issued a warrant from the NSW Commissioner, but maybe it's something to consider if we need official muscle.'

I considered her words, 'Yeah. Maybe we should get Andy, or probably Charlie, to put that in motion, but there's always my warrant card and I think that an ACP Commander trumps a NSW Senior Constable any day.'

Sandy grinned, 'True, you can 'trump' me any day darlin', but let's line all our ducks up well before we get there. We need to do a lot of homework first.'

I looked around at Dell and Bree, since Alex was busy at the wheel doing a great job of guiding us through the maze of shifting sands. 'Sandy's right and we need to come up with a workable plan to tackle this little problem we've been handed. I've promised Andy we'd keep it as low key as possible, but you all know my feelings about domestic violence! So we're going to help Kelly regardless of whose toes might get trodden on, and being a copper won't help this sick bastard; he goes down!

So, could everyone have a think about how we can do this without making a big fuss? We'll pool ideas and come up with a plan in the next day or two. But in the meantime, I think we all agree that haste is required?'

There were nods all around so I broke up the meeting by relieving Alex on the wheel and checking the best anchorage for us. There was a bay just south of the cutting that had two pristine, white sand beaches, as well as being more protected than the tiny bay right beside the canal entrance. On the approach, an island with shallows all around it had to be given a wide berth, but otherwise the run-in was straight forward and with plenty of light left in the day, we anchored just off the beautiful, white sand beach.

The beach ran up into a low plateau of limestone that had been heavily scoured by rainwater runoff over the years, and was difficult and uncomfortable to walk on, so we stayed on the beach. Jasper and Krazy loved the sand as usual and scampered about like overgrown kittens, making darting, mock attacks on us and chasing each other.

As we were walking, one other small yacht pulled into the far end of the second beach, but they anchored well away from *Firebird*. We had a quiet night with minimal booze consumed and not much fooling around, and everyone was in bed by 10:00.

I'd set the perimeter defence system as well as telling Jasper to conduct roving patrols, but we were undisturbed by any intruders, human or animal.

First light saw the boat a veritable hive of activity with everybody busy. The ladies made breakfast, while Alex and I pulled us in closer to shore, then broke out all the bottom scrubbing gear and prepared the Nardi Extreme 260 dive gear.

This Surface Supplied Diving Apparatus or SSDA equipment, allowed two divers to operate supplied with endless clean air from hoses leading to a surface-mounted 12-volt compressor. The system's limitation is the length of hose available and the depth, which is 15 metres with the Nardi unit. The twin hoses were custom-made 25 metres long and could be extended another 17 metres each if necessary, but they became a bit cumbersome to move around with at that length.

Although she already had some knowledge of weapons, Alex had been coaching Bree in the use of the large arsenal of guns aboard and under his expert guidance, she'd become very handy with both the PMR .22 magnum pistol and the 9mm mini-Uzi sub-machine gun.

Therefore, she was appointed as croc watch and posted on top of the coachhouse with instructions to shoot at any croc or shark she saw.

That freed up Alex to take the other set of dive gear to the other hull. Sandy and Dell would scrub the water line while Alex and I did the rest of the bottom which was out of reach of the surface. I should have expected the pair of them would jump in naked, much to Bree's amusement and Alex's embarrassment, but everyone worked happily and surprisingly quickly and we ended up with both hulls clear of all the crap that had been starting to slow us down.

Morning tea time saw the job finished and with the kettle on and a fresh batch of hot scones cooking, courtesy of Bree, the girls dressed while Alex and I rinsed off and packed away the dive and cleaning gear. There was no time to sit and solve the world's problems if we were to get through the canal safely, so I fired up the engines, hauled the anchor and drove out of there while the others scoffed the scones.

The actual canal was just 1850 metres long, but great care was necessary if there was any current still running either way. As we entered from the west, it was slack water, but that happy state wasn't going to last so I pushed the throttles open and we scooted through the stark, but picturesque canal worn into the limestone rock the islands were made from.

Even before we had covered that short distance, the tide had turned and the first stirrings of the massive force of water were just starting to be felt when we popped out the other end like the proverbial cork out of a bottle.

CHAPTER 6...

From the Hole-in-the-Wall to Cape York was a straight course of 368 miles which should take us 27 to 28 hours to cover at our standard cruising speed, so we settled back into cruise watch mode with just one person at a time doing the 06:00 to 12:00 watch then the 12:00 to 18:00 one.

Night watches always meant two persons for safety and the same six-hour period seemed to work well for us. Until a couple of years ago, I'd been unused to having crew aboard to share watches with, so when I did gain some crew, almost by accident, this system just happened, and since it suited everybody, we kept it going. The two pussies were always ready for some company and their company and playfulness helped to pass the boring early morning hours when the body's circadian rhythm was at its lowest.

The rest of the day was, in fact, just as relaxing, as if we had stayed holed up back at the Wessel Islands. Since the wind was brisk but steady from the south, it meant no sail adjustments were necessary, and we were able to make our set cruising speed target without using an engine. The autopilot was left in charge with the chart plotter to keep it honest and the radar with an intrusion alarm set, stopped us running into anything harder than a wave.

That meant the crew were able to lay around doing nothing for as long and hard as they felt like it. The nominal person on watch only had to poke a head up every so often and look around, check the electronic stuff was still electronicing, then get back to the serious stuff like sunbaking, eating and yarning about nothing much. A few ideas did pop up about how to tackle the PM's Lord Howe problem as it had come to be called, and these were seriously and carefully considered. By the end of the day, the better ideas had been melded into one and a plan formed which was quite interesting and seemed to have a high chance of success.

Sandy was our media-watch person and routinely trawled the various sites for items of interest to us. One item she read out to us, came out of Indonesia, where the usual bunch of do-gooders were protesting the announcement that in one of the most rapidly processed drug trials ever, seven persons with Australian citizenship were scheduled to be executed by firing squad within the next four weeks. They had been found with very large quantities of the new 'Super MDMA' ecstasy drug which was incredibly potent and instantly addictive from the first dose.

The quantities were too large to be for personal use, so they were obviously dealing, which is an automatic death sentence in Indonesia. We had little to say about that item of news, except how it tidied up a potential loose end.

We were rather more interested in her next item of news which referred to a stalled investigation into the death of a tourist on Lord Howe Island several weeks ago. Despite a full team of detectives and forensic investigators moving onto the island for weeks, they hadn't been able to come up with a motive or a perp. The victim, a young German female tourist, had been found naked, savagely beaten, raped and strangled. It was also reported there was evidence that some of the injuries had been inflicted post-mortem, but the report thankfully refrained from going into further detail.

'I'm glad about that!' Bree muttered, echoing the thoughts of the rest of us.

Dell added her thoughts, 'I thought even that was a bit much. It's a bit co-incidental that Lord Howe, the island of zero crime where people don't lock doors, suddenly has a gruesome murder. I mean, we get a call from Andy about his sister being bashed up, then we find out this poor girl has been strangled just two weeks ago. Is it only me who thinks there just might be some sort of connection here?'

Her words sparked a whole new train of thought in my mind and they weren't nice ones as I looked at her carefully.

'That's a very nasty thought you just had my dear lady, but I think you're brilliant.'

She looked a bit flustered. 'It was only a random thought, Harry. I haven't actually connected any dots yet.'

I smiled to settle her down. 'No rush, but take your time and put that fine mind to work, finding, then connecting those dots. Tell me when you see what it spells out.'

While she mulled over what she'd said, it was Bree who asked, 'But if all those investigators have been on this case for two weeks, they must have considered the same connection and rejected it.'

'Ah yes. But what if they don't know what we know about the attacks on Kelly? That information is very limited in its distribution. Therefore, it would mean there isn't a dot for them to connect!'

'Oh. I hadn't thought of that. Good point. So there could actually be a connection?'

I smiled grimly. 'There just could be. We'll have to be very careful, but this escalates things a great deal. It's a very small step-up from wife-beating to murder. We need to find out all the gory details of what he does to Kelly when he attacks. Probably the only way to get the right story is to ask the lady herself. I need to check back to Charlie or Alice about the safest way to make contact.'

So it was back to the SatPhone.

'Hi Charlie, how're things going?'

'Hi Harry. Pretty good thanks. May I presume you're calling about the Boss's personal problem?'

I laughed, 'To the point as always. Yes, Charlie, you may. I need to urgently talk to Kelly while she's alone. Do you know when that would be?'

'Yes. I have the schedule here. After the latest incident, best time would be 9 to 10, 11 to 12, 1 to 3, 4 to 6. Try to avoid having her call you. Is there an additional problem I need to know about?'

'There could be, but we're still working on it. You should have a go at connecting the same dots we just did. Look at Lord Howe news items going back two weeks from yesterday and see what you think, but don't call Kelly with any of this. We're on the case and have an initial protection plan which we'll put into place very soon, so keep everyone else out of it, including the Boss. Only discuss your thoughts with Alice and me. Is that acceptable?'

'Yes, understood Harry. I can appreciate what you're saying. I'll be in touch shortly. Bye.'

I returned to the impromptu planning session. 'OK. I have Kelly's best contact schedule and as it's just after 16:00 here, Lord Howe is just 30 minutes ahead, so we're in a contact zone now. I'm going to call her to get this extra info, unless anyone else has any other thoughts?'

Heads were shaken, so I went into the saloon to call, making sure the recorder was on.

'Hello?'

'Hi Kelly, my name is Harry Stevens and I believe Andy has mentioned my name to you. Are you able to talk freely?'

'Yes, he has and yes I can. However, for verification, what's the name of your dog?'

I laughed, 'Very clever. It's not a dog, but a cat and his name is Jasper. Will that do?'

'Oh yes, Harry. It most certainly will. Thank you for calling. Andy said you are coming here from Indonesia, but do you know when you'll arrive?'

'We're halfway across the Gulf at the moment, so at least another five to six days, I'm afraid. I have several very clever investigators working on your situation as we speak, but I also have some very personal and awkward questions I need to ask if we're to help you. Your answers will be a great help. Can you be very open and honest with me?

'Understood Harry. Yes, ask whatever you like. You've impressed *the hell out of Andy. He reckoned you saved his life 3 or 4 times, and has told me to trust you implicitly, so go ahead and ask.'*

'Great, thanks Kelly. Now, this last attack. I need you to describe exactly what happened, as in; tell me exactly what Darryl did to you.'

'I understand. Sparing no gory details, here's how it went.'

To her credit, Kelly gave an incredibly detailed description of the attack, including the most useful prelude to it, where several good clues lay. I'm sure she must have felt embarrassed at times, because I certainly was, but this was exactly what we needed and my concerns grew rapidly as her story unfolded. I also became convinced we were unfortunately, on the right track. It was a very lengthy story, so I was very glad the recorder had grabbed it all.

'Do you feel that you're safe at the moment?'

'Yes, I do. I'm usually good for at least a week or two after one of these events, although I have noticed the time between them has reduced. I've also noticed that Darryl has started to be more uptight all the time now.'

'Think back about two weeks when that girl was found dead. Did you notice anything odd about Darryl's behaviour around then?'

'Yeah, there was one odd thing, although I realised later I'd seen it a couple of times before. He came home a couple of nights before she was found with blood specks and odd stains over his shirt and pants. He said he'd had to break up a fight and stuff must have wiped off one of the men.'

'OK. That'll do for the questions. Now for some interim insurance; I'd like you to mention to Darryl, that your cousin Sandy is coming to visit and you've offered to put her up at your place. Is that a logical move for you to make if a cousin you really liked, called like that?'

'Sure, that would be the normal thing to do. I do have a cousin, but haven't seen her for years and Darryl has never met her. He might be a bit pissed, but there again, he fancies himself as God's gift to women, so he may also think he can get into her pants as well. You'd better tell her to expect it, but what's her full name? I should know that.'

'True,' I chuckled, 'her name is Sandy Thomson and she's actually a Queensland Police Inspector, but you'd better not tell him that. She'll be posing as a school teacher on leave. Physically, she can handle herself very well, so if she doesn't like something which Darryl tries on, he may regret it. But let's just get her there first. We were hoping her presence will be enough to deter him from having another go at you until we can work out the best way to take him down.'

'That's not a bad plan, Harry. Having another girl in the house will certainly keep him quiet for a while. Or at least until she knocks him back once too often.'

'One last question, Kelly. Is Darryl capable of having reasonably normal sex with you or anyone else for that matter?'

Her reply was rather more enthusiastic than I expected. *'Oh, yes. When this red rage isn't on him, he's usually quite gentle and actually rather good.'*

'I've just had a thought which will improve the timeline. In about 3 day's time, we have to put into Yeppoon to refuel before heading directly for you. I can put Sandy on a plane to Brisbane, then to Lord Howe. That'll get her there days earlier and she'll be arriving like a normal tourist, rather than as a boatie.'

'That won't work, Harry. Flights out of Brisbane are only on weekends. She'll have to go to Sydney.'

'Oh, OK. Thanks for that. Anyway, I'll call in a day or two with details when we get it organised. Otherwise, if it's urgent, please call this number at any time, day or night, if you have any concerns and we'll push on as fast as possible.'

'Thanks Harry. You make me feel better already and I'm really looking forward to seeing you and Sandy! Bye.'

I sat a spell trying to put her story into perspective, but the elephant in the room kept blowing its schnozzle, demanding attention. Kelly's relating of the finale to his wife-beating act was chilling and fitted the sketchy details in the news broadcast, so my next job was to call my contact at the ACP to find out more.

The old girl, Mavis, although I don't know if she is old or not, but she sounds like she is at times, was in good form this afternoon and quickly found the full account of the murder.

'How about I email the whole report to you, Harry?' she said dryly. *'Modern technology is a wonderful thing!'*

That set her off chuckling at having scored one off the great Harry Stevens, smart-arse scourge of her division, and when she'd recovered, I floated the idea which was slowly but surely firming up, based on more solid evidence.

'That's a very worrying thought Harry,' she said, all business as usual now, *'but your reasoning is sound as usual and I'm inclined to agree with you. You'll need to put as much evidence as possible into the report before their Lordships will give it a guernsey. For what it's worth, I'll support it openly when it gets that far.'*

'Thanks Mavis. I appreciate that. It's a very dangerous situation when the henhouse is guarded by the fox!' That one cracked her up as well, but I added, 'I'll go over this report with the crew and with what Kelly told me earlier, I think there will be too many points that match to be ignored.'

'I agree, but we need to convince their Lordships. But be very careful, Harry. You could be on some very unstable footing with this one. Keep me updated daily, please. Bye, bye.'

I waited until the emailed report arrived, then printed it out and re-joined the crew yet again.

'OK. This is the full account of the murder of that girl on Lord Howe. Concerningly, it also mentions there have been a series of violent sexual assaults on young female tourists over the past two years, including one rather more recently, who has disappeared. All the others have recovered from their attacks. In all those cases, the assailant made his attack in such a way he was able to remain un-recognisable and was careful to wear a condom and not get scratched. Therefore, apart from the fact that the bad guy is male, there are no leads to chase.'

'What about the timing of the attacks?' Sandy asked. 'As in, the spacing between them?'

'Good question and I'm sure it is answered somewhere in the report which appears to be very thorough. Anyway, we need to go through it first and see what matches up to Kelly's story of her assault. I'm betting there will be a whole heap of similarities which will at least give us an MO, and if we're lucky, a pointer in the right direction.'

I addressed Sandy again. 'I'm afraid my cunning plan is going to throw you into harm's way, my dearest lady.'

She raised her eyebrows questioningly, 'How so, O Lord High Poohbah?'

'I had the thought that to act as a block against Darryl getting wound up against Kelly before we get there, I might send you in first, posing as Kelly's cousin who she hasn't seen for years. Kelly is telling Darryl this evening that you're coming and you're going to stay with them. She thought it was a great idea, but suggested Darryl might either be a bit pissed at having someone else in the house, or be really happy because he has another female to try to drag into bed. Kelly said he fancies himself as quite a cocksman!'

Sandy had a good laugh, then said, 'Well, it sounds like it's a done deal. So in that case why don't I jump ship at say, Cairns, fly to Brisbane, then to Lord Howe? That'll get me there days ahead of you guys, and I'll be seen to be arriving on my own without a hit squad backing me up.'

'Well, actually, you have to fly out of Sydney because Brisbane flights are only on weekends. But the bit which concerns me,' I said, seriously for once, 'is that Darryl is sounding more and more like a real nut case and capable of anything. You may find yourself in an awkward situation if he takes a fancy to you. And you can't afford to step out of character too early before we've had a chance to sniff around and find out what's really going on.'

She smiled gently and patted me on the arm, 'I know the drill, dearest. If I've got to take one or even two for the Company, then so be it. I can play my part....'

'Hmmm! Kelly was almost enthusiastic when I asked if he was capable of having normal sex. She thought he was rather good when he wasn't bashing her up or trying to choke the life out of her!'

Sandy giggled, 'Well. That's even better then. It means all the ones I get to take for the Company will be good ones!'

I pretended to give her an affronted glare, 'Hang on there! What happened to, 'the one I have to take.....' where did 'all the ones' come from?'

That drew a laugh which lightened the mood, but I still wasn't happy about sending my lovely lady into trouble by herself.

It was Dell who came up with the next excellent suggestion. 'With Sandy leaving us at Cairns, we'll be a bit shorthanded, plus it seems this little caper is escalating into something a lot more dangerous. Why don't you call Dave and Corrine to see if they can fly up to Cairns and join us? It occurred to me we could use Dave's muscles and boat skills and certainly most of Corrine's many and varied skills. We have the beds.'

Sandy and I looked at each other. 'Brilliant, dear lady. I'm sure they'll help. I'll just go do some planning, then I'll get you to do some on-line booking if you would. I'm sure you're much better at it than I am.'

Dell and Sandy came with me, and we crowded around the chart-table, booting Krazy cat out of the way, much to her disgust. Dell manned the computer, while Sandy and I figured schedules and timing. Twenty minutes later, we had a complicated plan, but it seemed workable. While Dell continued making bookings on the internet, I found the SatPhone under various pieces of paper and punched in a well-known number.

CHAPTER 7...

'*Are you a Seeker of enlightenment, young man, or just after a good time?*' came Dave's deep drawl.

'Very funny, Dave. How's it all going down there?'

'*Good thanks mate. The Indonesian loot is all in storage awaiting your return from the paid junket you're all on. The Auction House people are going nuts over the stuff we brought back. Nobody's seen anything like it! Ever! Every time they release a bit of a teaser photo, the press and collectors go wild, so the return is going to be pretty huge by the sound of things. The auction people aren't in any hurry since the delay is whipping up a buyer frenzy. And how about you guys? Where are you?*'

'Halfway across the Gulf. We ran into an un-forecast cyclone and had to lay up in a creek for a couple of days.

'*Shit! That must have been a bit exciting! Any damage?*'

'Nah! Couple of scratches is all. But what I'm really calling about is, this junket has become a lot more serious. We got a call from Andy to help his little sister who's married to the copper on Lord Howe. Apparently he's been bashing her up on a regular basis for quite a while now and there's a good chance he's also been a very naughty boy with the visiting maidens for the last couple of years. The current score is one dead, one missing and eight or ten severely roughed up, but left breathing.'

'*Bloody hell, Harry! The man sounds like a psychopathic serial rapist!*'

'Yeah, that's a fair description, although so far, there's nothing to connect him directly to any of the bad stuff, apart from the wife-bashing, but we're putting together an MO which points the finger very firmly his way and it just might be good enough for us.'

'*Bastard! I hate those pricks as much as you do! So, where do you want us, and was it with or without Seeker?*'

I laughed. 'Good on you Dave! As it happens, if you and Corrine would like to make your way to Cairns by Monday, we'll be stopping briefly at the Cairns Marlin Marina at or around 02:00 Tuesday morning. Sandy will be getting off and you will be getting on to replace her. Sandy and Corrine will then be flying to Sydney, departing Cairns at 05:05 Tuesday on Virgin, then getting the 11:25 QantasLink flight to Lord Howe Island with their restricted 14 kilos of checked luggage and 7 kilos of carry-on.

Sandy will brief Corrine on the way, but she should be prepared to pose as a young writer seeking tranquillity and inspiration on Lord Howe Island. A villa has already been booked in her name for a month, with the option to extend if necessary. She'll have to keep on with the role-playing, since there's a strong possibility she'll be accosted by our suspected perp, Senior Constable Darryl Fitzgibbon. According to Kelly, he will most likely make a play for her, even though Sandy will be staying at their house, acting as Kelly's cousin. I'll have a couple of small jobs for Corrine, so she will need her complete First Aid Kit and her set of picks. You needn't try to bring any guns. We have all the weapons we'll need.'

'*Slow down, Harry. I'm trying to write all this shit down.*'

'Sorry to be so long-winded, but some of this stuff you need to know about now.'

'*Yeah. That's a long list, but no problem. We were wondering what we were going to do next, so just as well you called. Anyway, we'll be at the marina at 02:00 next Tuesday. I presume you'll just park against the outer arm near the entrance and not bother coming inside?*'

'Yeah. That's about right. We didn't want to waste time and a taxi can drive all the way around the arm.'

'*OK mate. Let us know if things change, otherwise we'll see you there. Cheers.*'

'Thanks Dave. Cheers for now.'

Feeling greatly relieved that Corrine and Dave were going to join us, I went back out and thanked Dell for so efficiently looking up flight times and making all the bookings, including the villa, using the boat's Platinum card.

I spelt out the schedule to them, just as I had to Dave, and everyone was happy with it. 'So, we just crack on as we have been with the minimum of delays. I'd like everyone not on watch to get as much sleep or at least rest, as possible.'

Sandy nodded toward Jasper, who was lying on the huge day bed at the rear of the cockpit, with little Krazy curled up against his furry belly. 'Jasper's going to be very disappointed if we don't stop at the creek on Cape York to let him make contact with his mate, the croc.'

I grinned at her. 'Good point. It was a pretty magical encounter that night. I still have trouble believing I let Jasper make me sit there with those monster jaws just a couple of centimetres away from my legs, while he went to pee and have a feed! Then when the bugger opened his eyes, looked at me, yawned and went back to sleep; just because Jasper had told him that all was well.'

Sandy laughed, 'We'll be famous, or Jasper will anyway, when we release that video. I don't know if she told you, but Tracy put a video together of the whole thing from start to finish, both with what she shot with the UHD hand-held, plus some of the footage from the masthead camera. She added titling and tidied it all up so it looks very professional, but made it even more scary! She left it with me to do as I saw fit, so it would be a shame not to show at least the interested naturalists and animal behaviour people.'

I nodded, 'That's true. I wouldn't mind having a look at the whole thing. It'll probably give me nightmares...again. But it should only be shown to the right people, and on condition we protect Jasper and conceal the location of the croc.'

'Agreed. So how about we put in there for a couple of hours. That should be enough time for Jasper to at least make contact if his mate is still there. And I'll shoot video if he comes around, of course.'

'OK. I guess a couple of hours isn't going to make that much difference.'

Sandy smacked me lightly across the arm, 'Lighten up, big boy, and stop worrying about a few hours. There are higher things in play here than keeping to your timeline, and making fresh contact with the croc would be an amazing thing.'

So that pretty well took care of Saturday evening after we tidied up the trip-plan, had a light tea and a couple of NQ teas, then the off-watch headed for bed. Somehow, Sandy left me asleep and took the midnight to 06:00 watch from Alex and Bree so I had one of the best night's sleep for a long time. It also restored much of my humour which may have been the reason behind the scheming of the two ladies.

By the time the big island called Muralug was rising above the horizon, it was early afternoon and we were making good progress. Our objective was the small creek which flowed into the sea on the east side of a ridge that poked out from the beach a short way. It was the last little cape before the big one that everyone wanted to stand on the tip of, and although the entrance was shallow, we had no trouble slipping in over the tumbling mess of small waves breaking across its mouth.

Minutes later, we were anchored in about the same spot as when we'd first come this way from the other direction, and although no one had said anything to him, Jasper was on high alert, standing up in the bows as we drove in across the bar, then swapping ends to peer over the sterns. Several times he made a very loud, yowling sound that echoed off the steep hill right beside us. We only intended to stay for a couple of hours, just to see if the croc turned up, so we didn't get too settled.

We'd decided to have a late afternoon tea and Bree was cooking up something that smelt great, when Jasper gave a series of short, sharp yap sounds and stood, almost quivering with excitement on the outer edge of the daybed.

'Hello,' said Sandy, quietly getting to her feet and flicking the camcorder on, 'this might be some action.'

Moving slowly, we stepped toward the rear of the cockpit, not seeing anything at first, until Alex quietly said, 'Straight astern, Commander, about 30 metres out. Eyes only.'

Then we saw them, looking for all the world at that distance, like a pair of seed pods floating with the current, except they remained the same distance apart. Jasper yowled again and though Krazy was beside him, she remained quiet and un-moving. The pair of seed pods weirdly turned to seemingly float across the slight current, tiny ripples marking their position more distinctly, until a second pair of rounded objects appeared about a metre and a half ahead of the first pair.

'Nostrils,' the big man said quietly, 'he's getting game by coming up and showing himself more, but he's a very, very big fellow! I hope you trust Jasper's opinion.'

'Well, it does look like he might be Jasper's mate alright,' I commented as the four objects continued to float across the gentle tide flow toward us. 'I certainly hope he is! If not, he could rip the boat apart if he got pissed off with us!'

Jasper didn't seem to have any doubts about the big croc's identity, as he trotted down to the stern boarding platform, mewling loudly all the way. Wisely, Krazy and the rest of us stayed where we were. When the croc was just four or five meters away, he lifted his head and most of his upper body to the surface, revealing his enormous length, with just the tip of his massive tail twitching lazily to propel his streamlined bulk through the water.

Nearly up to the boarding platform, his huge jaws parted slowly in what looked like a yawn and he gave a soft, coughing grunt that one could imagine passed for a greeting, if such a thing was protocol for crocodiles to say hello to another species. He lifted his head higher and moments later, had slid most of his metre-long head up onto the stern platform, forcing Jasper to step nimbly aside at the last moment and for the whole boat to lurch and dip alarmingly.

His head was, in fact, too long for just the stern platform, so he gave a slight flick of his tail and a quick twist of his body, which parked his snout up on the second step, with Jasper standing beside his jaw and close to one massive, amber eye. That eye then closed and opened a few times, whereby Jasper sat down and mewled softly.

I saw Sandy had caught the whole incident on video, although now Jasper and the croc were together again, nothing seemed to be happening, except Jasper had assumed his sphinx position right beside the croc's jaws, with what looked suspiciously like a grin on his face. I remembered I had a large, slightly smelly beef roast in the bait locker well past its use by date and was going to be used as crab bait, so I carefully dug it out from amongst the fish carcasses and to the horror of the rest of the crew, stepped slowly and quietly down until I was just above the croc's snout.

Jasper didn't move, but the croc's eyes were locked onto me and the large chunk of slightly smelly meat. I stretched down and held it near his nostrils, heard one sniff, then the bear-trap jaws opened slowly in what I took to be a 'thanks, that smells just perfect to me,' type of look, so I tossed it into his cavernous, creamy-white mouth.

He closed his jaws slowly, gave one convulsive swallow, then burped a noxious cloud of fishy smell, before closing his eyes and apparently resuming his mental commune with Jasper. I gave Jasper a quick pat, slowly retreated back up to the cockpit, then further back to the table where the others joined me.

Sandy poked me in the chest, a worried look on her face, 'You idiot! What the hell were you thinking, hand-feeding a wild croc of that size? You're not bulletproof, Harry! I don't want to lose you just yet, and not in the belly of a giant crocodile! So don't do anything like that again!'

I opened my mouth to protest that all was well, when Dell shook her head slightly, so I contented myself with a placatory, 'Yes dear!'

'Don't you bloody well 'yes dear' me either, boyo, or you'll be on a nookie-free diet for a week or two!'

In the face of such a threat, I shrugged helplessly, then kissed her in a flash of inspiration.

'And that doesn't change things either,' she retorted, heading inside to brew a fresh pot of tea.

I finally remembered the retractable and very expensive masthead camera, so I followed her inside to the chart table where I hit the right buttons, waited until it had woken up and unfolded itself. When it was ready, I tilted it down and aft, then zoomed in so that just the stern platform was in the UHD picture.

The only change to the scene since I left, was that Jasper had wriggled even closer to his mate and was resting his head on the croc's jaw, both with their eyes closed.

With a mug of fresh tea in hand, I looked around the crew for opinions and as usual, it was Dell who put the whole thing in the correct perspective by giggling. 'Well Harry. It doesn't look like we're going anywhere for a while! At least, not with a ton or so of croc hanging off our stern!'

The others thought it was funny as well and all had a good laugh, which I finally joined in, accepting the situation for the magical experience it really was.

CHAPTER 8

SUNDAY/MONDAY, CAPE YORK

As evening closed in, my plan to get on our way after a couple of hours was shot to bits. The croc was still parked on the stern and Jasper refused to leave him, even when tempted with food. Krazy cat lived down to her name and ventured down the stern steps to sit beside big brother and their giant, super colossal, new best mate!

After we'd had another lovely meal put together by Bree, and with no sign that Saltie and Jasper were going to part, I decided we should stand night watches as the situation was highly unusual and I wanted people around if and when Saltie decided to bugger off again. Therefore, Dell and I took the first watch, leaving Sandy to get a good night's sleep. Alex and Bree would be called for the midnight to 06:00 shift, if our visitor was still in attendance.

With the boat stationary, there was actually nothing to do except check on the communing pair of mis-matched creatures every so often and have a look around in case we had unexpected and unwanted visitors of the two-legged variety. Dell was still very excited by the croc's behaviour, not having seen him before, and wanted to fool around a bit. She and Sandy must have come to some agreement about this, as despite my own, unusual reservations, the bit of tit and bum messing about soon escalated into being more serious. When Dell told me that she and Sandy had been talking and that they had come to an agreement, I happily entered into the spirit of the occasion. And Dell as well, for that matter. It was a good thing the mozzies were absent, or we'd have looked a mess by morning. We couldn't use the stern shower to wash off as there was a crocodile lying on it, so we went below, one at a time to clean up.

Dell kept a steady stream of hot tea coming at me and wanted to snuggle a bit, in-between checks on our visitor who looked like he hadn't moved a muscle since he ate our spoiled roast and appeared fast asleep. Jasper lifted his head a few times to eye us when we came to check, but also refused to move. Little Krazy wasn't quite so in tune with all the crocodile interface stuff, and came back up to be with her humans.

When Alex and Bree came up to relieve us at midnight, I told him that if Saltie actually did leave, we were getting going, regardless of what time it was, and in that case, to start the engines and I'd be straight up. With all our nav aids and sonar, neither the shallow bar or rounding the Cape would be problems.

I shouldn't have been surprised when Dell followed me below, shed her clothes quicker than a quick-change artist, and climbed into bed in the middle, cuddling up to Sandy who half-awoke. I mentally shrugged, dropped my gear and claimed what was left of the bed, getting a pat on the bum from someone as I rolled onto my side to sleep.

It was good that I did get some sleep, since I was woken by the rumble of the engines starting at 05:30 and quickly pulled shorts on and headed topside.

Alex was just in the process of pulling the anchor up.

'Good morning Commander. The big fella slid quietly off just ten minutes ago, but it looks like he's still hanging around just upstream. Jasper's on the daybed, but seems settled enough to me. See what you think.'

'Thanks Alex, carry on please while I just check in with Jasper.'

'Very good. I have the forward-looking sonar on, as well as the radar in short-range mode. The tide is on the make and has been for about two hours.'

I noted that the anchor was just clanking home in its stowed position, so I left our departure from the creek in his extremely capable hands and crawled over the daybed to check on my big, mystical cat, who sat gazing wistfully out across the dark, still water astern of us.

I spoke softly to him as I stroked his silky black fur, 'It was good to see your big friend again, big boy cat. We might get back this way one day and see him again.' Jasper nuzzled my arm and mewled softly a couple of times. As Alex throttled up and we picked up speed against the run of the incoming tide, in the backwash of light from our stern navigation light, I saw the reflected gleam of a pair of eyes, very close astern, following us until the water shoaled and we punched through the small, breaking waves over the sandbar at the mouth of the big fella's creek.

Jasper made a final sound, then retreated to the saloon where he curled up on the dining seats and put his head down.

All three ladies stayed in bed, leaving Alex and me to tidy the boat up after our rapid departure.

'Good work Alex, getting going so quickly,' I commented. 'That will help make up a bit of time.'

The big man grinned, 'No trouble Commander, once I saw the big fella slip away, I reckoned the session was over. Quite an amazing thing to see, however. No wonder Dell was excited! The first video you showed us, plus this one will make you and Jasper real celebrities.'

'Yes, it will and I hate to think of the outcome if we did something as crass as release it on YouTube. I'm more than a bit wary about that side of it, although I'd like to share the experience with some animal behaviour researchers. I want to protect Jasper from those who would want to pull him apart, just to see why he can do all the things he can do.'

'Yes. There are people like that who would do things to him without regard for him as a complex, sentient creature.'

'Very well put Alex. I might use that line.'

It only took minutes for us to reach the Cape and round it, as despite the shallow water, we stayed close inshore, relying on our whole suite of sensors to make sure we stayed off the hard bits. In discussion with Alex, I decided we'd stay inshore as much as possible on our way south, to cut distance and time.

Monday dawned to a clear sky, and as we moved further south, the prevailing wind, an east-south-easterly, developed quite nicely, although it meant that we were sailing close-hauled or as close to the wind as we could. It was probably our worst point of sailing and threw spray over the decks which was pleasantly cooling, but meant that hatches had to stay shut, making conditions below a bit stuffy. As we were punching into the small wind swell, the boats motion changed to a more jerky, irregular one that made moving around more difficult and even lying in a bed or bunk was less comfortable. A least our speed was up above our 14-knot target average. We had lost about 12 hours with the giant croc, and although it was an experience nobody would have missed, we still had obligations and schedules to keep.

Still, if we could keep this speed, the chart plotter told me that we'd now make Cairns on or about 14:00 Tuesday afternoon.

We were well on our way when the girls decided to surface, all three looking refreshed and relaxed. In contrast, Alex and I looked and felt tired and gritty, so with little ceremony, I turned the boat over to Sandy, told her what the intention was, what direction to point the sharp ends, and returned to bed.

I was poked awake at midday by Dell, who enquired if I wanted to be sociable and join the ladies for lunch. She also told me she had changed the airline bookings and had called Corrine and Dave about the changes.

When I got topside, I grinned at her. 'Okay bossy bitch. What's the new schedule?'

That earned me a disrespectful smack across the arm, before she answered, 'Since it looks like we'll make Cairns a bit later, perhaps around 14:00 tomorrow, I simply put both flights back 24-hours and let Dave and Corrine turn up at the marina when they wanted. Dave said they'd probably still get there Monday to save changing another booking. All you have to do is call him when we're nearly there and they'll meet us as arranged.'

I complimented her on arranging everything, then turned to check our situation. The girls had the boat zipping along rather nicely and I complimented them on not having any sails flapping or luffing. I also noticed the wind had picked up and backed to be coming from the east so we were on a beam reach. That meant our speed had picked up, there were no engines running and the boat's motion was far more comfortable.

I checked the synoptic weather on-line and saw a small low had developed south of us and was moving slowly south, dragging our lovely beam wind and us with it. Our next waypoint was the very pretty Howick Island Group, we were now due to pass through at 02:00 next morning. Sandy and Dell had re-arranged the watch schedule so Dell and I shared the evening watch again and Alex and Bree seemed happy to stay with the early morning one.

It didn't matter too much, since Sandy was going to be leaving us soon and Dave joining us. I asked Sandy, in her other role as Chief Housekeeper, where she was going to park Dave.

'Logically, he should have the forward cabin here. Jasper doesn't often use the bunk, and we use the cabin even less.'

'Yeah, that'll do,' I said, 'it'll be good for him to bunk in cramped quarters again. He's been getting spoiled by that floating Italian mansion he and Corrine ponce around in.'

Night watches became quite busy as we sailed down the coast since there were many small islands to dodge and lots of areas of shoal ground which needed a wide berth. There was certainly no time for any more fooling around. Well, not much, anyway...

There was also ship traffic which had picked up a bit, with a few cruise liners going by in both directions, and in the darkness they looked like floating, multi-story islands ablaze with lights. Alex and Bree relieved us at midnight and Dell headed for her cabin while I had a shower and headed for ours.

TUESDAY

Unusually, I was allowed to sleep in until breakfast was ready and it was one of my favourites of bacon, baked beans, sausages and tomato. No eggs! There were several muttered commented about poor taste, but I liked that combo even though I also liked bacon and egg toasties.

After the feast was demolished, I kicked-back with my second mug of tea, and started to have a briefing with Sandy. We had a discussion about taking her gun with her, and while she insisted on taking it, I was concerned that if crazy Darryl found it, it would not only blow her cover but maybe cause him to do something really dumb.

Unfortunately, the official Sandy prevailed and she took both gun and handcuffs.

'I'll declare them properly to the aircrew as a serving Queensland Police Officer and as it is just a domestic flight, there's no check at Lord Howe, so no one will know I'm armed.'

'Well, when you get to Kelly's place at least hide them really well. Like maybe give them to Kelly to hide, because for sure, Darryl will search all your gear very soon after you get there.'

'Alright, dear,' she conceded. 'I'll do that. I just didn't want to be totally weaponless with that nutcase in the same house!'

'Yeah. I suppose you're right. Now regarding comms, remember there aren't any mobile phone services on the Island, so comms between you and me will have to be via Kelly's home phone for now, although Corrine will have a SatPhone. If it's an emergency and you can't use the house phone, then get to Corrine in a way which won't blow her cover and use it. We'll try to set up something better later on.'

I had a sudden thought and chuckled, 'I just remembered we're going to meet Darryl as soon as we get there since he acts as both the Immigration and Customs Inspector as well as his police duties. You'll get to meet him when he gets home from work tomorrow night.'

Sandy pulled a face, 'Gee! That's really something to look forward to.'

I ignored it and said, 'You and Mouse will have to be very careful since you aren't supposed to know each other. Unless of course, you get Kelly to 'accidently' meet her and invite her around for a drink or a meal or something like that. It might be a good way to kick things off with Corrine and Darryl if you all think it would work. I'll leave that up to you to decide, because this is really your show. We're just playing backup to this operation, because we do have a couple of heavies to subdue and a gem smuggling operation to pull apart. And don't forget you definitely don't know us boat people!'

She patted my cheek, 'Yes dear! We'll try not to cock things up too much.'

I ignored that as well, and tried to think of anything else, but the Darryl thing really was Sandy's show, and she and Kelly would have to work things out between them. Dell, Dave, Alex, Bree and I could only charge in to help if there was an emergency, in which case it would have to be with all guns blazing.

The easterly breeze held and even backed a little into the east'nor'east and strengthened, which really upped our speed and made the ride much easier. The girls took turns at the wheel, getting a real thrill out of hand-steering at speed and we were going so well by early afternoon, the chart plotter GPS readout predicted we could be in Cairns harbour by 13:00 that afternoon.

I held off notifying Dave and Corrine until we were close enough to be quite certain of the ETA, so in the meantime, we all enjoyed the smooth, powerful feeling of being driven hard and fast, while catching and passing the small swell waves coming in on our left rear quarter. As was usual on long trips, the at-sea routine involved lots of eating, yarning and playing with the two pussies. Despite Jasper's size and his occasional bursts of protective ferocity, when he relaxed, he was just an over-grown kitten and played accordingly. Although allowances always had to be made for his weight, the reach of his forepaws and the length of his claws; especially when he was batting at paper balls and dangled pieces of string and ribbons.

When I was reasonably sure of our arrival time, I fired up the Sat-Phone to call Dave and Corrine.

'*Gidday Harry. Where are you guys?*'

'Gidday Dave. We're really cracking on and have been for most of the day, thanks to a strong east'nor'east breeze and it looks like we'll be in Cairns at 13:00. We'll stay with the same plan, just do the crew exchange and piss off. Will that suit you two?'

'*Sure, no problem for us. We got into town yesterday and found a couple of good beds. We'll be on the harbour arm at 13:00, unless you advise otherwise.*'

'Great, thanks Dave. See you then. Cheers.'

With that loose end tidied up, we passed just inshore of the superb, but over-crowded diving sites of the Low Isles off Port Douglas, then stayed close inshore for the rest of the run down past a series of resort complexes that were dotted along the coast. The increasing profusion of tall white buildings ashore told the mute story of the raging development afflicting this once-pristine coast.

Passing Palm Cove, it was just a 40 minute run to Cairns Harbour, and the safe channel to the broad estuary off Trinity Bay. There was a fair amount of traffic; mostly small private fishing boats and commercial trawlers, so I left the sails up as long as possible as a personal challenge. As traffic became lighter closer in, I felt brave enough to run all the way into the huge, modern marina, executing a tight right-hand turn to head into the wind, just off the entrance.

With Alex and the girls standing by to slacken off the sheets, I quickly furled the screecher and the jib, then dropped the main halyard, before hitting the button for the furling winch to neatly roll the mainsail into the boom. The whole manoeuvre only took seconds, although they were very busy seconds. With the main river anchorage only 200 metres across from the marina, we drew several sets of claps, one muted cheer and three sets of 'smart arse's'!

My timing wasn't perfect and we weren't quite within reach of the outer arm of the marina, but starting the two engines only took seconds. With the crew quickly digging fenders out of lockers on the foredeck and deploying them over the side, I eased us alongside the marina arm. Dave and Corrine were waiting to take the mooring ropes and within a minute, we were secure and they had swung aboard to more good-natured cries of 'smart arse!' and 'show-off!'.

CHAPTER 9...

Although it had only been 10 days or so since we had parted company just off the coast of Timor, the reunion was quite enthusiastic.

After the initial greetings had been exchanged, I looked over at the wharf beside us. 'Where's the taxi? Do we have to call him back? We weren't going to stay too long.'

Corrine laughed, and pointed behind her at the huge building on the shore-side of the marina. 'No taxi, Harry. We walked over from the resort. That's where we're staying, so Sandy and I can spend the afternoon getting pissed in the bar and feeding up on mud crabs and oysters.'

I looked more carefully at the huge expanse of white building beyond the massed array of private, white-hulled fishing boats with their tall outrigger poles. 'Well, that really is convenient. Sorry to mess you around, although this seemed like the best opportunity to get both you and Sandy onto the island and get some protection in place for Kelly.'

Corrine gave me a little hug. 'No problem, Boss. We were getting bored once all the treasure had been unloaded and assessed, so this is just what we needed.'

Dave humped his bag aboard and with little ceremony, Sandy heaved hers over the rail, gave me a quick hug, a kiss and the same for the others, then hopped over the rail with Corrine in tow. I hoisted sail, Alex and Dave cast off and with an exchange of waves, we headed back down the estuary toward open water. Total time at the wharf was ten minutes, which must have been some kind of record.

Our next waypoint was Townsville and because the reef was still close-in all the way there, we had to stay alert for traffic and hard lumps like islands. There was no need to hug the coastline, so we were spared the pain of dodging too much, but there was a lot of boat traffic to watch, although most of it was commercial fishing boats. At our standard cruising pace, we were due abeam Townsville around 10:30 Wednesday, but found the good breeze was still blowing out of the east'nor'east so we were able to make good speed under sail alone.

Dave wanted to hear what had been going on, so I stayed on watch and let the others do as they wished. He brought me up to speed on the treasure hand-over and the intense excitement being generated by the auction house with their carefully calculated leaks of information.

'Fair dinkum, mate. You wouldn't believe the fuss that stuff is generating. Collectors are going nuts over the little teaser photos the auction house is dishing out, and the word is that because of the history and uniqueness of the pieces, it's going to bring in many times what we first thought. The crew are going to do very well out of it when we finally get it to auction. They'll all get way more than a million each; perhaps even two!'

'Bloody hell! I knew it was good stuff, but not that good. I guess that's why we mess around with boats and don't try to buy and sell fine arts!'

'You're not wrong there, old mate. But tell me about this fuss on Lord Howe. It sounds like there's two separate shitfights going on. Smuggled gems, bashed up tourists, a bashed-up wife, a missing girl and now a strangled girl! So, tell me your latest cunning plan. It all sounds a bit weird, even for you!'

Since Dave would be right in the middle of the mess with me, I laid it all out, making sure he understood exactly what had happened and what I'd planned in response.

'It seems that Sandy and Corrine are going to be on their own with this maniac Darryl. As in, we can't be seen to be supporting or even making contact with them in any way. This isn't like our normal team approach.'

'No, it's not and it bothers me, but it's like what we did on Bali. I couldn't see any other way to draw this character out to where we could step in and take him down. So to a large extent, the girls are bait. I thought that with Sandy right in his face all the time, he might leave Kelly alone. If he tries any crap with Sandy, I think she'll knock him on his arse and slap him in handcuffs before he knows what's going on.'

'Yeah, that seems likely, but if he behaves himself with Sandy, that means Corrine will be a target, especially if Kelly invites her to dinner like you suggested.'

I nodded ruefully, 'Yep. I'm afraid so. But you must admit, she is more than capable of looking after herself as well, and Sandy will be briefing her to not take any crap. If Darryl starts coming on too heavy, she can lash out as hard as she likes. I know she won't be taking any firearms to the island, but what knives does she have?'

He grinned, as proud of his girl's lethal ability, as was I. 'Apart from her First Aid kit, just her usual collection of ceramic cutters and stickers she tucks away in the most unusual places. She can throw them just as well. I set up a soft plastic dummy torso for her in the gym and she's been practicing heaps.'

'That's our girl! She'll be fine Dave, but we mustn't underestimate this maniac. It's almost certain he's killed twice and there's a long history of savage attacks going back even before he scored the island position. Sandy had Greg at Southport do some discrete checking into Darryl's last couple of postings and with each one, there's been a spike in attacks on young women in his area. So, when it's all put together, he looks like being a thoroughly bad one!'

'Yeah he does. But what about these other mutts we've got to take on? Is this gem-smuggling racket for real? And are these two caretakers going to be very tough?'

I laughed at his string of questions, 'Dell knows a lot more about the whole thing, having met them and seen the set-up, but from what I've gathered, they are a tough pair. Gerry Varley is an attractive woman who was 3IC in Terry bloody Xavier Johnson's Stainless Associates. Very tough personality and a good leader, with a hefty dose of the smarts. She's the brains on the island and her backup is a large guy called Steve Addy who is definitely muscle only, but he's apparently quite formidable. It'd be dumb to underestimate either of them, but I'd like to keep Gerry alive for a while to answer some questions which might help fill in some blank spaces.'

'I guess that's where Corrine's First Aid kit will come in handy,' he laughed, 'but do you have a plan to take them down, or even when would be best to do it?'

'Not complete yet,' I replied with a grin, 'and there's the start of an idea ticking over in my mind that could get us a heap of information if we can pull it off. But I don't have it all worked out yet, so hold off on the questions until I have it all up here.' I said tapping the side of my head.

The rest of the afternoon and evening passed pleasantly with happy chatter, despite the brooding menace, posed by Darryl, waiting for our two ladies. Bree kept us well fed, Dave offered to take the early watch with Dell, so I happily looked forward to a full night in bed, turning in at 21:00.

WEDNESDAY

I woke early, but refreshed, and as the first light of dawn pushed the dark veil of night back in the timeless cycle, wandered up top to find Alex and Bree on watch with Great Palm Island just coming up abeam. Hot on my heels, Dell wandered sleepily into the cockpit to say hello again, fetchingly un-dressed in a T-shirt and apparently not much else.

'I've slept enough for now,' she answered, when I asked if all was well, 'so I'll go get some teas.'

Not only did she brew up the teas, but she and Bree managed to find some crumpets in a freezer and after a forced de-frost, served those toasted and smothered with butter and golden syrup. Dave surfaced and joined in, before Alex and Bree drifted off to bed. With the breeze still holding steady out of the east'nor'east, we were scooting along at a good pace under sail alone, so I let Dave get some hand-steering time. The pleasure of sailing at a decent speed in near silence was something he really seemed to enjoy.

Our next significant waypoint was the beautiful Whitsunday Islands, but as we'd be abeam Hook Island at 01:30 on Thursday morning, I suggested to Alex that he track to the east of the cluster. I confirmed with him, that if conditions held, our refuelling and re-provisioning stop at Yeppoon would be around 06:30 Friday.

Once past the Whitsundays there were a bunch of small islands to thread our way through which would require a fair degree of alertness, but my trust in Alex's abilities was well founded and I slept well when he and Bree were on watch.

The day watch was allocated to just one person and was only for three hours at a time. I caught up on small maintenance chores under conditions like these, including engine oil and filter change, even though the good winds down the east coast had helped with keeping engine hours down. The other important job was to contact the Keppel Bay Marina to let them know we were coming in and arrange for fuel and re-provisioning.

They reluctantly accepted us at short notice, particularly with a 06:30 arrival, but were much happier when I said I was willing to pay for a 20-metre berth close to the shore, that we'd stay until Sunday and would require a hire car to go to the supermarket in Yeppoon.

The weather pattern which had helped us so much to date had changed, naturally, and the more usual south-east breeze kicked in, making for a hard slog to windward, so with plenty of fuel in hand, I decided to go back to running one engine constantly.

Despite having missed the sight of the main Whitsunday group of islands and their rugged peaks in the darkness, I reflected that this magnificent area with its natural beauty had become rather over-used and the mainland shores very over-developed, while on the opposite side of the continent, from Exmouth right up to the Kimberly coast was an un-touched paradise for boating.

I stopped that line of thinking since it was all too probable in the very near future, and despite the remoteness of the area, developers would move in and promote the hell out of that whole, beautiful and un-spoiled stretch of the Western Australian coast.

Past the Whitsundays, when I took over the morning watch, the fickle pressure systems changed the winds yet again and had them progressively coming from the north-east, then quite strongly from the north. That made for very comfortable sailing and peace and quiet returned as the engines were put back to sleep and our average speed increased again.

The course I'd plotted was almost a straight line between the extensive scatter of small islands, so there were minimal direction changes for the autopilot to make through Thursday until the final turn at High Peak Island on Thursday night, before the run in toward Yeppoon and the Rosslyn Bay Resort marina.

Since Cairns, Dave, Dell and I had been alternating the first watch so we each had a full night's sleep.

At some point, Dell mentioned she had good friends who lived in Gladstone, a retired couple, Liz and John, who had family scattered up and down the Queensland coast and in NSW.

'I hope you weren't thinking of contacting them?' I commented, smiling to take any hint of censure out of my words.

'No, not really I suppose,' Dell replied, 'although they would be very helpful getting supplies for us. Is there a supermarket at the marina?'

'No, there's none. But I've asked for a hire car of some sort so we can go into Yeppoon. There's a Woollies, a Coles and an IGA, so we can take our pick.'

She nodded, 'Yeah. I suppose will be safer rather than getting Liz and John to run us around. I trust them implicitly, but they don't know all my background and I don't want to have to start explaining it now.'

'Hmmm. Definitely safer.' I agreed.

Dell went to the galley to make tea, knowing my insatiable need for a regular supply of the stuff and returned with steaming mugs and a change of clothing, having reverted to her sleep wear of T-shirt and nothing much else. As we sipped the fragrant Earl Grey brew, she wanted to cuddle and I was happy to oblige, my appetite for tea matched by my appetite for lovely ladies. Once again, I gave thanks that my other lovely lady, Sandy, was so understanding. Still, a cuddle with a barely-clothed female was only misbehaving a little bit, and as we were still on watch, I tried to make sure things didn't escalate too much.

Nevertheless, what I was doing proved to be highly agreeable to Miss Petrie, and didn't feel all that bad to me either.

Decorum was restored by the time the midnight watch change arrived on deck and I happily handed over to Alex, showing him our position, proposed track and the waypoint for the last turn in toward the coast at or about 02:00. He and Bree were happy and relaxed and I felt grateful the big South African had proven so reliable and competent on the water. Bree seemed to have blossomed, now she had a good man to care for her and what looked and tasted like a promising career as a chef. She certainly got plenty of practice on a crew with such diverse tastes and was always trying something different.

Dell was sufficiently satisfied to go to her own bed for the rest of the night, which meant that I got hours of un-interrupted sleep and woke refreshed at 05:30 to feel the motion of the boat had changed and gladly accepted a steaming mug of sweet tea from a grinning Bree.

'All's well, Harry. I thought that you'd like a cuppa in peace before you come on deck.

There's nothing close to us and Alex doesn't mind waiting a while. We'll stay up for our arrival at Yeppoon since we want to go ashore for a walk.'

'Thanks Bree. Tell Alex that I'll do exactly as you suggested and will see him shortly.'

She smiled and left, allowing me to enjoy my tea in peace with no rush. I still stuck my head up through the big hatch over the bed to check what was happening outside, but apart from noting that we had made the turn in toward Yeppoon, the breeze was coming over our starboard quarter and we'd slowed down, there was nothing else to see.

The alarm panel mounted on the bulkhead beside the bed was showing all green and the compass repeater showed we were pointing in the right direction, so my confidence in Alex's abilities was renewed. Finally, after a pee and a wash-up, I ventured on deck, just in time to be presented with a plate of bacon, beans, sausage and tomato, my ideal brekkie. As had been suggested by the marina manager, we would go to the Fisherman's Co-op for refuelling first, before a small work boat would escort us to our temporary berth.

CHAPTER 10

Two women, one tall and well-built, the other shorter and slight of build, strode quickly back along the east arm of the marina, a duffle bag slung over the taller woman's shoulder. An observer would have noted that both ladies were very attractive and moved with the unconscious grace of fit, athletic persons. That was perhaps the only clue to the deadly abilities of the two, especially the almost child-like frame of Corrine, who had been a highly regarded sniper in Afghanistan, where she was also tasked with any necessary close and personal assassinations. She actually didn't like to kill, but didn't hesitate when the job was justified or those she regarded as 'her people' were threatened. She was also extremely competent at the job.

'Sorry for the short notice,' Sandy apologised, 'but as usual, Harry's cunning plans do seem to make some sense.'

Corrine laughed, 'Harry already apologised and like I said to him, we were getting a bit bored anyway, so this was the perfect solution. Besides, it sounds like fun!'

They grinned at each other, as despite their vastly different backgrounds, they had become very close friends over the last couple of years.

To remind herself, Sandy asked, 'What time does our flight leave?'

'Unfortunately, it's the early one at 05:05,' Corrine replied, 'so we need to be at the airport by 04:20. We might as well relax this afternoon. It's going to be a long day tomorrow and you might be heading into trouble from the start.'

'Yeah. I thought about that, so I brought my gun. Harry tried to talk me out of it, on the basis that if Darryl found it, there would be a lot more trouble, but I feel better having it.'

She suddenly giggled, 'Kelly told Harry that Darryl considers himself to be a major cocksman, and she warned me, he would probably consider any female staying in his house to be fair game.'

Corrine laughed, 'I'm sure you can convince him very quickly, that it would be a bad idea to try to mess with you!'

'Yes, I can. But I'm also supposed to be a harmless schoolteacher, so I'll have to be careful to stay in character and not come on too tough.'

'Yeah. That's a good point. But I hope for your sake he doesn't push it too far! It's all a big unknown with these psychos. You never know what's going to set them off.'

'I hope neither of us get to find out!'

'Amen to that, Girlfriend!'

Dumping Sandy's gear in their room, they decided to go swim and lie by the pool for a few hours. The poolside wet bar was a fair enticement as well, so they quickly changed into bikinis, pulled T-shirts over the top and went downstairs. The water was pleasantly refreshing, and the cocktails even more so, which lead to both becoming more than a little bit giggly.

They naturally attracted the attention of several guys and had to fend off some very pushy proposals. One in particular, a tall, muscular guy with a great tan, was very pleasant for a while and the girls enjoyed his company. But then he started trying to talk Sandy into a quickie in the pool, and while in very different circumstances she might have been tempted, she politely thanked him, but said no.

Apparently, 'no', wasn't acceptable and he started getting a bit physical, so Corrine got off her lounger, and stepped over to where the guy was sitting beside Sandy on hers.

She stood very close so when the guy turned his head away from trying to kiss Sandy, he copped a face-full of Corrine's diminutive body.

'I'm afraid my friend doesn't want to have any more to do with you, so please leave,' she requested nicely.

Seeing his plans for a bit of fun in the pool evaporating, he made the mistake of trying to push Corrine away, but the moment his arm lifted, one small hand with stiff fingers flashed forward into his upper belly. He made an odd sound, which didn't attract attention, then sagged back against Sandy's legs, an agonised look on his face.

'I did ask nicely,' she said to his face.

Afterwards, the barman who tried to wake him, reported that the guy had been chatting with two pretty ladies. They left and the guy lay down on the same lounge and went to sleep. The ambulance crew thought he must have had too much to drink and was affected by the sun, so when they finally revived him, they told him to go to his room and lie down for a while, although the ambos did notice he had trouble walking.

The girls had a beautiful meal in the restaurant, cut back on the drinks and managed to get a good night's sleep, before a quick shower to wake up and a hasty scramble to get a cab and make the run to the airport. It was only a 10-minute trip, especially at that hour, so they easily made the check-in. Sandy felt a bit of a pang of separation as the Virgin 737-800 lifted off with its load of yawning, bleary-eyed travellers heading south.

Sydney was cool, wet and dreary after the heat and vibrant holiday atmosphere of Cairns, but the girls knew they weren't there long enough for the depressing feeling to rub off on them. By the time they got into the terminal, claimed baggage and found their way to the other terminal, half the wait time for their Lord Howe flight had been burned-up. As part of their cover, the girls checked in separately, but had a coffee together before their flight was called for boarding. The flight to the island on the QantasLink Dash 8, was just under two hours and a snack lunch was served on the way by a remarkably happy flight attendant. The scenery out the window was monotonous in the extreme. A stupid little ditty sprang to mind, something that Harry would have said. '*Water, water everywhere, it's further than you think; I hope the bloody engines keep running or we'll end up in the drink!*'

When Sandy tried it out on the man sitting next to her, he gave her the sort of look normally bestowed on a certified idiot, then, shaking his head, went back to reading his Financial Review.

At a distance from the air, Lord Howe looks like a deep, emerald-green crescent set in an azure sea, and is the remnant of a 7 million-year-old volcano. Two high peaks dominate the southern end of the island, and a flat saddle between them had been utilised as the airstrip. Landing at Lord Howe was always a slightly nerve-racking experience for the un-initiated, since the airstrip runs across the narrow part of the island from beach to beach, and isn't very long to start with.

There is no dry over-run area and that in turn restricts the size of aircraft which can use the strip, and accounts for the very strict luggage weight restrictions imposed on passengers.

If there was too much weight on landing, then the beach and the water would get to show how effective they were at stopping an aircraft.

On this occasion, the pilots had done their weight and performance calculations correctly, bringing the aircraft to a safe stop with brakes and propellers, with a whole 20-metres of runway left. While they stood in line waiting to leave the aircraft, each girl put on her game face and adopted her planned alter ego, both having practiced their cover stories on their seat partners during the flight. The warm sea air which flooded the cabin when the forward door was opened, was refreshing and lacked the heavy humidity of Cairns, while the walk across the tarmac helped loosen up stiff muscles caused by the slightly cramped seating. Corrine, trotting along some distance in front of Sandy, hadn't suffered from space problems.

Ahead of them in the terminal, while they waited apart for their bags to be unloaded, were a small group of drivers with small people-movers from the various resorts, waiting to pick up their guests. There was even one holding a sign for Corrine, a pleasant-looking middle-aged woman. Sandy was just about to ask her if she could get a lift to the police station, when a tall, slim woman with broad shoulders, finely muscled forearms, and a startling shock of white-blonde hair pushed good-naturedly through the pick-up squad, glanced around briefly, then strode straight to Sandy. Maintaining separation, Corrine collected her bag and went with the woman who introduced herself as Jill Slade, the co-owner of the apartments. She led the way to a small bus where a young couple already sat, gazing with lustful intent into each other's eyes, apparently honeymooners! They drove off before Sandy came out.

'Sandy?' the tall woman enquired quietly, a beaming smile on her face.

'Hi Kelly,' Sandy replied warmly, happy to see her charge still in one piece, and holding her arms out for the expected show-hug and air-kiss, but was surprised and pleased when Kelly grabbed her in a real bear-hug.

'Oh Sandy! Thank goodness you came. Since I called Andy, I've been really worried Darryl might find out somehow and blow a mental fuse. But now you really are here, I feel better already.'

She finally let Sandy go, collected Sandy's duffle and headed for the parking area outside. Safely in private in Kelly's little car, they were able to talk more openly.

The first thing Sandy wanted to know was, 'How has he taken to my coming here?'

'He was a bit put out at first, then when I showed him the photo you sent through, he changed his mind and said it might be good for me to have another female around for a while. It was actually an odd thing for him to say, so I have concerns about his intentions. Please be careful.'

Sandy smiled grimly, 'Yeah. Harry passed on your warning, so

I'm prepared for anything. The only thing is, I need to stay in my role as a meek Primary Grade School Teacher, so I can't get too heavy with him until we're ready to take him down.'

Then it was Kelly's turn to look grim, 'That's what I'm afraid of. He really does think he can do anything and get away with it!'

Sandy patted Kelly's arm reassuringly, 'I'll be okay. But we have to wait until he does something really bad before we nail him. Otherwise, he'll just wriggle out of any minor charges with a smack on the wrist. We want to put him down properly.'

Kelly nodded, 'Good. That's what I wanted to hear. Quite apart from beating me up, he can't be allowed to continue killing and maiming girls, here or elsewhere! By the way, wasn't someone else coming with you? Was there a change of plan?'

Sandy laughed, 'No change. She came on the same flight and you walked past her as you were coming in.'

'Really? I was looking for someone really big and strong! You know, like a Russian wharfie, from what Andy's told me about all the things she's done.'

'That'll make Corrine laugh. She was the small, petite one who left with the lady from the Retreat Apartments.'

'Oh, that's great. That's Jill Slade. She and her husband George are lovely people. They own the apartments and keep them in beautiful condition. They're less than 400 metres up the road from us. So what's Corrine's story?'

'Since she can get away with looking a lot younger than she is, she's posing as a young writer who has come to Lord Howe to get away from the noise and distractions of the city, while hoping that inspiration comes knocking on her door. She's here for backup for us, as well as presenting another pretty face who might stir Darryl into ill-considered action. She's quite deadly in hand-to-hand combat.'

'Wow! I didn't realise. You seem to have a lot of faith in her!'

'We sure do. She doesn't hold back when necessary. There are some stories to tell that'll curl your hair, but maybe at a later time.'

'I'll hold you to that,' Kelly said seriously. 'Andy said she was an assassin in the Middle East war?'

'Yeah, she was. And the squad sniper. She's amazing with a .50 calibre Browning M2.'

Kelly blinked a few times. 'Wow again! I can't wait to hear her stories.'

'All I can tell you now, is that she's the one Harry pulled out of an ambush under fire after she was shot and was bleeding out, but pinned down by Taliban gunfire. He got shot as well, but kept running back and forth, Corrine over his shoulder, while firing back at the bad guys. He drew their fire until the rest of the squad got to better cover, then managed to get clear with a badly wounded Corrine still over his shoulder. She was still alive, but they almost lost her for a while. They were both medically discharged after that and Harry scored the maroon ribbon for his efforts!'

That widened Kelly's eyes. 'Holy crap! **That** maroon ribbon? The real deal?'

Sandy nodded, 'Yep. That's the one. But he won't talk about it. He reckons he was stupid to get shot like that and should have done things better. Naturally, Corrine doesn't agree and was quite happy with the outcome. The pair of them have quite a history together, even before then, but they won't talk about it in open conversation.'

'I guess I can understand that. Anyway, we'd better get home and settle you in before his Lordship arrives. He didn't expect to be late today, but because he wears so many hats in his job, he never really knows. I try to plan meals which can either be easily reheated or cooked quickly when he shows. Unfortunately, my planning doesn't always work and that can be enough to set him off into a rage.'

Sandy looked at her carefully. 'You don't show any bruises at the moment, for what that's worth.'

By way of answer, Kelly undid several buttons of her shirt and slipped it down off one shoulder, showing a large purple and yellow bruise extending down her bicep. After doing the buttons securely up again, she pulled her shirt tails up to expose her tanned and ridged belly and yet another very large bruise on the left side, spreading across her midriff.

'Bloody hell, Kelly. Both of those must really hurt! They're right on serious muscle.'

She poked a face, 'Yeah. Tell me about it. This is what finally brought me to my senses and made me call Andy for help. There are a few more I could show you, but suffice to say they hurt just as much. I live on Panadol Forte and a good friend lets me have a yippee weed biscuit occasionally which really does help!'

Sandy raised her eyebrows. 'Yeah. I've heard they can be really effective sometimes.'

Kelly nodded, 'I don't have one very often. Just when the bits he's hit, stop me moving around freely. Darryl's an important person in the island's administrative structure, doing Customs, Immigration as well as Policing, so I'm supposed to be a bit of a social butterfly!'

Sandy gave a soft chuckle, 'Sorry. I really can't picture someone like you sitting around doing the tea and cucumber sandwiches routine with the blue-rinse set.'

'Well, it's not exactly like that, but you get the idea.'

At which point, Kelly started the car and slowly drove the two kilometres back to town. The road scenically curled around the south east end of the airstrip, the beach just a couple of metres away, and she looked carefully left and right before crossing.

After backtracking along the other side of the airstrip, she then followed the western shore of the island, where the shallow water in the beautiful lagoon actually did have a turquoise shade, before turning into a side-street, then around a curve. They pulled into a driveway that was heavily-shaded by masses of trees, including the ubiquitous Kentia Palms which are the Island's only export to the rest of the world. The house, attached to the rear of the Police Station, was of simple construction as all building materials had to be imported by the fortnightly supply ship. Brick anythings are very rare and lightweight composite materials are the norm.

The house was immaculate and certainly comfortable enough, as Kelly showed Sandy to her room, which was quite large, bright and airy, with a double bed and a brightly-coloured doona cover. A guest bathroom was just beside it and she had it to herself because Kelly and Darryl had an en-suite. The lounge room was also bright, airy and cheerful, but when Kelly served tea, they took it out to the real social centre of the house; the outside patio where a gas BBQ was located near a large table with eight chairs. The outlook was a lush, tropical-looking garden, almost overgrown with Kentia Palms, sheltering under larger trees which looked like Moreton Bay figs and created a slightly dim, green-cavern look that proved cool and extremely restful.

'Do you need a hand to put dinner on?' Sandy asked, noting the time.

'No. It's all OK, thanks. I've made a salad to go with the lamb chops I'll do on the BBQ, but I won't put them on until Darryl gets home. He doesn't get upset about irregular eating hours, since it's always because of his odd work times. It's only stuff I muck up that sets him off.'

Sandy felt a surge of sympathy for this lovely woman who, like so many others, had put up with what must have become a living hell, before mustering up the courage to speak out and let someone else know what was going on.

Soon after, there was a crunching sound from the driveway leading around to the back of the house, and a man appeared on a bicycle, a form of transport which Sandy had already noted was by far the most popular on the island.

As he dismounted, she took in the police uniform with Senior Constable chevrons on the sleeves, although he wore uniform shorts. He was of average height, about 5'9" in the old scale and of a very muscular, stocky build with tousled blond hair and disconcertingly pale blue eyes which seemed to hide his inner self.

His arms were long and his hands very large, but for all that, he had a pleasant, open face with a quirky grin on it at the moment, as he parked the bike and said, 'Hi ladies, I'm home. You must be Sandy.'

Sandy stood and shook his hand, feeling the massive strength in his fingers, although he politely didn't try to crush hers. 'Hi Darryl," she said quietly, 'I'm pleased to meet you and thanks so much for having me here.'

He was openly giving her an approving and detailed up and down inspection as he said, 'Oh. No problem. It'll be nice having a fresh face around for a few days or so. I don't really get to know the tourists while they're here and as for the locals, we all know way too much about each other already. Isn't that right, Kel?'

Kelly hurriedly smiled, 'Yes. That's right. The village is small and everyone is very close, but it will be good to hear a different opinion about things. Anyway, can I get you a beer, Darryl?'

'Yeah. That'd be good, thanks. I'll be sociable with Sandy for a few minutes, then go and change before dinner.'

He looked her over again, before saying, 'So you're the long-lost cousin. How come Kelly's never mentioned you before?'

Sandy smiled easily, 'We haven't made contact for nearly 20 years. We were quite close as teenagers, when we went to the same school for a while, but then Uni, work and life took us in different directions. My parents died when I was young and I was raised by a series of rellos, so I was always moving around. The last of them died recently, so Kelly is about the only family I have left. I'm a Primary School teacher, but I felt I needed to get away from work for a while so I've taken a six-month sabbatical.' Sandy realised she was babbling, but Darryl's steady stare with those pale blue eyes was very unsettling, so she continued, disconcertingly aware she was sounding just like a nervous Primary School teacher.

'I thought of Kelly, traced where she was and called to see if I could visit. Gee, the restriction on visitor numbers makes it a bit hard to get in, but I must have just made the 400 allowed.' Her attempt to deflect his interest wasn't really successful, as he brushed that comment aside by saying, 'Oh, you would have been allowed in regardless. I am in charge of Immigration after all.'

'That's right. Kelly mentioned you have to wear a lot of hats, as well as being the law-enforcer. But there can't be much crime here in such a small community?'

His eyes briefly glittered with a strange emotion, before he blinked and the brief insight into his twisted mind passed, as he replied, 'No, not very much. But people in any community have all sorts of secret lives which sometimes cause problems. Although to be honest, I have more trouble with golfers behaving badly at the 19th tee when there's a tournament on.'

'Really? Do you get lots of visiting golfers?'

'Every November there's a Golf Week run by the Club which draws a lot of mainland visitors and it usually stirs things up for me. Otherwise, no. There's not a lot of crime. People don't bother locking their house doors, for instance, since they all look out for each other.'

Sandy was about to ask if the savage bashing, rape and murder of a young, female tourist qualified as a crime in Darryl's book, but decided sarcasm would be way out of character.

Kelly returned at that point with a tray, balancing a beer for Darryl, glasses of wine for herself and Sandy and a plate of lamb chops for the BBQ. Declining Sandy's repeated offer of assistance, she quickly booted the thing into life, put the chops on, and joined in the conversation, which had turned to the subject of the rat plague which had developed on the island. For the rest of the evening, Darryl proved to be a pleasant host and a good conversationalist, to the extent that Sandy had no further opportunity to ask about the murdered girl.

The evening wrapped up quite early because both Sandy and Darryl were tired and Darryl had an early start on the morrow.

CHAPTER 11

FIREBIRD, FRIDAY, YEPPOON

As promised, the marina map clearly marked where everything was and at that hour, the fuel wharf was vacant. The amiable young fellow who took our mooring lines and passed the fuel nozzle up to me, carefully wrapped in rag to soak up dribbles, was most curious about the amount of fuel which kept flowing into our tanks, but the sight of the orange cockpit bladder tank satisfied his curiosity.

Finally, we were full of fuel and after swapping two drums of used oil for two new ones, the marina work boat appeared and a pretty young lady in work clothes invited me to follow her. It turned out that my generous offer to pay for a bigger berth had given us prime position in a 24-metre slot closest to the shore, since there were no big boats in at the time.

Other staff were on hand to take our lines and with a tide range which could be up to 4.7 metres, they were careful about safely securing us. Fortunately, all the marina arms were of the floating variety which meant the walkway was always at the same relative height to the boat, regardless of the tide state. I went up to the office to check-in and see if my request for a car had been successful, and was pleasantly surprised to find that the more expensive berth allowed us access to a small SUV vehicle for the duration of our stay.

On impulse, I told the staff we'd stay two nights, departing first light on Sunday, which pleased them and would no doubt please the crew since there was an excellent restaurant and bar near the office as well as showers and a laundry. Back aboard, the news of our extended stay did indeed delight the crew, so Dell immediately gathered everyone's washing and headed for the laundry, while Bree finished her shopping list and checked if anyone wanted something special. She and Alex volunteered to do the shopping run, and I was happy to hand over the boat's unlimited credit Visa card.

Twenty minutes after tying up, Dave and I were kicking back in the cockpit, with little to do while the other three did their stuff. After chatting for a while, Jasper politely reminded me that he'd love to have a walk by chewing rather firmly on my big toe, so I fitted him with his wide, studded collar, attached the length of chromed chain which seems to reassure ordinary mortals when they get close to him, and took him for a walk up and down the long arm of our side of the marina. He considerately managed to poop over the side without falling in, then happily trotted along beside me out to the far end, then back in to our berth.

We only met a few other crews, all of whom gave us a wide berth by backing up a side walkway as Jasper padded past, a dopey grin on his face. The only exception was a little girl who spotted Jasper before her mother did and had her arms wrapped around his neck before her mother finished climbing down off a large cruiser. When Mummy turned around and spotted her dearly beloved hugging what looked like a small black panther, she promptly chucked a wobbly and sounded off like a fire-truck siren!

'Emily! Get away from that vicious creature immediately!' She turned her attention on me next. 'How dare you allow such a vicious, wild animal out in public! I'm calling the police!'

By this time, the vicious, wild animal was lying on his back, four paws in the air and his tongue lolling out, while the screeching, wild-eyed woman's rant spluttered to a stop as she took in the scene of her daughter bouncing up and down on Jasper's belly, while bracing herself by hanging onto both his forepaws.

'Actually, madam,' I politely replied, as she drew a breath, 'I am the police and I have a permit for this so-called vicious animal who is at present being used as a trampoline by your daughter. I might add that both seem to be enjoying themselves immensely; something I think you would do well to note, if you cared to be quiet for a moment and see the pleasure your daughter is getting from playing with my cat.'

She drew another breath, apparently to give me another serve, when little Emily stopped laughing for a moment to cry out, 'Mummy! Look! Isn't he beautiful, and he's purring, just like Ginger, my kitten!'

The woman favoured me with her best chook's bum expression, but then grudgingly declared, 'Yes. OK then. You do make a good point and he does seem to be well-behaved. Emily likes him well enough, but it gave me an awful scare!'

In my best British accent I said, 'My humble apologies. I was merely taking Jasper for a walk. He's been cooped up on board for several days without a chance to have a run on dry land. I'll take him over to the park after it's dark.'

She gave a shaky laugh, 'Oh that's alright, Mr.....ah...I obviously over-reacted. I'm sorry too, as I've come to trust Emily's judgement in such matters. She always seems to know when something isn't right about someone, man or beast.'

I gravely inclined my head in acceptance of her olive branch, and hoped that I wasn't bunging it on too much when I said, 'Stevens, Harry Stevens, at your service, and my cat, Jasper.'

I addressed Jasper, still flat on his back, with Emily now lying along his chest, her little head with its mop of blonde curls, tucked under his chin, 'Jasper. When you can get up nicely, please say hello to Emily's mum.'

That request gained me a strange look from Mum, which quickly turned disbelieving when Jasper slowly and gently rolled sideways so that little Emily was carefully deposited on the warm wood of the decking. He then rose to all four feet in a smooth, lithe motion, stepped carefully over Emily and sat in front of Mum. His huge right paw, claws carefully sheathed, was lifted to her and she was so surprised she shook it.

'How did you do that?' she gasped, 'I'm a behavioural psychologist and I know that animals can't understand complex spoken language!'

I smiled gently as Jasper returned to gently nuzzling Emily, who hugged him hard around the neck, 'No. Of course they can't, but I have no explanation to offer, so we must accept that there is much we have to learn about nature and all its creatures. Still, we mustn't delay you any longer. Come Jasper. Say goodbye to Emily please, pussy.'

That was cause for my dear, obedient cat to let out a loud 'merowl' of protest, before he nuzzled Emily one last time. As we turned away, Emily called, 'Can I come and visit Jasper again? Please Mister?'

I turned and smiled at her, 'Of course you can Emily, any time; but you need to ask your mother first. We're on the catamaran *Firebird* closest to the shore and Jasper and his kitten, Krazy are there most of the time.'

I resumed walking, and Jasper finally dragged himself away from Emily, picked up the end of his chain in his mouth, then turned and walked sedately beside me back to *Firebird*. When we were out of earshot of Emily and her mum, I said, 'You enjoyed that, didn't you furball?' A soft 'huff' was the stern reply.

As I stepped aboard, Dave looked up from reading the newspaper. 'What's with the shrieking female? You didn't flash her or make one of your disgusting propositions, did you?'

I grinned, 'Nah. Nothing exciting like that. Just another Jasper encounter with a little girl and a very protective mum, who I think has become a new Jasper convert.'

'Ahhh...One of those. That explains it.' And went back to his reading of the latest trouble and strife around the world.

Happy to disturb him again, I said, 'While I think of it, Jasper and Krazy might have a small visitor in the form of an 8-year-old girl called Emily. Jasper will look after her.'

'Good oh. Is mummy OK?'

'Yeah, pretty good actually, for a head-shrinker. A bit twitchy, but easy on the eyes. I'm not sure if there's a Mr, but they came off a large cruiser out toward the end of the arm.'

'Great. Jasper can play with Emily while I impress mummy with my sparkling repartee!'

'Just as long as that's all you try to impress her with!'

"How could you think such a thing, Mr Stevens! I'm shocked and disappointed.'

'You could be both if Mr Psychologist takes exception to a blonde-haired boat-bum cracking onto his wife.'

Dave laughed, 'That'd be the multi-millionaire blonde-haired boat-bum doing the cracking, if you don't mind, Mr Stevens! It makes all the difference!'

He wasn't kidding. I knew the war loot we had taken from previous ops had made the four of us multi-millionaires in our own right, although interestingly, while Dave and Corrine had spent some of the loot on a bigger boat, we all kept the same lifestyle and had made very little change in our habits. To an extent, being members of the Special Marine Strike Force took us into enough trouble and gave us enough excitement, to very nicely fend off boredom and keep our minds active.

I was still standing while all this rubbish was being bantered about, so I spotted Emily and Emily's mum strolling down the marina arm toward us, with what looked like a bag of laundry in her arms.

'Speak of the devil, old son, here they come now. Looks like they're on the way to the laundry.'

Emily squealed with delight when she spotted *Firebird* with Jasper in his sphinx position on the day bed, which projected out almost overhanging the walkway.

'Hello again, Mr Stevens,' mummy said. 'We're on our way to do the washing.'

I inclined my head in greeting. 'And very good facilities they are too. Our crew put some on earlier before they went shopping.'

Dave stepped up beside me and I saw mummy's eyes drawn to his very impressive physique, with a tanned and perfect six-pack belly, since he hadn't bothered putting on a shirt.

'May I present my colleague, David Robson, who is assisting me on this cruise. He left his own boat at Southport to come up here.'

She nodded, her arms still full of the large bag of clothes, 'I'm pleased to meet you David, and I'm sorry I didn't introduce myself earlier, Mr Stevens. I'm Carly Richards and of course, this is Emily.'

Dave said hello, obviously admiring Carly's very tidy body which was displayed nicely in a T-shirt and tight shorts, an outfit she hadn't been wearing when Jasper and I encountered her. Then Emily piped up, 'Can I come and play with Jasper again? Please Mr Stevens?'

'Sure, you can, Emily,' I said, 'but have you asked your Mum?'

That formality was quickly disposed of and Carly shrugged helplessly. 'I'm sorry to impose Mr Stevens, but she's been pestering me since we met. Perhaps if she played with Jasper while I put the washing on, if that wouldn't be asking too much?'

'No problem Carly, and it's Harry, if you would. Perhaps when the washing is on, you might like to come and have a cuppa with us while the machine does its thing. Jasper will look after her while you put your laundry on.'

She smiled and it was like the sun just rose again, transforming the severe face we'd seen so far, into someone totally different. 'That sounds like a great idea, thanks Harry, and I do believe Jasper will look after my little girl.'

Dave chipped in, interrupting the stream of heavy looks passing between himself and Carly, 'Count on it, Carly. I'll go put the kettle on, so you'd better get to the laundry.'

'Oh...yes. I'd better do that,' she said, looking somewhat flustered. 'Err.....thank you.' She turned and wandered toward the admin building, as Emily scrambled up the steps and hopped onto the daybed with Jasper.

Dave put the kettle on and lined up the mugs. 'Shot duck, I

reckon,' he said with an evil grin. 'I might just ask her if there's any leaking taps that need fixing while Emily plays with Jasper and Harry supervises the kiddies.'

'Steady on,' I cautioned, 'we don't know about Mr Richards yet.'

'Nah. She's sweet. No wedding ring and that finger is tanned, so she hasn't just taken it off. I reckon he's gone, one way or the other.'

I shook my head in mock wonder, 'And you have the hide to throw off at me for liking the ladies!'

'Yeah, yeah!'

With Emily giggling and rolling around the day bed with Jasper and Krazy cat joining in the fun, we waited for Carly's return.

It wasn't long before we saw her walking back down from the admin building. However, right behind her was the unmistakably huge figure of Alex towing a four-wheel handcart piled high with boxes of goodies. Bree and Dell followed, and it was comical to see the looks on their faces when Carly hopped lithely aboard *Firebird* ahead of them.

'Our crew have just arrived back with the shopping Carly, so I'll let Dave get you that tea or coffee while I give them a hand with all the stuff to be put away.'

She quickly stood and said, 'Oh, I'll get out of your hair.'

'No need,' I smiled, 'just sit there and relax. We won't be long.' I introduced everyone, then let Dave chat to her while I helped the others move a mountain of groceries and other stuff aboard. At least they hadn't forgotten the dark rum liqueur used in my NQ teas. Carly was distracted from Dave's attempts to separate her from her pants, by the endless stream of stuff coming aboard, while I was conscious that after re-fuelling, we were already down to our loaded waterline, so this additional necessary load would bog us down even more.

Still, there was no way we were going to Lord Howe without being totally self-sufficient, so with good grace, I let the flow continue, until finally it was all aboard. We joined Dave and Carly around the cockpit table, except for Bree who stayed in the galley to whip up lunch for everyone. During the meal, we found out Carly was married to a casual helicopter pilot named Rod, who was away on a job, but was expected back in a few days.

In return, I dispensed the official cover story that we were a diverse group of dive enthusiasts and were on our way to check out some of the best dive sites in the South Pacific, notably around Vanuatu. I added that we were fresh from doing the same thing around the Indonesian Archipelago, but wanted a change of scenery.

I was also careful to stick as closely to the truth as possible, remembering Carly was a trained psychologist who would spot a lie very easily. I didn't want some wrong words to start somebody thinking we might be anything other than the dissolute bunch of pleasure-seeking boat-bums we said we were. It turned out Carly also did contract work, so between the two jobs, the Richards family lived very well and were easily able to afford the boating lifestyle.

With lunch disposed of, Carly went to fetch her washing and on the way back, tried to collect a violently protesting Emily, so for the sake of peace, we agreed she could stay until either her spring ran down or Carly came to collect her.

With Emily and Jasper transferred to the bow trampolines where they had a bit of a kip, Alex asked, 'What's the plan, Commander?'

'Stay here today, tonight and all tomorrow. We leave early on Sunday, tracking coastal to the northern tip of Fraser Island, then straight for Lord Howe. That's a total trip of 683 nautical miles, and should take 50 hours or so, which will put us on Lord Howe on Tuesday morning. Until Sunday morning, everyone can do as you please. We have unlimited use of the car, so some sight-seeing might be fun. Otherwise lay about, eat, drink and enjoy.

CHAPTER 12

YEPPOON, AND AT SEA

Until Sunday morning, the crew kicked back and relaxed, following the soldier's principal that one should eat and sleep whenever possible. Several car trips into the surrounding area were interesting and with some difficulty, I persuaded Dell to avoid contact with her friends, Liz and John who lived just down the road a couple of hours.

Much use was made of the marina restaurant and bar, however, so Bree had a bit of a break from cooking as well. Dave and I checked over all the mechanicals and rigging on *Firebird* and only had to replace a couple of sheets which were showing signs of chafing. The chandlery had good stocks of the best braided rope, so I was happy to make the replacements. The engines had been given oil changes recently and checked out perfectly. Following protocol, I placed a call to the Lord Howe Island Port Operations manager and in reply to the cheerful person who answered, said that we were leaving Yeppoon on Saturday to head his way.

'No worries, skipper. What's your boat, how many aboard and any animals?'

'*Firebird*, a 60-foot catamaran which draws just over half a metre with the boards raised, there are five adults and two cats. The cats are used to being left aboard at times so there's no issues with them jumping ship. We're making a documentary of the best diving spots around Australia and Indonesia, so we'd like to book a mooring for a few weeks.'

'Yeah, righto. The lagoon is quiet at the moment, so there's no problem with the mooring. With that draft, I can give you one close to the jetty, but the normal time limit of a stay is 2 weeks. Is film-making the main reason why you want the longer stay?'

'Yes. We need the best conditions to get the best video, so if we have a few cloudy days or it's so windy the water gets murky, then we can't shoot and lose time. We might even need 4 or 5 weeks if you can allow that.'

'Hmmm....Yeah. Why not. The island's pretty quiet at the moment since it's outside peak holiday time. I'll give you 5 weeks, but if you finish sooner, please plan on leaving. You can always come back.'

'No problem for us, thanks Officer. I appreciate your generosity and we should be there on Tuesday morning.'

'Good work, skipper. Anytime between 08:00, and before 16:30, will make the entrance to the lagoon much easier and safer. Call me on marine VHF Channel 12 on approach and as you're coming from Australia, you aren't under quarantine, but your cats must stay aboard at all times. I'll see you at the jetty after you pick up your mooring, which will be a yellow buoy, number 15, not far out from the jetty, but I'll be in touch when you come in. Anything else?'

'No, that's great, thanks. We'll talk on Monday. Bye for now.'

With Carly's husband still away, we invited her to join us at least for meals and she seemed to like the company so much so, she was with us most of each day. Emily certainly loved the extra chances to play with Jasper and Krazy. We said our goodbyes after dinner in the restaurant on Saturday night and dawn on Sunday saw us backing quietly out of the marina berth. Once clear of the moored boats, tied fore and aft to fat piles set in the muddy bottom of the little bay, we were out into the clean water of the passage inshore of Great Keppel Island. Its rugged beauty, glorious white sand beaches and excellent diving for all levels made it a popular destination for tourists, while an increasing number of private homes were also being built.

The resort was still being re-built after a cyclone wreaked havoc on the island and was only partly functional.

We skirted the small, rugged Hummocky Island, which brought back a flood of bad memories for both Dave and myself, from the time we were on the run from the combined forces of most of the bikie gangs in SE Queensland. That unwanted attention had, in turn, forced us to resort to some very nasty tactics to stay alive and remain one step ahead of the horde, hellbent on murder! Despite our past exploits, neither of us relished the thought we might have to do the same again one day.

It didn't take our experienced crew long to settle back into cruise mode, but with the south-east breeze well-established, we had an uncomfortable ride. We had to push straight into it, running both engines without any sail raised since they would just create drag and slow us down. The usual soft, swooping ride we were accustomed to when sailing, was replaced by a stiff, choppy movement which grated on nerves and made moving around unpleasant.

No wonder so many cruising sailors only ever sailed downwind!

By the time we reached the dangerous, nine-mile long fingers of sand shoals reaching NE from the tip of Fraser Island, we were totally over punching into the choppy little wind swell.

After talking it over with Dave and Alex, I decided we would follow the coast down to a point somewhere between Coffs Harbour and Port Macquarie, before turning east for a much more comfortable run to Lord Howe.

In the last of the evening light, we gave the Fraser Island sand-shoals with their unpredictable breaking waves and ever-changing water depth, a wide berth before we gratefully turned to the south, then southwest down the flat coast of the largest sand island in the world. The run down the coast would still have us on a beat to windward, but at least we could have sail up to ease the load on the engines. The final leg east to Lord Howe would be a far more comfortable beam reach, which was our fastest point of sail.

The extra distance would add about 100 miles to our journey, which meant about an extra seven hours sailing and meant we would be dropping anchor around 14:00 Tuesday afternoon.

As darkness fell, we moved a little further offshore for safety, although there were no hard bits to run into for a while. We were still close enough to shore to see the occasional little cluster of twinkling lights showing where campers had set up on the beach, braving the indigenous dingos that had become a real nuisance, mainly because they had become so used to campers feeding them. They now became quite stroppy when they weren't fed, and often resorted to helping themselves; a big concern when young children were around.

We needed the engines on again to clear Double Island Point, but once around that, we were able to bear away, turn the engines off and sail again, even though we were on a close reach with the wind about 40° off the port bow, our worst point of sailing. The only compensation was the dramatically-moonlit, steep forested slopes which came right down to the beach. In turn, it ran uninterrupted for 50 kilometres to the Noosa heads bar. Midnight had the lights of Noosa off to our right and as Sunday night gave way to Monday morning, we laid a course for Cape Moreton, just off Queensland's capital city, Brisbane.

Monday morning breakfast was enjoyed still under sail, as the Gold Coast showed its mix of natural beauty and urban ugliness in the orange light of the new day. Ten hours later, on Monday afternoon, we reached Coffs Harbour, where I had to decide whether to call in to top off the fuel tanks, or push on. A careful check of fuel remaining showed we really had plenty, so after a brief of the crew, I announced we would turn to the east'sou'east and as a north easterly breeze was now blowing, we would head straight for Lord Howe Island.

I was also concerned about Sandy and Corrine, although Corrine had called in on the SatPhone just to say they'd arrived okay and Sandy had been collected by a tall, blonde woman who presumably was Kelly.

The new wind direction meant we could make a good speed under sail alone, so the new ETA at Lord Howe became 16:30 tomorrow, Tuesday afternoon.

There wasn't a lot which happened on that ocean leg which took just under 23 hours. We were escorted by a pod of dolphins for about 30 minutes, just after we'd set course for the island, and the magnificent animals departed as quickly as they had arrived. I shared the first night watch with Dell, and after the others had gone to bed, she let me know that she was more than a little bit frisky, but I gently suggested we might put that lovely thought on hold, at least until we were off watch. She was partly mollified by the idea that maybe we were going to get together later on, and made no further personal demands for the rest of the watch.

It was fortunate that Dave and Alex had volunteered for the second night watch, leaving Bree get a full night sleep, since a hint to Dell was like a full-blown promise! Once we'd handed over the watch at midnight, she followed me down below, shed her clothes and slid into bed beside me. I knew she and Sandy had been discussing this situation on several occasions, so felt no qualms about indulging in an extended session that left both of us exhausted and asleep in seconds.

TUESDAY

Dawn arrived with a cloudless sky and surrounded *Firebird* with a gently heaving ocean, empty of all other signs of life, apart from a solitary wandering albatross, a magnificent roving sea-bird with a wingspan up to 3.5 metres.

Its course took it close astern of us and we watched in silence as it casually trailed a wing-tip feather lightly across the face of a wave.

'How do they fly for so long?' Dell asked, totally in awe of this beautiful bird with its extended black line above its eye that makes it look like a permanent frown.

'It's a form of flight called dynamic soaring, and it requires the birds using it to follow a swooping, semi-circular flight path along the backside of waves. It wasn't until recently when scientists worked out how they did it. Before then, it was assumed they used the updraft in front of the wave to soar on. They can fly without flapping their wings for many hours at a time, provided the wind blows and there is a reasonable wave height to make the dynamic soaring thing work.'

'Well, whatever they do, they certainly look beautiful!'

The one we were watching suddenly broke off its flight pattern and flew around the bows, continuing the banked flight path to come around the stern again. I had a sudden insight and noticed Jasper standing up on the daybed, the outer edge of which hangs out over the water and shelters the RIB.

'No. It couldn't be,' I muttered half to myself.

'What's that Harry?'

'Albatross are rarely interested in ships or boats, unless they drop food overboard, so I was wondering why this fella is circling us, but then I saw Jasper standing up there on the daybed and I thought perhaps he was doing his weird, mystical communication thing again.'

'Well, he's done it with a croc, that I've seen, and you told me he did the same thing also with seals and two orcas. Why not with a bird?'

I shrugged, 'I guess there's no reason why not. He's a pussy cat full of surprises!'

While lacking the drama of the croc or orca encounters, it was nevertheless a video moment so I grabbed the camera from the chart table and gave it to Dell, while I booted up the faithful masthead camera. I set the auto-track function, locked the cross-hairs on the bird and let the software do its magic.

The majestic bird flew two more circuits of the boat and looked like it was about to exit stage left on its way, when it suddenly tightened its curved flight path around the stern and angled in toward the daybed. When it had been flying about a hundred metres away, it just looked like a big bird, but as it approached the boat, slowing and descending, we realised just how big a 3.5 metre wingspan bird can be when it's up close and personal!

'Holy crap, Harry! It's going to land!' Dell gave a delighted squeal of surprise as Jasper also realised that the bird's wings were a lot wider than the daybed and he dropped flat as the albatross flopped awkwardly onto the padded bed, one wing smacking Jasper across the back of his head.

Stunned by the happening, we didn't move as the bird calmly composed itself, made a very complicated manoeuvre to carefully fold both long, skinny wings, before fussily tucking them in against his or her body. He or she gave several little wriggles to get them seated comfortably, then squatted down and closed its eyes.

Jasper's reaction was to slowly sit up now that the scything wings were safely tucked away and contemplate his latest new friend. Little Krazy cat wisely stayed perched on top of the instrument panel in front of the wheel, where her little mouth chattered continuously but quietly, at the sight of this huge bird, just within reach for once. But maybe the sight of that massive yellow beak with the sharp hook to its tip that made her cautious.

'That is fantastic!' breathed Dell. 'Do you think it wants to be fed?'

I looked at Jasper. 'Let's wait 30 minutes or so and see. If it's still there then, we can try some baitfish.'

So, we sat; Jasper sat; Krazy chattered to herself on and off and the subject of all the attention, the huge, white and grey albatross, apparently slept peacefully. Dell and I soon grew tired of sitting still and quietly resumed our normal watch-keeping routine. After a couple of hours of total inactivity, the big bird opened his eyes, gave a slightly startled squawk and looked over at Jasper before standing up, spreading its wings into the breeze and departed; just like that! Only the masthead camera recorded the event, although there wasn't much to be said for it.

'Bree will be really pissed she missed seeing that,' Dell commented with a grin, 'even though bugger-all happened.'

'True, although Jasper must have had something to do with it landing in the first place.'

Dave was the first to wander out, yawning and scratching himself in the manner that was both a standard and necessary practice for males everywhere. 'Morning, you two.'

He glanced around at the empty, gently heaving ocean and grinned, 'I see we haven't sailed off the end of the earth yet, so it must have been a quiet night.'

Dell was busting to tell him and said excitedly, 'You missed the albatross who came to visit Jasper.'

'Really? He's done it again?'

'Well, we think so. The bird was about to fly past, when it suddenly curved around the bows and came in to land on the daybed where Jasper is now. He didn't do much while he was here; just slept. Then he woke up, squawked, and lifted off.'

'I've never known them to land on a small boat like this unless they're totally exhausted, and even then, he would have landed on the water.'

'Even though he had a sleep, he didn't seem to be exhausted, so we reckon it was Jasper calling him in.'

Bree and Alex wandered out then and had to hear the story again, and Dell was right, Bree was pissed she'd missed the big bird and moseyed in to start a late hot breakfast, grumbling about missed opportunities. I went to the chart table which was the electrical and electronic nerve centre of the boat, stopped the masthead camera, stowed it under the retractable cover and played the UHD vision of the albatross on the saloon widescreen monitor so Bree could watch from the galley.

That mollified her considerably and she finished serving breakfast in a much happier frame of mind. 'Can I get a copy of that video, please Harry?' she asked.

'Of course. In fact, what I should do for the rest of the day is put together all the video of Jasper being mystical. There were the seals in Bass Strait, the Cape York croc, twice, the Indonesian orcas and now the albatross.'

She grinned, 'That'll keep you busy until we arrive at the island all right, so I'll keep you well fed.'

'But you already do that!' I protested in mock horror.

'Don't worry. I'm sure Lord Howe will give you plenty of exercise so you don't have to worry about your waistline!'

I gave her the finger and she laughed, causing me to reflect that she was coming out of her shell quite quickly since we had returned to Australian waters after the Indonesian mission. She and Alex had proven themselves to be an indispensable part of the crew. In her own way, Dell fitted that description just as well, bringing her razor-sharp mind and knowledge of the criminal side of operations, gained during her time as the Chief Investigator for the Combined Union Super Funds.

CHAPTER 13

Although I missed Sandy's company and her incisive way of thinking, I was well-satisfied the crew I had would be up to facing a set of largely unknown problems. We had all talked the possible scenarios through many times, as well as picking Dell's brain for any little detail we might have missed. Therefore, we tried to relax by settling down on the forward trampolines, which turned into an unplanned little party which in hindsight, wasn't a bad thing to happen.

I know it certainly eased a lot of tensions which had been unconsciously building up for days and as our late afternoon arrival time approached, Dell let me know that she wanted an in-depth tension-relief session. With Dell and me, sex seemed to be a given these days, particularly as she seemed to be randy all the time and it didn't matter what time of day it was when she wanted looking after. Still, it passed the time extremely pleasantly since she was an excellent bed-companion, as well as a happy and cheerful crew-member. Knowing it was with the knowledge and the blessing of my dear Sandy certainly helped. When I re-surfaced, leaving Dell still asleep, apparently very well de-tensioned, I found that because Dave was bored, he had taken over the watch and was hand-steering.

'This sailing caper is pretty neat,' he commented, knowing that normally I'd bite, but I just smiled my best Mona Lisa one and patted him on the head.

'Good dog! Now you're learning about REAL boating! If your 'floating Ferrari' wasn't so much fun, I'd talk you into a big cat.'

Dave grinned as he faked a backhander to my cheeky head, 'Yeah. Sometimes I'm tempted, but even a big cat can't go 80 knots!'

'No, it can't. But how often have you been able to do that on *Seeker*? You have to wait for near calm conditions.'

'True, but speaking of boats, have you considered upgrading *Firebird*? Just like us, you can easily afford to get anything that takes your fancy.'

'That's true, although honestly, I haven't really thought about it at all. I will admit that it'd be nice to have even more room occasionally. Anyway, what would I upgrade to? I need to keep it to a manageable size for a small crew.'

'Yes, but with Sandy a permanent part of your life, and Bree and Alex apparently very happy to live aboard, there seems to be plenty of crew for a bigger boat.'

'Yeah, OK. So just for the mental exercise, since there's nothing else to do, what's your choice of a good size which doesn't look like a four-story block of flats?'

'Funny you should ask that! I was doing some internet surfing while you were playing games with the delectable Dell and came across three that would float your boat, so to speak. One in particular is called a Sif 80, designed in Amsterdam, but built in South Africa. Eighty feet long, all carbon-fibre, very light and designed to be very fast. They talk about comfortably exceeding 30 knots under sail alone, so that would tick all the boxes, as well as your personal 'need for speed'. The layout can be changed around to suit your decadent lifestyle and still leave heaps of room for additional cabins and beds.'

'Decadent lifestyle! So says the man who has a stateroom larger that most one-bedroom units on land! Anyway, what's this thing look like?'

'Very low profile, very sleek and clean. Definitely you! Go boot up Mr Google and check the history menu. You'll see it under Sif 80. You've got a couple of hours to have a good look before we run into Lord Howe Island.'

I shuddered. 'I do wish that you wouldn't talk about running into things like that. Bad karma!'

I did as he suggested however, and immediately was very impressed by the design of the much larger boat. It would certainly sail a lot faster than the current *Firebird*. I briefly thought of how the sail plan could be modified to allow for smaller sails, but as that would need the addition of a second mast which was less efficient than just one, that thought was put aside for possible discussion with the designers. Still, the powered boom-furling mainsail on *Firebird* had worked out very well, so maybe a bigger one wouldn't be too much to handle with a small crew. Dave was right in that the accommodation plan could easily be modified to allow Sandy, me and the pussy cats to have the very spacious stern half of the starboard hull to ourselves, plus a decent walk-through robe and a generous en-suite. The cabins forward of that with their own companionway access could be shuffled around to allow two twin bunk cabins, each with their own en-suite.

The port hull could keep the standard layout of large stateroom aft, another double forward of that, then a decent laundry plus workshop, and a twin stacked bunk cabin with its en-suite right forward. All cabins had an en-suite for a total of 12 beds and 6 shower/toilets. The saloon with galley was impressively huge.

Reluctantly, I saved the data and resolved to talk to Sandy about the idea ASAP. Reflecting on what Dave had said, while I was certainly attached to my present boat, he was right in how my lifestyle had changed quite radically since the days of exploring the Australian coastline with Jasper as my sole companion. Now there was Sandy as a seemingly permanent part of my life, missions with the Special Maritime Strike Force and Alex and Bree who appeared to prefer to live aboard and take what came.

I freely admitted that I liked my new lifestyle much better than the old one, so was I even daring to think about upgrading my lovely boat? Hell, yes! Certainly cost wasn't a consideration, even though the increase over *Firebird's* initial cost would be huge.

I really liked the look of the Sif 80, having always believed that a boat had to look good as well as perform well. As well, in a practical sense, the sleek, low-profile design would assist it going to windward, as well as lower drag at anchor in a blow.

Even the layout was close to being what I wanted, so the changes would be minimal. I made a mental note when I had some more time to check for any other 80-footers from some of the other manufacturers. Cannon and OutReacher came to mind as being reputable builders who offered very fast cats, but whether they made any in that size I'd have to check.

My rare bout of introspection was broken by Dave calling out, asking if the island was showing on radar yet. I flicked the power switch and within seconds, the screen showed several targets directly ahead, so I re-joined him in the cockpit. Visually, the only signs were several streamers of cloud on the horizon, being pulled downwind by the strong winds aloft. Over the next 30 minutes, the mountain fingers which looked like they were anchoring the cloud streets, slowly lifted their shaggy green bulk above the horizon. At that point, I went back inside to use the marine band VHF radio to call the harbourmaster. He must have had the mic in his hand, replying almost immediately, and it was the same, cheerful voice who I now realised was the dreaded Darryl, but all he told me was that he'd meet me on the jetty after we'd moored, and I should bring the boat's papers with me.

After negotiating the passage into the lagoon via the north pass through the fringing reef, we found the correct mooring buoy. I left the crew to tidy up while I lowered the dinghy and motored the short distance to the end of the long jetty where a lone figure stood beside a bicycle. On first inspection, he was of average height, but of a very muscular, stocky build, with tousled, blond hair and disconcertingly pale blue eyes, which did a good job of hiding his inner thoughts. His arms were quite long and his hands were very large, but for all that, he had a pleasant, open face with a happy smile on it.

'Welcome to Lord Howe Island, Mr Stevens. That's a good-looking boat you have there; was it an easy trip?'

'Thanks, Senior Constable. Yes, it was a very pleasant run, once we got down to Coffs Harbour. We were butting a headwind before that, which wasn't so easy or comfortable.'

'Yeah. I can understand that. Still big cats ride well.'

He'd been efficiently looking through the boat's papers as he spoke, ticking items on a form held in a clipboard, before going through the crew list.

'Are all the crew divers, Mr Stevens?'

'Yes, but I normally play topside safety and let Mr Robson, Mr Chetty and Miss Petrie do the diving. Miss Welsh joins them at times when we think another attractive female body provides a good counterpoint to the underwater visuals. We find around wrecks is a good place to have the two girls up front.'

I noticed that his pale eyes took on a strange glitter for a few moments as I waffled on about the girls in front of the camera.

Seriously, he said, 'That almost sounds a bit manipulative. Don't the ladies mind?'

I laughed, 'Good grief, no! The pair of them are the biggest pair of exhibitionists I've had the pleasure to work with. Do almost anything if a camera is pointed at them. Ha, ha!'

'Who do you work for, if I may ask?'

'Oh, we're strictly freelance. This series is going to be offered to the Travel Agencies Association as a promotional tool. My contacts with them suggested it would be a good idea and should sell well, so here we are.'

'And where were you before this?'

'We've been up the east coast of the mainland, then across the top end, but the waters are usually too murky for video work in the summer. The west coast was stunning, however, particularly the Kimberly region and the Montebello Islands. We scored some amazing footage. Then we wandered around the Indonesian Archipelago for a while and I must say that as much as I love Australia, the whole area is quite superb! We cleared in-bound Customs in Darwin, then called at Yeppoon for refuel and re-stocking. That was our last port as you can see by the log entry.'

'Yes. All is very much in order. It's rare to see such well organised documents and records. Have you been in the Service?'

I gave a little self-depreciating laugh, 'Oh no. Nothing exciting like that. I was just a working boy until an inheritance made this lifestyle possible. Now it's girls, booze, boats and more girls and booze. Ha, ha!'

He made a polite noise, but that strange glitter in his eyes made a brief appearance until he blinked and it disappeared. 'Sounds fascinating. I'd like to see some of the video you shoot here, if you wouldn't mind. The Island Management Board might like to buy some fresh views of the underwater attractions, so it would be good if the pretty girls are in that segment and show up well! And perhaps there could be another short version of that one for private showing.....If you know what I mean?' He finished with a smirk.

'I'll be happy to try to accommodate that request, Senior. Especially since you've been so helpful in allowing us to stay longer.'

He grinned, 'No problem then. This way I can tell the Board if they ask, that you're doing a job for us as well, so we can hardly kick you out, now can we?'

He held out a very large hand to seal the deal, and I braced for a hand-crushing contest, but he was very controlled and only squeezed gently. 'Well. I'll let you get back aboard. Please make sure your two cats have no opportunity to get ashore. I see that one is quite big. Is that the Chausie cross?'

'Yes. He grew even bigger than expected, but he makes a good guard-cat so we don't have to worry about un-invited visitors!'

I deliberately left the heavily veiled threat hang in the air, since I'd picked up a few unhealthy vibes from his questions. Particularly the one about the girls underwater and cameras. I made a mental note to chat to the girls about what they might have to be prepared to do, to at least get the video clip rated R-18+, although I had doubts about Bree getting too adventurous! I was also glad we had two UHD underwater cameras aboard to hopefully be able to generate some good video of both reefs, fish, wrecks and girls. As a parting gesture, Darryl handed me a multi-page document which gave a lot of information about the island, where to eat, find entertainment and all the touristy, scenic things to do.

'I'll be seeing you around, Mr Stevens. I wear a lot of hats on the island.'

I smiled pleasantly, 'I look forward it, Senior Constable. Thank you for your assistance.'

He mounted his official bicycle, and headed back down the jetty and home where my lovely Sandy was waiting, while I re-boarded my official dinghy and returned to the crew.

'All OK with Darryl?' Dave asked.

'Yeah, no problem. He's very pleasant on the surface, but definitely twisted in the head. In return for allowing us to stay for at least 5 weeks, he strongly suggested that the Island Management Board would appreciate a video highlighting all the good diving sites around the island and the girls should feature front and centre. He also wants one which would be rated at least R-18+ for more a private viewing! That's the price of his co-operation.'

Dell giggled, but Bree was a little more dubious, especially about the R-rated version. 'Terrific Harry! Now we're making porno movies for a serial killer! What else is this assignment going to involve?'

I gave her a wry grin. 'That's an interesting way of putting it, and I must admit I hadn't seen that request coming. Unfortunately, it will be necessary to have something to keep Darryl happy for a while.'

'And what would we have to do in the R-rated one?' she persisted, still looking concerned.

I shrugged, 'Whatever you and Dell come up with, I guess. I thought to take him at his word and simply show more of you two. I certainly don't intend to let it become a male/female thing. You'd have to lose your bikinis at the very least, although I wouldn't plan on getting too heavy. Maybe a bit of girl-on-girl fooling around and don't worry about trying to qualify for the XXX-rating. Needless to say, the one for the Island Management will feature you ladies being decorative only. As in, playing with the fish and peering at the coral.'

She poked a face. 'Yeah. I guessed that bit. And in the 'R' one, I suppose there'd be lots of close-ups?'

'Oh, yes,' I said cheerfully, 'that'll be a given. Although, since we're making it, we can avoid close-up facial shots if you like, because in all honesty, the audience for that one won't be looking at your pretty faces very much! If you'd be more comfortable with Alex behind the camera, that's fine by me.'

Dell was still a lot more enthusiastic about the idea than Bree was, but at least she agreed to talk it over. As the conversation ran down, everyone admitted they were tired, so by mass opinion, we decided to postpone any exploration of the island until tomorrow.

One highlight was when Corrine checked in via the SatPhone to say all was well with her, she'd already been contacted by Kelly and was invited to dinner tomorrow night. She was to pretend they had a chance encounter at the Co-op, and that was the reason for the invite. We agreed that a meeting of our own, sometime after tomorrow night's dinner would be useful, otherwise a phone call would do it.

WEDNESDAY

It was a slow start to the day which had dawned cool, grey and dismal with regular squalls chasing each other in from the south-west, dragging their opaque curtains of rain like dull, grey skirts. In fact, no one was inclined to go anywhere or do anything until it cleared up, which made for a very relaxed morning for me, listening to the rain washing the salt build-up off the boat. Sometimes, it doesn't take much to keep me happy. In between showers, Dave, Alex and I checked carefully around the boat, but found nothing that needed maintenance. The weather also scuppered any chance of shooting some underwater video, a job I wanted to get out of the way sooner rather than later.

After a lovely morning tea of fresh scones, jam and cream, Dell and Bree outlined the little acting session they planned for when the weather improved. 'We can shoot both of Darryl's videos over the reef just out from the anchorage,' she said, 'or anywhere else we happen to be, although we'd prefer to be in shallow water wearing just the hookah gear, or even without. We can both hold our breath for a reasonable length of time. But if we did need an air supply, would the pump run from the RIB, or do we need to move *Firebird?*'

'No need to move, it'll fit in the dinghy OK because it only needs a good battery to run. It's a good idea about being in shallow water over the local reef, though. The light will be better, the colours more vivid.'

After kicking ideas around for a few minutes, they settled on having Alex on one camera, one of them would hold the other, with myself staying up top on shark watch. The normally impassive Alex had a growing grin on his face as the discussion progressed, which he quickly removed when Bree glared at him.

'I'd plan on your little bit of play-acting to only last about 5 minutes, and the other portion with bikinis on will be longer. However, it'll take a lot more time than that to shoot enough good video for editing. We can do all that on the boat's Mac computer. But even though the water stays gin-clear here all the time, all that will have to wait until the weather settles. In the meantime, and when the showers stop, shall we go ashore and have a closer look at this fascinating island which is in the process of trying to end a rat plague?' That last little piece of information was an effective change of subject away from 'making a porno movie for a serial killer' and drew a series of expressions of disgust from the two girls.

'How come a plague, Harry?' Bree asked.

'Apparently, in 1918 a ship called the *Makambo* ran aground on the reef, and was stuck for a few days until it could be repaired and floated off. In those few days, a number of rats escaped the ship and took up residence. Because there weren't any natural predators, they bred rapidly and over-ran the place, wiping out a lot of the native species of birds and animals. There's been a massive baiting program going on for years, and it's finally starting to show good results. The Island Management Board expects to eradicate the last of them within a few months.'

CHAPTER 14

While we waited for the weather to clear, I thought of a treat for the crew, and called ashore and made a booking for dinner at one of the best restaurants, which was located at a resort not far from the jetty. I then called a planning session to shape our primary campaign, namely, to sort out the legacy of the late and very un-lamented Xavier, gemstone smuggler and killer. Fortunately, someone was thinking since Bree said, 'If we're going to a restaurant tonight, we should do something to disguise Dell. It was only a few weeks since she was here but what if Xavier's two caretakers decide to have a night out as well?'

I mentally kicked myself. 'Good point, Bree. I should have thought of that! As our resident SFX girl, do you have any ideas?'

'Actually, I do. Although instead of a make-over, I thought the hide-in-plain-sight plan might be more effective.'

As everyone looked blank, she hurried on. 'What I mean is, I could trim Dell's hair a bit, then wrap her head tightly with a silk scarf, as though she's recovering from chemotherapy. The tightly wound scarf will alter the shape of her head, as well as providing a focal point for people's attention. A very brightly-coloured scarf would be even better at catching the eyes of others. Then a bit of judicious make-up and her mother wouldn't recognise her.

'That's brilliant!' Alex offered, in support of his lady's cleverness.

'Absolutely,' I said admiringly, 'that's really good. Can I leave you to work with Dell to make it happen?'

'No problem, Harry. It'll be done in time.'

'Great! So...I thought after dinner, we might go for a bit of a walk to settle the food down and should we happen to just wander past the house which Dell went to, as an early recon, that could provide some useful info.'

'Yeah. Good idea, Harry,' said Dave. 'I feel we've been behind the eight-ball so far and this will be more pro-active. We need the intel, but don't forget Corrine will be having dinner with Darryl, Kelly and Sandy tonight.'

'No. I hadn't forgotten, so if we need her, you get to lurk in the shadows outside her unit!'

He grinned, 'Thanks mate. That'd probably get me run off for being a stalker!'

Dell laughed, 'Well, you are, aren't you?'

Dave poked his tongue at her. 'So, we need a plan to tackle the two caretakers. Dell, you said they were both very tough characters?'

'That's right. The woman in charge, Gerry Varley, is big-framed, strong and has had some martial arts training. She mustn't be underestimated at all. Her partner, Steve Addy is just muscle; not too smart, but not stupid either. Be careful of him as he's been linked to several disappearances in Melbourne. He has a reputation for enjoying bashing people to excess, if Xavier wanted information from them. It wouldn't be any loss if he disappeared.'

'Good points. We'll look at what to do with him at the time, but we certainly can't afford to create any fuss when we move in. So… I'm thinking maybe instead of trying to force our way in with a home invasion assault, why not try stealth.'

That thought earned me some blank looks, so I continued, 'How do you think they'll have reacted to not hearing from Xavier for a few weeks?'

Dell thought a moment. 'They'll be a bit concerned and may even have tried to contact him. Xavier kept a tight rein on things, so they were used to hearing from him pretty often, especially when a shipment was due.'

It was my turn to have a think; an action prompting Dave to sarcastically remark, 'Oh, bugger! Now the plan really goes down the gurgler! Harry's thinking!'

'Smart arse!' I looked at Dell, 'I don't suppose you remember when the next shipment's due?'

'I do, as a matter of fact since I did the scheduling. Yesterday was the first Tuesday of the month, so it will be this Friday night.'

'Right. And does the collection team bring the package straight to the house?'

'Pretty much, although it might take a while for them to get back to shore, and the drop isn't at an exact time, so there can be a variation of several hours, although the earliest would be about ten pm. But regardless of the pickup delay, the fisho's would never keep it overnight.'

I smiled, happy my scattered thoughts might just come together. 'Good. So how do you think the caretakers would react to a message from Xavier, saying his normal channels of communication have been compromised? Therefore, since he needs to have a meeting with his most trusted crew, he's sending his Executive Assistant and a male escort to take over the collection operation for a short time. On Friday, Miss Varley and Mr Addy have been booked on the Qantas flight to Sydney, then Melbourne the same afternoon, but Miss Petrie and Mr Stevens are arriving tomorrow morning, for a handover. For security reasons, they shouldn't be met at the airport and will make their own way to the house to receive a briefing on the current state of affairs.

Miss Varley and Mr Addy will be booked in at the Crown Towers, in an executive suite, all expenses paid. A limo will collect them at 09:00 on Saturday, to be brought to Head Office for a confidential briefing on a sensitive matter which can only be handled face-to-face.'

I finished and looked enquiringly at Dell, who considered the scenario. 'It just might work, Harry. So long as they don't know Xavier's dead, and I don't see how they could. If I used the last set of code words which were current when I was with him, they'd have to accept the message. They wouldn't dare check back because of the 'compromise in communications'. There's no reason why they wouldn't accept the message at face value, especially if I've been sent as the temporary replacement, because they know me and that I know the whole operation. Two total strangers would be suspicious.'

She sat back, smiling. 'I reckon it's a go.'

'Excellent! Can I get you to make the phone call to them and do the flight bookings? You need to be able to give them tickets. Even though they won't be leaving the island at this stage, book the Lord Howe to Sydney and the Sydney to Melbourne portion of the flight plus the hotel. The SatPhone has an un-traceable number, listed somewhere in Uzbekistan, which is probably something Xavier would do anyway.'

'You're right. That's exactly what he'd do. I'll make the calls now, then print out the e-tickets and hotel confirmation. I'll also write up a note from Xavier with his signature establishing our credibility.'

'Brilliant, Dell! Go for it!'

While she attended to those pieces of deception, Bree took over Sandy's role as media watch and passed on a few facts about the island, adding to the stunning vista laid out in front of us. 'To our right, the whole southern end of the island rises to towering, rugged heights of 875 metres or 2,871 feet, with numerous near-vertical cliffs which drop to the sea. Just north of those heights, a narrow saddle virtually at sea-level provides the only viable place to put the airfield, although even that was angled to make it just long enough for the twin-turboprop airliners that service the island daily. The low plateau between the western lagoon and Ned's beach to the east is where the scattered population of around 380 persons lived. The whole island, which is about 10 kilometres long, is part of the weathered rim of an old volcano with the northern end of the island elevated, but much lower than the southern end.'

She stopped reading for a moment in surprise, then continued, 'It says here that some of the best dive spots are right here in the lagoon, especially in two deep holes, Erscott's and Comet's, or along the edge of the fringing reef. Then there are the Admiralty Group of islands just off the north end of the island, and Ball's Pyramid 20 km south, although it's rated as a deep-water dive.'

We gave her a clap as her recital ran down and she blushed.

'Thanks Bree. It sounds like we needn't go far to get some good video of coral and fish, with maybe the Admiralty Islands if we think we need some variation. In any case, to maintain our cover, we're going to have to do some serious diving, or at least look as though we are by going out there, although we still need heaps of video. And don't forget, we don't know who those fishermen are doing the pickups of the gem drops every month, so we have to look like what we claim to be all the time.'

The others nodded seriously, accepting that we were on the job now, although there was no reason not to enjoy ourselves.

Dell came back after a lengthy time on the phone, internet and computer, with a number of pages.

'OK,' she said with a proud grin. 'They totally bought the story about comms being compromised. I hinted Xavier strongly suspected there is a traitor in the camp and while it could be his 2IC, Con Theodopolous, there are several other candidates. Gerry hates Con with a passion and has her own corporate ladder to climb, so she's ready to shaft him any way she could. They'll expect Harry and me to come knocking on their door sometime around 15:00 tomorrow. They have a bed we can use; just one queen, I'm afraid Harry, and will be packed ready to catch the afternoon flight out on Friday. Gerry also hinted a drop was imminent, but was quite happy when I said I knew because I was the one who set the schedule. The code words were correct, so there were no obvious suspicions or bad questions.'

She floated a brief letter across the table to me and it was an authorisation to pass over the caretaker role to herself and an operative named Harry Stevens for a short period while they visited Melbourne for personal consultations at Head Office. Miss Petrie and Mr Stevens were duly authorised to conduct all island-based business as usual. The signature was a complex scrawl, but Dell assured me that it was quite indistinguishable from Xavier's.

'The only snag I could see would be Julie, Xavier's Company Secretary. She also has lofty ambitions about climbing the corporate ladder and was looking who to shaft and what dirt to hold on everyone else. There'll be a problem if she's still in the office.'

'Nope! Not a problem. Once we had Xavier secure, I spoke to my people and she was rounded up a couple of weeks ago. She's being held in custody and strict isolation. Because she knows the whole operation, she'll be a witness when this mess is finally wrapped, but only after the interrogation squad has wrung every drop of information out of her. She'll probably be offered a plea bargain in exchange.'

Dell looked very relieved. 'Thanks Harry. I was getting jumpy about the idea of Julie being on the loose with an even looser lip!'

She checked the papers again, then slipped them into a large envelope and sealed the flap since we wouldn't need it until tomorrow.

That broke up the meeting and everyone drifted off to do their own thing for a while, myself included.

Without saying anything to Dave, I sat at the chart-table and drafted up a query to Le Tromp Yachts in Amsterdam, OutReacher Catamarans in France, Daedo Yachts in the USA and Cannon Boat Company's new owners in France. The models I was interested in were the Le Tromp Sif 80, OutReacher 7x, Daeddo D80, and the Cannon Boat 78.

The Sif 80 and the new Cannon Boat 78 were probably my first choices, with the Cannon producing a proven fast performer, but all the sail handling was done in the forward cockpit, at the base of the mast, fully exposed to the sun and weather and even spray.

In the emails, I asked each of them the current build program & status, and in the case of the Sif 80, asked about modifying the cabin ahead of the starboard master to create a private office space.

Another question I asked about the Sif 80, the Daeddo D80 and the OutReacher 7x was if the cutaway section of the cockpit roof over the helm position could be filled-in with a sliding hatch overhead with an inset glass panel. I asked Cannon if they would delete the forward cockpit and fit an aft steering station in the cockpit, with the powered sail controls worked from there, and with a sliding hatch to allow the helmsperson's head and shoulders to poke out, just below the boom.

I'm not normally an impulse buyer, but Dave's argument made a lot of sense and the bigger, faster boat would be much better for what we tended to do once or twice a year. The other item I put in all four emails, was the request that sail-handling on all had to be set up to be comfortably possible by a male and female couple. This also meant I required a quality, powered boom-furling setup with all the advantages we were still enjoying on *Firebird*. As an afterthought, I included in all emails a question about propulsion options.

The weather made an abrupt change and cleared to a beautiful afternoon, with no wind. On another impulse, I stirred the troops by suggesting we take the RIB out to the fringing reef and shoot some video. There were a few grumbles, mainly from Bree, who hoped we'd be too busy to do the nude underwater video stuff.

'Look at it this way,' I said reasonably, 'if we can get an hour of video recorded, we've got something to show Darryl if he gets pushy. We can shoot in the same area with you both in bikinis, then you and Dell can do the scene you spoke of earlier. It sounded good to me.'

Bree pulled a face. 'Harry, any naked girl would look good to you, regardless of what she was doing.'

However, she went with the flow and shortly, she and Dell, both in tiny bikinis, plus Alex and myself, two anti-shark, 12-gauge bangsticks, two sets of scuba gear and both cameras, headed the few hundred metres out to the reef.

CHAPTER 15

After a bit of scouting around, we found a small sandy area with a beautiful selection of coral on three sides. The water was only about three metres deep over the sand and not much less over the coral. The girls decided to just use basic snorkelling gear, and as the dive masks were a good disguise, Bree reluctantly allowed me to dive as well with the second camera. There were also re-assured by the presence of the two bang-sticks with a 12-gauge shotgun cartridge in each.

'But Alex does the nude close-up's, thank you Harry,' she said sternly. 'One camera will be quite sufficient for that.' An evil grin was my answer, as Alex and I strapped into our gear, checked each other for correct attachment and function, and slid over the side.

We let the girls get used to swimming around with bikinis on for a while, and the stunningly-clear water, with the profusion of fish life in the full spectrum of colours, made for a videographer's dream. Both girls worked really well with the cameras, and without being too blatant, came across as very sexy. Even the ultra-modest Bree, seemed to unwind in the beautiful environment, and was comfortable with many close-up passes.

The fish were totally unafraid and large and small ones crowded around these newcomers to their world, nuzzling the girls and the cameras. Bree wasn't happy when a couple of small reef sharks came around to see what was going on, but they were just inquisitive and swam lazily around Dell with none of the jerky, over-excited movements which could mean they were looking to bite something.

I experimented with different camera angles, and felt we had some really good video. The girls must have worked something out while floating on the surface catching their breath, for suddenly, four pieces of bikini floated down. Luckily, I had my camera pointing up at the time, at the lovely silhouette of the two girls, and caught the whole undressing sequence. They came together on the surface, and slowly descended to the centre of the sandy patch, performing an intricate, and highly erotic ballet. The weightless aspect of being underwater, lent a totally different aspect to the usual girl-on-girl fooling around, and Bree seemed to have lost all inhibitions. She didn't even seem to notice when both Alex and I moved in to get some close-up shots, and looked to be enjoying herself immensely. At some point, their fooling around turned rather more serious, and was faithfully recorded. Their unexpectedly super-erotic performance had the usual effect on the fit of my shorts, and I was glad to see Alex wasn't immune to their antics either.

But finally, all good things came to an end as both girls reluctantly released each other and separated. Dell pointed to the surface, drawing her finger across her throat, so Alex and I collected their bikinis, and joined them in the dinghy. They were strangely quiet on the short trip back to *Firebird*, and huddled close together in the bow, not bothering to get dressed. They washed each other off on the stern steps, then went below, leaving Alex and me to rinse off the gear and ourselves. Dave gave us a hand and asked, 'Were there any problems? The girls seemed very subdued.'

I chuckled and shared a grin with Alex. 'I think what you saw was embarrassment. I think they surprised themselves, once they got used to the environment.'

Alex agreed, 'I don't think Bree has ever done anything like that before, and I agree with you, Commander, they both enjoyed themselves immensely.'

We had a private man-chuckle, but made no mention of it when the girls re-appeared.

A little later, cleaned up and dressed presentably, we went ashore dry, and walked the 500 metres to the resort where the service and food were even better than their website claimed. Dell was definitely un-recognisable with the bright orange and peacock-blue scarf wrapped tightly around her head and with a slight trace of some sort of white make-up base on her face and the painted-on, dark shadows under her eyes, she looked to be knocking at heaven's door, instead of beating a hasty retreat from it!

As Bree astutely pointed out, most people don't like to stare at a cancer victim for various misguided reasons. Or maybe they were just being polite; but either way, she didn't get any obvious second glances or significant looks. Afterwards, we wandered aimlessly for a while, but then, as we passed a typical LHI residence, well separated from its neighbours and surrounded by lots of trees, Dell said quietly, 'That's the house'.

There wasn't much to see which might have been out of the ordinary. The yard was neat with mown grass and trimmed hedges, while the house-paint appeared to be in good condition. Lights were on in several rooms where the curtains were carelessly not closed properly. Strains of some pleasant, light classical music, playing over a decent hi-fi system, drifted out a partly open window. A worn set of car tracks down the side of the house led to a carport set well to the rear of the house, with a battered old Toyota Hi-Lux ute parked under it. We kept moving slowly, making sure we didn't stare at the house any more than the others in the street, chatting quietly as would any group of tourists having a wander after dinner.

Back at the boat, we compared notes on what we'd seen and put it all together.

Dave asked, 'Going with the plan you've put in place should save any immediate physical rough stuff, but once you're inside, what's the plan from there? Tomorrow's Thursday, so once you and Dell check in there tomorrow afternoon, the caretakers will expect to be doing a hand-over, then packing a couple of bags before heading for the airport on Friday afternoon. I guess I'm asking; when do you knock them off?'

'To keep things peaceful, I think we're going to need Corrine's help with some knock-out drugs. We don't need the guy, Steve Addy, so to save later problems, he can be eliminated first off. He won't know anything Gerry doesn't, so he's surplus to requirements. Gerry's the one I need to interrogate to get all the knowledge of Xavier's pipeline, and it would be easier with Steve out of the way and Gerry drugged. She sure as hell won't tell us anything willingly.'

Dave checked his watch, then said, 'It's probably too early to call Corrine. She'll still be enjoying Darryl's exciting company. Leave it an hour or so, otherwise call first thing in the morning.'

I nodded, 'Yeah, good thinking. I'll try in an hour. I'd like to give her plenty of warning.'

Dave grinned, 'Oh, she'll be ready! She loves using that little kit and her pharmacist friend likes the challenge of making up the various compounds. When they're together, they become like a pair of evil witches, chucking over increasingly potent concoctions and the weird effects they should produce on their victims.'

I laughed with him, 'That's what we need. I think Gerry is going to be a bit of a tough nut to crack.'

THURSDAY

The weather was clear when I stuck my head up through the top hatch at dawn, although a fresh breeze was blowing from the east but that hardly stirred the crystal-clear waters of the lagoon. With no creeks or rivers feeding the various bays and the lagoon, the waters around Lord Howe Island stayed clear, even after rain, as we had seen yesterday afternoon. A few small fishing boats with keen anglers aboard were heading out for the day, although it was way too early for the charter boats. On impulse, I went aft and dug out a mask, snorkel and flippers, and jumped over to go check the mooring. Unlike anchoring, where I knew the chain and anchors were in top condition, here I was asked to trust someone else's ground tackle. Therefore, I checked. The water was cool, but immensely refreshing and with renewed vigour, I stroked slowly down the heavy chain, thick with barnacles, weed and a stunning collection of crustaceans who fed on the growth. They were, in turn, continually thinned out by a collection of little fish with beautiful colours. Schools of larger fish slowly cruised past, not in the least afraid of my presence, although they deferentially scattered when a metre or so of the silver axe-handle shape of a large barracuda cruised past on breakfast patrol. He kept his huge jaws, full of wickedly sharp teeth, gaping slightly open, and one black, fathomless eye fixed on me. I had no desire to have a pissing contest with him about who was the apex predator on his territory, so I hung on the chain and stayed still until he arrogantly flicked his tail, accelerating instantly to a blur which disappeared into the distance.

By the time I'd reached the huge square concrete block which comprised the immoveable part of the mooring, underwater peace and tranquillity had returned and the slow, unafraid parade of fish life continued. After re-filling my lungs with fresh air, I carefully checked the various fittings on the mooring and decided I was happy to have *Firebird* stay there if one of the island's notorious storms blew up suddenly.

As I hauled myself out at the stern again, I was presented with a steaming mug of tea by Dell, who'd been sitting with Dave.

'All good below?' he asked.

'Yep. We shouldn't have any problems if a blow does come in. There's a massive concrete block which looks in good condition and the chain and fittings look okay.'

He nodded, 'That's good to know. This wouldn't be the easiest place to bail out of if there was a sudden on-shore blow. Much easier to double-up on the chain lashings and stay put.'

'True. I reckon it'd be very choppy and windy, but a westerly gale wouldn't stir up any sort of a swell in these shallow waters, so *Firebird* would ride it out alright.'

Almost as an afterthought, Dave said, 'I called Corrine. She was just awake and said it was a very interesting evening. Darryl behaved himself, just, but she could see that there was some madness lurking in his eyes and every so often it seemed to blaze out. They're her words; not mine! But all in all, she said even though he comes across as everybody's friend, he's a very scary dude and she wouldn't like to be on the receiving end of one of his rages. She doesn't know how Kelly has put up with him for so long.'

I chuckled, 'According to Sandy, when they had their first little chat, Kelly suggested that when he was rational, he was very good in bed.'

Dave looked incredulous, 'That's a piss-poor reason for hanging around a serial rapist and killer, and just waiting to get beaten up!'

'Alleged, my dear Dave, alleged serial rapist and killer, but proven wife-basher, and don't most battered wives tell a similar story?'

'Oops! My bad. PC rules and you're right.'

'Of course, I am. In this case at least. Now, how are we going to hook up with Corrine? Did she have a plan for that?'

'Yep. She wants me to go to her unit this morning and collect an aerosol spray she and her mad pharmacist mate cooked up. It's a mix of some stuff called Remifentanil, Propofol and something else she didn't say. A quick spray into a person's face, takes effect in a couple of seconds and will render them incapable of doing anything for about 30 minutes. If they aren't unconscious, they might as well be, and there's a total loss of memory afterwards, even though all the other effects can be reversed very quickly with an injection.'

'It sounds like the brew she's used before,' I commented, 'although I don't remember the aerosol spray, or that it worked so quickly.'

Dave grinned, 'No, it's what her mate came up with. This brew is a new one and they won't say what this other drug is that makes it work so fast, but they could make a fortune selling it, legally or otherwise. Anyway, we have it, or will, once I go pick it up.'

'Excellent. It might give us the edge we need to get in there without using too much violence. This island is just a small village where everyone seems to know what everyone else is doing and I wanted to avoid stirring up loud trouble. Two new faces can be explained fairly easily, but not a firefight on this peace-loving island.'

He looked at me thoughtfully, 'You do realise there's one glaring hole in your cunning plan?'

'Let me guess. Dell and I didn't arrive on the Thursday aircraft, so how are we going to explain just turning up?'

He gave me a strange look. 'Yeah. That's the problem. Enough people would know you two weren't on the aircraft, so you can't get away with that story.'

'Well, I think we can. We've only told Varley and Addy we're flying in and they certainly won't be telling anyone else. Therefore, we can tell anybody who really asks that we came with friends by private yacht. So as far as they're concerned you're the owner of *Firebird*.'

'What about Darryl?' Dave asked. 'He met you when we cleared in and your name is on the boat's papers.'

'True. But he's very unlikely to be coming around to Xavier's house, because there's no connection. But even if he does, it won't matter to him how I got there. I mean, he won't be comparing notes with others how you got here. So apart from the two in the house, everyone else knows I've arrived by boat.'

He nodded thoughtfully, still trying to find something in the story sequence that might bite me later. 'OK. That should work.'

I grinned, 'With a homicidal Darryl prowling around, it'd better work!'

Dave left shortly after to meet with Corrine and collect the latest of her first aid kit surprises, while Dell and I packed a bag with basics and a few essentials. For immediate back-up, I chose to take the two PMR 30 pistols in .22 calibre, one for each of us, since Dell had been doing a lot of practice and was getting pretty good. I tossed in an Isis suppressor for a 'just in case' situation. When they surfaced for breakfast, I briefed Alex and Bree on what was happening.

'Will you be requiring our assistance in taking over the Xavier house?' was Alex's question.

'I'm hoping not, thank you Alex, since I want to keep from creating any sort of fuss which might attract Darryl's attention. We have two parallel missions running, with Sandy and now Corrine keeping close to the Darryl one, so we don't want to stir that pot until we're ready. If Dell and I can take over the house without raising anyone's suspicion, then we can use it as an on-shore base of sorts to support Darryl's take-down. In the meantime, you're both back-up if things go pear-shaped. We've done the planning, now we just have to run with it and hope for the best.'

We had just finished morning tea when Dave returned.

'All good?' I asked.

'All good, thanks mate. I have the spray.' He undid his backpack and pulled out a soft, zippered purse. From it, he took a small aerosol container less than half the size of a normal one with a colourful label declaring it to be 'Aussie-made Bug Spray, guaranteed 100% effective against all types of pests'. Across the lower part of the label was a stern warning... Caution – inappropriate use of this product could be injurious to someone's health!

It raised a chuckle to see that Corrine's chemist mate had a macabre sense of humour.

CHAPTER 16

Despite too many years spent conducting military operations in someone else's desert, the wait until ops kicked off at about 15:00 was still just as nerve-wracking. On reflection, it was a bit silly really, to make all those plans, then to expect some of the people involved, who didn't know what those plans were, to fall in with them anyway.

No wonder the saying, 'No plan survives first contact with the enemy', so accurately describes the opening stages of any hostile encounter.

After the earlier discussion about the plan with Dave, I added what I hoped would be a useful refinement, by having him run Dell and me across the lagoon in the RIB and drop us off on the beach closest to the road leading into the airport. It was an easy 200-metre walk to the terminal, where we firstly looked like departing passengers, then as the 36-seat QantasLInk Dash 8 Q200 turboprop landed, we mingled until we were part of the arrivals. I noted the line of resort and accommodation drivers waiting for their fresh customers, and started asking for a ride. In typical friendly and helpful LHI manner, the first driver I spoke to said that she'd have room for us and would be delighted to drop us off at the house.

'Know them well, do you mate?' the cheerful woman asked.

I sensed a bit of a trap closing and hopefully dodged it by saying, 'No. Not really. It's a company house and we're just relieving the other two for a week or so.'

I think she would have carried on probing, except that her four guests turned up, bags in hand and she had to do the meet and greet bit.

Once loaded, she said to me, 'I'll drop you off first since our resort is just a bit further on from your place.'

I gave her my best beaming smile, and said that'd be lovely and we might come down to her resort for a good feed one night.

'Oh, not a problem. Our chef specialises in seafood. He really is a marvel!'

Although the distance wasn't far, it took a while because there's a 25 km/h blanket speed limit on the whole island, and most people either walked or rode bikes. Still, it was a pretty drive and soon we were pulling up in the same shady street we'd last seen in the dark, two nights ago. In daylight, the house still looked neat, the yard tidy and generally un-threatening. So we slung our backpacks and as planned, Dell took my small carry-on bag as well as her own, so my hands were free.

I'd have thought that with the super-slow pace of life on the island, the pair we were 'relieving' would have been ready and waiting at the front door, but there was a bit of a wait after I knocked, before I heard one set of footsteps approaching on what sounded like bare floor-boards. It was opened by a rather pleasant-looking woman in her mid-thirties. She wore what seemed standard island dress of shorts, a T-shirt and bare feet. Her legs and arms were long, slim and well-tanned.

A rather stiff smile of welcome was pasted on her face, and she had just started to say, 'Welcome...' when I did a quick draw that Butch Cassidy would have been proud of and squirted her full in the face with the 'Bug Spray'.

She screwed her face up in annoyance and started to say, 'What the f......?' when her legs seemed to collapse from under her and she slid quietly, and more or less gracefully, to the floor where she sprawled carelessly on the polished board floor.

To cover the odd noises and her exclamations, I said loudly, 'Good to see you too, Gerry! Nice place you have here.'

Dell bent down and checked her pulse and breathing, giving me a thumbs-up when vital signs proved to be where they should be.

'Where's your partner, Steve?' I asked her unconscious form, motioning to Dell to help me carry her into the lounge area just inside the entryway. An unconscious body is the most difficult and awkward thing to pick-up and carry, but we managed to get her more or less into a high-backed lounge chair which had its back to the hallway that stretched to the back of the house, with several doors opening left and right off it.

'Second door on the right is the operations room and office. Steve's probably in there,' Dell murmured in my ear.

Accordingly, I drew the PMR 30 from the uncomfortable position tucked down the back of my shorts, and screwed the suppressor onto the threaded end of the barrel. It doubled the size of the weapon, but reduced the sharp crack of the magnum .22 cartridges to a loud thud which wouldn't carry outside the house. Motioning Dell to go ahead and turn the knob, I stepped into the room to see a burly man with a flowing beard, in the process of getting up from the chair behind the desk, alarm showing on his face. Unfortunately for him, he was also groping at his waist with his right hand and I caught a brief glimpse of gleaming black metal.

That was more than enough provocation for me to pull the trigger and for the neat little PMR-30 to spit a double tap which took Steve high in the chest and pulled him up short. Despite the small size of the rounds, they were hollow-point magnum loads and to be on the safe side, I placed two more rounds into his head and it really was game over as he slumped to the floor behind the desk. None of the rounds were through-and-through since they lacked the mass of the bigger calibres, but the end result was the same; just without the usual mess to clean up.

Dell squeezed in behind me, her pistol in hand and darted around the desk to check Steve's status, while I scanned the room in case of unexpected visitors, of which there were none.

'He's finished!' she announced, looking a bit pale, but otherwise holding up well as she handed over a chunky, but compact pistol. It was a Glock G32 in .357 SIG calibre, a rare gun and calibre to find in this place, more powerful than the 9mm it closely resembled, but much less than the classic .357 magnum.

'Okay. Let's secure Gerry, then we'll look at the disposal of Steve.'

Gerry was still sleeping peacefully in the lounge chair, so I took a chance and hit her with another brief squirt of the aerosol, before tying her wrists, elbows and ankles with large cable-ties. A piece of gaffer tape with a small hole poked through it with the tip of a pen acted as a gag. We then hunted through the house and found a large plastic drop-sheet which served nicely to dump Steve's body on so it didn't leak any other body fluids. So far, we'd been lucky that the usual bladder and bowel loosening hadn't happened yet, so I was glad to get him bundled up in the plastic with many metres of gaffer tape to make the cocoon more secure. The keys to the Hi-Lux ute were in the ignition and I wheeled it around to the back door where we struggled to get the bright-orange, plastic-wrapped bundle into the tray. A smelly old tarpaulin roughly pulled over the plastic roll made a good disguise and I parked the ute back under the car-port.

Then it was time to collect our thoughts, and for me, the first step was to go and brew up some tea. The house was quite neat and tidy, having been kept in good condition, and without the expected mess. The kitchen was well-stocked with utensils and the fridge full of food. Maybe Gerry had been stocking up for us.

The fifteen minutes spent having a cuppa was well worthwhile and Dell's colour returned.

'OK. What's the plan now stage one is complete?'

'We have two objectives and the first one is to interrogate Gerry. I'm wondering if getting Corrine around here may be worth the risk since I don't want to be stuffing around with her. We need to hear the truth about the operation as she understands it and things like any code-words for the drop hand-over and the combination for the safe I saw set into the desk.

The other objective is to go through all the paperwork in the house to see what else we can learn about the smuggling operation.'

I dug in my small backpack, found the SatPhone and called Dave to report progress.

'*Glad to hear all's well, mate. What can we do to help?*'

'After dark, we need to move the body down to the beach and I'll get you to run it out past the reef and give the gents in the grey suits a feed. But before then, I'm thinking we might take the chance and get Corrine around here to help sort out Gerry. Do you know what her plans were?'

'*Yep. She's waiting for your call. She's only about a hundred metres away and she reckons she can slip into your backyard without much exposure.*'

'Good oh, thanks Dave. I'll give her a call. If you guys sit tight for the rest of today, you can come ashore about 21:00 tonight. A single vehicle going to the beach and back at that hour shouldn't raise too much attention. In the meantime, we'll wring Missy out for info and search this house for more. Call if there are any problems.'

'*Will do and good luck. Later, Harry.*'

Corrine was indeed waiting and said she'd be with us in five.

It was even less than that and she scared the crap out of Dell and me by appearing soundlessly in the office we were just starting to search.

'Back door was unlocked', was her brief statement, grinning at our reaction.

'Great to see you too, Mouse. And that you survived Darryl. But business first; let me show you our sleeping beauty.'

Looking more like a trussed turkey, Gerry was still out of it. 'Righto Boss. What would you like to happen?'

'Basically, we need to hear all about the operation, any code words for the hand-over of the ship-drop and the combo of the safe. I don't want to have to sort through any bullshit, so load her up so she tells Uncle Harry everything.'

She nodded, 'No problem, but she'll be very disoriented afterwards, with this on top of the good stuff you sprayed earlier. I presume it worked well?'

'Terrific! She went down like a sack of spuds and hasn't stirred since. And I'm not terribly worried about after effects. She may end up with her boyfriend Steve.'

Corrine shrugged, 'OK. I'll bring her out of the Remifentanil hit first, then hit her with the tell-all drug, but we'd better remove the gag first. She may projectile vomit.'

I removed the tape, possibly a little rougher than I should have, just before Corrine deftly prepared two injections and slipped the first one into the webbing between her third and little fingers. It took about three minutes before she suddenly tried to jerk upright, but the restraints were still in place. Her eyes were jacked wide open and staring wildly around the room, looking terrified as if she'd been ripped from the jaws of death.

Corrine waited another minute before slipping the next injection between two toes. It took about a minute before she settled down and relaxed, her eyes half-closing.

'Who are you guys?' she asked in a woozy, husky voice. 'And where's Steve?'

'Steve's just outside in the carport and won't be joining this session.'

'What session? Why am I tied up?'

'You've been struggling so much, we had to do that to protect you from yourself.'

'Bullshit! You're supposed to be taking over from us. And this big bitch is Xavier's main squeeze. She knows everything.'

Dell stepped forward smiling, 'Not exactly everything Gerry. There are a few things we need to verify. As you've been told, we know there's a traitor in the ranks and we're in the process of weeding out the bad eggs.'

Gerry suddenly lost her bluster and looked very worried. 'But we haven't done anything! We just process the stuff when it comes in once a month.'

'OK. Maybe you are clean, but we need to check the password for the fishermen, the combination for the safe and where all the sensitive files are stored.'

'Sure, whatever you want.'

And that was all it took to open the floodgates. Luckily, Dell was on the ball and found a writing pad in the kitchen to take notes. She virtually wrote flat out for five pages worth of stuff before grinding to a halt. She scanned it quickly for glaring errors, but found none.

'OK Harry. This stuff confirms everything, but I'll just go check.'

She took the pad and went back to the office, reappearing a few moments later with a triumphant grin and a thumbs up sign.

I addressed Gerry again. 'You've confirmed the drop is tomorrow night, Friday, so I'm afraid we'll have to keep you isolated until then.'

'Can't I give you guys my word that I won't try to get away?'

I shook my head, 'Sorry. Xavier would have my nuts if something was wrong and I didn't find out. You know what he's like.'

Gerry's shoulders sagged, 'Yeah. I sure do know what he can be like. Go on, do what you have to! But I need to go pee before anything else.'

'How many toilets are there?' I asked.

'Three. One in the ensuite in the master bedroom, one out back on its own, and one in the guest bathroom down the hallway.'

Cutting her hands free, I re-formed her ankle tie in the form of a hobble, and asked Dell to take her to the toilet.

'Clothes off before you bring her back out, please Dell, but don't remove the hobble. You'll have to slice her shorts off with a knife' I instructed.

She grinned, 'No problem, Boss.'

'Hey, hang on. What's with the no clothes bit?'

'That's the deal, take it or leave it.'

Dell led her away grumping and grumbling.

'Can you knock her down tonight so we don't have any trouble?' I asked Corrine.

'Yeah, I can, but I could also come here tonight and help with the guard duty.'

'Thought of that, but what if Darryl decided to come visit? It might be too soon for you to have made any good friends.'

'Yeah. I guess I'd better be in my unit in case.'

'We'll be right if you can knock her out or at least slow her right down. I'll really hobble her anyway, so it'll work out.'

Shortly, Dell called out they were finished. Gerry was glaring at me for leaving her naked, but I ignored that as I thought she looked rather good. But to me, naked ladies always look good, hobbled or not.

I taped Gerry's wrists together, with a nylon cable-tie over the tape to make sure she wasn't going to chew her hands free. I removed all toenail clippers, scissors and other sharp objects.

I also screwed the bathroom window shut as a precaution. She had a basin full of water to drink and a toilet to use or just sit on. What more could a naked captive want?

'If you try yelling for help, I'll tape your mouth closed and leave it like that, so your decision. Behave and you'll even get fed!'

There was some cursing, but before long she seemed to be resigned to her new situation. Interestingly, she still seemed to believe that although Xavier wasn't sure of her loyalty for now, when it was proven she was not the 'traitor', all would be well. That thought, as much as anything else, kept her in line and quiet, so I reinforced the belief as much as possible.

With Gerry reasonably well secured, I used Corrine to help us search the entire house for everything and anything which might be related to the gem smuggling operation. We started with the obvious, the safe in the office, and worked outwards from there. Corrine wasn't needed to crack the safe since Gerry had babbled the combination quite happily, so with her unerring instinct for where stuff might be hidden, she and Dell set out to scour the rest of the house, while I attacked the safe and the office files.

The combination worked and the metre-high door to the safe which took up all of one side of the desk underpinnings, swung ponderously open.

Unsurprisingly, most of the space was taken with stacks of Australian currency; banded piles of $100 notes which I started pulling out and stacking on the desk for counting. Several brown manila envelopes stuffed with papers promised payday, but I set those aside for later reading. The thought crossed my mind that Xavier really must have trusted Gerry to leave all this cash available, as a quick count revealed a total of just over $2.6 million, a very tidy sum in cash, and far better than a poke in the eye with a burnt stick! But still...

It was not what I expected from another of Xavier's famous 'stashes' and in light of his other ones, it wasn't much more than emergency champagne money.

There weren't even any gemstones waiting for onwards shipment and that was a surprise, particularly given his love of investing in the best gems.

On a whim, I dug a powerful LED torch out of my backpack, got down on the thick mat and examined the interior of the safe very carefully. Most of the interior shape was the same as the external, allowing for the thickness of the steel and fire-proofing, but from the lower position, I noticed a rectangular section, about 100mm high and 200mm deep, extending the full width of the interior and forming the upper rear of the interior. Putting the torch into spot-beam mode, I carefully examined the steel box and discovered a very small pinhole about 10 mm in from the right-hand edge and about the same distance down from the roof. With a by-now-familiar tingle of excitement, I awkwardly extricated myself from my position, half in the steel box, and went through the desk drawers. In a tray of the usual bits and pieces like paperclips, paper clamps, pins and other crap, I found what looked like just another partly-straightened slide-on paperclip.

Oddly however, it was the only partially-straightened slide-on paperclip in the tray and when I dug it out, it proved to be made of such a very tough and hard wire that I didn't have a chance of bending by hand.

With a tingle of anticipation, I dug it out of the tray and crawled back under the desk and half-way into the safe again. With the torch held in my teeth, I managed to slip the end of the wire into the tiny hole and pushed it all the way home. There was a quiet click of finely machined parts, and as I withdrew the probe, the entire front face of the box swung open a small amount, hinged on the left. The workmanship was of the finest watchmaker standard, since there had been no hint of the hinge line or the door line either when I'd examined it earlier. The mechanism was well oiled and I swung the door silently open all the way. Lined up inside the cavity were a series of black velvet bags with their necks tied with red, white, green and blue woven silk cords. They were lined up in two rows of ten bags per row and each bag was about the size of my fist.

I needed to clear some desk space, so I stacked all the cash back in the safe, then lifted the bags out, keeping them in the same order, just in case it meant anything. There were seven white tie-cord bags, five red ones, five green ones and three blue. For some reason, one of the blue-tied bags had an orange cord tied around it as well.

I started with a white one and surprise, surprise, it contained a handful of dull, translucent whitish rocks with rounded corners. They ranged in size from a small chook egg through a pheasant, pigeon, then slightly smaller, but none less than the diameter of a 20-cent piece. A quick check showed the other six white-tie bags contained similar-sized stones, although one was a real whopper which was the size and shape of a large chook egg.

With my mind reeling at the value of the diamond collection, even in an uncut state, I opened a green corded bag to find emeralds, as expected. There weren't many per bag, but they were very large in size and in their uncut condition, gave no hint of their possible eventual magnificence. The red tied bags contained a similar selection of very large rubies.

As I turned to open the last three bags, I felt a real surge of excitement that brought me out in goose-bumps, something I hadn't felt in many a long day, as I realised we might have stumbled on Xavier's major nest egg after all.

Going right back to the first stash which Dave and Corrine had discovered on the original *Seeker*, we knew Xavier loved precious stones, so this should be the elusive master cache I had felt sure should exist somewhere.

I had always prided myself on being highly dispassionate about most things, but I noticed my hands were trembling slightly as adrenalin flooded through my system, causing my fingers to fumble at the draw strings of the first of the three blue-tied bags. It had just one cord tied around its neck and not unexpectedly, contained a handful of what I presumed to be large sapphires which were pretty even in their rough state.

The second bag had a double blue cord around it and contained a collection of quite large, dirty-looking stones which were roughly hexagonal in shape and around 35 to 40mm in size. On closer inspection, I saw some were speckled with deep blue, while others had a gold speckle.

I was quite intrigued by the blue and orange-tied bag and what the tie-cords might signify, but delay wasn't productive so I just opened it. Inside were five large stones with three of them looking like elongated pear-shapes or very thick teeth from an ancient race of smallish dinosaurs. They were about 60 to 80mm in length and about 35mm wide. They had a rough surface and were coloured a deep amber-pink or salmon shade. They didn't look like any sapphire that I'd ever seen, but the contents of the previous bag weren't very inspiring either. The other two were angular, crystalline lumps of rock, coloured a deep salmon shade, and about 35mm square.

As I went to put these attractive, but unexciting rocks back in their bag, I felt a large lump still in there. Scrabbling around showed a second, smaller velvet bag with an irregular lump in it, was tucked deep inside the bigger bag and didn't want to come out. Pulled free and opened, it contained a single stone that was roughly hexagonal in shape and looked a bit like the stones in the bag with the double blue ties, but instead of being a dirty grey/brown colour with coloured flecks, this one was a translucent pinkish/amber shade like the others in the amber-tied bag.

It looked to be about 50 to 60 mm across and about 15 to 20 mm thick and superficially, was quite pretty. I slipped it back into its little bag and tucked it back where it came from.

Several thoughts ran through my mind and I spent some quiet time going over each one before I flicked through the papers in the Manila envelopes, then decided to go find the girls.

CHAPTER 17

I found them digging through the second of three bedrooms, a cardboard box full of papers sitting on the end of the unmade bed. The scattering of dirty clothes across the floor, along with the dirty plates, mugs and glasses piled up beside the bed, suggested this had been Steve's room and Gerry didn't share her bed or anything else with him.

The grey colour of the once white sheets supplied part of the reason.

'How's it going ladies?' I asked as they seemed to have turned up little of interest. But I've found hidden extra safes in stranger places.

'There doesn't seem to be much of value in here,' Corrine said, 'although we got a lot of stuff from Gerry's room but we haven't gone through it yet. How about you?'

'I've only done the safe so far, but that's produced a good haul. You'd better note where you're up to and come look.'

That got their attention and in short order, they were crowding around the desk looking at our haul.

'Holy crap, Harry! Is that all money in there?' Dell asked, eyes wide open. 'I wasn't allowed in here last time, but things have changed in the few weeks since then.'

I laughed at her amazement, 'Yep, that's all cash. About $2.6 million Aussie dollars by my very rough count. But that's not the real find.'

Corine looked at me. 'You've done it again, haven't you? You found Xavier's main stash!'

I tried to look modest, but failed miserably. 'I cannot tell a lie. I applied my naturally developed detective skills to the problem and came up a winner.'

'Cut the crap, Harry!' was Corrine's retort, as she eyed off the twenty cloth bags on the desk. 'Where were they?'

'There's a hidden compartment built into the upper-back end of the safe with a very close-fitting door opened by a hidden latch. It's a beautiful piece of work, but the contents might be a lot more so! I don't think Gerry would have even noticed the little compartment, let alone known how to open it.'

'That's right. She didn't make any mention of it when she told us the safe combination,' Corrine observed.

To show the collection to the girls, I started as before with the diamonds, although there was none of the excitement and startling beauty of looking at cut gems. Therefore, the imagination had to work hard to picture the finished product, and with the large lumps of dull, whitish stone, if there were no major flaws or inclusions to reduce the cut size, the result would be utterly stunning.

'These are much bigger than the ones we've got,' Corrine said in awe. 'I can't imagine what they'd bring at auction if they were cut properly first.'

'It's hard to tell in their uncut state, but I suspect Mr Jacobs will go nuts when he sees them.'

Corrine looked at me sharply, 'So you've decided we will keep these?'

I nodded, 'I had a quick look through the papers in those envelopes, and they seem to be related to the various sources of gems being fed into the smuggling pipeline. My people and Interpol will love the information, but it will be impossible to prove which particular gem had been stolen from which mine. They can be classified by areas, but cannot be classified by an individual mine. Therefore, they're in limbo as far as ownership goes. We found them, the previous owner is deceased, therefore we hang onto them.'

Corrine looked pensive for a moment, 'Good call, Boss. I reckon that'll work. We say nothing about them, right Dell?'

She shrugged, 'Yeah, OK. I can keep my mouth shut. Good luck to you.'

I picked up on her tone and said, 'That'll be 'good luck to us', dear lady. You're a part of this crew, you've done your share of work, so you get to share in the 'spoils of war,' as I like to put it.'

Dell's face brightened considerably, 'You mean I get a share of this? Including the cash?'

I shrugged, a devilish glint in my eye, 'You can have all the cash for your share if you want. What's your call, Mouse?'

Corrine was way ahead of me as usual, and deadpanned, 'Yeah. That sounds fair, Boss. $2.6 million in cash instead of a share in the contents of those bags? Yeah! No problem for me.'

Dell's quick mind processed the interchange and decided that we were taking the piss. 'You evil mongrels! Obviously you think the rocks are worth a lot more than the cash. So, can I still really have a share of everything?'

I laughed, 'Yes of course. We wouldn't have let you accept just the cash. You get a seventh share of the whole pie the same as the rest of us. There'll be more than enough to go around so there's no need to niggle about who did what to earn a share. That's the way we always work.'

She still couldn't grasp what was involved, so I tried again, 'We don't really know their value since all the rocks are uncut, but as I see it, they're all very large; they've all been smuggled because they are special in some way, and they all had been collected by Xavier personally, as being the best-of-the-best! We won't know the true value until we get them valued professionally. But I would feel confident in saying you should end up with something well north of a million or two as your share. That includes some of the cash as well, although because too much cash is very hard to get rid of these days, we may have to make a quick run to Vanuatu to get rid of it.'

Dell looked puzzled, 'What's with Vanuatu?'

'We all have bank accounts there since it's tax free and we can withdraw from anywhere. They don't ask awkward questions about large amounts of cash wandering in through the door, so that's where we stash all our ill-gotten gains.'

'Oh…. Can I open an account there too?'

Corrine said, 'Sure thing, I can set it up tonight from my unit. Just give me all your details and I'll get it done.'

'OK, thanks. That'll be great.'

I quickly went through the rest of the bags of stones, explaining my puzzlement about the amber-coloured stones as well as the hexagon-shaped ones.

'Did you say you had a gem expert who could check all this stuff for you?' Dell asked.

'Yeah. Mr Jacobs is a lovely old Jewish gentleman. We've put two lots of loot through his shop so far and he arranges the auction process and security. He's helped make us all rather wealthy, so hopefully, he can do it again.'

Corrine said thoughtfully, 'One thing stands out for me, Harry. The last two bags of loot we sold were cut stones. These are all uncut, so won't the value be a lot less?'

'I've read up on that a bit,' I replied, 'and it all depends very much on the quality of the uncut stone. If the uncut one is of very high quality with few, if any inclusions, then it will still have a very high value, although not as high as if it were cut properly. But it started me thinking that maybe we could take a punt and spend the extra money to have them cut properly.

As I said earlier, I reckon because they are in Xavier's personal stash, they will be of superior quality and therefore will gain a lot of value by being cut. Personally, I think we should take the risk. The value increase can be considerable if a stone is really special. However, we all need to talk about it and consider carefully as we all have to agree on a course of action. It'll be difficult to get Sandy's opinion at the moment, so if necessary, I'll take a chance and vote 'yes' for her. '

'Is there any way to find out in advance roughly what the cut product would be worth?' Corrine asked. 'That would be a good way to decide whether to cut or not.'

'Yes. I've read that a good cutter will use experience and modern tools like 3D modelling to determine how best to cut each stone, but the buying public's opinion dictates which cuts are more desirable and therefore more expensive. Mr Jacobs will know the best thing to do and how to go about it. I trust him implicitly to do the right thing by us.'

'So why don't we take a photo of each stone and email him? That would be a start,' Dell suggested.

I grinned, 'Or I could take the lot and fly over to see him. That trip would fit in with the new drop of gems from the fishermen tomorrow, which has to be delivered to Sydney. I'll have to check with my people to see how they are going to play the Sydney end, and I'd only be gone for two or three days which would get them off the island.'

Corrine considered my comments. 'As much as I hate to admit it, that might be the best thing to do, although you'd better get Dave to stand in for you here in the house. But speaking of the fishermen, didn't Gerry say they get $500 each for the privilege of working for Xavier?'

Dell looked at her notes from the interrogation, and nodded, 'Yes, here it is. They're the Foley brothers and aren't the sharpest knives in the rack, although they seem to have been doing this for several years.'

I thought a moment, then said, 'I think we'll need to keep this operation going for a while longer to give my mob and Interpol time to trace the supply and smuggling lines back to their sources. At least another month, if they're having trouble tracing links to people.'

Both Corrine and Dell grinned, as Corrine replied, 'I guess I can put up with another month here, but what about the Darryl problem?'

'We'll have to take that as it comes, but let's finish what we can of this one first. After we complete the hand-over tomorrow night, we pay the Foley's with cash from the safe and I take the package to Sydney on Monday like Gerry said she or Steve used to.'

'It sounds like a good plan. It'll get that ball rolling and get them away from here like you said. A final big payday from Mr Terry 'Xavier' Johnson will set us all up very nicely. He must have been skimming these shipments for years to build up this many prime stones.'

Corrine looked thoughtful for a moment, then went on, 'Just thinking; you brought *Dragonfly* with you, didn't you?'

'Yep. We didn't offload it anywhere. Dave's been bitching that he has to share a cabin with a small coffin.'

'Do him good, the pussy! Anyway, I thought it might be able to supply useful Intel to your people if we were to launch it tomorrow night and have it track the Foley's boat out to the rendezvous. If we can get some clear IR video of the transfer, including the name of the ship and any faces involved, that should speed up the backtracking process. What do you think?'

I gave her an appreciative smile, 'I think I should have thought of it much earlier! Good one. OK, we have plans and I need to talk to Dave, but tonight will do when he comes to collect the ex-Steve. Then again, I might call him soon and suggest he brings Jasper for a beach run. I also need to talk to Mr Jacobs and make sure he'll be in town on Tuesday morning. As for transport, we transfer the Friday booking for two to the Monday flight. Anything else?' I asked both ladies.

'What about Gerry?' Dell asked. 'She's quiet for now, but she'll be getting sick of being tied up like that. She'll need feeding soon as well.'

'Yeah, yeah! I guess I was hoping she would just fade away, but that's not going to happen, is it?'

Both girls shook their heads.

'OK. What more can we get out of her?'

Dell consulted her notes again. 'Nothing obvious. We have all the contact details for the Foley's hand-over and the details of the

Sydney contact who normally takes the gems, but you'll be passing that info onto your people I guess.'

'Yes, they can work out how to pick him or her up. So, you're saying we don't need her at all.'

'No. Although she could be handy in case something goes adrift; like with the Foley's for instance. Surely you aren't just going to shoot her?'

I smiled grimly, 'Yes. I did think seriously about that, but now I think we'll hold her until Monday, then I'll escort her to Sydney for hand-over to the ACP. They'll have to keep her in strict isolation until this is all wrapped up, but that's their job. We can't look after her any longer than Monday, and that'll be difficult enough. Mouse, you'd better think of a tranquiliser which will keep her docile, but she can't appear drugged or drunk or they won't let us on the aircraft.'

Corrine smiled wolfishly, 'I've got just the thing. She'll be a docile as a lamb, but will be able to talk and function reasonably well. And it should last 4 or 5 hours, so plenty of time to get to Sydney.'

'Brilliant! Thanks Mouse. Now I'd better make a few calls.'

CHAPTER 18

THURSDAY, LORD HOWE ISLAND

'Good afternoon. Jacobs' Fine Jewellery. This is Miriam.'

'Hello Miriam, this is Harry Stevens. I hope I find you and your Grandfather well?'

'Oh, hello indeed, Mr Stevens. A pleasure to hear from you again. We have finally finished cataloguing all those beautiful items you brought to us and I must say that both Grandfather and I have never been so excited about an auction before. He looks years younger and is having the time of his life arguing with the auctioneers. When will we see you again?'

'Well actually, very soon. I wanted to see if you and Mr Jacobs would be available next Tuesday morning. We are still in the middle of the other job I mentioned, but we have come across something which needs your very expert advice. If you could spare me the time, I can be there by 10:00 Tuesday morning.'

She laughed, *'Oh dear, Mr Stevens. Every time you call to ask for an appointment, it usually means something very interesting has occurred and you bring us some treasure. You don't need to ask! But I ramble on too much. Of course, we will be delighted to meet you on Tuesday at the time you suggest. If you need to change that time, please call this number at any time. I shall inform Zaydee, and he will be very excited.'*

'Thanks Miriam. I look forward to meeting with you again. Until then.'

'Thank you Mr Stevens, and likewise.'

My next call was to Dave, to suggest that when he comes ashore tonight, he bring Jasper since we could use his presence, but to let him have a run on the beach first if nobody was around. I quickly updated him on the extent of Xavier's stash and my plan to take Gerry to Sydney on Monday and turn her over to my ACP colleagues. I also mentioned I was going to the Gold Coast to turn the stones over to Mr Jacobs and Miriam to get the appraisal under way, and would he stand in for me from Monday arvo onwards till I got back.

His other job was to plan the launch of *Dragonfly* tomorrow night to track the fishermen.

'I'll get Alex and Bree onto it,' he replied. 'I know Sandy had been teaching Bree how to set up, flight program and launch it. Alex was always peering over their shoulders, so I think that between them, they'll have it covered. Do we know what boat these clowns are using?'

'According to Gerry, it's a 20-foot alloy, centre-console jobbie, with a white hard-top shade-shelter and a pair of 150 Mercs hung on the transom. It's one of the few local boats to have radar, since the beacons marking the channel into the lagoon are unlit.

It normally lives on a trailer parked in the front yard of their house, and they launch at the boat ramp just the other side of the jetty. Bree and Alex should be able to see them launching by using the IR camera on the masthead. If they're ready, it will give them time to launch *Dragonfly* and for the auto-track function to lock onto the boat.

The task is to track their pickup boat to the RV, get some close-up of the actual exchange, including the ship's name and any crew visible. Gerry said they aren't normally out more than two hours, so with a full tank, *Dragonfly* should have plenty of endurance.'

'OK, mate. That's plenty to go on, so I'll brief them now and I'll see you tonight on my garbage disposal run.'

'Thanks Dave.'

My next call was to my handler, a lady of indeterminate age who was briskly efficient regardless of what time of the day or night I called, and was well-known for making dry, and often sarcastic comments about my experiences and spending sprees. I held off telling her I was going to get a new, and much bigger boat. I can take only so much crap from her in one sitting! She is also a marvellous organiser and a superbly reliable backup when push came to shove.

I spelt out the situation, omitting mention of the hidden stash of uncut gems, but included my movements on Monday with a witness who had to be kept in total isolation until the gem pipeline investigation had been wrapped up. I was confident Gerry knew nothing about the gems in the hidden locker, which meant there was no one left alive who did, apart from our crew.

'*You have been busy again, dear boy,*' *she replied, having told me once, that as she had an eidetic memory, she never took notes of my reports. 'So apart from Miss Petrie, who I presume is still in your Protective Custody and behaving herself, then if Mr Addy is no longer an issue, Miss Varley is the sole operative still at large?*'

'Yes, Miss Petrie is behaving herself and has in fact, made herself into an extremely useful team member on this operation. As for Miss Varley; well, she's not really at large. As we speak, she's cable-tied wrists and feet, hobbled, gagged and confined to the guest bathroom. We left her without clothes so she can use the facility without needing help and so far she hasn't made a mess.'

She gave a throaty chuckle that sent a tingle down my spine, 'You do employ some interesting methods to restrain your prisoners, Harry. In this case, one could almost accuse you of humane treatment!'

'Ha, ha! Very droll. I do have a reputation to live down to, you know, so don't spread around any soppy stuff about being humane! Anyway, I'll have Miss Varley with me on Monday if someone can meet us to take her off my hands. I presume you'll be picking up the courier once Miss Varley has identified him or her. I'll also have a pouch of all the papers we could find which relate to Xavier's operation, as well as the UAV video of the drop of the stones off the ship.'

'*I think you can take it as locked-in, Harry, so I'll bid you farewell. But do try to stay out of trouble and look after Jasper and Krazy.*'

Which reminded me that now the official business had been taken care of and the kitchen table was covered in notes on various bits of paper, I could indulge myself for a short time and check my emails to see if any of the four boat-builders had responded. The house had a computer with satellite internet connection so I made use of it and was pleasantly surprised to see all four had responded. A Sif 80 by the Dutch team LeTromp, still on top of my list, was under construction at the moment at their new yards in South Africa. It was hull #2 and was a spec-build by the company, and had only proceeded to hull lay-up stage. The company said that they would be delighted to incorporate my modifications into the build and suggested a visit to their head office and a chat with the designer would see all my wildest ideas incorporated for a price.

I was greatly heartened by this highly co-operative response.

The next email was from the Cannon Boat Company who declared that their design didn't lend itself to any serious modifications, but they would be happy to place me in the order queue. I was disappointed in their attitude, but they weren't the only ones selling boats.

My next choice would be the OutReacher, a boatyard with an impressive list of fast cruising catamarans sailing in all parts of the globe. They also responded with a very positive attitude and said anything was possible and again invited me to visit the shipyards in France to have a chat with the designer. However, they said that response to the 78-foot cat had far surpassed all expectations, so they were looking toward buying into an established yard in South Africa for additional building capacity. They would be delighted to add me to their order book, but delivery would be some two years hence.

The Daeddo 80 team from the USA with their dramatically futuristic offering, were equally as encouraging as the Dutch and French teams, but on reflection I crossed them off the list as being a little bit too radical. Nevertheless, some of their propulsion ideas were very interesting and prompted another round of internet searching.

If I wanted to have a boat in a reasonable time-frame, that only left the LeTromp team with their Sif 80, and this won me over by being already under construction and their co-operative, can-do attitude.

Making a rare and insanely-impulsive, command-level decision on the spot, I emailed back to say I would like to secure Hull #2 and would be in touch to discuss the short-handed sailing and general boat handling modifications I needed, adding that I wasn't able to visit their Head Office. I also asked what they required in the way of a holding deposit.

I fired that one off, then also thanked the other three companies for their response and wished them well.

By that stage, the day was nearly done and with the girls still searching the house, I settled at the desk and started going through the papers which were in the safe. I hit pay dirt almost immediately with some lists of the mines which had unknowingly contributed their best stones to the pipeline. The lists went back many years and I was staggered by the quantities of stones which had been funnelled through the island in that time. One cryptic list was in a code of some description I couldn't make any sense of, so I set it aside for Corrine and Dell to look at.

After ploughing through piles of paper, there was still no way to tie any particular set of stones to an individual mine. I had more luck though, with tracking the shipments from Lord Howe to Sydney, where they were apparently split up into smaller parcels to meet orders from customers. This shed a new light on the whole system and shot down my idea that Australia was merely a way-station in the pipeline.

It now appeared the Sydney base was the distribution hub for customers around the world. There were even suggestions that rough gems were being stolen to order, which lent a whole new slant to the operation.

I showed Corrine and Dell when they came in with very few additional papers, but neither of them could add any more thoughts to what I'd worked out. From her time with Xavier, Dell hadn't learned these sorts of details, so it began to look as though he might have been involved in the operation to a much greater extent than we'd thought. I still felt there was someone else who had set this up in the first place, and suggested to the girls that we all go through the papers again, in the hope we could pick up a name out of all the data.

I drafted up an email for my controller lady with a summary of the new information which seemed to name a few people in Sydney as well as some hints of a central address and fired it off to her.

With evening well established, I decided to accept Corrine's offer to help with guarding Gerry through the night, so she and Dell set to making the beds with fresh sheets and in the case of Steve's room, a new pillow and blanket as well. The floor was mopped with a strong cleaner and a liberal dose of air freshener helped to clear the musty, rank odour.

I left the sleeping arrangements to them and was surprised to find I'd been allocated the bed in Steve's old room, which was a double anyway.

The evening meal was a simple one of sausages I grilled on the gas BBQ out on the back patio, together with a tangy salad Dell put together from a well-stocked fridge.

'What about Gerry?' Dell asked.

I must had mellowed after a long day, as I said, 'I'll go and see if she wants to be civilised.'

When I entered the bathroom and turned on the light, she was curled up on the floor as best she could and looked very cold and very unhappy. She immediately started making noises through the tape gag, so I held up one hand.

'Hold it and listen up! If you're hungry, and promise to behave, I'm prepared to partly free your hands, put some clothes on you and let you join us at the table. If you want to keep on with the aggro, you can have some leftovers where you are. So what's it to be?'

To get an answer, I carefully peeled the strip of tape off her mouth, but held it ready to slap back on if she started winding up to scream. My concerns were unfounded, since she was almost pathetically grateful, a sentiment I immediately distrusted, but went along with for the moment, in case it was an example of the Stockholm Syndrome. The residue of the drugs Corrine and I had injected seemed to be still slowing her down, which encouraged me to take a chance.

I knew her muscles would be very stiff after 5 hours tied up like she was, so I cut her hand and arm ties and helped her to her feet. Thankfully, she'd kept herself clean. I couldn't help but take a moment to appreciate her finely-shaped and toned body, although I could see she would be very strong and a real handful if she was given the chance when the drugs wore completely off.

For now, however, she was docile as I let her shower, then helped her to her old room to put on a pair of track-suit pants and a warm top. She passed on panties and a bra, although she didn't need the bra, so we headed for the kitchen where I sat her down at the table, but looped a pair of long cable ties around her elbows and the chair back. I added another one that joined her elbows in front across her chest, which had the effect of making the use of the knife and fork very awkward, but much safer for us. The hobble was back in place around her ankles.

She attacked the sausages and salad as though she were starved and said nothing until her plate was cleaned. Then she looked around the table.

'I recognise you,' she said to Dell, 'but I don't know you other two. What's going on? Someone said something about Xavier looking for a traitor in the ranks, but if he suspects Steve and me, then why ask us to go to Head Office?'

I decided that being semi-ignorant about things would be best under the circumstances.

'I don't really know, I'm afraid. Dell, Corrine and I were sent here to relieve you, but Steve took exception to our presence and as Corrine is Xavier's personal enforcer, he paid a rather high price. Under the circumstances, my new instructions are to escort you to Sydney to be passed onto another of Xavier's inner circle who will escort you to Melbourne. If it helps, I've looked at papers and your record, and I've advised Xavier you appear to be blameless. Steve's reaction to our arrival was highly suspicious and his demise may well have resolved the problem. Xavier is well-pleased with the situation, but still needs to talk to you in person.

My personal advice is to go with the flow and I believe if you don't play up, or make any trouble, then all will be well for you.'

She looked a bit dumbfounded for a moment or two. 'This is all a bit much to take in all at once. Are you saying that this...girl here killed Steve?'

Corrine gave one of her Mona Lisa smiles, while I cautioned, 'I'd be very careful not to upset Corrine, if I were you. I have personal knowledge of fifty terminations she has performed in her career, and there are rumoured to be many more. Xavier doesn't hire amateurs, although it would appear that Steve unfortunately fell into that category. Or maybe he just got greedy.'

'Yeah! That'd be stupid fuckin' Steve,' Gerry replied, eyeing Corrine with a look of respect and awe. 'He always was ambitious and looking for a fast buck. Anyway, thank you for telling me all this and on consideration, I'd be a mug to fight with you. I mean, you are just the messengers, aren't you?'

I smiled, hopefully sincerely, 'That we are, and on Monday, we fly out. I may as well use Steve's ticket, since seats are restricted. Tomorrow night, the next drop will occur and you can introduce Dell and me to the Foley brothers, so they don't get excited about strange faces suddenly appearing.'

Gerry appeared to be on-board with all of this and promised to behave. 'Can I have the arm and leg restraints off, please? I've promised to behave.'

'I'll remove the elbow one, but the ankle strap and the hobbles will have to remain. Remember it's only Dell, Corrine and me who think you are innocent. Xavier is the man who calls the shots, so if he says 'keep her restrained' then that's what happens. We don't dare defy him in any way; you know what he's like, and somehow, he always finds out.'

Gerry nodded ruefully, 'Yes, I sure do. So okay... but do I have to be tied to the toilet as well?'

'No. We'll skip that bit, but you will have to sleep in the bathroom with the door locked from the outside and the window screwed shut from the outside.'

Her shoulders slumped, 'Can I at least have some seat cushions from the sunroom to sleep on? Please?'

'Of course. That's not a problem. We don't want to make you more uncomfortable than necessary, but we all need our rest as well.'

She nodded, 'Yeah, OK. I can understand that, but you'll have to trust me tomorrow night when the Foleys come around.'

I lied smoothly, 'I'm sure by then we will have established a degree of mutual trust that will render restraints un-necessary.'

'Thank you Mr Stevens, for your consideration.'

Dell had already gone to set up the make-shift bed in the bathroom, with cushions, a pillow and a couple of blankets, so soon after, Gerry was locked into her cell and we waited for Dave to arrive on rubbish collection and disposal duty.

His arrival was announced by a soft knock at the back door, admitting a cheerful Dave and the huge form of an equally genial Alex, with the sleek, black shape of a grinning Jasper pushing in past them to greet us enthusiastically.

CHAPTER 19

'Did he have a good run?' I asked Dave.

'Hell yeah! I told him to avoid any people he saw and since there were no alarms, I figure he obeyed.'

After saying hello, Jasper disappeared to explore the house, an environment he was unused to. He paused at the door to the guest bathroom, sniffed, then growled softly. It wasn't so softly that it didn't provoke a tremulous call for help from Gerry. With the slightly nasty side of my personality briefly gaining the upper hand, I opened the door to let Jasper and Gerry see each other.

The responses were slightly different as Jasper gave a much louder and more threatening growl, even to the point of dropping into a crouch, the precursor to an attack spring. Gerry's response was to give a thankfully quiet scream of terror, as if she didn't want to provoke the black monster glaring at her from two metres away. She was sitting on the toilet seat, and promptly drew her legs up as if that would stop an attack.

Without taking my eyes off Gerry, I reached down and laid my hand on Jasper's back, bristling with raised fur, an action which stopped the growling, but not the glaring or the attack pose.

With a trembling finger she pointed at Jasper, which is never a good idea, and asked in a hoarse whisper, 'What the fuck's that?'

'That, dear lady, is your new night-guard. He belongs to a friend who's dropped by to visit and will be making sure you aren't tempted to misbehave during the night. I'm afraid he doesn't seem to like you, for some reason, so I really wouldn't try his patience or his willingness to do you some extreme harm. He has a number of kills to his credit and a lot of severe mauling's as well.

I'm going to leave him just outside this door all night. He won't be sleeping, so please don't be tempted to test his resolve.'

'You can't leave him there by himself. He might break in!'

'No, he won't do that, you have my guarantee. So long as you don't try to break out. Then the shit, will actually hit the fan, so to speak.'

'Okay, but I'm very unhappy about this new arrangement, Mr Stevens.'

'Be as unhappy as you like princess, but suck it up and live with it.'

I nodded at her and closed the door, almost bumping Jasper's nose in the process as he gave a last few growls, before following me quietly back to the kitchen.

I beckoned for Dave and Alex to follow me into the office where I'd already stacked the bags of uncut stones in my small backpack.

I pulled out a few bags and showed them some samples, and Dave was highly un-impressed by the dull, misshapen stones.

'Is this the fabled Xavier retirement fund?' Dave asked sarcastically. 'If so, I'm glad we have all that other loot waiting for us. This lot looks like it wouldn't bring ten cents!'

Alex had said nothing up to now, but then he stepped forward, 'Excuse me please Commander, but may I take a look at the bag of the biggest diamonds?'

Wordlessly, I handed it to him, watching as he carefully dug out what looked like the biggest, turned on the desk lamp and held the stone against its surprisingly bright light, squinting closely at it as he turned it every which way. He then searched through the desk drawers until he found a large magnifying glass, then resumed inspecting. Finally, he grunted in satisfaction and turned to us, a small grin on his face.

'Forgive my theatrics, Commander, but I have some small experience with stones like these. Before it was strongly suggested that I leave South Africa, I was a specialist geologist working in the

Kimberly mine, the original diamond mine in that region. This particular stone, which I'm guessing would measure at least 130 carats, appears to be colourless. If cut carefully by an expert cutter, it would have a possible yield of 85%, an un-precedented amount, and would produce a cut diamond which would purchase two or three new boats for you, easily.

You can see how its basic shape is very close to a classic pear or teardrop, so if there are no flaws, and I can't see any at this stage, then minimal faceting and polishing would result in a very large, finished stone of enormous value. And that's just this one stone. The others in that one bag, although slightly smaller, appear to be equally as pure and well-shaped.'

He carefully replaced the egg-shaped and sized stone back in its soft bag, a cheerful clink sounding as it re-joined the company of the others.

Dave looked a bit sheepish, but contritely said, 'Me and my big mouth! I didn't know about your past, Alex, but I owe you and Harry an apology. Maybe Xavier's legacy will be our big payday after all.'

Alex gravely nodded. 'Yes, I do think so. If all these stones were chosen for their special qualities, then this could be a collection the likes of which the world has never seen in one place!'

I took the opportunity to satisfy some of my curiosity and found the bag tied with the blue and orange ties. handing it to him, I said, 'Please take a look at the stones in here, Alex. They are unlike anything else; in particular there's one I can't identify, it's wrapped separately.

He took the bag and carefully shook the rocks out on the table. Once again, the five large salmon-coloured stones that looked like dragon teeth lay glittering under the strong, white light of the desk lamp. Alex stirred them gently, a rare smile on his normally impassive face. 'Oh dear Commander, these are very special. They are sapphires, of course and while normally not as valuable as diamond, they are of a very rare colouring called Padparadscha. That rarity makes them very valuable indeed! No other gemstone has such a colour, which is a mix of pink and orange, and of course, being a sapphire, the stone is very hard; almost as hard as a diamond. As usual, the size, cut and clarity combine to make the value, and these appear to be near-flawless.

The size of these five pieces also sets them apart from all others as most Padparadscha are less than 10 carats in weight. If cut to retain most material, which is the usual thing to do, these will be at least 30 or 40 carats each, maybe more. They could be worth tens of thousands of dollars per carat.'

Unusually for Alex, he hardly paused to draw breath before continuing, 'These two angular lumps with the pretty colourings are the same material, but can be cut into different shapes. Still very valuable.'

When I was sure that he had stopped, I suggested that he look in the small velvet bag which was tucked inside the larger one. Curious, he extracted the large, hexagonal dirty-looking stone with the deep pink/amber patches.

After a few moments of peering at it, with and without the aid of the magnifying glass, he chuckled, 'You have just come into possession of possibly, the only known example of what is widely believed to be a non-existent gemstone. A serious collector would pay almost anything for it.'

'OK. C'mon Alex! What the hell is it?'

'Oh sorry. It's a Star Padparadscha sapphire. The star effect is created by internal 'silk', which are rutile needles within the stone crystal. These microscopic needles intersecting at 120 degrees inside the sapphire create a six-rayed star effect seen within the stone when a direct light is overhead.

When the star effect is combined with the Padparadscha colouring, it's a combination which has been presumed non-existent. Rumours float around occasionally about someone finding one, but I've never met someone who has even seen one! Truly, these things aren't supposed to exist at all.'

Almost reverently, his big fingers carefully slipped the Star Padparadscha back in its bag and tucked it back where it came from. He then looked up with a gleam in his eyes.

'Well Commander, you've really done the job this time. The value of stones in those bags, when cut properly, will make the entire haul from Indonesia look like beer money. That's my considered opinion, but I presume you'll be getting your professional jeweller friend to verify all that?'

I nodded, still a bit stunned by Alex's calm appraisal. 'Yes, I will, of course, but I must admit you've blown me away with your statement about the value of all these. However, you said that is the value of the cut stones, not left rough.'

'That is correct. Although, I must say that because of the excellent shape and condition of the rough stones, they would attract a premium price, but you would certainly see a big increase in value if all were to be cut, despite the cost of having an expert cutter do the job. Doing so would certainly would be my strongest recommendation.'

I looked at the others and they all looked a bit shell-shocked, until Dell voiced what must have been a common opinion. 'It's hard to imagine the value of these could exceed the value of those beautiful gems you all recovered from Bali and the pirate's base. Can we afford to get them cut? It must be a very expensive process.'

Alex nodded, 'Yes, that's correct. But considering the basic shape of the rough, it means that far less cutting is needed to produce a magnificent gem. Therefore, the cutting and polishing process should be faster, cheaper and produce a larger, more valuable stone.'

I looked around at four of our team of seven. 'The five of us need to consider what we do with these stones. We could get them all cut and take the risk that some might be damaged by bad cutting or flaws, or just cut the ones which are going to cost the least, and leave the rest uncut. Or we could sell them as is, uncut. That makes three options.

Alex will tell Bree when he gets back aboard later tonight, but letting Sandy know will be more difficult.'

'I can drop around to Kelly's in the morning,' Corrine offered. 'If necessary I can slip her a note.'

'Okay. But only if it seems a natural thing to do. Really, she'll go along with any scheme that is going to increase her nett worth, although...I suppose you'd better tell her I've ordered a new and bigger boat!'

Dave laughed out loud. 'You're a sneaky bugger! I didn't think you listened to my suggestion at all! What'd you decide on?'

'The LeTromp Sif 80 you showed me. I checked out three others, but LeTromp have the second one already started in their yard in South Africa which was to be a factory demo model and they were delighted to incorporate my changes for the right money. So I said I'd take it. I emailed them earlier; now just waiting on their reply.'

Alex was most interested. 'That will be a much bigger boat than the current *Firebird*, Commander. Do you think it will need a full-time crew?'

I looked at him; huge, competent and even-tempered, but answered, 'The list of changes I've asked for are intended to make it as easy to handle as possible. But I will admit that sail handling could be a problem short-handed, so I'm thinking maybe a couple of competent persons who are familiar with big cats would be a real asset. Do you think you and Bree might like to stay on with us?'

His usually impassive face broke out into a beaming smile that utterly transformed him. He seemed to be at a loss for words, so he just stepped forward and shook my hand for a long time, which from Alex, spoke volumes.

'Well, I guess I can consider those positions filled. You do realise that with your shares from the last operation and this one, the pair of you could do anything you like, including getting your own boat?'

He nodded and with a hint of a gleam in his eyes, said in a husky voice, 'We both realised that, for the first time in either of our lives, and thanks to you and the Major, we can do whatever we want.

However, we have also decided that what we really want is to stay close to the only two people who have ever given us a real chance at life and been totally fair-minded toward us. Therefore, we would be happy and honoured to stay on as crew. *Firebird*, whatever her size, has become our home too.'

For Alex, that was the longest and most emotional speech I'd ever heard, but I was very glad to have his and Bree's support. That was also a good cue for Dave and Alex to finish their duty for the evening and dispose of the late and grossly un-lamented Steve. Rounding up Jasper, who kept stopping at the bathroom door to growl at Gerry, Dave and Alex fired up the Hi-Lux ute and drove away in a cloud of noxious smoke. Fifteen minutes later, the ute was returned, but the driver disappeared just as quickly, so after dividing the night into three watch periods, I left the girls chatting and went to bed.

THURSDAY

I woke to feel Corrine gently shaking my arm. 'All OK Harry,' came her soft reassuring voice. 'Everything is quiet inside and out.'

'Thanks Mouse. Give me a few moments to catch my scattered wits and I'll be on the ball.'

'No worries, Boss. I'll hang around until you're up and running, then I'll disappear.'

'Thanks. You've been a great help as usual. See you again on Monday with your first-aid kit.'

'No problem. Cheers, Big Dog.'

Soon after, I dragged myself out of bed, washed, then dressed. All was as quiet as promised and a prowl around showed that Corrine had left, Dell was in bed asleep and Gerry was quiet in the bathroom. Putting the kettle on, I went out the back door and walked around the house. At 03:00, not much was happening on Lord Howe Island,

and certainly nothing was stirring at the ex-Xavier house. I checked the guest bathroom window and wasn't surprised to see that the glass had been cracked, although the window was too small to climb through. Screwing the sliding frame to the surrounding fixed frame had made things more difficult for a potential escapee, although a healthy fear of stirring up the 'devil cat' may have accounted for the window glass being just cracked and not broken right out.

The faint whistle of the kettle called and minutes later, I was sitting at the kitchen table with a hot, sweet mug of tea and nibbling on some chocolate chip biscuits. My peaceful planning session was interrupted by a soft knocking from up the hallway, and naturally it turned out to be Gerry, cold and uncomfortable, in need of a hot mug of coffee. In a relaxed mood, I let her out and even cut the hobble from her ankles without being asked.

'Aren't you afraid that I'll run away?' she asked, making herself a coffee, since my good nature only went so far!

Casually, I took a sip of tea before replying, 'Nope! You wouldn't get far and the mess would be very nasty. It'd be blamed on a rabid dog attack, of course, which would mean every dog on the island would have to be rounded up and tested.'

I smiled to myself as she nervously looked over her shoulder up the dark hallway.

'Nope. He's not up there. When he heard the window glass crack, he went outside, where he still is – waiting for you to do something stupid!'

I eyed her firmly muscled body speculatively. 'You've got a bit of padding here and there, so since he hasn't been fed for over 24 hours, he'll certainly eat some of your plumper bits for breakfast. He's actually very partial to bum cheeks and the back of the thigh.'

I noticed she was getting paler as I spoke, but the images inspired by my last few words were too much and she made a bolt for the sink where the remains of last night's meal joined the recent coffee grounds. Once thoroughly empty, she rinsed her mouth carefully, before turning to me.

'You're a bastard! Why did you have to say shit like that? Anyway, what is he and where does he come from?'

'I think you should be careful about who you call names,' I said mildly. 'If he thinks you're trying to harm anybody in this house, or trying to leave the house, he'll attack without further warning. I wasn't kidding when I said he had several kills to his credit. And none were clean, if you know what I mean.'

I nodded toward the sink as she went pale again, but she fought the bile back down and refused to succumb a second time.

'OK. I get the picture, but I'd still like to know what he is. I've never seen anything like that, except in a zoo.'

'Alright, I'll tell you this much. He's an Indonesian jungle cat who was crossed with a large domestic breed of cat, except instead of becoming smaller, the strain reverted back to nearly pure jungle cat, but with the better domestic traits. He's normally even-tempered and very affectionate with people he likes, but if he decides you're on the shit list, then, I'm afraid, your arse is toast. Pardon my mixed metaphors. He'll spend the day outside, watching and waiting for the slightest excuse to have a go at you.

Step out any door without an escort and you won't even see him coming. I've been told it's like being hit with a truck, except that trucks don't eat your best bits afterwards.'

That last was too much for her weakened gut and she made another dash to the sink, even though there was nothing left to bring up.

Finally, able to leave the stainless sanctuary, she was too wrung out to curse me again and slumped down in her chair, waving her hands weakly.

'OK. Enough already with the hungry pussy tales! I'll be good, but no more crap about the cat!'

I shrugged, 'Good oh. I selfishly wanted to spare my girls and myself from having to clean you up, or dispose of your carcass after you thought you were cleverer than I was and tried to leave.'

Gerry held her hand up as she hung her head, obviously fighting the wave of nausea that had swept over her yet again. 'You have my word I won't attempt to leave without you holding my hand.'

Finally, her comment struck me as funny so I laughed, 'You're a good-looking woman, Gerry, despite the tough image, but I'm not aiming to get too close to you. But there again, maybe that would be the best way to keep you close. Just remember, it's not just me and my buddy's cat you have to worry about. Muck up too much and Xavier will be all over you like a bloody rash.'

She gave a shudder, 'More like a bloody octopus, you mean! And nearly as cold and clammy!'

There was no point disputing that assessment so I let it slide.

'I might go back to bed for a while, if that's alright?' Gerry asked.

'Yeah, sure. But you'll be locked in and don't forget the cat is outside, because he won't have forgotten you.'

'I think I've got it, Mr Stevens, but thank you for reminding me!' she replied. She sounded a bit narky for some reason!

It was around 05:00 and with Gerry locked in believing that Jasper was waiting, salivating outside her window, I thought it safe to get my head down as well, so went back to bed. I'd no sooner turned the light out, when a naked, and very female body slipped in through the open doorway and joined me. I've always believed it's only polite to do the right thing by a naked lady who joins you in bed, so I went ahead and upheld that fine, long-standing belief.

In fact, the first time around was so good, I had to make sure it wasn't a fluke and did the right thing again. Dell thought it was a bit of alright as well, and happily went to shower and get breakfast ready while I dozed for another 20 minutes or so.

FRIDAY, LORD HOWE ISLAND

Dell checked on Gerry, but discovered she didn't have much of an appetite for bacon, sausages, baked beans and tomato and was staying in bed a while longer.

No matter; meant there was more for me and Dell.

We left the bathroom door open for Gerry to come and go as she wanted, but she mostly stayed where she was. There wasn't much else to do that day until the Foley brothers came calling later in the evening, therefore I took to the office and went through more papers. The only thing I learned was, that the whole operation appeared to be set up by Xavier developing a string of bent mine managers to look after the supply side and a network of gem dealers, auction houses and private collectors who didn't ask too many embarrassing questions where a particular gem came from.

There was reference to something called 'a facilitation tariff' which I wasn't sure about, but thought it would reveal itself in due course.

The other exciting email was from the LeTromp headquarters in Amsterdam, to say they would be delighted to confer ownership of the project named Sif 80-2, currently under construction at the company's new boatyard at St Francis Bay in South Africa for the initial sum of 1.7 million Euro, which converted to close enough AU\$2.8 million. They thoughtfully included in their email their bank account details for a direct transfer, as well as a list of the changes I'd said I wanted, for me to check. A series of progress payments, thankfully a lot smaller than the deposit were listed, as well as an invitation to call or visit them anytime. I sent an email to my bank in Vanuatu, asking them to transfer the sum of $2.8 mill to the Le Tromp account, and noted that the earliest time to call them would be at 19:30 this evening, which was still well before the Foley boys were expected to drop by.

I fiddle-farted around until tea time, stowing the bags of uncut stones securely in my carry-on luggage then weighed it carefully, not surprised that they used a fair portion of my 7-kilogram carry-on limit. I also took the precaution of taking the stones out of their fancy white velvet, draw-string bags and put them in kitchen variety zip-loc plastic bags. If asked, I was going to declare them as amateur geological samples, but first I checked there wasn't any prohibition on the taking of rocks away from the island.

Dell had made a simple evening meal from the well-stocked fridge and pantry and Gerry decided to join us, rather hungry after losing all her meal from last night. It was a very quiet occasion as I briefed Gerry on her role when the Foley's came to exchange a parcel for cash.

'Why do I have to say you're taking over for a while? Why can't I just say that you're relieving us for a week or two?'

'Because I don't know what Xavier wants,' I explained, 'so this way, both of us are covered. If you're back in a week, happy days! We'll be delighted to get back to civilisation. If it takes longer, then the Foley's won't get upset. Xavier has gone to a lot of trouble to set up this whole operation and he won't be pleased if we upset the pick-up crew.'

'Yeah, all right. I guess that makes sense.'

'Good. So just vouch for Dell and me, and say you'll be back soon. If they ask about Steve, he's had to fly out early.'

She gave a short, humourless laugh, 'They won't be worried about Steve, they hate his guts! They've had a few run-in's over the last couple of years.'

'Good. That makes it easier. Just play it low key. Do you normally invite them in?'

'No way! They come to the back door and we have to leave the outside light off as well as the kitchen light. I give them the cash in one envelope, take the package and open it after they leave. There are two packages inside, and the bigger one goes to Sydney unopened. The small one I leave in the safe for when Xavier comes, which is about every second month, but I guess things are a bit buggered up at the moment.'

I smiled grimly, 'Yeah, that's for sure! Anyway, I've got to make some calls, so hang with Dell until I get back. Dell will feed the cat shortly, so you might like to wait in the bathroom when she does. He doesn't like the look of you for some reason.'

Dell got the message and said, 'I'll look after things, Boss, but don't be long.'

'No, I won't. Just feed the kitty and keep him outside until Gerry goes in the bathroom. In fact, it might be better if you go in there now, please Gerry. Just in case.'

She didn't need to be told twice and it was almost comical to see that she left the kitchen in almost indecent haste, and moments later, we heard the bathroom door bang closed.

'I'll be in the office, but I'll get their money ready first. You'd better make feeding Jasper-type noises to justify all this play-acting and keep Missy quiet. She's obviously terrified of him.'

Dell grinned and gave passable imitation of a Jasper yowl, then banged the kitchen-screen door a few times. 'There...that should do the trick.' she said softly.

I smiled back, then went to the office where I opened the safe, found the broken pack of $100 notes and peeled off ten, then put them in an envelope. I took it and left it on the kitchen table, then returned to the office, closed the door and called Le Tromp in Amsterdam. I made immediate contact and in moments was speaking to Chief Designer and founder, the boss man, Hugo LeTromp himself. Being Dutch, he naturally spoke excellent English, which saved me having to attempt to use my virtually non-existent Dutch.

Following a brief exchange of pleasantries, Hugo took the time to work through all the mods I'd suggested. Extending the master cabin into the next cabin forward to make a large walk-through dressing room and storage area was no problem, and even adding a pair of fold-up berths for emergency accommodation could be added. The for'rard cabins could easily be converted to two spacious twin-berth cabins with their own en-suite.

The port hull would keep the standard layout of large stateroom aft, another double forward of that, then a large laundry and workshop, and a twin stacked bunk cabin right forward. All three cabins would have an en-suite each.

There were no problems moving the galley up to the saloon and a wheel could be added to the saloon nav station for bad weather steering. What I had thought would be one of the biggest changes, that of eliminating the twin rear-set, outside steering stations, and creating a much better protected, bulkhead-mounted steering station in the cockpit, with full overhead cover and a sliding hatch, plus a forward armoured glass windscreen, wasn't a problem at all.

Covering the cabin and cockpit top with solar panels, and fitting a targa bar to hold the satellite comms gear and the various antennas wasn't a problem either, although I was sure I heard the clicking sound of the calculator keys adding up the cost of all my extras!

He asked for photos and descriptions of my current setup so they could duplicate them more easily. He strongly suggested the single, very tall mast be retained since this added greatly to the extraordinary performance of the boat under sail. My very expensive mast-head camera could be added at the change-over if I could provide the measurements of the mounting brackets and wiring needs.

In response to my concern about sailing short-handed and trying to handle very large sails, he proposed a very innovative electro-hydraulic drive arrangement for all halyards, sheets and the roller furling of the three roller-furling sails ahead of the mast; the huge

Code Zero or the Screecher, the 155% reaching Genoa and the self-tacking inner jib. The massive mainsail could certainly be set up on a custom boom-furling arrangement, and this too, would be driven and controlled by an electro/hydraulic drive unit.

'Therefore, Mr Stevens, even on such a large catamaran, just one person can control all sails from either the cockpit steering station, or the saloon navigation station with just buttons and mini joy-sticks! To further assist the helmsperson, a sail position graphic and a UHD camera will display the position and set of all sails on the main 4K LED monitor. The hydraulics would, of course, have triple redundant pumps, as well as a central back-up pump which would still allow sail furling, just more slowly than with the individual setup.

We recommend using a new main sheet traveller car which has a remote push-button, instant release to de-power the main in a squall gust. It has a back-up system in case of malfunction in the form of manual access to the traveller sheet. Also, for an emergency, every winch or drive will have a hand crank fitting built in. Already, there are two very large and strengthened clear view panels over the interior helm station, to enable visual sail setting, so the boat can be easily sailed by one person. In your case, I would suggest adding UHD cameras to aid with docking from either steering station, but the engine control system incorporates a wireless remote to allow full engine and rudder control from anywhere on the boat.'

'One last suggestion about the rigging. You have a carbon mast, and for longevity, we strongly recommend that the standing rigging be solid rod. There is a small weight penalty aloft, but a big reduction in windage compared to synthetic. Sheets and halliards should be Dyneema where they will be used exclusively with the hydraulic drives or winches, and for handling with bare hands, the type with a polyester sleeve. Your suggestions for the propulsion system are easily accommodated. We have had talks with a Scandinavian company who can do all of what you require and more. We believe you will be delighted with the result. I have just emailed their proposal for your approval.

We can apply all of your minor fitting and setup preferences as the *build progresses, if you'd care to photograph and document the features you wish duplicated from your existing boat.'*

I'd been frantically scribbling notes, but was happy to give him the go-ahead on all his suggestions, and promised to get all the other little features that suited my style of sailing, photographed, documented and emailed to him.

Without my asking, Hugo suggested that a reasonable time-frame for completion would be 4 to 6 months, because the new yard was very efficient and because the area had become a major centre of boat-building activity, they could pull in more labourers as required.

'Much of the moulding work has already been completed, all the fittings are on hand, and the carpentry is all done in-house. There should be little or no delay to blow-out the time-frame or the cost, apart from your special requirements.'

That was good news, since I was starting to get excited at the prospect of becoming used to such a big and fast boat. We signed off soon after, with Hugo expressing his appreciation for the prompt payment of the deposit.

I finished off my notes, stacked them tidily, and went to re-join Dell.

'Just in time, Harry. It's 21:30, so the Foley's could be here at any time.'

'Oh, sorry. I didn't realise how late it is. Time flies when you're having fun spending several million dollars.'

She blinked, but said, 'I'll go roust out Gerry. I'll tell her Evil Kitty had been locked away until after the Foley's have been.'

I grinned at that, 'Good thinking. She might have wondered why the Foley's weren't shredded.'

Gerry was very subdued when she followed Dell back down the hallway, maybe sensing the brief encounter with the Foleys might be her last bit of business on Lord Howe.

We sat around the table with the light out as required, not having much to say, until there was a soft knock at the door. I let Gerry open it and stood beside her in plain view. In the dim light, the brothers looked to be shortish, stocky men with broad shoulders and broad bellies to match, suggesting a powerful fondness for beer.

'Who's that?' came a gruff challenge from the older one. I presumed he was older as, in the dim light, he seemed to have more grey hair than his brother; or maybe he just worried more.

'This is Mr Stevens from Head Office. He's relieving me for a few weeks while I go to the mainland. His partner is Miss Petrie, she's Mr Xavier's personal assistant. They are considerably more senior than me so watch your manners and do whatever they say. They've come straight from Mr Xavier.'

His answer was a grunt, but he must have accepted the change in management, for he thrust a black, plastic-wrapped parcel at Gerry, who made a point of handing it ceremoniously to me. I made my own point by tossing it casually to Dell, who in turn, handed me the envelope. I passed it to him and he took it without a word. The pair of them, scruffy, smelling strongly of fish and in bare feet, spun around and melted into the night without a sound.

I closed and locked the door. 'Well. That was a painless transaction. Good job Gerry, and I can see why they don't come inside. It wasn't hard to guess their occupation.'

Gerry made with a rare grin. 'You did well. They normally don't even speak at all. Will is the older one and Jack the younger. I've never heard him speak.'

I looked at my watch. 'OK. That'll about do me for one day. I'm afraid I've got to lock you in for the night,' I said to Gerry, 'but I won't tie your hands. I'll have to put the hobble on, though, and remind you that the bad, black pussy cat will be in and out of the house all night, so please be a good girl. There's just two more days to get through, before we fly to Sydney on Monday, and you fly on to Melbourne alone. Xavier will have a man to meet you at the airport, so just go with the flow and behave. All will work out just fine.'

Maybe my reassurances were convincing, as she meekly submitted to the cable-tie hobble and then to being locked in the bathroom.

Dell and I took turns at making snuffling sounds outside the door, and I asked Dell if she could make with another Jasper yowl outside in the yard near the bathroom window. She did and it even raised the hackles on my head. I couldn't see what Gerry thought of the performance, but there wasn't a single sound from her for the rest of the evening.

With that chore taken care of, Dell and I went into the office to see what sort of a Christmas present the Foley's had brought us.

The package was bulkier than I expected, but some of that was just waterproof plastic wrapping. Not that water would worry the stones, but the layers of plastic and tape did provide padding. As Gerry had said, there were two parcels inside; the larger one to be passed on and a smaller one for Xavier, which now explained the curious references about the 'facilitation tariff' in the papers I'd been reading. I pushed the larger one over to Dell. 'Look after that for me please, dear lady. My bag is a bit heavy already.'

As she nervously poked and prodded the tightly wrapped parcel, I took a knife from the desk drawer and slit the wrapping on the smaller one, to reveal a length of black velvet cloth wrapped around a series of lumps. Unrolled, the lumps appeared to be three large rubies the size and shape of small chook eggs and four deep orange-coloured stones that I thought might be diamonds. They weren't all that much smaller than the red stones and roughly measured 60 x 45 mm. Someone had gone to the trouble of grinding a tiny flat on each orange stone, so I dug out the powerful magnifying glass Alex had used, swung the strong, white desk lamp toward me and peered into the depths of the larger one.

It was a weird experience; like looking into a brightly-lit, orange room through a small outside window. The clarity of the stone seemed perfect, which made it seem like it was hollow. There were no marks or inclusions of any size I could see, and the roughly oval shape suggested to my untrained mind, that it could be cut with minimal wastage. The other three were only slightly smaller, but all appeared to my unskilled eye to be flawless. Certainly, their colour was stunning, a brilliant, almost luminous deep orange like scattered clouds above a sunset in the tropics.

'I've never seen an orange diamond before, if that's what it is. I didn't know there was such a thing.' I commented to Dell as I passed the stone and the magnifying glass over. 'If they weren't in Xavier's personal parcel, I'd say they were pretty, but worth bugger all! But someone's gone to the trouble to separate them from the others, so they must be a little bit special. Or maybe it was a slow month for smuggling special gems and they threw these in to make up the parcel.'

Dell looked up from her peep-show into the orange depths. 'I don't know, Harry. They look too beautiful to be cheap. But I reckon it'll need your expert to decide.'

'Yeah, that's right. Mr Jacobs is going to have a lot to do on Tuesday. Anyway, I'm for bed. It's been a long and busy day and I'll call Dave in the morning about the *Dragonfly* flight, or he can just tell us when he gets here late morning.'

I shoved the bundle of stones in the thigh pocket of my cargo pants, checked the safe was locked, did a quick lap around the house to make sure Gerry was quiet, scratched on the bathroom door a few times until I heard a whimper, then headed to bed.

Naturally, Dell had beaten me to it, so faced with the choice of being rude by going to the other room, or being polite, I did what my dear, departed mother always said, which was to always be polite. I'm not sure that Mum had in mind this particular situation when she said that, but I wasn't complaining. Nor was Dell.

CHAPTER 21

I was up pre-dawn next morning, as usual, sitting in the kitchen with the back door open, having a mug of steaming Earl Grey, when to my delight, Sandy appeared, a big grin on her lovely face. Slightly emotional greetings over with, we got down to swapping stories.

'How's Darryl been behaving and how did you manage to slip away?' I got in first.

She grinned at my impatience, 'I've started the habit of getting up a bit earlier and going for a walk. I do the same in the evening after tea, if nothing else is going on. That gives me the ability to check in with you, or to see Corrine. It doesn't matter if I'm seen with her since Kelly invited her to the house and they got on very well. She's been a couple of times now, and Darryl rather likes having her around.

As for his behaviour, so far he's been okay, but Kelly reckons an eruption is getting close. She knows all the signs and thinks this one will be a real ball-tearer; so to speak!'

'So he hasn't chucked the heavies on you yet?'

She chuckled, 'No, not yet. But I reckon that's even closer. He's laid some heavy hints that a threesome would be a good way to relax, and it probably would be; for him! He loses his temper very quickly now about stupid little things, so I can see that Kelly is right. She's a lovely girl and I'm so glad we're in a position to help her, but I fear that for now, it's just going to have to play out. At the moment, she'll do anything to keep him settled and avoid the eruption, which is why I think she'll push for the threesome to happen very soon. But we still can't move in prematurely because we can't prove he's done anything wrong.'

I could see the thought of being helpless was really getting to her, but she was right. Until Darryl struck out at someone, he was bulletproof.

'Yeah. I understand. Just be very careful my darling girl. If he starts to rough you up, in bed or out, don't hold back. Bash him and we'll sort things out later. Call me on the SatPhone and I'll come straight over! If necessary, he can join Steve in a swimming lesson just off the reef one evening.'

She smiled, 'OK, Boss. I'll do that. Now, what's been happening with you?'

I chuckled, 'I won't take up your time now to show you, but I've found Xavier's main stash!'

Her eyes lit up, 'Wow! Is it really good?'

'We think so, there's some cash, but the rest of it is in gems again. This time, they're all uncut so it's hard to tell how good they are. Apparently Alex used to be a geologist and worked for a diamond mine in South Africa, so he had a quick look and said they are all very special as they had been set aside especially for Xavier. They should be worth a huge amount, but we won't know until I take them to Mr Jacobs on Tuesday.'

'Woo Hoo! But what's this about Tuesday?'

I quickly told her about having to shoot Steve; keeping Gerry quiet with Jasper's help and the belief she was going to see Xavier; deciding to use the airline tickets to take Gerry to Sydney and hand her over my mob, then going on to the Gold Coast to hand all the gems over to Mr Jacobs for assessment.

'So we're going to keep them?' she asked with an avaricious gleam in her eye.

I grinned, 'Yes, my darling, money-grubbing millionairess, we are. Just Xavier's stash, since no one still alive knows about them. Gerry doesn't since she didn't find the hidden compartment in the safe. Oh, and there's nearly $2.6 million in cash in the safe as well. We could hand it in, but only Gerry knows about it. We might have to put some in an account for her, but we'll have to go to Vanuatu to get rid of it. An Aussie bank would be screaming terrorist plot in ten seconds if we trundled that lot through the door!'

'Yep! You're right there. Maybe we can take a real holiday and make a cruise to Vanuatu, without being on the job. Speaking of being on the job, has Dell been looking after you properly? I did have a long talk with her before we split in Cairns.'

I patted her hand and kissed her. 'Yes dear, she has been a good girl and my needs have been well looked after. It's a pity you've only got Darryl to do the same for you.'

She gave a throaty chuckle, 'Kelly still keeps going on about how good he is in bed when he's not too uptight, so I guess I find out very soon.'

I nodded, still uneasy about Sandy, literally in the very dangerous hands of Darryl, the serial rapist and murderer.

To lighten the mood, I said casually, 'Oh, by the way, I've just bought us a new boat.'

She blinked in surprise, searching for words, before saying, 'You've bought a new boat! What is it? How? Why?'

I grinned at her bewilderment, then relented and explained all. I blamed it all on Dave, of course, but when I showed her some photos of the Sif 80, she changed her mind dramatically. 'But can just you and I handle it? It looks gi-bloody-normous!'

'A good question and, yes, it is big, but the way it will be set up, we can handle it just fine. However, Alex and Bree didn't really want to go anywhere else, even though they can afford anything, so I asked them if they wanted to stay on as crew and they've jumped at it! Given the size of the thing, we could literally have a football team aboard and still have elbow room!'

She was very happy about Alex and Bree, and continued to look excited which was even better, but then asked the typical question all females ask when their mate spends money, 'Dare I ask what this monster is going to cost?'

'Well. I just transferred $2.8 mill as a holding deposit, then there will be progress payments as the build proceeds.'

She hit my arm in that slightly painful, but affectionate gesture I'd come to know so well, 'Bottom line dear Harry, bottom line! Emmachisit?'

'Probably nudging $8 to $10 million Aussie, by the time we've both finished setting things up properly the way we want them.'

'I take it we have no trouble affording that?'

I smiled, 'No dear. It isn't a problem.'

'So am I going to be very wealthy all over again?'

'Yep, I'm afraid so.'

'Oh, goody! I'm getting to like this.'

'What, even dealing with Darryl?'

'Everything comes at a price, dearest. No pain, no gain, as some fool once said.'

At that point Dell wandered out to see who the other voice was and they had a happy reunion. I was pleased the two ladies got on so well, and it occurred to me that I hadn't mentioned to Dell she'd be welcome to stay aboard the new boat, but I'm sure she had plans of her own, especially when she had her share of the newest batch of loot.

Then it was time for Sandy to head back to Kelly's before Darryl started wondering where she'd got to, given that the island wasn't that big.

That was also time to let Gerry out of her bathroom isolation, remove the hobble and have breakfast. Dell did the honours with the food and Gerry helped her to produce my favourite feast of bacon, sausages, baked beans and tomato. The girls liked it too and chatter around the table was a lot livelier than it had been.

When plates were clean, I said to Gerry, 'There's nothing special to do today or tomorrow, so you're free to wander about the house as you want. Just don't try to go outside for any reason. The cat is prowling around, and will attack without any warning. I'll ease the hobbles a bit more, but they'll have to stay on just in case you get a change of heart.' Mugs of tea and coffee finished, and with a bit more animation, Gerry helped Dell clean up the kitchen, then went to do the same to herself and the reminder that the 'bad cat' was still hanging around, was more than enough threat to keep her from doing anything silly.

She decided to pack early, and Dell supervised her in the master bedroom where she packed a small suitcase and dug out a comfortable travelling outfit. With that task completed, her earlier upbeat mood seemed to have evaporated. Before Dave arrived at 11:00, I asked Gerry to return to the bathroom for the duration, something she did without complaint.

When we were in the office, the first thing I wanted to know was, 'How did *Dragonfly* go?'

'Really good. Alex and Bree are a great team and Bree is right up to speed on it. As you suggested, we just waited with the masthead camera trained on the boat ramp until they appeared, then launched the UAV. Bree took it up to 2000 feet, set an orbit, set the cameras to track mode with the boat as target and left it to sort itself out.

Once they went out through the North Passage, she brought it down to 1000 feet. With the stabilised camera, the zoom let us just about count the length of the whiskers on the fisho's chins, so she kept it at that height. They went around the north side of the island and headed up to the north east. There wasn't much breeze, but there was a decent swell running, so there might be a bit of a blow on the way for us to look out for.

They only went 18 miles out, then stopped. Bree widened the orbit and went higher so they wouldn't hear the engine, then this container ship came into sight on a south-west heading which kept it well clear of the island and Ball's Pyramid. Bree moved the auto-track to the ship and dropped down again, so we have some really sharp, close-up video of the ship, its name and the crew. She even sent it past the bridge to see who was there, but only one dude was on watch, although she got good shots of two guys, Asian origin, walking out to the stern railing with a bulky package. It had a square box fastened to one side with a small antenna poking up out of it and a green flashing strobe. They tossed it overboard and went back inside the accommodation block.

The pick-up boat was only about half a mile away, and it moved in straight away, fished it out and buggered off back to LHI. We caught all of it in close-up detail and I've got the whole thing on a 32 GB flash drive. It's raw footage and un-edited.'

I nodded appreciatively, 'Perfect! Thanks Dave. I'll hand that over to my mob, together with Gerry and the gems. Sounds like an ancient pop group. Thank Bree for me and for doing a really good job. I'm very glad they wanted to stay on as permanent crew.'

'So, what's the go with the new boat?' Dave asked.

I went through what I'd done and what I wanted and showed him the emails. He agreed the sail handling arrangement would make short-handed sailing do-able and the extra space would be stunning! 'When's delivery?' he asked with a grin.

'Hugo reckons anywhere from 4 to 6 months, but he did say all the mouldings are done and ready to be fitted. The changes I wanted wouldn't add much time to the build, and in any case, now the thing was sold and they have my money, he was going to throw a heap of labourers at it, so it could be as little as 3 months. I did say that I'd pay extra if they could work 7 days on it, so that might speed things up.'

Dave grinned, 'The overtime will cost a bomb, but I guess Xavier is paying for it ultimately.'

'That's the way I looked at it, and with all this extra money coming in eventually, Sandy and I aren't broke. Still, there was a bit of sticker shock when I made the transfer of $2.8 mil as a deposit!'

'Yeah, I know just how you feel. Corrine and I had the same feeling paying out $10 mil for *Seeker*. But that's what money's for and it seems like we've got more coming in.'

'We do,' I said, 'but this could be the last of the easy gems we pick up. We might have to work for a living after this.'

He shook his head, 'Nah! Corrine's still got a few emeralds

squirrelled away in a safe deposit box and I'm sure you've done the same and have a 'safety collection' tucked away somewhere. We'll get by. But tell me; how are you going to collect it? Do we all fly to South Africa and sail it back?'

I nodded, 'Yep That's my first choice. The yard will arrange delivery if necessary, but I'd rather like to be the first to sail it. Once we have the teething problems sorted, it should be a quick downwind trip back to Aussie.'

Dave looked happy at that. 'Yeah. That's more like it. If we drop down a few degrees of latitude, it should be solid westerlies all the way to Tasmania. Didn't you want to go back down there and do some exploring?'

'Yeah, I did actually. Sandy and I wanted to have a good look around Macquarie Harbour and then go down to Port Davey in the south-west. I was actually headed there when I got hooked up with Janice and her daughters, so it'd be good to finally get to complete that particular trip.'

'Sounds good. Corrine and I might bring *Seeker* down as well.'

'That'll be good too, but if you're both already on-board *Firebird* then we can plan to go to Strahan, but we'll have to clear Customs in Fremantle first.'

'Ah, yes. I'd forgotten about that. But what about Jasper and Krazy?'

'I've been thinking about that, and one option is that we take the current *Firebird* to South Africa and sell it there. The yard could transfer a lot of our specialised gear like the mast-head camera to the new boat.'

'We could do that, but it might be a lot cheaper and easier on everybody if we fly to SA, the pussies were boarded for a while, then were sent to meet us in Fremantle, for instance.'

'Way too sensible, Dave. That plan could even work.' I conceded gracefully.

We chatted for a while longer, indulging in the happy pastime of talking about boats and planning fit-outs, before Dell interrupted our delightful contemplation of pleasures to come, with the down-to-earth announcement that it was lunch-time.

The weekend passed relatively quietly, to the point of being boring. Gerry became increasingly irritable, shuffling around the house in the hobbles, and annoyed Dell and me with her constant complaining about being restrained. Pointing out that she was being given a lot more freedom than Xavier wanted didn't help, so on Saturday night, I had Dave bring Jasper ashore and leave him with us for Sunday. That was a bit like taking a shotgun to a knife fight; Gerry was reluctant to even leave her bathroom, with Jasper free to wander in or out of the house as he wanted. He knew not to show himself to anybody wandering past on the road, and certainly no visitors came around for a friendly cup of tea and a chat.

MONDAY

It was, therefore, with a distinct sense of relief, that Monday arrived, along with the promised bout of bad weather. Strong winds and cold rain lashed the island, encouraging Dell and me to stay in a warm bed, until Gerry's whinging prompted me to call out that she should get her own breakfast.

'Your door isn't locked, so stop being a pain in the arse and get up. And while you're on the job, we'll have a tea and a coffee please.'

I heard the bathroom door open, followed by a shriek. 'But the bloody cat's looking at me,' she complained.

'Well, look back at him. He's probably making sure you're still as horrible as he remembered. He knows you're allowed to move around the house. Just don't try going outside. C'mon, Gerry, chop, chop. One coffee, one tea. You can do it!'

'Bastard's still looking at me,' came the grumble, but at least there was the sound of the kettle being filled. I didn't really expect her to bring us tea and coffee in bed, but before long, she shuffled in, carefully trying not to spill any. After handing them over, she perched on the foot of the bed, looking wistfully at the bare upper half of both Dell and me as we sat sipping the reviving hot brew. She seemed on the verge of saying something profound, but the moment passed, and with a trickle of tears down her cheeks, she rose without a word and shuffled out, her faithful, but unwelcome black shadow at her heels.

Later that morning, Dave came ashore with a small bag of gear and was introduced to Gerry as another of Xavier's operatives.

'Christ, how many more of you are on this bloody island?' she demanded.

'Enough.' was the unencouraging reply.

I brought Dave up to speed, although there was little to do unless Darryl arced up while I was gone, then Dell ran Gerry and me to the airport, where Dell gave me a hug and a kiss as she dropped us off at the terminal where our red-tailed bird sat waiting. Check-in was uneventful with minimal baggage checks apart from very careful weighing. The incorrect name on my ticket was quickly fixed and we boarded on time.

The seats in a Bombardier Dash 8 weren't really designed to be sat in for 1 hour and 45 minutes, but there was little choice, so an occasional walk up and down the aisle helped ward off cramps. The scenery 25,000 feet below, was monotonous in the extreme and my travelling companion had little to say, although at one point, she asked plaintively, 'Will I be alright, Harry?'

For once I could answer her honestly, and said, 'If you're prepared to go with the flow, then I can truly say you'll be alright.'

She looked at me strangely, but replied, 'That's not exactly what I asked, but I'll accept it at face value. Thank you.' That was the extent of conversation for the rest of the flight and finally, we were touching down in Sydney, a strong west wind blowing. Disembarking at the domestic terminal, we had the usual wait until our bags were spat out of the maw of the handling facility. I'd already spotted my contacts. A young guy and his female partner who slowly moved closer to us, just like everybody else trying to grab their bags two seconds before someone else.

However, there was another young man who sidled up to Gerry and said, 'Got the stuff?' Gerry wordlessly pointed at me, so I smiled brightly, dug the plastic-wrapped parcel out of my carry-on bag and handed it over, saying as I did, 'Hi. I'm Harry, the new Steve. Is this what you're after?'

He blinked in surprise, but took the parcel without fuss and turned to walk away, but two burly men with expressionless faces, smoothly intercepted him before he'd gone ten paces and steered him outside where a black car waited, doors open.

Gerry seemed to miss the last of this byplay as she was in the process of grabbing her suitcase before the conveyor belt re-absorbed it back into the system. As she turned from the carousel, a couple stepped close, the woman flashed her credentials and quietly said, 'Miss Varley, I'm Sergeant Jones of the Australian Commonwealth Police and this is my partner, Senior Constable Corbett. Would you mind coming with us, please? My superiors would like to have a confidential talk with you. This way if you please.'

Gerry only had one frantic moment to ask, 'Is this all right, Harry?'

I nodded, 'They're the good guys, Gerry. Go with the flow. All will be well, I promise.'

I handed the fat bundle of papers and the flash drive to Senior Constable Corbett with a reminder that Gerry was to be held incommunicado and the papers were to be handed by him personally to my Controller and no one else. He nodded acknowledgement, and added, 'No problem, Commander. I'll make sure it happens just that way.'

Nobody around us seemed to either notice or care as Gerry was quietly escorted away, leaving me to collect my bag and head back into the departures terminal to catch my flight to Brisbane.

CHAPTER 22

I had a pleasant and delightfully uneventful evening at a so-called, upmarket hotel that had severe delusions of grandeur, but at least had a good bed, restaurant and bar where I taught the barman how to make North Queensland Tea, that happy blend of black tea and a double shot of dark rum liqueur.

I decided to hire a car for the drive to Southport, so was easily able to make my 10:00 appointment with Miriam and Mr Jacobs at their modest shop in the main street of Southport.

Being Tuesday, the shop was open for normal business, so with a pleasant and competent shop assistant looking after the walk-in trade, the delightful Miriam escorted me to a back room, which was well set up for inspecting precious gems. The elderly, but still spritely Mr Jacobs, hurried forward to shake my hand. As had become the norm, their welcome was quite effusive, which was appropriate given the stunning array of fabulous gems and jewellery I'd passed across the waxed wood counter. And in return, of course, they had helped make me and my crew rather wealthy.

'My dear Mr Stevens. Wonderful to see you again. You must be wondering about the auction and I can report that all is finally arranged. I have papers for you to sign and it is scheduled for the 23rd of next month, which is just six weeks away. I do hope it will suit you, but the auction house had to set a date.'

I smiled at his enthusiasm. 'I'm sure it will be fine, Mr Jacobs. We certainly hope to be able to attend, but circumstances may well conspire against it. In which case, I'm sure you and Miriam will represent our interests most effectively.'

I don't know why, but in the presence of Mr Jacobs, I feel obliged to talk like him, all old world, courtly and stuff.

He nodded and smiled, then scolded Miriam for not bringing tea. 'But I do have tea ready, Zaydee. See, here it is on the coffee table.'

A set of comfortable chairs surrounded a lovely polished redgum table, set under a pair of skylights in the middle of the room, so we sat while Miriam played Mother and poured the tea.

Mr Jacobs then proceeded to tell me how the auction of the pirate's treasure we'd seized in Indonesia was going to be presented. Finally, Miriam had to stop the flow of words by saying, 'I'm sure that Mr Stevens knows what is in the auction, but he has other business with us this day, Zaydee.'

Mr Jacobs looked enquiringly at me, so I said, 'Miriam is correct. I do have other business to conduct with you and it may take some time.'

'Oh. I must confess I have been so wrapped up in this amazing auction, that I tend to think of little else. My apologies. Now, what did you wish to discuss?'

I had my backpack with me, so I dug into it and produced the first seven white cord tied bags and set them on the table. In the privacy and security of my overnight hotel room, I'd changed the stones back into their cloth bags from the plastic zip-loc ones, when it became obvious that nobody cared about a bunch of dull, coloured rocks.

Miriam removed the tea things to make room, fetched a rolled-up length of black velvet cloth to lay across the table, then joined her grandfather in staring at the bags. Finally, Mr Jacobs let out a pent-up breath.

'Oh, Mr Stevens; surely you can't have done it again? We haven't even disposed of the magnificent pieces from your last round of escapades...now we have more, if I'm not mistaken. Let us see, let us see!'

His fingers were having trouble untying the drawstrings until

Miriam gently nudged him aside to complete the job. They emptied each bag, lined up the stones, then made a relatively quick visual inspection of each, as well as weighing and measuring them for carat size. Miriam kept them in order and made copious notes, while I settled back in my comfortable chair to enjoy watching them work. I also enjoyed watching Miriam who had always been very easy on the eye and had a superior intelligence which made her even more appealing. I idly wondered if she had a boyfriend.

Finally, they were finished with the diamonds and Mr Jacobs looked both exhausted and exhilarated by the experience. He looked at me, shaking his head with a tired smile and said, 'Once more, Mr Stevens; you've done it again. To see one pure, white diamond of very large size and excellent shape which might cut with minimal wastage, is rare and exciting. But to see 29 of them in one place is beyond imagination!'

He paused, seeming to collect his thoughts, before continuing.

'We have a peculiar situation, whereby if these stones were to be placed on the market all together, they would lose a considerable value. Therefore, I would suggest that, if you are not in a hurry for the funds, they be released slowly.

Just one stone of this size, properly cut, could fetch $6 to 8 million, so to maximise the yield, we should release them perhaps in pairs, with 3 to 4 months between.'

As usual, Mr Jacobs' numbers had my mind spinning. 'You've raised a point I've been discussing with my colleagues. Should we have these stones cut to increase their value, or try to move them uncut?'

He and Miriam exchanged glances, studied the stones arrayed before them in their dull, frosty-white forms, then Miriam spoke.

'I think I can safely speak for my Grandfather when I say the value of any of these stones will be greatly increased by good cutting. So much so, that the cost of cutting would be relatively insignificant. It would appear each stone has been carefully selected to be an outstanding example of shape and size. Which means that when cut, there would be minimal loss of material to produce a finished stone and the end result would be quite stunning, due to the lack of inclusions and the fact they are colourless.

However, the cost of cutting all these stones will be considerable. Are you prepared to handle that?'

I thought quickly, 'Are we talking tens of thousands, hundreds of thousands or more?'

'Oh, nothing like that!' exclaimed Miriam. 'But a good cutter will charge roughly $400 to $500 per carat, and for a big, complex stone, maybe more.'

Mr Jacobs had recovered his composure, picked up a pear-shaped lump of opaque rock the size of a chook's egg and carried on. 'If you were to allow up to $600 per carat, that would easily cover it, so this particular stone, which is just over 50 carats, would cost you perhaps $40,000 to cut.'

He noted my raised eyebrows with a smile.

'Yes, it does sound a lot, but bear in mind that the resulting cut stone, plus some smaller ones cut from the trimmings, would bring some three to five million as a minimum! If you take my suggestion and only release two at a time, I'd further suggest we choose two which will cut the same. As a matched pair, they should be worth even more per carat!'

He smiled again as my eyebrows tried to shake hands with my hairline.

'And there are 28 of those clear diamonds! I can see why we should drip-feed the market. That's a lot of money!'

His smile was a near-constant feature as he contemplated the rows in front of him. 'Yes, it truly is. A matched pair of, let's say 35-carat pure, white diamonds, could easily bring 8 or 9 million dollars at auction.'

I couldn't think of a suitable reply and I was glad I'd shown him the most valuable stones first.

'Once again, I'm glad you still are able to be surprised by things in my world, Mr Stevens. I can only speculate about how you came to possess these stones, and perhaps I shouldn't know, but it is your world and you seem to know it very well. As I know mine, I might add.'

I thought briefly about what he'd said, before replying, 'After what you have done for my colleagues and me, I feel I do owe you an explanation as to how I came to be in possession of them, but perhaps that should be held over for a later time. Here and now, I have more stones for you to evaluate, but firstly a question. If you think the stones are best sold in cut state, then where and who would do this work? I obviously wouldn't know where to even start looking, and don't know who's good or not. Also, do we have to look in Europe for a good cutter?'

'Ah. Now that is a very good point and is where we are most fortunate. A very dear friend, Teresa Rubens, who I worked with for many years in Tel Aviv and some other places, followed me to Australia only two years ago. She was the premier cutter with the largest diamond firm in Tel Aviv and was in constant demand to handle the largest and most difficult stones. The relentless pressure wore her down and she left the trade, but since coming here, she has set up a small workshop and I send a few stones to her. She doesn't want to become mainstream again; just wants to keep her hand in. It is my humble recommendation that you consider using her for this work.

As there is no great hurry, she can set her own pace.'

I shrugged, 'I have no idea, so I'll be guided, once again, by your opinion. If she will take on the job, that's great. Where is her workshop, by the way?'

'Oh...Right here in Southport! Sorry, I forgot to mention that bit. You should meet with her; she's a very interesting person.'

'I would very much like to meet the person who's cutting my stones,' I replied with a grin.

'Good, good. I'll set it....' He stopped in mid-sentence, thought a moment more then went to the phone, where he called, spoke quietly for a few moments, then returned.

'We're in luck. I just called Teresa and she is free this morning. I managed to stir her interest sufficiently, that she is on her way as we speak. She'll be here directly.

Now, I take it you had some more stones to show me. I should have known you would have more, you bad boy!' The last was said with a smile and a distinct note of affection.

'Yes, I do have a lot more,' I said, amused to see their eyebrows lifting, 'but as they are all uncut, perhaps it would be best if we wait for Miss Rubens to arrive.'

'Ah...yes! All uncut! Yes, you are right. We shall try to control our curiosity and impatience.'

The pair of them didn't take to patiently waiting at all and kept fidgeting and fiddling with one white diamond after another. I was amused to see that when they'd finished, the stones were lined up in four rows in strict size order, largest at the back, smallest to the front.

To tantalise them further, I took my time about removing all the other bags in my carry-on bag and lining them up, the ones with red cords in front, then the green corded ones, then the three blue, one of which had an orange cord as well as the blue one.

Another round of tea was served and we'd just finished when there was a soft knock at the door and the shop assistant stepped aside to allow a woman who was attractive, very short and most surprising, probably younger than me, to step inside.

'Mr Stevens, please meet Teresa Rubens. Teresa, Mr Stevens is the owner of a most remarkable collection of uncut stones of undisclosed origin. We have taken a quick look at the white diamonds, but he appears to have many more to show us, which is the reason why I thought you should take a look now.'

Finally Teresa had the chance to speak, and with an affectionate glance at Mr Jacobs, she held out her slim, tanned hand and shook mine with a firm grip, saying in a strong, husky voice, 'It is my pleasure, Mr Stevens to look at what you have brought. I have heard about your previous offerings and if these are anything like them, then they will indeed be special.'

'Thank you for coming at such short notice, Miss Rubens. I thought I would have to communicate with an expert cutter on the other side of the world, not one here in town and in person! Your opinion will be invaluable, although Mr Jacobs and Miriam have done their usual wonderful job of explaining the situation with cut or uncut gems.'

She smiled at my politeness, then true to her calling, directed her attention to the arrayed ranks of frosty rocks on the coffee table. 'So...this is what has dragged me away from my marvellous new adventure novel this morning. The sizes...Incredible!' She also couldn't miss the line-up of white velvet bags on my side of the table and her eyes widened in awe.

Turning to Mr Jacobs, she said, 'Hiram. Thank you for calling me. Now let's see what we have.'

She carried a small, but apparently heavy aluminium suitcase with the obligatory extending handle, large wheels and a badge on the lid stating that it was made by 'Kruss'.

After Miriam had brought out a small table to sit it on, Teresa opened it to reveal what proved to be a small, mobile gem-testing kit. At least I recognised a very flash stereo microscope when she set it and several other un-identifiable items out on the table.

Twenty minutes of peering, prodding and testing later, she sat back and regarded me with what I took to be an excited gleam in her eyes. 'May I ask how these stones came into your possession, Mr Stevens?'

I hedged for a moment, 'Please, call me Harry. Mr Jacobs has asked the same question and as yet, I haven't given an answer due to a number of other factors involved.'

She gave a tight smile that didn't quite reach her glittering green eyes, 'Very well Harry, and please, call me Teresa. My question of origin is due to the fact that uncut stones have no identity worth talking about, but on occasion, they do have some characteristics which can suggest their origin.'

I cut in before she said too much, 'Are you saying that you can say exactly where those stones came from?'

'Not that exactly, I'm afraid. But I can often place them from a particular region with some certainty.'

'Can you identify the mine of origin?' I asked, fingers crossed under the table.

She smiled a much warmer smile, 'No way. I could guess, but could be totally wrong, so I won't even try.'

Much relieved, I sat back, until she said, 'However, by the huge size and quality of all the pieces, I would hazard a guess that they have been stolen to order from various mines. However, if that is the case, establishing ownership would be quite impossible as the mines didn't know they had them in the first place, so there are no records. It also means that when they are offered for sale, there cannot be any certificates or provenance, apart from what Hiram and myself are able to state from visual identification. This may or may not affect the value of the stones, although personally, I don't believe it will have any serious impact on pieces such as these.'

She grinned mischievously, 'May I take it that my educated guess as to their origin is correct, and perhaps I have eased your mind as to the legality of owning them?'

I inclined my head, 'Thank you for that, Teresa, and indeed you are correct. However, due to matters which are still proceeding, I cannot confirm or deny anything more about them. Please forgive me for not being more forthcoming with that information, but I hope to be able to tell all three of you the whole story soon, but not today I'm afraid.'

'Then we'll accept your statement and I'll personally hold you to it, as will Miriam and Hiram.'

I thought I should toss in the big question, and asked, 'May I take it that you would be willing to cut these and the other stones?'

Another enigmatic smile. 'Not so fast, Harry. I need to look at these more carefully before I reach a decision. My hesitation comes from not knowing if they will cut properly. It appears most unlikely, but if many are flawed, then I'd probably say no, it's not worth it as there's no return for either of us. And I need to see what you have hiding in those other bags.'

By way of answer, I leant forward and emptied the contents of the five bags of rubies onto the cloth. All three were momentarily riveted by the sight, then Teresa's professionalism took over as she worked her way through a quick examination of each stone.

Her summation was short and sweet, 'Truly stunning! The best of the best, one could say. As with the diamonds, they will cut beautifully with minimal wastage, as the basic shape is already there.'

Miriam moved the rubies onto a tray and set them aside with the trays of diamonds, creating room for me to extract the emeralds from their five bags. Finally, her summation was the same, 'Prime examples of classically perfect stones. I don't try to suggest value; that's Hiram's job, but if I were to guess, then I'd say these could set new records!'

Miriam efficiently cleared the collection again, then I emptied out the last three bags of sapphires. With Mr Jacobs and Miriam looking closely over her shoulder, Teresa quickly separated the roughly hexagonal ones from the salmon-coloured ones.

In silence, she carefully made her inspections, before finally looking up to deliver her assessment.

'The hexagonal shapes should be star sapphires, although I won't know until they are given an initial polish. The cutting process is very complicated and therefore costly and the stones aren't very valuable, although these are large. If I can preserve most of each, then they may bring enough to make it well worthwhile.

The salmon-coloured ones are rather different. They are called Padparadscha sapphires and are rare enough to up the price sufficiently to get excited about. The size of these, as well as the clarity and colour depth, will make them quite valuable. Well worth cutting.

The hexagonal pinkish/amber big, flat stone is a real anomaly. I believe and I think Hiram agrees, that it is a very rare example of a stone which isn't supposed to exist. It could be a Padparadscha

Star sapphire, and as it appears to be well-coloured, large in size, and with a good rough shape, could fetch a very high price, if only because if its extreme rarity. Cutting and polishing this, while trying to preserve as much mass as possible, will be a real challenge.'

Miriam moved in again with a tray, loaded them up and cleared the table. Teresa started to say, 'Well, Harry. I must say that is an incredible collection of....', when I stood up and the thigh pocket of my cargo pants made a 'clunk' against the side of the table.

'Oh bugger!' I exclaimed. 'I clean forgot about these ones that came in late. The red stones may be good, but the yellows aren't much chop I'm afraid.'

'No matter,' Teresa said, sitting back down, 'dig them out while I'm still here. Might as well see everything.'

So, I did and partly unrolled the newspaper-wrapped bundle, finding the three big rubies at that end. Teresa didn't spend much time on them, and said, 'Near perfect quality, same as the others, just bigger. No trouble selling them, but as Hiram would have said, you'll have to move them in small lots.'

I nodded, 'Yep. I understand and it won't be a problem. We can afford to wait, especially after the pirate treasure and the other gems sells.'

'Good. That's a big help if there's no pressure to move them prematurely. Now is that finally all?'

'Not quite; just these orange hunks of quartz or whatever-they-are's. You better have a look anyway.'

I had trouble with the wrapping, and ended up ripping it off. The remaining four stones, about the size of walnuts, were finally revealed. I had forgotten how deep and intense was the orange colour. Almost apologetically, I handed them to Teresa, who nearly snatched them from my hand and placed them under the microscope. She then used her other instruments on each of them, before sitting back, a twisted grin on her face.

'What did you think these were?'

I shrugged, 'I didn't really know. Just orange quartz, I guess. I mean, I've never heard of an orange stone of any description before, so I thought they were just pretty rubbish.'

She smiled at me, her eyes dancing with excitement. 'These, my dear man, are natural, un-treated, orange diamonds and in this size, shape and colour are utterly unheard of. There has been only one example that was over 4 carats, and that's 'The Orange' at 14.82 carats, a magnificent stone that went at auction for $35.5 million, or $2.4 million per carat. These appear to be near flawless, and if so, are as rare and valuable as red diamonds! I believe you have had some experience with those?'

To say I was blown away was an understatement! It's one thing to think that something is valuable and have the thought confirmed, but to think something is junk and find out they are near priceless, is a shock to the system.

'You look a bit shocked, Harry,' Teresa grinned.

'Yeah! I am, and I don't mind admitting it. I truly thought they were just pretty quartz.'

'Well, I guess that's why you are here,' Teresa said lightly.

I drew a breath, calmed a moment then asked, 'Rightie-oh. Where do we go from here? Teresa, are you prepared to cut however many stones Mr Jacobs deems worthy, and depending on your own assessment, of course?'

'On that basis, yes, I'm willing to do that. But understand that some may be rejected as either too risky, or too flawed. Bear in mind, however, that rejects can often be broken up and cut into much smaller stones. The average engagement ring is only 1 to 1.5 carats and a lot of smaller stones can be cut from just one of these big stones, so even a reject wouldn't be a total loss. I can pass any like that onto other cutters I know will be happy to make something out of not much.'

At that point we shut down the meeting, after Miriam had photographed all the stones and drawn up an inventory.

Teresa was to take all the stones to her workshop for a better evaluation, following which, she, Miriam and Mr Jacobs would confer as to the timing of a staggered release program.

Miriam wrote out a receipt for all the stones, a painstaking operation that took 30 minutes.

I signed the papers for the auction of the pirate's treasure and the gems from Terry and Paula.

Therefore, by early afternoon, I was in my little hire car, heading up the M1 motorway to Brisbane where I'd stay overnight, ready to fly to Sydney in the morning to catch the Wednesday flight back to LHI.

CHAPTER 23

SATURDAY, LORD HOWE ISLAND, SANDY

Since talking to her beloved Harry that morning, Sandy had been made even more aware of Darryl's instability by overhearing several vicious, but short arguments he had with Kelly. During dinner on Friday night, she had tested his mood by suggesting maybe it was time for her to go back home. He had reacted really strongly to her statement, and to her surprise said she was welcome to stay as long as she wanted.

'It's good for Kelly to have her rello's around her, instead of just me all the time.'

If the invitation was issued by a normal person, Sandy would have felt very welcome and settled, but it was quite the opposite when issued by Darryl.

There were raised voices in the bedroom that night after the meal, including the sound of a slap on bare flesh, but nothing more appeared to develop, so Sandy stayed out of it.

Saturday dawned overcast and raining, and although it was forecast to clear later that afternoon, Sandy thoroughly enjoyed the lie-in, listening to the patter of the raindrops on the galvanised steel roof. She also waited until Darryl had left for work, before she went to check on Kelly.

She found her still in bed, trying to ease the pain of a fresh crop of smacks and a couple of fresh belt weals across her bum. She asked Sandy to rub in some cream she had which contained a pain blocker, and after that was done, she said she felt better. Sandy was still just wearing a T-shirt as a nightie, and while Kelly was lying back waiting for the cream to work, she said to Sandy, an embarrassed look on her face,

'I don't know any other way to ask you this, but tonight, Darryl wants the three of us to go to bed together.'

Since Sandy was expecting it, she didn't need to pretend surprise and or disgust, but to make Kelly feel better, she said, 'OK. Darryl has hinted a couple of times he wants to do it, so I'm not surprised. Is that what last night's argument was about?'

Kelly nodded miserably. 'Yeah. Sorry about that and about having to ask you, but he made me promise to ask. In fact, it went beyond that and I had to insist you joined us in here after dinner. He might even want to do it earlier if he gets all his work done quickly.'

Sandy hugged a very distressed Kelly and tried to settle her down.

'Look it's Saturday, so I suppose he goes to the Golf Club after work for a few beers?'

Kelly just nodded agreement.

'OK. I've seen when he comes home with a skinful, he's usually in a mellow mood, so let's just get this over with. If he wants to go to bed straightaway, let's just do it.'

'Are you sure? I hate asking you something like this.'

Sandy nodded and made a weak joke, 'Don't beat yourself up, Darryl does enough of that! But seriously, it's not like we're being raped or anything. That is, I presume and hope he doesn't get off on stuff like that?'

'No, he hasn't so far. It's usually just straight sex.'

'So, does he really think he's going to look after two of us?'

Kelly grinned for the first time, grabbing Sandy's hand and squeezing it hard. 'That's his problem. I reckon he'll be a shot duck after just one!'

The both had a laugh over that mental picture, and Kelly got up to get breakfast for them. Sandy openly admired her long, lean body with the good tan which almost, but not quite, managed to disguise all the bruises, marks and scars from Darryl's version of being a loving husband. It was a peaceful morning with the rain steadily falling and Darryl occupied with business. They were delighted when Corrine dropped in mid-morning for a coffee and a chat.

'I just had Darryl around at my unit,' she announced, 'and he invited me to come around tonight for drinks and a bit of a party, so I thought I'd drop in to see what the go was.'

Kelly and Sandy looked at each other and started laughing. Sandy composed herself and explained their reaction.

Corrine grinned, 'The rotten shit! He really must fancy himself as Mr Super Stud if he thinks he can handle three of us! Or, does he plan on getting his rocks off by watching us play together?'

Kelly grinned, 'I truly don't know. He might just be thinking it, although he's never suggested anything like this before. But it still might be safer if you stayed away.'

Sandy agreed with Kelly, so Corrine accepted their advice and left soon after, with the advice that because Darryl had been very insistent she join them, he might be a bit upset by her non-appearance. As an afterthought, she passed over a jar of the Green Gold ointment for Kelly's injuries.

'Use it very sparingly,' she advised with a grin and a side glance at Sandy. 'There are side effects which Sandy will explain. I might drop in tomorrow if I don't get arrested and dragged here tonight by his Lordship.'

The afternoon dragged slowly, the rain easing and the sun breaking fitfully through the rolling mass of dark clouds. Kelly made a lovely roast lamb dinner for the evening meal and they also made an early start on the wine stocks, starting with a chilled Colombard Chardonnay that went down very easily.

By 17:00, both girls were in a very mellow state, the dinner cooked, but turned off since there was no sign of Mr Super Stud.

'OK. I'll go do something mundane and warm the roast back up. If Darryl's coming home at a reasonable time, it'll be soon. Otherwise it'll be when the Club closes and he'll be pissed!'

And that was the way it played out. The girls had their dinner in peace, made up a plate for Darryl in case he was interested, but when he still hadn't turned up by 22:00, they went to bed. Sandy read a book for a while, and had not long turned her light out when Darryl came home, sounding quite drunk and falling over everything. He ignored the kitchen where the light was left on and his dinner in the oven staying warm, and headed straight for the bedroom.

There was no attempt to close their door, so Sandy was treated to the full range of Darryl's verbal, then physical abuse of Kelly, although it didn't sound too bad.

Then came the words she was hoping she wouldn't hear.

'Where's that cousin of yours'? I told you I wanted you both in here tonight, so get your lazy arse out of bed and go get her! I'm in the mood to have some fun.'

'Why don't you just have me tonight, sweetie?' she heard Kelly ask plaintively. 'We can have a lot of fun.'

'All in good time. I want to see that Sandy in here, then I'll decide who's first. You probably don't think old Darryl can handle two women! I'll show you! Go on! Fetch!'

Moments after the last smack of a hand on bare flesh, Kelly, naked and shaking, limped into Sandy's room, whispering hoarsely, 'Sandy! Are you awake?'

'Yeah. I'm awake and I heard it all,' she answered wearily. 'I'm coming. Go back in and I'll be right behind you.'

'I'm so sorry I dragged you into this. I just should have kept my mouth shut!'

'That's enough of that. I chose to come here and I had a good idea what to expect, so stop with the what if's and get back in there now, before he gets more upset.'

With one loud sniff, she turned and went back to the bedroom, Sandy close behind, wearing just her sleeping T-shirt. The sight that greeted her almost brought on a fit of the giggles, but she managed to stifle that insane impulse.

Darryl was stretched out on the bed in all his naked glory,

sporting a fairly creditable erection and with a look-what-I've-got grin on his face. If he thought the sight was supposed to turn Sandy on, then he was sadly mistaken. Still, she felt obliged to go through with the farce for Kelly's sake and also to keep Darryl as calm as possible.

'Ah, there you are Sandy,' he slurred, 'I think it's time we got better acquainted. Why don't you join Kelly and me on the bed? And you should lose the T-shirt on the way; there aren't any secrets in here, are there Kell?'

Kelly sent Sandy to the other side of the bed, while she draped herself across Darryl in an effort to get him to have her first, but he wasn't going to be distracted now he saw Sandy naked for the first time, so with resignation, she submitted to his very clumsy and un-coordinated efforts. His breath would have stripped paint, so she turned her head to look at Kelly who was sitting on the side of the bed crying silently, several fresh red marks on her body.

Since she was expecting this and had prepared, it wasn't the ordeal it could have been, and she made sure his grunting movements came to a thankfully quick end. Typically, he rolled off her and was snoring almost before his head hit the pillow.

When she was certain he was staying asleep, she went and showered, before joining Kelly in the kitchen, having to forestall another round of 'I'm sorry' from Kelly.

'Look. That wasn't so bad. He didn't hit me, he didn't last long, and by taking the precaution of using some KY first, he didn't hurt! To tell the truth, his breath was the worst part. It was an experiment on my part, anyway. I wanted to see if he moved into the strangulation mode at some point, but in this case, he didn't.'

'That was a drastic experiment, wasn't it? I mean, what if he'd become violent?'

'Then I would have reacted a lot differently and I was hoping you would have assisted me by bashing him over the head with something hard!'

'Well I certainly would have!' Kelly assured her. 'But I was surprised he finished so quickly,' Kelly ventured, 'he normally lasts a long time.'

'Do you think that it's to do with him being pissed or feeling the pressure to attack a young woman again?'

Kelly thought a moment. 'Yes, that could be it. Even though being pissed hasn't made a difference in the past. So maybe he really is getting close to going off the deep end again?'

'That's what it looks like to me. But I'm a bit concerned he might have Corrine in his sights next.'

Kelly thought a moment, 'I guess if you think about it, that's more likely than trying to pick on a total stranger. Now he's met her, and clearly fancies her, she'd be the prime target, especially living on her own. But I thought his next melt-down would still be weeks away, but maybe it's much closer. He hasn't had another female in the house before, so it's hard to judge with his normal routine messed around.'

'Yes, you could be right. But we really don't know much more than before except that Darryl is quite a big boy, isn't very inventive and has very bad breath!'

The girls went to bed after that, and the rest of the night passed peacefully.

SUNDAY

Peacefully, that is, until Darryl woke around 09:00 and interrupted Sandy's lie-in, by insisting on having a return bout in bed, claiming to have been deprived of the good time he'd promised himself.

Once again, for the sake of keeping the peace, Sandy submitted without saying a word and while his breath was worse than the previous night, his performance was considerably improved with the lowering of his blood-alcohol level. While the experience was well short of being enjoyable, at least it could be said it wasn't unpleasant.

He also lasted a lot longer. When he'd finished, he got off her, and without bothering to wipe himself, headed for the door with the parting words, 'You're a cold bitch, aren't you? One day soon missy, I just might crack that reserve. Anyway, I'll be back.'

Sandy was watching him and once again, caught the brief flash of what she took to be madness in his eyes. She held her tongue, not being ready to take the arsehole down just yet, but she promised herself a decent slice of retribution when she did.

Soon after, Darryl went to work, letting genuine peace settle temporarily over the unhappy house. Kelly wandered into the bathroom, while Sandy was doing another very thorough clean of herself.

'I tried to talk him out of it, but it's like trying to stop the tide!'

Stepping out of the shower cubicle, Sandy gave her a brief hug, 'That's alright. It's a nuisance more than anything at this stage, so I can easily put it aside. So long as he doesn't get violent. Which reminds me, we must check on Corrine and let her know what's been happening.' That thought resolved itself when the girl herself turned up while they were having breakfast, but before they had a chance to tell her about last night and this morning, she spoke.

'I just had dear Darryl banging on my door,' she announced, gratefully accepting a mug of steaming coffee from Kelly. 'He gave me a big serve for not being here last night, the cheeky bugger! So I told him I don't do threesome's or foursome's, and his reply was that he was quite happy with a twosome. This guy just doesn't quit!'

Sandy could see Corrine was quite upset and understood why. In a normal situation, the local law would be the one to go to for making a complaint against some swinging dick who wouldn't take 'No' for an answer. But when the copper is the guy doing the harassing, a feeling of helplessness settles in.

'That's unfortunate,' she said to Corrine, 'because we really aren't ready to move in on Darryl yet, since there's no hard evidence of serious wrongdoing.'

Corrine gave a short laugh, 'There was a heap of hard evidence in his pants just an hour ago! I'd say he was rather well hung by the look of it.'

Sandy looked at Kelly. 'He shouldn't still be hard! Not if he's gone straight there from here.'

Kelly had a sudden thought and cursed, 'Oh, shit! Hang on a tic!'

She left the room, then was back, a small packet of pills in her hands. 'The bastard! He's had these for a long time, but never used them before. Sildenafil! That's Viagra isn't it? There are three pills missing, so that's why he was confident he could handle two or even three of us. And that's why he had an erection when he was talking to Corrine.'

Corrine looked at the other two, 'So what happened here last night?'

Sandy told her, 'He smacked Kelly around a bit, then I got to take one for the mission. That wasn't a problem, but then he popped up this morning and wanted a second round so I copped him again. He was very pissed last night, which might have slowed him down, but not this morning. Sounds like it might be your turn next.'

Corrine got a look of disgust, 'Great! Just what I need. The randy copper from hell! Sorry Kelly, no offence intended.'

Kelly flapped her hands helplessly, 'None taken. I just wish I could deflect him a bit better from you two.'

Sandy smiled, 'Well sweetie, we're here to deflect him from you, until he slips up and we can nail him on a serious charge. So, I guess at least in my case, the plan is working.'

It was Corrine's turn to grin, 'Yeah, OK Girlfriend. I get the message. You've taken two hits, I've had none! But I feel the balance is about to be redressed if his Lordship's appearance this morning is any indication.'

'Anyway, tomorrow morning, before they leave, I'll go for a walk to see Harry and discuss all this rattle. There seems to be some bad weather heading our way as well. Dave mentioned the swell was up on Thursday night.'

Sandy nodded, 'Good. I might pop around early as well.'

Kelly looked pained, 'Are you sure there's nothing more I can do to help? I feel helpless with you two copping the hard stuff.'

Both Sandy and Corrine giggled, 'Good pun, Kell! I'm sure you meant to use it!'

CORRINE, TUESDAY

She started another quiet day the same as the previous few, with an hour of hard exercise which left her sweating heavily in the high humidity, but feeling much better mentally. A quick shower washed the sweat off and a light breakfast of fruit set her up for the day.

As part of her cover, her routine was to sit down with her laptop after breakfast for one hour of writing. It was a task she normally dreaded, but as she got into telling the story Harry had suggested, she began to like what she was doing and found the words flowing more easily.

She was totally immersed in the plot, when there was a knocking at the front door.

Saving her work, she found Senior Constable Fitzgibbon on the doorstep, cap in hand.

'Good morning Miss Johns, I thought it was high time I called on you again,' was his opening remark as he rudely pushed past her.

'Uh...umm...yeah! Terrific. Come on in, Officer. What can I do for you?'

He gave an evil grin, 'We'll get to that. But firstly, I'm a bit annoyed you rejected my invitation for Saturday night. Why was that?'

For a few moments, she regarded him rather like a shark sizing up a fat cod for a meal, but then dropped back into helpless female writer mode. Darryl blinked a few times, not sure of what he'd seen, but the look was gone, replaced by something far less predatory.

'Gee Darryl, I wasn't sure about going to a party. I'm really getting on with my book now I'm on the island and I wanted to keep going while the ideas were flowing. That's why I came here.'

'Yeah, well, you need to understand that when I issue an invitation, you need to respond without argument. Get that?'

'Well, sure. I hear you, but what if I don't want to?'

He shook his head, the evil grin back in place, 'Nope! Not an option! What I want, I get! Do you understand what I'm saying?'

Corrine let her shoulders slump, looking dejected. 'Yeah, I get it! All you guys are the same. You see a young, single girl and the first thing you want to do is get into their pants!'

Just then, the SatPhone rang, so Corrine grabbed at it like a lifeline, while Darryl waited impatiently, fumbling with his belt buckle.

'This is Corrine.'

'..... Oh, hi Mr Edwards, good to hear from you, but can I call you back. I have a guest.'

'.....Yes, I'm making some good progress, but I'll tell you more later if that's alright?'

'.....Thank you. Bye now.'

'Who was that?' Darryl asked. 'And how come you've got a satellite phone?'

'Just my editor. He insisted I stay in touch, so supplied me with this. He's been chasing me for the first part of my book, but it's not ready yet.'

'That doesn't matter now. Just get in the bedroom.'

With a resigned look on her face, Corrine walked ahead of him down the short hallway to the bedroom, slipping out of her top as she went, then letting her shorts drop to the floor, exciting Darryl even more when he saw that she wore nothing underneath.

Ten minutes later, a red-faced Darryl stormed out the front door, still tucking his shirt in. Corrine trailed behind, unconcernedly naked and trying, with limited success, to suppress a fit of the giggles.

'I'll be back, missy!' he barked over his shoulder. 'This isn't finished by a long shot. Just consider yourself lucky today. And next time I call, you be ready!'

He snatched up his bike from the front path and steered a wobbly course down the street.

Corrine was still standing in the open front door, watching his unsteady progress, when Jill Slade, the cheerful owner of the apartments, came around the corner. Without batting an eyelid at her naked guest, she said, 'Oh dear. Our stalwart Darryl is having another case of erectile disfunction again, is he dearie? Or was it the dreaded premature ejaculation this time? No, don't tell me; I can see now it was PE. Just some still left around your left hip. Yep, that's got it. Awfully sticky stuff it is; gets everywhere!

Now George and I wondered how long it would be before he came to see you, and I've just won the bet! That's $50 he owes me. Now, are you alright? Apart from needing to wipe just a bit more off from under your lovely little left boobie?'

'Yes, I'm fine thanks Mrs Slade. He hardly touched me.'

'Well, with a lovely body like yours, it's no wonder he had a case of PE, but it always makes him terribly angry. We pity that delightful wife of his, Kelly. She really is such a lovely girl, and he treats her terribly! So, if you're alright, I'll go and tell George he owes me $50! Bye dearie and do be careful around Darryl. He's very unstable, you know!'

Corrine started to say, 'Yes, I do know now!' but Mrs Slade was already marching across the lawn toward their owner's unit, yelling out, 'George! George! It was PE, not ED, you silly old fart. That's what you've got and now you owe me $50 as well. And don't think you're paying it off in kind either; you kinky bugger!'

Still laughing, Corrine closed the door, checked herself all over for more streaks or splatters, before calling Harry back.

'.........Yeah, It's me. I got lucky. One glance at my ravishing body and our boy had a severe case of premature ejaculation!'

'.........No, I'm fine, but that was luck, not good management, since he left here in a screaming temper. If you can warn Kelly and Sandy, he might head their way later on when he recovers, to try to fix the problem. If he does, he won't be gentle about it!'

'………. Funny you should say that, because Mrs Slade probably heard it all and saw him go, so she's a reliable witness and told me it's a regular occurrence anytime a single girl is staying here. She also mentioned he lets his fearsome temper loose way too often.'

'………No! He didn't get anywhere near close enough to try grabbing at my neck, thank goodness, or I'd have had to take him down!'

'………No Boss. I truly am OK. He literally didn't touch me, unless you want to count being sprayed from neck to knees. Mrs Slade thought it was funny.'

'………Yeah, that's no problem. I'll drop around tomorrow afternoon as soon as you're back.'

'………Anyway, I'm going to clean-up and get dressed. You warn Kelly and Sandy. This might be the trigger that sets him off, what do you think?'

'………Yeah! That's right. Travel safely. Bye now.'

WEDNESDAY, LORD HOWE ISLAND

After a busy and tiring day of airports and aeroplanes, I was clear of the LHI terminal by 15:00. Darryl was there to check new arrivals and vaguely recognised me with a little wave. Officially listed as being attached to a visiting yacht, I didn't count towards the maximum limit of 400 visitors staying on the island at any given time.

I bummed a lift with a small group of visitors going to one of the resorts, and was grateful to be let off at the end of my street as a steady drizzle was setting in and the wind was picking up.

Dave and Dell were happy to see me and demanded to know all about the valuations. In turn, I demanded a mug of tea in my hand before I said a thing about gem stones, although I did ask Dave about the weather.

'Yeah, there's a bit of a blow heading our way. The Met boys are calling it an 'ex-tropical low' which as we both know means it's a cyclone that's formed where it isn't supposed to be! Anyway, the mooring is very secure as you've seen; no other boats near us, and Alex and I have hooked us to the mooring with chain and doubled up the nylon rope snubber. Upper decks are clear of loose items and lashings doubled on everything else.'

'Lovely work, thanks mate,' I replied to his report, gratefully accepting a steaming mug of tea from Dell. But before I had a chance to fill them in on the details of my quick trip, the back door opened to admit a slightly damp Sandy, looking as beautiful as ever! Hot on her heels was Corrine, so I was able to bring everyone, except for Bree and Alex, up to date in one telling. After settling them down with tea and coffee, I told the tale of the showing of the stones and meeting Teresa Rubens, the feisty little cutter who provided much of the suggested values of the stones. All four were surprised at the extreme reaction by Teresa, Miriam and Mr Jacobs to the orange diamonds, and absolutely blown away at the possible value.

'Unfortunately, kiddies,' I said in my best patronising tone, 'it would appear we really have cracked the best of the best. The orange diamonds would be the real stars of the show, if they cut well and are near flawless like Teresa thinks and hopes. Mr Jacobs suggests that while we should be selling the cut stones either individually or in pairs, but well-spaced out in time, the oranges could be presented as four matched stones with the same cut. Based on that, the $2+ million per carat or $140+ million for the four, could go a lot higher. And that's just the four oranges!'

'The sapphires, while not terribly valuable in their own right, will still attract a high price because twelve of them are Star sapphires, and the others are this weird name, Padparadscha sapphires, which refers to their unusual salmon-pink colour. There is one large sapphire which is a Star and Padparadscha-coloured, which apparently is not supposed to exist. Therefore, it could pull a high price just because it's unique.'

'What about the diamonds, rubies and emeralds?' Sandy wanted to know, her eyes shining with excitement.

'Ah...yes. Those. Well, as we guessed, they appear to have been stolen to order as the diamonds appear to be D-flawless or very close to it, which means no colour and no inclusions. Depending on how they cut, if they are around the 20 to 25 carat mark each or better, then each pair should fetch from 5 to 8 million at auction. Each stone would cost between $600 to $800 per carat to cut.'

'The emeralds also appear to be the best of the best with very big size, the best pure-green colour, with deepish colour tone and a vivid saturation, or so Teresa says. Could bring $50 to $70K per carat easily which would translate to $1.5 to 2 mil each.

Most of the rubies are large, well-shaped for cutting, and some are rated as the very rare Top-Colour. As such, they could bring up to US $1,000,000 per carat, although most are classed as very good colour or better. As small stones, they would fetch $18 to $20K per carat, but in this size, about 20 carats, Teresa or Mr Jacobs wouldn't guess. My thoughts, formed from listening to them, is that they'll go for $100K or more per carat because they are so clear and free from all but microscopic inclusions.'

I paused to drink some tea while the others chattered excitedly.

'Just remember, apart from the oranges and the Star Padparadscha, all the others will have to be drip-fed into the market, one and two at a time.'

'Meaning?' Dell asked.

'Meaning the proceeds will come in over perhaps a couple of years, although there will be a nice little return from the first sales, plus the impending auction which should re-fill the coffers. It's been a bit concerning, since after paying the new boat deposit, I reckon I'm down to my last ten million or so.'

There were hearty 'yuk, yuk's' all round at my sparkling wit, although I could see Dell trying to add up stratospheric numbers in her head.

'Don't try, dear girl,' I said kindly, 'we'll only know what the trade thinks the stuff is worth when the hammer falls at auction. Everything else is pure pie-in-the-sky speculation.'

She grinned ruefully, 'Was I that transparent? I was just wondering if I'm going to come out of this OK, financially, I mean.'

I nodded, 'I think I can safely say that you won't be hurting. As for the official stuff, I can't say, except that Sandy and I will be putting in good reports about your excellent co-operation.'

She teared up immediately and it was several minutes before she was composed again.

'OK. Now how are things going with Darryl? I saw him briefly at the airport, but we didn't speak.'

'He's started flexing his muscles,' Sandy said, 'by wanting a threesome, with Kelly and me, then tried to include Corrine as a foursome. I ended up with him last night and again this morning, but he was quite well behaved, with no tendency to get violent.

Despite that, Kelly still feels he's moving close to a break-out, where the impulse to strangle a young girl becomes overwhelming. We're concerned he's starting to pay a lot of attention to Corrine. He mentions her name more often each day.'

Corrine nodded, 'I agree. He ordered me to bed yesterday morning, but I must have looked too young and appealing and he became over-excited. He shot his load all over me without even touching me. I guess I fit his ideal rape-strangulation profile of a very young, helpless girl. If he tries to strangle me, I'll have to take him down.'

I wasn't happy with this escalation of Darryl's interest in Mouse. 'Hmmm…The situation does sound like he's working up toward something. I don't want any of you getting hurt, but I suppose there's no other way, for the moment.'

Sandy shook her head, 'No dear man, there's not. If we fight back now, we can shut him down, but what do we charge him with? Terminating him would be the final solution, although the NSW Police investigation may well turn over some nasty facts. Also, at this stage it might be a bit extreme for just demanding sex, although anyone with breath as bad as his deserves a fitting punishment!'

That we were able to laugh at stuff like this, was encouraging.

'OK, this was always yours and Corrine's show, so how do you want to proceed?'

'Pretty much as we're going. One objective has been met; in that Kelly hasn't had a bad beating since I came to stay. Minor slapping around stuff, but compared to what he used to do before, this is nothing. I'm relying on Kelly to warn me when she thinks he's about to really lose it and do his Jekyll and Hyde imitation. I just hope we can grab him before things go too far.'

'Risky game, my dear, and from a military point of view, not really much of a plan. Still, I appreciate your problems, although we obviously can't sacrifice Kelly or anyone else just to catch the bugger!'

'Of course, we can't do that! But as I see things, there are only two options. If we're going to get him brought up on official charges, we need to have rock-solid evidence. The only way to get that would be to interrupt him in the process of raping and strangling someone. How do we get that? I'm stuffed if I know!'

I considered her words. 'You're right, and that option really is being caught between a rock and a hard place. That leaves just one other choice...a pre-emptive strike to take him down terminally! The body would have to disappear of course.'

It was Dell who expressed what everyone felt about that plan.

'But that's premeditated murder! You can't do that!'

I nodded soberly, 'That's right. Unless....'

'Unless what?..... Oh! You mean go way back to Plan A and use Corrine as bait? That was the plan when you both decided to come here in advance.'

Sandy looked thoughtful. 'I suppose now Darryl's showing a lot of interest in Corrine, it wouldn't be too hard to set him up so she could do a permanent number on him.'

'That's the idea, but you two need to work out a plan as soon as you can. I'll add my ten cents worth when you're ready, so you do what's necessary, but please be careful.'

She smiled as she and Corrine stood to leave, 'Yes Dad, we'll look after ourselves.' They hugged and kissed everyone, then slipped out the back door.

Dave decided to go as well and called *Firebird* on the SatPhone for Alex to come and pick him up at the jetty in 15 minutes. His small bag was packed, so with a cheery wave, he left Dell and me to carry on pretending to be Xavier's island collection crew.

Naturally, that meant sitting around twiddling our thumbs as we actually had no work of any description to do. Papers had been gone through exhaustively and handed over to my mob, the house had been searched very thoroughly, the Foley brothers pickup had been paid for and there was no reason for them to come around to the house.

So, we went for a walk, with the idea it would help with overall fitness and fill in time. As nice as the island was, there was a limited range of activities if we were to stay for a month or two, so I was hoping we could soon get out of Paradise and back to playing boats again, without planning to avoid the bad guys every day.

Of course, that little plan depended on whether the papers I'd handed over in Sydney had been read carefully and acted upon or not.

With nothing left to do concerning the wrapping up of Xavier's smuggling scheme, it was natural that Dell and I would pool our thoughts about fixing the other main problem, that of Darryl and his murderous impulses.

THURSDAY

Domestically, Dell and I shared the master bedroom and each other, as well as the basic chores around the house, although I didn't bother with maintenance since we weren't going to be there that long. On our walks, it was inevitable we would come across Darryl in his official role sooner or later, and on just our first walk, as we arrived at Ned's Beach, he turned up quietly on two wheels.

'Mr Stevens, I believe,' he said cheerfully, 'off the large catamaran moored in the lagoon. I hope the mooring is proving satisfactory?'

'Indeed, it is Senior Constable, and we appreciate being close to the jetty. This is Miss Petrie, one of the crew whom you didn't get to meet the other day.'

Dell smiled at him and shook hands politely.

'Very good to meet you, Miss Petrie, as I believe you are one of the lovely ladies to appear in the underwater videos Mr Stevens is making for the Island Management Board. I'm looking forward to seeing the outcome of your efforts.'

He turned to me and with a smile asked, 'I suppose the weather hasn't been very kind to you for underwater video work so far? Have you had any chance to go diving yet, Mr Stevens?'

I nodded, trying hard to look enthusiastic. 'Actually, we did make a start, but just in shallow water on the lagoon fringing reef. There was a short break in the weather one afternoon last week, and I took the chance to get some video. Despite the rush, it turned out rather well, so we're hoping for even better results with late morning sun. I must say, the fish life is amazing. I think your Management Board will be impressed. We certainly were.'

His smile was almost convincing, but there were still the flashes of crazy in his eyes.

'I'm very glad to hear that.' He gave Dell a long, searching look.

'I hope you feature prominently in these videos, Miss Petrie. You would be very attractive underwater.'

Dell smiled seductively. 'Thank you Senior Constable. I did try to put on a good show, along with my good friend Bree. It seemed to work out really well, although we've not starred in a commercial video before.'

He dragged his pale blue eyes up from Dell's tight shorts and tiny top. 'You do look slightly familiar, Miss Petrie, or maybe it's your name? Have you visited the island before?'

Dell was smart enough to know that Darryl could have remembered her name from the hurried visit she made with Xavier just weeks earlier.

'Yes, I have, Officer. A couple of months back, I came here briefly with the owner of the house off Bowker Ave.'

'Ah...yes. A strange gentleman if I may say so without giving offence. I know he's not here this time, but will he be returning anytime soon?'

I picked up the ball from Dell and replied, 'No. We don't believe so. In fact, we're looking after his house for a few days while his usual staff take a break on the mainland.'

'Right...So you know Gerry and Steve?'

I smiled guilelessly, 'No, I didn't before Miss Petrie was asked to look after the house for a while, but Miss Petrie does, of course.'

Dell gave him a beaming smile, 'Of course. I've done some casual work for Mr Johnson, and because we were coming here anyway, he asked me to house-sit for a few days while his staff took some leave, so Mr Stevens joined me. It's a break from being on the boat all the time.'

'Yes, I guess it must be.' He looked at me directly with those creepy pale eyes, 'I hope your cats aren't getting too restless being confined to the boat all the time? I wouldn't want them swimming ashore to have a run on the beach.'

'Oh, no! They're used to being on the boat for extended periods.'

'Good. I wouldn't like to think about the size of the animal who made those huge pawprints on the beach a few nights ago. Or about what mischief it might get up to while having a romp ashore.'

I let that one slide through to the keeper and regarded him calmly. 'Well, we mustn't detain you any longer, Senior Constable. No doubt we'll be seeing a lot more of each other before we have to leave.'

He gave a mocking salute and an enigmatic smile, before pedalling off.

'What the fuck was that all about?' Dell demanded, worry and fright chasing across her face.

I grinned to settle her down, 'That was just a bit of muscle-flexing Sandy talked about. Darryl was telling us that he thinks we're bullshitting, but he's not sure what we're up to. We can expect him to be watching us like a hawk from now on, so we'll just keep on doing what we've been doing.'

'But that's going to restrict our movements, won't it? What about Dave coming ashore to see us?'

'That's expected. He knows we're off the boat, and to make a point, we should have Alex, Bree and Dave over for dinner tonight. Remember, he's one man and can't be watching us all the time.'

'Well, how about Sandy and Corrine coming over? How would we explain knowing them?'

I shrugged, 'Everybody on this very un-private island knows everybody else's business, so what if we were to just meet them on a walk, for instance. I should have told her yesterday, but I can call her now and let her know. We can maybe bump into them this afternoon.'

We were back at the house minutes later and I called Corrine on the SatPhone, but when she answered, she sounded somewhat strained.

'*This is Corrine.*'

'.........*Oh, hi Mr Edwards, good to hear from you, but can I call you back later. I have a guest.*'

'.........*Yes, I'm making some progress, but I'll tell you more later if that's alright?*'

'.........*Thank you. Bye now.*'

I disconnected, and looked at Dell. 'That's odd. We haven't used a code like that for a long time. I think Darryl is there again, although she didn't want immediate help; there's a different code word for that. We'll have to trust her ability to cope with trouble and check-up later.'

CHAPTER 25

I then tried Kelly's number, relieved when she answered.

'Hi Kelly, it's Harry. Is everything alright there?'

'Oh, hi Harry. Yes, everything's fine. Why, what's happening? Do you need to talk to Sandy?'

'No, you can tell her. Dell and I met Darryl on our walk a bit earlier, but I just had a message from Corrine that Darryl is around there now, wanting sex again. After that failed attempt the other day, he's going to be a lot more insistent this time.'

'Oh, bugger. Yes, he will be very...ah, forceful. I don't know if Sandy told you, but he's been taking Viagra as well, to make sure he doesn't blow his chance again, excuse the pun. He wasn't too bad last night, and we both only had him once, but was very excited this morning and didn't want either Sandy or me, something which has become almost regular, although it's mostly Sandy he wants.'

My heart sank to think of the slimy Darryl with my lady, but I had faith she'd take him down if he got too rough.

'Ok, Kelly. It sounds like you two are getting an easier time at the moment, but I don't like the way Darry's become so focused on Corrine.'

'We're worried too, although Sandy keeps reminding me that Corrine can and will look after herself.'

'That she can, but I'm still concerned.. Anyway, I'll be in touch. Take care.'

CORRINE, THURSDAY

Corrine spent a quiet morning doing some washing and getting into her writing. She was still enjoying acting out her cover story, and found making up characters to fit a story line was fun. That was until there was a knock at the door and to her dismay, the unwelcome form of Senior Constable Fitzgibbons, a manic leer twisting his normally pleasant face into something which sent shivers down her spine.

Despite her war experience where she had many close encounters with very bad persons, most of them were at least rational. Coping with a certifiably insane man who regularly erupted into killing rages, while trying to maintain her cover personality as long as possible, was something else again.

'Hello, Missy,' he grunted, pushing past her. 'I did say I'd be back.'

'What now, Officer?' she replied wearily. 'Didn't you have enough fun last time? Why can't you leave me alone?'

'Oh, that was just a warm-up, Girlie. I'm prepared now, so this'll be the real thing. I hope you don't have any plans for the next couple of hours, because you're about to find out what a real man is like.'

She made the mistake of sneering. 'What real man? Is there someone else outside?'

The blow from his huge right hand, in the form of an open-handed slap across the side of her head, took her by surprise. Dazed and disoriented, she fell to the floor, feebly clawing at the polished wood floor-boards to move away. Bending down, Darryl easily picked her slight body off the floor and flung her at the two-seater lounge, her head once again bouncing painfully off the back-rest. With his nose almost against hers, he hissed, 'Nobody slings off at me! Especially some little snot-rag of a girl who doesn't know her place! You thought you made a fool of me last time, but that won't be happening again. When I leave here, much later, you never forget your experience with Darryl Fitzgibbon!'

Corrine was still conscious, although her limbs were un-coordinated and her vision was fuzzy. She was dimly aware of her shift being ripped apart, and being half-dragged into the bedroom and tossed like a doll on the bed. Aware of what was coming, she relaxed as much as possible, not able to rely on any sort of premature ending to the unpleasantness. As her head cleared and strength returned to her limbs, she fought to conceal her recovery by not responding to his efforts at all. Keeping her eyes closed, she tried to ignore the gusts of foul breath washing over her, as Darryl proved that his earlier promise of longevity wasn't an idle boast. Feigning unconsciousness seemed the best idea, so she lay inert and finally it was over.

'Must have hit the silly little bitch too hard,' she heard him mumble as he rolled off her and started dressing. 'Better keep her awake next time. She'd be alright if she was moving a bit.'

Moments later, the front door crashed shut and she was able to drag herself off the bed to the shower.

I'd done all I could for now, so Dell and I had lunch. We had just finished and Dell was clearing away, when the SatPhone rang with my Controller on the other end. She seemed to derive vicarious pleasure from my assorted exploits and happenings, which led me to suspect she either was an ex-field operative, or had always wanted to be one.

'*Thanks for all the material, Harry. We've been going through it carefully and it's given us really good detail about the various personnel involved which means we should be able to wrap up the supply end fairly soon. At this stage, we would like you to stay there long enough to make one more pick-up. However, you need to know that it appears Xavier had a partner in the whole enterprise, and it's someone who's still active on the Island. We don't have a name yet, but he or she will* be very clever, and in a position where they can cover their tracks easily. It also means they may well be onto you, or at least very suspicious. You may need to pull your head in for a while if that's possible.'

'Thanks 'M'.' *She loves to be called that!* 'I'm glad the stuff is useful, but I'd rather like to have the name of the partner. I don't suppose it could be our serial rapist/murderer?'

'*We truly don't know, although that does seem unlikely. Unfortunately, no real pointers to the identity. Anyway, this was just in the nature of a 'heads-up'. Do watch your back, dear man. We don't want anything untoward to happen to you.*'

With that, she was gone, leaving me with a major puzzle. I ran the information past Dell, but she couldn't think of anything which could point towards anyone in particular apart from Darryl.

'Logically, it should be him,' she offered, 'but it could easily be anyone in a position of reasonable authority.'

For a change, I tried some 'what if' brainstorming with Dell, a useful trait I'd learned in the desert when we were trying to get a lead on a particularly troublesome band of Taliban.

'What if,' I began, fixing Dell in my sights to hold her attention, 'the partner is someone we would normally never suspect.'

Dell cranked her very fine, analytical brain into gear, 'But would it need to be someone who is associated in some way with this operation?'

I grinned to see she was playing the game. 'No, not necessarily to all outward appearances. They would have to appear innocent-looking, so they could move around without comment from anyone at odd hours.'

'OK', she said, 'turn it around a little. Who do we know who's associated with this operation, still on the Island and still breathing?'

'Ha...bingo! The Foley brothers are the only ones we know about. That means Will Foley is playing a very good part if he's the partner!'

'Right! So how do we prove it?' Dell asked.

'Damn! I was hoping you wouldn't ask that. I'm buggered if I know!'

'Yeah, we can hardly go ask him to tell us.'

'No. You're right, we can't.......hang on! Or can we?'

'What are you thinking?'

'Corrine and her first aid kit. She's coming around sometime later, or we'll meet her on our walk. But we need some information first.'

I dug out the SatPhone and dialled the last number called, pleased to hear the dulcet tones of my lovely handler.

'Yes, Harry?'

'Sorry to disturb you again so soon, 'M', but can you find out rather urgently where the Foley Brothers live in the island. Asking Gerry would be the quickest way, if she's accessible. I have a theory that Will Foley could be our silent partner and need to confirm or disprove the theory as soon as.'

'*No trouble, Harry. I can make her as accessible as we need. Would you care to hold the line? She's just down the corridor having another debriefing session.*'

'Is she being co-operative?'

'*Surprisingly so, as it happens. We're learning a lot and gradually the whole mess is un-ravelling. But let me send word; won't be a minute.*'

In fact it was less than a minute that she was back on the line.

'*Ned's Beach Road; fifth house on the right from the lagoon. There's an aluminium boat with a centre console and a fixed bimini over the steering position. Will that do?*'

'That's terrific 'M'. We'll find it. We just need to ask Will a few questions.'

'*I won't ask how you expect him to answer those questions, but good luck. I expect a full report of all these comings and goings in due course. Bye Harry.*'

The final ingredient in my latest cunning plan slipped in through the back door around 15:00, in the slim shape of Corrine. 'Hi guys. How're things going?'

'Cruisie, thanks. I called Kelly and all was well there as of a couple of hours ago. But what happened with you and Darryl?'

'Ah... I thought you'd pick up on that. He came fully prepared this time. Anyway, I copped a long session with him and I've sort of just got myself back into shape. He caught me a good whack to the side of my head which knocked me loopy for a while.'

'Aww, shit Mouse! Are you alright now?'

'Yeah, I think so. Still a bit sore, but a couple of aspirin and a long shower fixed most of it. Seeing that bastard breathe his last will fix the rest.'

'Hmmm. Apart from whacking you about the head, did he try the strangulation thing?'

She shook her head. 'Nope. Just finished his business, jumped up and left.'

'Ok. I'll wait to see if Sandy comes around, or you can pass your info on if you see her first. But is he likely to want a repeat session tonight?'

'I wouldn't have thought so, but maybe those pills really pump him up. However, Kelly said the fortnightly supply boat is in, so that would tie him up the rest of the day and well into the night.'

'Great! That's is a relief. My Controller called me earlier and advised the papers I handed over suggest that Xavier not only had a partner, but that person was and is still living on the island!'

'Wow! That's a surprise. Any idea who?'

'Suspicion only, but we think it could be Will Foley, as unlikely as it sounds. So the plan is to go ask him what's going on.'

She gave a feral grin, 'Ah.. that is indeed a cunning plan, and I presume you need me to use my lovely little first aid kit?'

'Yes please, Mouse. He needs to be compliant, no lies or evasions and to forget all about the interrogation afterwards.'

'Too easy, Boss. I've got just the right stuff, but how do I get to him to administer it.'

'I was thinking of a late-night visit; some knockout spray if necessary, then an injection of your wonder stuff. You should knock out Jack as well so he doesn't interfere, but I don't think he's involved.'

'Yeah, that could work. When do you want to do it?'

'Let's go tonight. This drizzly rain is probably part of the storm moving in and as the sea is already rough, they shouldn't be out fishing.'

'OK. I'll be back at 23:00, Darryl permitting!'

That was a good point and I wondered how potent those blue pills were.

'Just a thought, Mouse. It's a bit wet to be walking this afternoon or tomorrow, so why don't you visit the Co-op in 30 minutes and be prepared to meet some old friends? A meeting like that in front of others will be remarked on.'

'OK. No problem. See you there.'

Promptly at 16:30, Dell and I were wandering the aisles of the store, selecting a few items we didn't need, in the long-established manner of shoppers who don't make lists and stick to them. Dell was terrible like that, and several packets of porkie crackle and some potato chips were the first things added to the carry-bag. With a view to making a tasty feed for the evening meal, I managed to add a few salad items and two very nice-looking pieces of rib-eye fillet steak to the non-nutritional stuff, but not before three packs of Crown Mints joined the porkie crackle.

Corrine wandered in, poked around at a few things and like Dell and me, selected some things for the evening meal. Then she apparently caught sight of us and made a huge fuss about co-incidences. Several shoppers and the check-out lady watched with amusement as the three visitors carried on with stories of mutual friends and who'd done what to whom, and how often! As we checked out, we swapped addresses, something that's notoriously difficult to pin down on Lord Howe, since there are no house numbers, only street names.

Therefore, someone's house will be known as 'the third on the right, up from the corner, with the black, half-cabin boat on a trailer in the front yard'. I wrapped up the deal by inviting Corrine around for the evening meal, then went back and found another piece of steak from the display. As we left, I told her loudly to 'come around for drinks as soon as you're ready'.

For appearances, she did go home from the Co-op, then openly walked the short distance to our temporary residence. That was a good excuse to fire up the BBQ to do the steaks properly, and fortunately it was under the shelter of the back patio, since the rain was increasing and the wind rising. While the BBQ was heating, I called Dave on the SatPhone to get a weather check and a report on conditions on-board.

'That sub-tropical low is moving our way at the moment, but is expected to curve away to the north-east before it hits us. We're still under a strong wind warning, rising to Force 7, strong gale force by late tonight. Alex has double checked all lines and we're riding easily. Just noisy, as you well know, so we're alright. The worst of it will be over tomorrow after the system passes north of us, so there'll be a minor wind shift, but the lagoon gives really good wave protection; pity about the lack of wind protection! Pussies are settled down OK. We'll stay aboard for both comfort and security.'

'OK, thanks Dave. Just wanted to check on things. Corrine's having dinner with us since we've formally 'come across each other' in the Co-op. Now the whole town knows we know each other, but that's no hassle. There's not been any further action from Darryl, so he's probably still playing around with the supply boat.'

'Yeah. That'd be about right. They had trouble there earlier when some mooring lines broke in a squall and for a few minutes, it looked like it was heading ashore, but things got sorted out and they look secure again.

'Good oh. We're hoping to have a bit of a chat with the Foley boys tonight. There's some suspicion Will Foley is Xavier's partner in this business, so hopefully, we'll have more info in the morning.'

'That's interesting. I wouldn't have picked him, but I suppose that's

the idea of a sleeping partner. Anyway, go carefully and we'll talk in the morning. Cheers, Harry.'

By then, the BBQ was quite hot enough and Dell had already slapped the thick, juicy steaks on. She looked like she knew what she was doing with them, so I left her to it and cracked a beer from Steve's stock, kept in a separate bar fridge out on the patio. Corrine had whipped up a salad, so we set the table and sat out there, keeping Dell company while the delicious aromas of the cooking rib-eye's were swirled tantalisingly around us by the rising wind.

The steaks were excellent, the salad very tangy with an Italian dressing and the second beer cold. Looking around, I reflected that in other circumstances, a man could want for little more than two lovely companions, a terrific feed and a cold beer. Sometimes, the simple things are the best.

Finally, with pleasantly full stomachs, we considered that the rain, a solid cloud cover and the noise of the wind crashing and banging through the trees, added up to an excellent night for a bit of skulduggery!

CHAPTER 26

As usual when she had to work, Corrine refrained from alcohol, and I restricted myself to just the two light beers.

'What's the plan, Boss?' Corrine asked when we'd cleared the remnants of the meal away and were kicked back with teas and coffee.

'I thought we should visit at around 02:30, when they should be dipping into a deep sleep cycle. Later would be better, but as fishermen, they're used to getting up at odd hours, so hopefully this weather will keep them in bed tonight. If you can keep Jack asleep for an hour or two, that should be plenty of time to ask Will a few questions. But I'd really like it if he doesn't remember our visit clearly or at all, particularly if he is the silent partner.'

She grinned, 'No problem with that. It'll mean a bit of a cocktail of drugs, but the worst he'll feel will be tired and some vague memories of strange dreams.'

Dell asked, 'What's the go if he is the partner?'

'Excellent question, and the short answer is, it'll depend on the situation he can describe for us. He must have been trying to get in touch with Xavier and Head Office, but with Xavier gone and Miss Julie in custody, all he'll get from a phone call to Head Office will be a well-informed female ACP operative telling callers that the office is closed temporarily for water damage repairs. We need to find out what his role is as a sleeper; like, is there something else going on we haven't come across yet? Otherwise, why is he a sleeper in the first place? Then there must be something else happening! Nevertheless, hopefully we'll find out after he's suitably drugged.'

Dell posed another question, 'Should we try to get some sleep first, or stay up?'

Corrine and I exchanged grins. 'In the desert, we had a standing rule that you eat when you can and grab sleep when you can. Just in case you can't do it later.'

Corrine added, 'I've got my gear, Boss, so I'll grab some kip here in case Darryl decides to drop around for some light relief after playing with the supply boat all day.'

'OK. Good thinking. We want to head out by about 02:15; it's not far, and there are several sets of rain gear in the hall hanging locker.'

Without further ado, Corrine rose, collected a shopping bag that had been parked just inside the back door, and disappeared into the spare bedroom.

'She seems very competent,' Dell remarked.

I chuckled, 'In the desert she was far more competent than anyone else in the team and has some very scary abilities. It has also been suggested she has the condition ASPD or Anti-Social Personality Disorder although I dispute that.'

'And ASPD is?'

'Basically, a person with ASPD is supposed to show a lack of concern for the feelings of others. They are alternately called psychopaths or sociopaths, and can be skilled manipulators who flatter and lie their way into people's lives. As the name of the condition suggests, they have little to no regard for social norms, and are able to cause pain without experiencing remorse or guilt.

Based on that description, I think Mouse shows very few of those personality traits, apart from being able to kill people without hesitation if she believes they are a menace to her immediate family or friends. That definition includes her military unit members and people she works with, but it doesn't pay to really offend her! I've seen her really cut loose on people who have done the wrong thing by her and it wasn't pretty.

I mean, could a person who is supposed to not have any feelings for others, have a caring and loving relationship? Yet she does with Dave and has for years. Sometimes the psychiatrists need to take a step back and admit there is a lot they don't know about the human brain processes.'

Dell gave me a calculating look, took a breath and said, 'With respect, my dear man, from what I've seen, most of that description applies equally to you, and I don't have any problem with the way either you or Corrine behave. In fact, I feel incredibly well protected and in my situation, that's very comforting. So, thanks to both of you.'

I pondered her words, then nodded agreement. 'Anyway, time to get the head down and get some rest while we can.'

Dell pouted, 'Do we have to really have to sleep all the time until 02:00?'

'Yeah, That's the idea.'

'How about some relaxation first then? Ease the pre-mission tensions?'

I pretended to consider, 'Oh well, that's different.'

Promptly at 02:00, a disembodied voice spoke from the bedroom doorway, 'Awake, Boss? 02:00.'

'Awake, thanks Mouse,' I replied, sliding out from under what seemed like several of Dell's lovely limbs and heading for the ensuite after poking her in the ribs before I went. Her first response was a bit slow, so I did it a few more times until I was requested to stop in very un-ladylike language. I dressed in soft, dark blue tracksuit pants that don't rustle when you walk and had Dell do the same. A tight, dark-colour sweater on top completed the outfit.

Corrine on the other hand, preferred a mottled, dark-grey, skin-tight body suit that clung to every wrinkle and as usual, one look almost made me grab her and return to the bedroom. She claimed she had virtually unrestricted movement in it, and it was rustle-free. Also, on more than one occasion, a bad guy had spent a few vital seconds looking at her body, and failed to live to regret his lack of more positive action. On schedule, we pulled on the wet-weather gear and left via the back door, Corrine with her first-aid kit in a bum bag strapped around her waist.

The Foley's house was a typical Lord Howe, un-pretentious three-bedroom house, with the equally typical fishing boat on a trailer in the front yard. The same applied to the lack of security when Corrine went to make a quick recce, while Dell and I sheltered under a tree. The rain and wind, as forecast, had eased off a little but there was still plenty of noise to cover any we might make. Having shed the rain gear as soon as we arrived, she appeared at Dell's elbow, a dark shadow amidst darker shadows and it wasn't until she murmured the doors were unlocked, that Dell noticed her. Dell's reaction was almost comical, but I left her to steady her heartrate and start breathing again, and bent close to hear Corrine's Sitrep over the patter of raindrops on the leaves above us.

'Great security, Boss. All doors are unlocked and both targets sleeping. No other persons inside. As discussed, Jack has been immobilised for about an hour or two and Will has had his injection. He will be awake, aware and compliant very soon, so we can move inside out of this rain.' Entering via the kitchen door, I noted that the house was remarkably tidy and clean, with none of the expected smell, slop and mess generated by two male fishermen living together. I risked a quick sweep of a shaded torch which showed the kitchen spotless, floors dust-free and the lounge room clean and tidy. Corrine put her lips near my ear, a not-unpleasant position, and murmured, 'I noticed that too. The bedrooms are the same. Not quite in character, is it?'

'No, it's not. But lead on, Mouse.'

We went down a hallway and passed one open door where heavy breathing sounded from the occupant, to the next door where the heavyset, bearded man lay in his bed, eyes open, but un-focused. His breathing was easy and slow and he showed no alarm as three, dark, menacing figures entered the room, balaclavas covering their faces, but slowly turned his head to look at us. We took the risk of turning on a small, heavily shaded bed light.

Corrine briefly shone a small, pencil torch in his eyes to check pupil dilation, then said in a soft, but normal tone, 'OK Boss.'

I stepped forward, looked him in the eyes and asked, 'Are you William Foley?'

He blinked, then replied in a flat tone, 'Yes.'

'What do you do for a living?'

'Fisherman.'

'Is that your boat in the front yard?'

'Yes.'

I worked through several more innocuous questions and all were answered in the same way, so I cut to the interesting stuff.

'Do you pick-up a parcel dropped off a cargo ship north of the island once per month?'

'Yes.'

'How are you notified of the time and date of the pickup?'

'I get an email from the shipping agent in Mumbai, India.'

'Do you have records of his name, contact details and shipments!'

'Yes, in the filing cabinet in the front office.'

Bingo!

'Have you heard from your partner Xavier lately?'

'No. He always calls every two weeks and visits every two months.'

'Who came up with this scheme to smuggle stolen stones?'

'Jack and I did. He's the smart one with numbers and read about the trade in stolen uncut stones, but Xavier had the contacts, muscle and funding to kick it off.'

'How do you split the proceeds?'

'Xavier insisted on talking his share in uncut stones from each shipment, so there are always two parcels. However, there are extra stones in Xavier's parcel to cover our share, since Jack said we should stick with cash for our take. Every second month, Xavier arranges a funds transfer direct into our bank accounts in Singapore.'

'Where are your bank details and passwords?'

'Jack keeps everything in the filing cabinet. That stuff is under 'B'.

'Are the passwords there as well?'

'Yes.'

Corrine darted away, presumably to the front room office, while I asked one final, fateful question. 'Why are you still involved in the gem smuggling? Surely Xavier was more than capable of running it, and he had his two workers set up in a house here, so you weren't really necessary. Gerry and Steve could have done the pickup's.'

Will's lips twitched as though he had almost smiled. 'Xavier hates snakes...'

For a moment my mind went blank and I looked at Dell for inspiration, before the light of clarification went on. 'Oh crap! There's a second smuggling operation! Live reptiles out-bound!'

A few more questions revealed that as live snakes and unique Australian lizards were in such huge demand in Asia, Europe and to a lesser extent, the USA, the prices paid were astronomical. A breeding pair of lace monitors were worth around $113,000 in Asia. Worldwide, the trade was estimated as being worth $24 billion annually, which made it as good or better than the much higher risk of drug smuggling. Apparently, even bob-tailed lizards or shingle-back skinks could bring up to $10,000 each in Japan.

Contrary to the very cheap, nasty and cruel methods employed by other smugglers who didn't care if only 50% of their stock sur-vived the journey, the Foley/Xavier operation carefully cooled the reptiles down and placed them in heavily-insulated boxes where they entered a state of hibernation which didn't require them to take food or water for weeks. They were flown to the island, stored at the Foley's house in the garden shed which was insulated, airconditioned and solar-powered to avoid detection. There they were stored until the next cargo ship which dropped off the stolen stones, made the pick-up of the reptiles. With the co-operation of the helmsman on watch, they deployed a rake-type scoop over the side to retrieve the floating buoy that was attached to the floating box of hibernating live cargo.

As I sat back and digested this latest bombshell, Will Foley's eyes closed and he appeared to drift off to sleep, so Dell and I went to see how Corrine was getting on in the office.

She looked up from a pile of papers dug out of the open filing cabinet beside the desk.

'How's the talkative Mr Foley?' she asked.

'I ran out of questions after he told us about the reverse reptile-smuggling operation he and Jack are running. Jack is also a lot smarter than they let on. It seems that with typical Xavier efficiency, the usual piecemeal reptile-smuggling was re-organised so a network of collectors provided a steady supply of the most sought-after reptiles, and also filled special orders for particular ones. The network sent their catches to a central depot and dispatch facility in Sydney, where they were actually carefully and humanely packed, cooled down, then sent here.'

Corrine tapped the papers on the desk, 'That explains the references here to outgoing shipments identified with just a three-figure code. It made no sense before, but that's all dropped into place now you told me. Cunning buggers! It also might explain their bank account balances!'

My ears pricked up at the sound of loose money. 'What did you find?'

She grinned, 'How about the boys have around $10 million each in their investment accounts? And another $2.5 million each in working accounts!'

'Wow! They must be letting it build up. Will mentioned Xavier transferred money to them after each gem shipment, so that, plus the reptile smuggling has been very lucrative!'

'A damn sight more for Xavier though,' Corrine said. 'He would have to get a share of the reptile trade as well.'

'Bugger! I didn't think of that. We should wake him up and ask about that too.'

'Ahhh...not if he's drifted off to sleep, Boss. That means the drug is wearing off, so we'll have to finish up here quickly and leave them to it.'

'Can't you just give him another hit so we can ask some more questions?' I pleaded.

'No way! It really doesn't work like that. If we mess around with the procedure now, he's likely to wake up remembering everything. And we don't want that!'

'Hmm…No we don't,' I admitted. 'OK. Let's go, as soon as you've covered all traces of looking at their bank accounts.'

'Oh, I've already done that. I took the liberty of transferring $12.5 million into each of our bank accounts, which cleans them right out. We can split with the rest of the crew later. I also left some traces which suggest it was Xavier's secretary that did the deed, so that'll drive them nuts trying to track her down. You said your mob have her in safe custody?'

'Yep. She's well looked after and can't talk to anyone who cares. But that's a rather nice bit of loose change for a wet evening's work!'

Both girls grinned as Corrine closed out of the bank login and shut the computer down leaving it exactly as it was. All documents went back in the filing cabinet, but not before Corrine had photographed every page for me to send to my Control in the ACP.

I was still coming to grips with the ease that Corrine showed every time she found money in someone else's account and managed to pinch it without leaving a trace who did it! We double-checked each room to make sure that nothing was left out of place, noted that both brothers were snoring softly, wiped fingerprints off everything we might have touched and exited by the back door.

The rain was still tumbling down, although as forecast, the wind had eased somewhat, making the walk back to the house a little more pleasant. Picking up a share in $25 million might have had something to do with the warm, fuzzy feeling as we splashed through the puddles.

CHAPTER 27

Friday dawned overcast and drizzling, so after a quick pee, I returned to bed and managed to catch up a few more hours of sleep. It would have been more, except that we were rudely awakened again by a loud banging on the back door. Pulling on a pair of shorts, I blearily wandered out to see what the fuss was about, and was bailed up by a pair of spitting-angry Foley brothers.

They no longer made any pretence of being shy and quiet, pushing rudely into the kitchen, before rounding on me, demanding to know where Xavier was.

I played dumb and said, 'In Melbourne as far as I know. At least, that's where he was when he gave me this assignment. He's certainly not here, but why do you need him? What's wrong? You seem a little upset.'

'Upset! I'll bloody give him upset if I ever catch up with him again. Where's that woman you came with? Maybe she'll know.'

I shrugged, 'I doubt it, but if it'll make you happy, I'll go and ask her to come and speak to you. She's still in bed...we had a guest for dinner and it became a late night.'

The draining rack full of plates and cutlery supported that reason, as did some empty beer bottles by the rubbish bin.

'Humph!' Will grunted. 'Well, go on. Get her.'

'Bloody hell, you're a pushy bugger! Keep your panties on! She'll just tell you the same story, but I'll get her anyway.'

Dell was dozing when I went in, but quickly woke and pulled pants and a top on without delay. Back in the kitchen, she told them the same story I had, then suggested they keep trying to phone him. That seemed to infuriate Will even more, and Jack had a few rather un-complimentary words to say as well. With a last look around, as if we might have been hiding Xavier in the pantry, they abruptly left, muttering curses and banging the door behind them.

In the disturbed wake of their departure, Dell looked at me and grinned, 'Corrine did her job on the computer really well, I reckon.'

'Yeah. It must have been a shock to their system to find all their money had disappeared and what seemed like Xavier's, or at least his secretary's fingerprints all over it! Lots of luck to the Foley's for their attempts to find either of them.'

Dell looked thoughtful, which usually means that she was about to say something I should have already thought of. 'What are your plans for them? The Foley's, I mean. Are you going to notify Customs, Parks & Wildlife or whoever is concerned with reptiles?'

That was my cue to look thoughtful. 'I'm not sure, since my mob and Interpol have requested we keep the gemstone pipeline in operation for another month, so we can't really turn them in at this point, as much as I'd like to. But there is the start of a cunning plan in the back of my mind, which might have two good outcomes.'

She chortled with glee, 'Oh goody! I'm starting to really love your cunning plans! It usually means payback time for some dickhead!'

I shared her grin, 'Hopefully, you'll be right.' Then I proceeded to explain how I thought it should go down and Dell tried, but couldn't find any major flaws in the idea. Action depended on several other factors, so I grabbed the SatPhone and started dialling.

My ACP Control was delighted.

'*Oh, Harry. You are a naughty boy! But the Customs and the Wildlife section of the Dept of Environment and Energy will be delighted with the plan! It'll make them extra happy to hear we will underwrite some of the cost, although I'm thinking we might drag the RAAF in. That will keep the costs down for us and the Dept of E & E. Just let us know ASAP about the load size.*'

'Thanks 'M', I'll get back quick as I can.'

My next check was with Corrine, and I was relieved to hear she was alone and hadn't heard from Darryl yet, although midday was still an hour away.

'*So what's up, Boss?*'

I told her about the morning visit by two totally pissed off Foley brothers, looking for Xavier.

'*That's beautiful! Still, they aren't dills, those two. The electronic fingerprints I left were very subtle, so they've done well to pick up on them and to try and find Xavier or Miss Julie. But what else is on your mind?*'

I chuckled, 'You know me too well! I want to give these clowns another good kick in the guts, since I'm not convinced they've been hit hard enough. I thought we might make another excursion tonight, if you're up to it. Full covert recce with no contact this time. Go in at 02:00 again. Sound good?'

'*Yep! No problem. I'll come to your place again, but not until kick-off time. See you then.*'

A further check with Kelly and Sandy revealed that last night, Darryl had been quiet and surprisingly pleasant since his encounter with Corrine. Still, Kelly didn't trust the lack of aggressive behaviour and had warned Sandy to be especially watchful.

Rain was still falling and was forecast to continue into this evening, accompanied by quite strong winds again, so that suited our little excursion, but made for a dull, slightly boring day. Dell suggested that a fair chunk of the afternoon could be more pleasantly utilised by having a bit of a fool around, and that turned into an extended romp accompanied by sound of the relentless rain beating down on the corrugated iron roof.

We went for a wet walk later and bought some fresh fish fillets from the Co-op and I tried them on the BBQ, wrapped in aluminium foil with butter and lemon, with excellent results.

In preparation for the evening, we went to sleep early, although I was awake when a slim figure slipped into the bedroom at 01:45.

SATURDAY

'Awake, thanks Mouse,' I said, poking Dell in the ribs gently.

Corrine laughed at her startled reaction, then retreated to the kitchen to brew some tea as a sleep-chaser, while Dell and I peed, washed and dressed.

'No rain gear tonight,' I warned Dell. 'We're going just on a recce and staying away from the house, so we can't have plastic rain gear that makes a noise. Therefore, we're going to get wet. At least it's warm out.'

Corrine wore her skin-tight outfit again and looked terrific, while Dell and I just had the same soft pants and dark jerseys as last night. We wore our balaclavas rolled up like watch caps until we reached the target, so with our dark sneakers splashing through the puddles, we walked quietly the few hundred metres to the mark.

Lights were out in the Foley residence and Corrine reported the only sounds inside were that of snoring. Therefore, we headed for the target, a long solid-looking shed, the size of two, twin-car garages set end-to-end well back from the house, and almost concealed from casual sight by trees and bushes. The roll-up doors at one end were electric, and the man-door in the side had a very substantial padlock on it, but unfortunately for the Foley secrets, it was no match for Corrine's lock-picking talents.

Curiously, or perhaps, ominously, there were no windows, but once inside, we chose to use shaded red torches anyway. Straight away, the cold hit us like a hammer, our breath steaming in the chilly air. Four split-system air-con units purred quietly away, keeping the sub-tropical warmth at bay. Our dim red light revealed rows of boxes, neatly stacked waist high in multiple rows down the centre of the space. The front area of the shed, closest the roller doors, was dominated by a very large workbench with piles of packing material scattered about. A small bench attached to the left front side wall had a collection of quality hand and power tools neatly laid out, or hung on shadow boards. The boxes weren't heavy and were made of very substantial double-walled cardboard. Where the top flaps folded over, there were quite large gaps, which at first glance seemed as though they were badly designed, but given the contents, there was a natural airgap that didn't look suspicious.

There was some cryptic, coded, alpha-numeric printing on the top and sides of each, along with very large and very red printing; 'This side up' and 'Cool to +6° C only'. How they were described on a cargo manifest would be a job for later, but by the sheer quantity of boxes, it was obvious they had come in on the supply boat.

We needed to look inside one, even though I was wary about breaking any hidden seals, but then Dell found one at the front on the far side that was opened. Looking like it was set up for twenty small, slim bottles of wine, were cardboard dividers holding twenty lizards, eyes tightly closed, each very carefully wrapped in clean, soft cloth. Their little heads poked out into a common area just under the top flaps where they would get plenty of fresh air.

'Why so cold?' Dell murmured. 'I'm fuckin' freezing!'

'The low temperature puts the reptiles in a state close to hibernation where they can survive without food or water for weeks at a time. This is a very sophisticated smuggling operation and the mortality rate would be very low. Profits will be correspondingly high because of it.'

Corrine was doing a box count and as soon as she was finished, we replaced everything as was, and left the shed. We carefully retraced our footsteps to the road, then headed for home. Corrine came in to dry off, change and warm up, using the guest bathroom, while Dell made tea and coffee. The cheeky little bugger called out for me to give her a hand getting out of her skin-suit, which had a single, small zipper down the back from collar to below her waist. With that pulled down, the wispy scrap of material peeled off to reveal a very bare and damp Corrine. I handed her a towel just as Dell came in to deliver the steaming mugs, and with a big grin, she stayed to admire the drying-off process, something Corrine didn't seem to mind either.

I ended up beating a hasty retreat, the two girls following a few minutes later, laughing at my discomfort.

'What's the plan now, Harry?' Corrine asked.

I checked the time, 04:15, and replied, 'I've been told to call ASAP with the information, but I've never called this early, so 'M' won't be on duty.'

I placed the call anyway, and was delighted when my favourite Control lady answered within moments, and hardly sounded sleepy.

'Good Morning Harry. Wet the bed, did we?'

'Lovely to talk to you, too 'M', at this hour, but you did say to call ASAP!'

'I did, and you have. What do you have for me?'

I accepted her shortness and proceeded with my report. 'The reptile operation is very sophisticated and should have a low mortality rate due to the mild refrigeration of the packaging and the smuggled subjects. There is a stock on the island of some 185 boxes, mixed loads, we suspect, although one box we checked had 20 lizards in it. That adds up to a huge number of reptiles.

Each box is around 0.5 m^3 giving a total volume of 92.5 m^3. We have not been able to determine why the stock has built up so much on the island, but it would appear imperative to return them to the mainland ASAP.'

'Copied all. What's your action proposal?'

'We'll attempt to decoy the smugglers out of the way for a few hours tonight. I suggest a large cargo aircraft which can use this short strip be available from late this afternoon. A RAAF C-130J Hercules would do the job if it can fit the strip. It should have the internal volume for the load. Can you check that and get back to me?'

'Well, if you keep your panties on, I'll check for you right now.'

For the next few minutes, I could hear her in the background, haranguing some hapless person, who had dared to be asleep, but then came back.

'That was an RAAF C-130J Crew Chief. He says if they can top-up

their fuel there, which I know they can, then they can land and take-off with a light load. Will that do the job?'

'That'll be lovely. I need them to be on the ground here late this afternoon, shut down, refuelled and waiting for my contact. If the Skipper can carry a SatPhone, I'll call him with instructions, but nobody is to leave the aircraft. Only the Skipper talks to anybody on the ground and the story for the refueller is that it's a hush-hush Joint Forces exercise. That'll be sufficiently vague to confuse the issue. Don't tell the crew in advance the cargo is reptiles; I'll do that before they load.'

'Copy that.'

'Another item; please ask them to borrow the longest, open glider trailer from the RAAF Richmond Gliding Club and bring that. Also ask them to chuck in an extra ten troops to help with the loading and unloading, but they should all be in civvy clothing.'

'Copy that.'

'I presume you will set up an emergency collection at your end, but remember the little buggers will start to revive if things warm up too much, so temperature control is critical.'

'In hand, Harry. Any more?'

'Apart from the fact that I don't wear panties; negative for now. Just let me have the phone number ASAP.

'Will do Precious. Hold the line again.'

I suppose the Crew Chief was still awake, since she came back to me just a couple of minutes later with the satellite number.

'The Skipper will be Squadron Leader Karleigh Maxwell. They'll be on the ground there by 16:30 LHI time. Fuel top-up is being arranged, but expect a lot of questions. They are doing this as an act of faith at the moment, so tread carefully and give them good answers! These boys can be a bit sensitive if they think you're trying to give them a snow job! Anything further?'

'No, Thanks 'M'. Lovely piece of organising.'

She gave that throaty chuckle, 'It was rather good, now wasn't it? Let me know how it works out. Bye now Commander, and do take care.'

CHAPTER 28

SATURDAY, THE ISLAND

'OK, Harry. So, you get to play with the big boy's toys yet again. Lucky you!'

Dell raised her eyebrows questioningly, so Corrine responded. 'During the operation we were on just before the one where you were involved, our dear Harry got to play Admiral with a fully-crewed RAN patrol boat. Sent it here and there, shot up people, boats and a camp and had a lovely time, didn't you, dearest Big Dog?'

I looked up from sketching timelines on some scrap paper. 'Sorry. Just making sure all the timing of this fits and will work. Then there's just one more job for you, Mouse, before you can get some rest before tonight.'

She looked intrigued. 'OK. Hit me.'

'When we interrogated Will last night, do you remember if he said anything about how they were notified of the next delivery of stones?'

'I remember that,' Dell chipped in. 'Will said it comes in direct from the shipping co-ordinator in Mumbai, in the form of an ordinary-sounding email. However, the word 'merchandise' has to be in it, as well as the GPS co-ordinates, plus a date/time group of numerals without a space.'

I switched my gaze. 'Mouse? Did you hear something similar?'

Corrine nodded slowly, 'Yeah. Dell has it about right. The code word and the one set of time/date was proof.'

I suddenly felt excited. 'Alright, here's what you do, young lady. Then you can go home and have a rest before tonight.'

I laid out the rest of the plan and Corrine's part in it, before she rounded up her gear, disappeared into the office for ten minutes, then gave us the thumbs-up as she slipped out the back door and went home. Dell and I kicked the plan around a bit more, but there wasn't much to refine, so with first light turning the eastern sky a beautiful, soft shade of salmon-pink, we went for a walk. The rain had stopped, the wind had abated as well, and although the sky was still overcast, the cloud-base was much higher, holding promise of rapidly clearing weather.

We walked for an hour, trying to relieve the tensions of the last couple of nights, and making sure there weren't any loose ends that could trip us up. I shamelessly used Dell's sharp mind as a double check to my thoughts and plans, while remaining mindful of the fact that the far more serious situation with serial killer Darryl, was still festering away in the background.

'I guess so long as Darryl stays quiet today, we can clear out most of the Foley's business by tonight,' Dell commented.

'Yes. But they won't be a happy pair of campers later tonight. I wonder if they'll connect the RAAF visit with the continuation of their troubles? I mean, when they discover they've had visitors, there'll be some evidence that the critters didn't just evaporate, so someone had to move them. Which begs the question; where did they go?'

'The supply boat is still here, isn't it?' she said, 'Dave said the bad weather caused some delays, so why should they suspect the RAAF? If the locals think the aircraft is staying overnight, they won't be hanging around watching and waiting for some action, therefore, they won't see any loading activity. But even if someone does spot something, it could just be associated with the Joint Forces Exercise. It would take a very good imagination to connect the RAAF with transporting reptiles!'

'All that's true,' I said, thinking hard, 'but I wonder...The supply boat is supposed to leave this evening, so given the size of the load, it would be the logical way to move them. If they focus on who might have nicked their stock and loaded it on the boat, that should keep them busy. But I wonder if we can lay another false trail pointing towards Xavier? I must say that even after his gory demise, he's proving to be most useful!'

Dell went a bit pale at the memory of several giant Komodo Dragons, their fangs ripping into Xavier's lily-white body and turning a pristine Indonesian beach bloody red.

To distract her, I said, 'Regardless, we'll have to keep all movements as quiet as possible. How the Foley's react to this latest attack, will be the key to their chances of living to a ripe old age! If there's the slightest chance they'll connect the dots and raise a fuss, I'll terminate them myself!'

Dell's eyes widened at the tone of my voice, so different to my usual laid-back approach. 'Look. If they make a fuss, Darryl gets involved, and that part of the operation is blown immediately. My people want us to stay here until the next shipment is due, go through the motions with the Foleys to collect the shipment, then shut everything down at this end. By then, all the overseas feeder pipelines should have been closed down and their principals locked up or worse.'

'OK, Harry, for what it's worth, I can't see any basic flaws in the plan, so we'll wait and see, I guess.'

Back at the house, I called Dave and asked that he and Alex come ashore late afternoon and walk up to the house. I also spoke to Bree and gave her a set of instructions which she said wouldn't be a problem and didn't need any extra help. This was one of those times when I felt I had set a bunch of random events in motion, and was only hoping the outcome would be favourable. Consequently, it was difficult to relax since my mind kept going over all the events which were in play, trying to see if I'd made a cock-up somewhere by forgetting something.

As a distraction, Dell said we should do the touristy thing and go for a paddle with the fish at Ned's beach, a suggestion that was so bizarre, it was actually appealing! We duly joined a bunch of other visitors in tossing chunks of bread and approved fish food to an amazing variety of fish, some quite large at 3 to 4 kilos, that slithered around our ankles in the knee-deep water. There was minor consternation amongst the group when several small Galapagos sharks joined the party, proving to be quite unafraid of and uninterested in the small forest of tasty human legs appearing around them.

While having a slippery fish rub harmlessly against your legs was one thing, letting a 1.5 to 2 metre shark do the same would lift skin and start a fast blood leak, which might be just a bit too tempting for a hungry predator.

Dell was having a lovely time, squealing with delight every time a large wrasse or bluefish rubbed against her legs, or popped it's head up out of the water to beg for food.

Finally, we tired of the play and made our way back to the house, getting some fresh long rolls and ham for lunch.

The back yard was reasonably private, or seemed to be anyway, so it seemed natural to peel off our damp, sandy swim gear and hose off under the rainwater-fed garden hose. That led inevitably to a round of fooling around, where Dell's greatest complaint was that the coarse grass tickled her bum. She obviously enjoyed the outdoor experience as much as I did.

Consequently, lunch was a bit late that afternoon, but eventually we were washed, dried, fed and clothed, just in time to receive a call from Corrine who sounded pissed.

'What's the go, Mouse?'

'I've just got rid of that fucking Darryl! Again!' she spat angrily. 'He took some time away from the supply boat loading, and the bastard came around, his system loaded with a triple dose of bloody Viagra and keen to prove again what a brilliant cocksman he is! Trouble was, because he overdosed, he came in the first two minutes, but was left with an erection that just wouldn't go away, although after the first hour, he started to complain!'

I'd put the phone on speaker so Dell could hear. 'I hope he

behaved himself,' I said, trying hard not to laugh, even though Dell was nearly choking on a fit of the giggles.

'Yeah, he sort-of did behave, but I tried not to laugh when he was still hard into the second hour and really starting to ache. He tried every-thing to get it to go down, including cold water, ice-blocks and even a whack with a cold spoon, but nothing worked! He insisted on seeing if re-insertion would help, but it didn't and just made him sore. I didn't mind those attempts all that much, although when he started to get really angry toward the end, he started to get a bit rough.'

'I hope he didn't hit you again!' I said, suddenly concerned.

'Nah! Nothing like that, Boss. He was just a bit.....rough! Hard to explain if you're not a girl. Anyway, he finally subsided enough to get his uniform on and hobbled away like he had a broom-stick up his arse and a magnum .44 down the front of his pants. You'd better check on Sandy and Kelly, but I think he'll be a shot duck for a while!'

I couldn't help a few chuckles, glad that she had survived unscathed, but concerned that he was still targeting her. 'Are you still right for tonight?'

'Yeah. No problem. I'll be there as soon as it's dark.'

'Good oh. I've asked Dave and Alex to come ashore around then to lend a hand. It may take a couple of trips, so if Darryl stayed home tonight, that'd be great.'

'I'll call Kelly now and give her a heads up. She and Sandy might be able to feed him a good meal and get him pissed. That'll keep him grounded.'

I laughed, 'See you, Mouse.'

'Seems like we're just getting away with keeping Darryl from flipping over,' Dell observed shrewdly, 'but it can't last. I mean, why did he think he needed three full-dose Viagra pills to visit Corrine? He must be having a severe attack of can't-gettit-up-itis!'

'Yeah, it does. I just hope it doesn't mean he's so uptight to stran-gle someone that those urges are messing around with his normal sex drive!'

We fluffed around for the next couple of hours until the distant thunder of powerful turbo-prop engines in reverse thrust echoed across the Island. Dell and I took the ute out to the airport at the standard speed of 25 km/h, arriving on the northern side of the runway in time to see the bizarre sight of the massive bulk of a Hercules C-130J-30, reversing backwards down the runway.

'What the hell's he doing that for?' Dell asked.

'I think it might be so he doesn't mess up the bitumen at the end of the runway trying to do a tight turn. He can drive it backwards, so he is.'

As we drove around the end of the runway, almost on the beach, the huge aircraft neatly made a three-point turn manoeuvre opposite the taxiway to the terminal, then drove forward onto the apron, before turning left onto the grass parking area. As Dell and I pulled into the parking lot, we were surprised to see fifteen or twenty twin-engine light aircraft lined up on the tie-down strip parallel with the runway. A small fleet of service vehicles from the various lodges were in the parking lot beside us and a crowd of cheerful, chattering pilots and crew were streaming out of the terminal toward them.

'Looks like a Flying Club or Association fly-in,' I commented to Dell as the happy throng flowed around us trying to find the right vehicle. 'We might just let them sort themselves out while our guys shut that monster down.'

The C-130 had shut down all four engines and a Crew Chief was walking around, putting wheel chocks in pace, covers on pitot tubes and such, while having a good look at everything, especially the tires. But because they were designed to do just this sort of thing, it would be odd to find a problem. While we waited for the fly-in crews to depart, a fuel tanker pulled up under one of the Hercules's wings and began the requested refuel. The Crew Chief was joined by one other airman in RAAF General Purpose Uniform blue camo pattern clothing, but as I'd requested, no one else left the aircraft.

'OK,' I said to Dell as the last of the visiting aircrew left the parking lot, 'it's show time! Let's go see what we've been sent.'

Leaving the battered Toyota where it was, we strolled through an open gate into the unpaved parking area beside the terminal. As we approached the hulking aircraft, a diminutive figure in GPUs and with three stripes on each shoulder tab, the middle one thinner than the outer two, stepped quickly away from the refuelling operation and approached, hands held out to shoo us away. Closer up, it quickly became clear that the 'he' was, in fact, very definitely a 'she', and in a crisp, decisive voice, she said, 'I'm sorry folks, I'll have to ask you to return to the car park. This is a restricted area for the duration and we're on an active mission, so please go back.'

A quick glance at Dell, then myself showed part of her concern; we were both barefoot, wearing creased shorts and a T-shirt each. Additionally, I hadn't shaved for a couple of days, so it was my turn to spread my arms and look innocent.

'Squadron Leader Maxwell, I presume,' was my rather limp opening line, but as her name was embroided on a rip-off tab on the upper slope of her right breast, and her rank on her shoulder tabs, she wasn't impressed with my display of insight.

'Yeah, but you still have to move back behind the fence...now!' Thinking she was about to have trouble, she made a fist and raised it to her shoulder. Immediately, the Crew Chief left the refueller and trotted over, towering over the pilot.

'Problems, Skipper?' he inquired in an easy tone.

'Hopefully not, Flight Sergeant Golding. These civilians have been asked to return to the car park.'

I tried again as the rather large form of the Flight Sergeant stepped forward.

'I'm Commander Stevens and I've come to see you.'

The Flight Sergeant was still trying to shepherd us away. 'C'mon folks...you heard the Squadron Leader. Let's keep moving back.'

Sometimes one has to make a stand, so drawing myself up as best I could in shorts and bare feet, I barked in best parade ground manner,

'As you were, Flight Sergeant. I repeat, I am Commander Stevens and I'm the one who requested you be sent here. For the duration of this deployment, I'm your superior officer, so back off!' That was at least enough to stop him in his tracks, but he looked at his skipper for guidance. Squadron Leader Maxwell had a frown on her face.

'Identification!' she correctly demanded.

Helplessly, I slapped at my empty pockets, the distractions earlier in the day causing me to leave my wallet behind. 'Sorry, left it back at the house, but.....'

'No but's, sir.' The Flight Sergeant resumed his move forward, 'I'll have to ask you to keep moving.'

I stood my ground until we were nose to...chin. Well, he was a bit taller than me.

I tried again, 'I repeat. Back off Flight Sergeant. I have information to give to the Squadron Leader; something I can't do with you in my face. Don't make me use the SatPhone.'

At least I'd remembered to bring that, so I whipped it out of my pocket in a quick-draw that Wyatt Earp would've been proud of and brandished it like a talisman.

He stopped and Squadron Leader Maxwell said in an amused tone, 'OK Flight. Let the gentleman have his say. He appears to have us outgunned at the moment, so let me hear him out. I'll let you fetch the M134 Minigun if he fails to convince me. But for now, just step back a few paces.'

Glaring at me, he complied.

'Now, Sir,' she went on, 'in lieu of formal ID, perhaps you can convince me of your real status.'

I thought briefly, then said, 'At approximately 03:45 eastern time, Flight Sergeant Golding received a phone call asking if a C-130J-30, could land at Lord Howe Island and collect a lightweight, but high-volume cargo. He replied that without knowing the exact weight of the cargo, it could if the fuel could be topped prior to the return. Further instructions were to load ten to twelve ground crew and to borrow and load an open glider trailer from the RAAF Gliding Club. The refueller was to be told the aircraft is on a Joint Services exercise; it was to be on the ground at LHI by late afternoon to await further instructions from Commander Stevens. A final instruction was that apart from post-landing checks and liaison with the refueller, no personnel were to leave the aircraft. How am I doing, Squadron Leader?'

She grinned, then snapped off a salute. 'Ten out of ten, Commander. My crew and I are at your service. Could we perhaps step into the terminal building for a briefing?'

I returned the salute, despite the lack of headgear. 'I'd prefer to step into your aircraft, if you wouldn't mind, Squadron Leader. Just for security. Too many curious eyes on this island for comfort, I'm afraid.'

She gestured to the aircraft and the Flight Sergeant led the way. 'Treat us just as casual visitors in front of the refueller, please Flight,' I said softly. The refueller, according to info Sandy got from Kelly, was a very genial islander who also ran a herd of dairy cattle which he milked twice a day and was the caretaker of the island's diesel electricity generators. He was equally at home topping off the C-130 with a carefully calculated amount of Jet A-1 turbine fuel, or filling the light private aircraft tanks to the brim with AVGAS aviation petrol.

'Roger that, Sir,' he muttered in reply, leading us to the forward air stairs. Inside the cavernous cargo hold, sat a very out-of-place glider trailer, battered and scarred from years of use, but still with the main features necessary. Some of the seats hinged against the side wall, were folded down where several young airmen and women, were playing cards. Several others were stretched out on the 12-metre-long glider trailer obeying the first rule of military service...sleep when you can.

Opposite the entry door was a very compact toilet and shower module, but the Squadron Leader wheeled left just inside the door, entering the flight crew rest area. A pair of drop-down bunks allowed for crew rest periods while a small table and fixed seats were in the small galley opposite. There was another toilet module built-in for crew use.

Since this was the new Super-Hercules C-130J-30, there were

normally just three crew; two pilots and a Crew Chief/Loadmaster. Of course, another 128 troops could be squeezed aboard, or up to twice that many in an emergency airlift.

Forward of the rest area was the cockpit and like everything else on this aircraft, I found it to be almost cavernous. The driver's chairs were of armchair proportions, with a third chair offset to the rear for an extra body. The extent of the view through the cabin windows was amazing. The right-hand or co-pilot chair was rolled back on its runners with a female wearing Lieutenant's stripes on her shoulders, slumped down in it, her feet propped up on the very cluttered and expensive instrument panel.

Cords trailing from her ears and a tapping foot suggested she was listening to music from some source.

'Hey, Mary!' Squadron Leader Maxwell called. 'Wakey, wakey. We've got visitors.'

In one smooth movement, the long legs swung down off the panel, the earbuds were swept out of sight and she stood facing us. She was a lot taller than her skipper with short, blonde hair and a supple, slim body, typical of the high standard achieved by RAAF aircrew who had to keep in good condition.

'Sorry Skipper, just chilling out for a moment.'

'That's cool. This is our contact, Commander Stevens and Miss Petrie who are about to tell us exactly what's going on, as nobody else has so far. Commander, Miss Petrie, this is my co-pilot Lieutenant Maryanne Marshall, or M 'n M for short.'

I didn't miss the not-so-subtle shot about secrecy, nor that I was going to have to tell all or the feisty little Squadron Leader was quite capable of taking her bat, ball, C-130J and going home. She waved me into the third seat, letting Dell find a switch panel to lean against.

She added, 'In here, you can drop the Squadron Leader, if that's alright with you?'

I relaxed a little, aware that I was depending on this woman to do the right thing and help us sort out a problem.

'Yep. Fine by Dell and me. I'm always happy with just Harry, although there was a time when I was an SAS Major, so we were the same rank. Since leaving the Military, the Commander rank doesn't seem quite right.'

Karleigh looked at me quizzically for a few moments, then said softly, almost to herself, 'Major Harry Stevens...SAS...Middle East. Holy crap! I know who you are and it's my very great privilege to meet you!' She grabbed my hand and shook it hard, while Maryanne looked at her as though she flipped out.

Karleigh noticed the look and said to Maryanne, 'This is Major Harry Stevens, VC. Taliban...trooper rescue...then squad rescue by playing at being a human target... wounded, but still managed to take out several high-ranking Taliban leaders while playing dodge-the-bullets!'

I got the same treatment from Maryanne, but without the vocalisations, for which I was thankful, because I still found the whole VC thing very embarrassing since I'd got myself shot in the process and received a medical discharge from the Service.

'Ever since I heard your story, ...Harry, I wondered. Did you ever catch up with the trooper you rescued that day?'

I laughed, 'Yes, I did. In fact, she's here in town at the moment and has been helping with this project which I'm about to tell you all about.'

Karleigh smiled, 'That's a co-incidence. We'd love to meet her, but even more, we'd like to hear all about this mission and what part we get to play in it. Like why the glider trailer and twelve airmen?'

'How about you call your Flight Sergeant in and I'll bring you all up to date on just some of the odd things which have been happening around here.'

The spacious cockpit filled up appreciably with the addition of the impressive bulk of Flight Sergeant Golding, although Karleigh and Maryanne were able to stay out of the way, standing to the outside of their seats, such was the width and headroom of the aircraft at that point.

CHAPTER 29

I took a deep breath, then started. 'There are several things happening on the island at the moment, but since you won't be here long, only one really affects you. Two locals, fishermen by trade and brothers by birth, are running a couple of smuggling operations. The one we're trying to do something about tonight, is live Australian reptiles being smuggled out of Australia to Asia and Europe primarily, with the USA as a lesser market.'

Flight Sergeant Golding and Flight Lieutenant Marshall recoiled in disgust, showing the standard human reaction to any unfortunate creature that has to crawl or slither. Squadron Leader Maxwell, however, showed strong interest, but launched into a bit of a rave.

'I suppose they're stuffed into socks, then jammed in some idiot's luggage. These arseholes really give me the shits! They just think of the money they might make and not the pain and agony they cause the animal. Like the Thorny or Mountain Devil who only eat small, black ants which are found in just a few localities. Take them away from their feeding grounds and they starve and die!'

She shook herself as if to settle her thoughts, then went on, 'Sorry! I hate bloody smugglers with a passion, but enough of that, where do we come in? Surely this would be a matter for the local copper?'

I made sure she had run down, then said, 'Yes, it should be, but that's another matter which you don't need to be involved with. And I'd appreciate it if there was no speculation about that when you return to base.'

She looked abashed, 'Sorry again. How about I let you deliver the briefing first?'

'No problem, but to answer your question, all of you and your lovely aircraft are here to haul all the reptile's home in one go, as quickly as possible. There are so many of them, adding to the pressing need to get them back in their natural habitat ASAP. We have a sting operation running as we speak, to deprive these clowns of their carefully hoarded stock and to get these creatures back to the mainland.'

Karleigh waved her hand around, 'But the cost of sending this thing is horrific. Who pays?'

I shrugged, 'Above my pay grade, I'm afraid. Maybe the Department of Conservation and Environment? But to get back to the nuts and bolts of the operation, we expect the two smugglers to take their boat out tonight. It's a false callout we've set up, so we don't expect them to be away for more than two hours. That's the time frame to load 185 boxes, roughly measuring $0.5m^3$.' I smiled, 'Hence the glider trailer which can be towed behind my Toyota ute.'

The expression on their faces was comical and it was the ever-practical Flight Sergeant who chipped in with, 'Just a quick mental check of the box count, Commander, and it all adds up to something like $92.5 \ m^3$! And that's more than half of our total volumetric capacity.'

'Yep! That was taken into account, Flight. We looked at using the C-27J Spartan, but it would have cubed out if some boxes are bigger than the average we worked on. Therefore, you guys got the guernsey.'

'So how many reptiles are in each box?' M & M asked. 'And what's the weight?'

'There was only one box open when we went prowling last night, and that had 20 shingle-backs in it. The weight was about 7 or 8 kilos, so I didn't think weight would be a consideration as the whole shipment shouldn't exceed 1,500kgs.

They are being kept refrigerated to slow their metabolism down and it would appear that considerable effort has been taken to ensure their survival. These people aren't silly; the more that die on the way, the less money they make. We didn't open any more boxes as we didn't want to alert the smugglers ahead of time. I can tell you though that this complex sting involves a parallel operation, so that's why this briefing is confined to you three. The troops are to help with the loading and mustn't be told what the cargo is, except that it is extremely fragile and must be handled with all due care. We also need to be as covert as possible and not stir up the neighbourhood at all.'

Flight Sergeant Golding nodded, 'I can handle that, Skipper. I'll make sure they keep quiet.'

Karleigh nodded, then turned to me. 'So, what's the plan, Harry? I assume you've worked something out?'

'Yeah, I have, but it depends on a lot of things going right. Basically, it's planned to go like this. We have a long-range UAV which will be launched from my catamaran at the same time the two fishermen launch their boat, and that's usually around 21:00; give or take. As soon as they are on the water, we load the troops in the ute, hook up the trailer and head for the house.

The UAV will track the boat out to a pre-arranged, but fictional rendezvous with a cargo ship, but when the ship fails to appear, the lads will turn around and come home, although because the UAV will be loitering overhead, my operator will give us plenty of warning via SatPhone of their return.

I estimate we'll have about two hours to clear the stockpile and eliminate most traces of the job. I'd like to leave a couple of small pieces of evidence which will point to the job being the work of another bad guy, so hopefully, he'll get the blame.'

'Is that why you want our troops in civvy's?' Karleigh asked.

'Yes. And it's why I suggested the refueller be told that you're on Joint Service exercises. I definitely don't want even the slightest hint of RAAF involvement in this operation, even though some people may wonder about a ute with a very long trailer moving through the village, but we want to keep a low profile as much as possible. Are you able to feed everybody on-site without having to go to one of the Clubs?'

'No problem. Plenty to eat, although I'd like to let them have a run outside once it's dark, if that's OK?'

'Sure, no problem once it's dark. I just didn't want any of them chatting to one of the locals and saying the wrong thing.'

'I'll guarantee it won't happen,' growled Sergeant Golding, looking grim, 'and they'll be quiet as mice on the job.'

I smiled at him, 'Thanks, Flight. With regards to transport, we'll have to be a bit naughty because there's only the one vehicle, a twin-cab ute, so we'll jam who we can in the cabin and the rest in the back tray. There's a blanket speed limit of just 25 km/h, so the risk level will be very low. Can I presume you're happy with that?'

Karleigh nodded, 'Yep! No problem, Harry. I must say that you get to play with some very strange toys at times. Catamarans and a long-range UAV sound like a strange combo, but fun.'

Dell gave a short chuckle, unable to refrain from scoring a couple of points, even though she wasn't on that particular operation, and said 'Only six months ago, I was told, he had a RAN patrol boat, two Browning .50 cal machine guns and a MK47 grenade launcher at his disposal, courtesy of the Navy Fleet Commander!'

That really raised some eyebrows, and I saw some tension leave Karleigh's eyes as she thought it through. If the Navy Fleet Commander was happy to dish out major equipment to this scruffy-looking, bare-footed boatie in front of her, he must have massive political muscle. Therefore, pulling a C-130J to Lord Howe island was nothing to be concerned about.

'OK, Harry. We're in, so what's the timetable?'

I checked the time and it was just past 17:30 local. 'Unfortunately, there's still some time to kill. The smugglers won't be heading out until around 21:00. How about you two come with us back to the house, and we'll put as many of your troops as we can in the tray laying down with a tarp over them. We'll come back for the trailer and the others after it's dark.

That'll save some time when we get the go ahead from our UAV operator.'

Karleigh thought about it for a moment or two. 'That's not a bad plan, Harry. I like the idea of saving time later. Maybe we could have a look at your boat and the UAV if we've got some time to kill.'

'No problem. I've got two of my crew coming ashore shortly, leaving the UAV operator and my cats aboard.'

'Oh, nice!' M 'n M said. 'I love cats and these will be real boat cats!'

Karleigh rolled her eyes good-naturedly, before turning to Flight Sergeant Golding. 'Flight, would you mind organising security patrols for the evening, please? Wide perimeter, I think and random mobile. Armed, of course. Split the remainder into two details; one to travel with M 'n M and me back to the Commander's house in about ten minutes. The other detail to be ready to go at......?' She raised her eyebrows at me, so I hastily added, 'About 21:00, thanks Flight. I'd rather not chance the smugglers spotting the long trailer. We'll try to travel dark and quiet, so several troops lying in the trailer will help dampen any noise from the sheet metal.'

He nodded, 'No problem, Commander. I'll make it happen.'

It was just ten minutes later, that Dell, Karleigh, M 'n M and I climbed in the old Toyota, with two girls and two guys laying down in the tray with a tarpaulin draped carelessly over them. As we drove slowly out of the airport area, I looked carefully around, but the place was totally deserted. The same couldn't be said for the Golf Club, the entrance to which lay just past the airport turnoff. It would seem that many of the visiting private pilots had accepted the invitation to cleanse their parched palates after the slightly harrowing flight from the mainland.

Another source of loud voices gargling down the brewer's best, was heard from the Bowling Club as we drove slowly along Lagoon Road to our residence.

I drove through to the back yard to unload in privacy, not surprised to see Corrine, Dave and Alex with their feet propped up and swigging the late Steve's beer. Dave hardly batted an eyelid as eight people climbed out of the ute, two of them officers in RAAF blue GPUs.

Following introductions, where Corrine copped her share of attention from Karleigh and M 'n M, Karleigh allowed her four troops two beers each, then she and M&M were taken inside by Dell to change into civvy's left over by Gerry, as they'd both insisted on getting involved in the Great Reptile Rescue as M 'n M took to calling it.

They returned looking vastly different out of uniform, as well as quite sexy in basic shorts and shirts showing a lot of bare skin. They both copped a mild degree of friendly joshing from the troops, showing that both officers were well respected and were good leaders.

'Is the RIB beside the jetty?' I asked Dave.

'Yep. You going out to *Firebird?*'

'Yeah. Karleigh and M 'n M want to have a look at the UAV, and M 'n M wants to play with the kitties.'

He laughed, but didn't say any more, so I took the ladies and we walked down to the jetty where the island supply boat was getting ready for departure. I was relieved to see that its crane hadn't been stowed yet and that one hatch was still open, with a flat-bed truck parked on the jetty. Slightly more alarming was that it was apparently hard aground, the tide being out.

A quick question to one of the crew having a smoke on the jetty cleared up that mystery.

'Normal procedure, mate' he cheerfully replied, 'the old girl usually takes the ground each trip. Depending on the tide. She'll be fine in another hour and a half. Then we'll be gone.'

'Mr Stevens,' came a familiar voice, 'you seem to have a knack of collecting pretty ladies. I'd love to know where you managed to find these two lovelies.'

I adjusted my expression as I turned to face Darryl, a clipboard in his hand and a leering expression on his face as he blatantly eyed the two RAAF Officers up and down. With one hand behind me, I gently patted the air to try to stop Karleigh or M 'n M from burring up at his patronising comment.

'Good afternoon Officer. These ladies just flew in and expressed an interest in looking at my catamaran instead of watching their partners getting pissed at the Golf Club. How could I refuse such charming and attractive ladies?'

I carefully allowed Darryl to assume the girls flew in a light aircraft, and not the C-130. After all, pretty girls in shorts and brief tops don't fly four-engine military transports, do they?

'How could you indeed, Mr Stevens,' he replied, his eyes still roaming over the girls, that weird glitter of madness, flickering like the distant lightning before a storm.

'Well, we shan't keep you from your duties Officer, although it would appear you are nearly finished. Take care.'

That last comment earned me a hard look as, with a last lingering look at the ladies, he spun around and marched stiff-legged toward the boat's gang-plank.

The RIB was tied to the jetty inshore of the freighter's bow, so in short order, we were aboard and buzzing across the lagoon on the short ride to *Firebird*.

'Ok Harry,' Karleigh said, 'that was seriously creepy and obviously, something is going on involving the local law. Is this something we need to know about? As in; is it going to affect this operation we're on?'

I was seriously tempted to tell all, as Karleigh impressed me as being a very cool hand under pressure.

'I'm sorry about the unpleasantness. Yes, that was creepy, and yes, there is something else going on involving the one and only police presence on the island. However, it won't affect the operation you're involved with.'

'Okie doke, Harry. But we'd like to know more when you can tell us, or if you need help, I have a certain amount of latitude in how I choose to protect my crew and aircraft.'

'Thanks, Karleigh. If anything erupts before you leave, I will ask.

But for now, let's just relax a little.'

At first, my passengers didn't know which boat we were headed for, as several other yachts had arrived in the last couple of days, but as we closed on my lovely catamaran and Jasper poked his sleek, black head around the side of the cockpit surround, Karleigh said, 'That's some boat, Harry. And is that a big black dog I can see looking at us? I thought you only had cats.'

With good theatrical timing, I replied, 'That's right. I do only have cats.'

There was silence from the pair as we swung around under *Fire-bird's* high sterns and Bree came down to tie us up. Quick intros and she led the way up to the cockpit where Jasper waited patiently to greet us, a pussy-type grin on his normally impassive face.

'Holy crap!' was M 'n M's response, while Karleigh stopped dead. 'That is a very big, very scary cat, Harry!' she said carefully, not taking her eyes off his, while I knelt down and accepted his affectionate nuzzles. Little Krazy cat came bounding out and never being one to stand on ceremony, went from one set of legs to another, purring and rubbing her face against every bit of human skin she could. Laughing, Maryanne scooped up the bundle of black fur with her myriad tiny white tufts of hair. Holding her up, the little puss batted at Mary-anne's nose with a soft paw, which seemed to be a signal to Jasper who stepped forward and held up his right forepaw to be shaken.

Maryanne carefully put Krazy down, knelt and gently took Jasper's huge paw, feeling the steely claws carefully retracted.

She looked up with an expression of pure delight on her face, 'He's absolutely beautiful! What's his name?'

'His name is Jasper and this is Maryanne, Jasper. The other lady is Karleigh and they are both friends; just come for a visit.'

Both ladies looked a bit puzzled by the way I obviously spoke directly to Jasper, but when he stepped around Maryanne and held his paw out to Karleigh, she too fell under his spell.

'Wow Harry! How did you teach him that trick?'

It was a common question from visitors and the answer was simple, 'Actually, he did it all by himself. I've never taught him anything. He'd probably tell me to get stuffed if I tried to.'

Jasper's response to that statement was typical; a loud 'huff'.'

Karleigh looked at me strangely. 'Did he just 'huff' at you?'

I nodded, 'Yep! That's his way of telling me to get stuffed. Cheeky pussy!'

His response was to huff again and park himself leaning against Maryanne's long, bare legs, making her laugh delightedly again.

'Is he for real?' Karleigh demanded, 'I mean, is this like a party trick? Because it's almost like he understands what you're saying.'

Bree replied for me, 'Oh, but he does understand what Harry says. He's carrying on a bit because Harry's been ashore for a few days.'

'Well, that's pretty amazing, but can we have a tour of your boat, please Harry?'

So, I dutifully did the tour guide bit, but it wasn't a chore since both ladies were really interested, especially in the self-supporting systems I'd designed to make us as electrically independent of a diesel generator as possible. Their attention was drawn to the very obvious coffin-shaped box taking up a fair chunk of estate in the saloon, with a pair of water proof Pelikan cases sitting beside it.

'Dare I ask what that is?' M 'n M asked. 'I'm presuming it only looks like a small coffin.'

I laughed with her, 'You're right, but that's the travel case for *Dragonfly*, our UAV. Bree's getting it ready to launch as soon as our smugglers launch their boat. When it's fully dark, Bree will set it up on the saloon roof and swing the main boom aside to clear the take-off and landing path.'

Bree opened the cases, first showing the dismantled *Dragonfly*, then the Ground Control Station and the second case with a large lithium battery for when *Dragonfly* was away from base power, and the various VHF, UHF and satellite antennas. She went through the performance figures which impressed the hell out of the two RAAF officers.

Karleigh looked at Maryanne, then said, Ah...Harry. Would it be possible for us to stay here with Bree and watch the UAV operation? You seem to have plenty of extra hands and we'd really like to see more of this incredibly capable UAV.'

I shrugged, 'Sure. That won't be a problem. The only rush is to clear out the reptiles before our boys get back, but you don't have to take off until you're ready. In fact, it will be much better if you don't leave immediately. Go tomorrow when you're ready, so long as the boxes are kept cool.'

'That's not a problem,' Karleigh answered, 'the APU is already running, so when the boxes are loaded, I'll just get Flight to close the rear hatch and fire up the air-con.'

'Can you call him to arrange that and let him know what's happening?'

She looked disconcerted, 'Ahh... Bit of a problem! We don't have a flash SatPhone like you and mobiles don't work on the island.'

'Does he carry a portable radio?'

'Yes. One in the Military UHF band. I didn't bring ours since I thought we'd be out of range with the mountain between the airport and the town.'

'No problem. Sit yourself at the Nav desk and we'll find you a radio.'

An array of radio head units ranged along the sloping face of the Nav desk, giving coverage from the bottom of the high frequency band, right through civil marine and air-band frequencies, to the top end of the Military UHF band with all the encoding necessary to talk to any civil or military unit.

I powered up the Elbit Systems PRC-710MB, VHF-UHF unit and selected the appropriate UHF military channel range.

'There you are. Just dial up the channel you're normally on and use the microphone or the headset if you want to be quiet. The antenna is on the mast, and at the high-power setting, it'll blast through anything.'

Karleigh looked suitably impressed, especially when the Flight

Sergeant came up instantly loud and clear. She explained the situation and that I'd be with the delivery crew. After loading, he was to button up the aircraft, air-con on and to keep all visitors, especially the local copper, away from the aircraft, quoting National Security issues as the reason. The display of loaded weapons was approved to enforce the security issue.

I dug out a hand-held UHF radio which I was sure would communicate with his and placed it on the desk in front of her, so she mentioned he could call her if there were any problems.

CHAPTER 30

The time was just 21:30, and I was back in the house with Alex, Dave, Corrine and Dell, but without my two RAAF pilots, when the SatPhone rang. In crisp language, Bree informed me that the masthead camera had allowed her to identify two persons matching the descriptions of the Foley brothers, launching their boat at the ramp just the other side of the long jetty.

She had *Dragonfly* set up and ready to launch, so would call back shortly with an update.

That was our cue to get ready and I knew Karleigh would have called the Flight Sergeant with a heads-up as well. Less than ten minutes later, the crisp voice of Maryanne Marshall on the Sat-Phone announced that the Foley's were presently tracking out through the North Passage, *Dragonfly* effortlessly keeping tabs on it by flying a wide orbit at 1,000 feet. The auto-track function had been locked onto the boat and was working flawlessly.

'I've gotta say, Harry, that from the little we've seen of this UAV, it's an absolute cracker! Bloody marvellous! Anyway, Bree has just reported that the Foley's appear to be taking the same course to the north-east as the last run.'

That was our launch signal, so with five up front and the four RAAF'ies in the tray, we headed for the Foley house, where I dropped the eight out front. Corrine would let them into the store shed, while I headed for the airport to collect the trailer and all the live bodies they could spare.

The roads were deserted at that hour, but I kept to the 25 km/h speed limit anyway. There were still sounds of revelry from the Bowling Club and even more from the Golf Club when I pulled into the airfield car park.

Two armed airmen were on the gate, but quickly stepped back and saluted when I announced myself. I drove up to the dark, hulking mass of the C-130J and parked stern-to the loading ramp. As I stepped down from the ute, the high-pitched whining of powerful electro-hydraulics sounded and thin, but ever-widening lines of dim red night light showed around the edges of the broad area under the aircraft tail as the ramp lowered.

Six hefty young airmen appeared, four in civvy's, pushing and pulling the glider trailer, guiding it down the ramp even before it bottomed out on the soft, sandy ground. In moments, they had mated it to the tow-ball on the back of the ute and an attractive young woman wearing the twin chevrons of a Corporal strode up, saluted and said, 'Ready when you are, Commander. I have four airmen in civvy's to go with you, which leaves four, plus the Flight Sergeant back here for security, although we are able to help unload and stow the cargo when it arrives. Will that be satisfactory?'

I smiled, 'Extremely so, Corporal and my compliments on organising that. If you'd have the troops get in, we'll be off. The clock is ticking on this one, so we need to move as quickly as possible, but the cargo is extremely fragile and must be handled very carefully.'

She cracked a brief smile, 'No problems, Sir. The Flight Sergeant has made some very dire threats as to what he'll do to the first person to mishandle just one item of cargo. But may I ask, sir, what is this cargo?'

'Can't tell you that, Corporal. But I can say that it consists of 185 boxes weighing 7 to 8 kilos each and sized at about $0.5m^3$ each. It is imperative that no box be damaged and none must be opened under any circumstances. I can add that the contents aren't hazardous to the aircraft as such.'

She grinned back. 'I'm afraid that doesn't help at all, Commander, except we'll be very busy. What's the time frame?'

'Two hours with the clock running right now.'

'Yessir. Crap! We'd better haul arse!'

Four husky lads scrambled in the ute, a bright, intelligent lad in his early 20's up front with me and commendably question-free, as we made the slow drive back to the Foley house. We passed no other vehicle, but who knows what eyes took in the strange sight of the long glider trailer trundling quietly along behind the battered ute. I wheeled in the Foley driveway and around to the rear of the back yard where the long, low shed sat half-camouflaged by the verdant green growth of bush. The roller door at the front was raised and a single, dim light served to help the loading.

'Quiet now, please lads,' I cautioned, 'no un-necessary chatter, please move quickly but do not drop any boxes! Clear on that?'

There was a muted chorus of 'Yessir, no problem.'

With twenty minutes elapsed, a human conveyor belt was set up, the boxes passed from hand to hand and stacked two high on the trailer. Each load was just 48 boxes and took fifteen minutes to stack safely. I took the four airmen back with me to speed the unloading and that was done in ten minutes. The round trip, from loading to unloading, took a total of 35 minutes. For the second trip, we chanced a third layer for a load of 72, leaving 65 boxes for the third and last load.

Dave, Dell, Alex and Corrine stayed to tidy up and remove all trace of the removal process, before locking up and heading back to their respective homes. I ran the last load out to the airport, un-hitched the trailer inside the big bird, and ran back to the jetty where Karleigh and Maryanne were waiting. A quick stop at the house for them to change back into uniform and it was out to the airport for the last time that night. I released them to depart at any time after 09:00, thanked everyone concerned and headed back with Bree's warning in my earpiece that the Foley's were pulling up to the boat ramp as we were speaking.

To be sure, I made a slight detour to approach the Xavier house from a different direction and didn't see any other vehicles. Dell had the house in darkness as I parked in the carport, and I locked the doors when I went in, even though it wasn't standard Lord Howe practice. Expecting visitors, we nevertheless went to bed and waited for the inevitable.

Strangely, it came more than three hours later when we had fallen asleep anyway, and took the form of a thunderous hammering on the back door and the furious rattling of the door handle. I waited a suitable length of time, before sleepily shuffling through the kitchen, saying, 'Hang on, hang on! I'm coming! Keep your bloody shirt on! This better be good to be waking a fella up at this ridiculous hour!'

I unlocked the door, to have it nearly knock me over as Will, then Jack barged into the kitchen, both red in the face from what seemed to be a combination of anger and exertion.

'Ah...What's going on guys? Where's the fire?'

Will's answer was to poke me hard in the chest. 'Don't you give me any fucking fire bullshit, you smart-arse prick! What's been going on while we were on a bullshit mission out to sea?'

I think I gave a pretty good impression of total bewilderment, but decided being too meek may work against me.

Putting on my best very-unhappy-Major look, I stepped forward and poked Will even harder in his chest, forcing him to stumble backwards into Jack, who fell over a kitchen chair and abruptly sat on his arse. Will spun toward me with murder in his eyes, clenched fists raised and screaming abuse.

Into this farcical mess strode Dell, both hands holding the small frame of a PMR-30 pistol out in front, the menacing shape of the suppressor pointing unwaveringly at Will's head.

'Back...up...the...bus!' she announced very clearly, the fact that she only wore very brief panties hardly distracted attention from the gun. That is, it didn't distract the Foleys, but then I wasn't the one with a gun pointed at me.

While Will pulled up short, Jack finally got untangled from the chair legs and turned to charge me down, so Dell calmly shot him in the shoulder. The muted bang was hardly audible over

Will's cursing, but the trickle of smoke from the muffler tip got his attention.

As did the aim of the gun which Dell swung from Jack to Will's crotch and he abruptly shut up. Behind him, Jack groped for an upright chair and sat down heavily, one hand clasped to his bleeding shoulder.

'You shot me!' He said disbelievingly, 'You dirty, rotten, fucking bitch! You shot me!'

'Yes,' Dell said, 'and if you say one more word or try to get up, I'll do it again. Now you, Bill or Jill, whatever your name is. You sit down as well and don't move until we sort out this cluster-fuck! Are you okay Harry?'

'Yep. I'm fine. Good shot, by the way, thank you. I like the much quieter sound from that Isis suppressor. It works well.'

Dell grinned, 'Yeah. It balances the weight of the gun better, as well.'

The Foleys looked at each other, trying to figure out what was going on, so I said, 'Righto you two clowns! What's the meaning of barging in like this and attacking me? Start talking or I'll turn Dell loose again.'

Behind me, Dell made a noise that sounded suspiciously like a stifled giggle, as Will haltingly stammered out a reply, 'We got a message in the usual way, that there was a special drop on tonight, so we went out as we normally do, but there was no ship at the RV point. When we got back we found someone had broken into our shed, and taken our entire stock of another operation we had going. They didn't leave many clues, but there was something left behind which pointed at Xavier being behind the whole thing! You two have come here straight from Xavier, so we thought you must know something about it.'

At the end of the table, Jack still sat holding his shoulder, a red stain slowly spreading down his shirt and the occasional drop sliding between his fingers.

'Excuse me, you bunch of fuck-wits. Is there any chance I can get some attention to my shoulder where smart bitch shot me?'

I looked at him. 'I'd watch my language, mate! The only medic here is the lady who shot you, so you might like to try being nice and apologising for bursting in here, screaming and yelling and accusing us of theft. If Xavier is involved in whatever it was that happened to you, we know nothing of his plans.'

I told the truth on the basis that it's much easier to remember.

'And while we're on the subject, just what was it that was stolen from you and what operation have you got going? I thought you were supposed to work for Xavier. Is this a bit of private enterprise?'

Jack shook his head, wincing as the movement disturbed his punctured shoulder. 'Nope, can't tell you that. None of your business.'

I shrugged, 'OK. As you say, it's really none of our business, but you've come around here, pushed your way in, attacked me, then got yourself shot for your trouble. It would seem to me you've already involved us in your business, whether we like it or not.'

The brothers looked at each other, before Jack spoke, 'Yeah, all right. I guess we did leap to conclusions a bit quickly. But you still aren't involved in our business and it's going to stay that way. We might take ourselves off home and try to figure out what the fuck's going on.'

'Don't you want Dell to fix your shoulder?'

Jack shuddered, 'No way! She's fixed it enough already. Will can take it from here.'

With that, they got up and left, a small trail of blood spots marking Jack's exit.

I re-locked the back door and put the kettle on for a brew.

'That went rather well, I thought,' Dell commented, as I made sure they had left.

I chucked, 'Yeah. It did go well. Although now they suspect Xavier's involvement, we're still the most likely culprits. I mean, who else can they suspect?'

'Does that mean you think they'll be back?'

'Hell yes! Either they're already thinking like I am or just about to. But they need proof that we were involved, and the first thing I reckon they'll do is chase up the supply boat's loading manifest to see if their precious inventory went out that way. When they draw a blank on the shipping manifest, my take is they'll assume the whole lot is still on the island...somewhere!'

I checked the time and it was 04:40. 'Squadron Leader Karleigh will be departing at 09:00, so that will remove the last of the evidence. Which reminds me, I'd better call 'M' and let her know where we're up to.'

I dug out the SatPhone, and speed-dialled the number.

'Good morning Harry. How are things in your South Pacific paradise?'

'Good morning to you too, 'M'. The operation was successful, and thanks to the RAAF, Squadron Leader Maxwell will be departing in 3 hours and 20 minutes, with her live cargo. However, it appears we've made a target of ourselves with the smugglers.'

'How so, dear man?'

'We've been leaving clues with them that Xavier was trying to cut them out of the gem business, and was also involved in nicking all their smuggling stock. At the moment, they aren't sure whether he's on the island or not, but because we're the only other people associated with him in sight, they're gunning for us.

Are you sure we have to wait for another delivery of stones before we take them out? I feel that we're just sitting here inviting them to take a shot at us.'

'Point taken, but earlier today, our international colleagues were still chasing down several key players in the smuggling racket and asked for more time, which we had to agree to give them.'

'But hasn't the word of arrests spread up the pipeline to alert these characters?'

'Not so far. The police are being very quiet and cautious, and that's why it's taking so long. Although they reported that someone had hacked

into the computers operated by the main overseas contact in India, and sent a false drop notice to your local fellas. I don't suppose you know anything about that, do you....?'

'Yeah, I do. We needed to get these clowns off the island for a couple of hours so we could nick their stock of reptiles, so that seemed to be the best way. The weather's been a bit too crook lately for them to go offshore fishing.'

'Oh, okay. That clears that one up. It was reported to be a particularly neat hacking job, as a matter of interest so I know it wasn't you. You're the nearest thing to a computer illiterate that I've ever seen!'

'Gee, thanks for the vote of confidence M. In fact, it was Corrine who did the hack. So, to get back to it, we'll have to go through with the next drop, is that right?'

'I'm afraid so, Harry. We need to keep the pipeline intact for one more drop, so even though your lovely UAV video gave us the ship and crew members involved, they won't be pulled until after the next drop.'

I gave a theatrical sigh. 'OK. Thanks for bugger-all, 'M'. If I come up with a cunning plan, I'll let you know.'

'No way! If it's anything like your usual cunning plans, I don't want to know anything about it! Talk soon. Bye Harry.'

I cursed the un-caring SatPhone before putting it back in its charging holder, then updated Dell, even though she'd heard most of the conversation.

CHAPTER 31

SUNDAY, THE ISLAND, EARLY AM

Dell and I had another brew in silence, while I mentally worked on my plan. I was about to start bouncing ideas off her, when a rather more polite knock at the door turned out to be Corrine who'd had trouble sleeping as well, but for different reasons.

'All quiet?' I asked.

'Yeah! No more Darryl the Viagra stud, thank goodness! How about you?'

'Not so quiet,' I replied, and then told her about the decidedly un-friendly visit by the Foley brothers.

'They'll be back and looking for trouble!' she stated flatly when I'd finished, drawing the same conclusions Dell and I had. 'I guess your Control still wants you to go through with another rock drop?' she asked.

'Yes, she does. Although I'm not sure if the local system with the Foley boys is going to work like it did. I mean, if they're so sure Xavier's behind all this trouble with their reptile smuggling operation, I can't imagine them handing over the stones to us, plus a cut for him as well.'

Corrine grinned, briefly looking like her normal self, instead of the target of a serial killer and rapist. 'OK Big Dog, I'm sure you've worked out one of your cunning plans to deal with this problem, so what is it?'

I shared her grin. 'Well, yeah, you're right Mouse. Dell and I have been thinking that based on what the Foley's said, we really are just sitting here waiting for them to take a shot at us, so I reckon we need to go pro-active!'

'Alrighty, please explain?'

'How about this; the Foley's are expecting a drop notification in a couple of weeks, we know the collection procedure from Will's interrogation, and you know how to hack their computer. So, what if they were taken out of circulation immediately on reptile smuggling charges. The dude in India who's been co-ordinating the gem stone operation receives the correctly coded response to his notification email. Then we go out in the Foley's boat and make the collection ourselves, now we know where it is and how to do it.'

I looked at both girls, wanting their sharp minds working on finding holes in my wild plan. There were a few moments of silence before Dell shrugged.

'At first thought, it seems like it should work all right. But what are you planning to do with the Foleys?'

'I thought my mob might want them back on the mainland to face wild-life smuggling charges. It's worth $210,000 each in fines and/or 10 years in the lock-up, so I'm sure they'd like to have them in hand. Not to mention all the info they can get about the gem smuggling operation.'

Corrine gave an evil grin. 'Well, I have a better idea. Now they don't have any money to pay the fines, it'd save everyone a lot of time and money if both were accidentally hit over the head by a falling palm frond and had to be fed to some of the grey-suited gentlemen who hang around the outer reef!'

To her credit, Dell only looked faintly shocked; I eyed Corrine thoughtfully.

'Tempting Mouse, very tempting! But we'd better think things through carefully, given that 'M' didn't want to hear about my plan.'

Dell chipped in with, 'Why not ask her if she'd like the Foley's served up on a plate as well as having the next stone drop go ahead as scheduled?'

I considered that suggestion. 'Not bad. Taking it further, I guess we could offer the option of two birds in the hand, or two disappearances in the bush, so to speak, if that would be more convenient. It would seem that as the main concern of our bosses is to keep the stone pipeline going a bit longer, these dicks aren't really necessary, and their welfare is of very minor concern.'

Corrine got quite emphatic. 'Go on, Boss. Get on the blower and check in. I don't like the idea of these guys running around free while they plan a hit on us. They're a lot smarter than people think they are.'

In the face of such perfect logic, I retreated to the SatPhone and called home.

'Hello again, Harry. I hope you haven't called to lay your latest plan on me.'

'Good morning, 'M', I hope you enjoyed your breakfast too.'

'Indeed, I did, dear man. The canteen does a lovely lamb's fry and bacon. But I expect you're about to ruin that pleasure with more vexing news.'

'Gee 'M', that's a bit rough! I was about to make you an offer you couldn't refuse, but if you aren't interested, we'll just go ahead and do what we think is best.'

'That's better! I can cope with you when you're back to being a smart arse, Harry! Please go ahead with your suggestions.'

With such encouragement from my Control, I laid out our suggestions.

'Interesting! From a humanitarian standpoint, we'd like to have the Foley's back here for trial, but as you point out, it would create a lot of opportunities for smart lawyers to get them off with a wrist slap. Therefore, I'll handball that detail back to you on the spot. Our primary objective is to let another smuggled stone drop occur, before we can wrap up the whole ring. Everything else is secondary. Is that clear?'

'Got that, thanks 'M', and we'll be in touch. Bye now.'

I reported the gist of the conversation to my small crew, and predictably, it was Corrine who was in favour of a pre-emptive strike before the brothers came knocking again.

'We have three handguns with us, two PMR 30's and a Glock 32 .357 SIG retrieved from Steve, plus there's still some of your knockout spray aerosol we used to barge in at first,' I said, 'but I'd like to think more about the pre-emptive strike idea.'

'Why wait, Boss? Why give the buggers a chance?' Corrine asked.

'Yeah. You're probably right....... Okay, let's plan on paying them a visit tonight.'

Corrine beamed; Dell looked worried; while I felt we needed to cover our two bases, so I fired up the SatPhone again and called Dave on *Firebird*.

'*Yeah, mate. How's it all going?*'

'Quiet now, but we had a bit of excitement early this morning with the Foley brothers dropping in to point fingers at us for nicking their smuggling stock. They got a bit pushy, so after we pushed back, they buggered off. But we expect a return visit at some point once they've done some searching around for where their stock might have gone.'

Dave laughed, '*I'll bet the supply boat will be the first suspect! Then they'll probably think the stock in still on the island. Hopefully, they won't think the RAAF could be involved in any way.*'

'They were my thoughts as well. But as they already blame Xavier for their troubles, it just leaves Xavier's local crew in the form of us to get some answers and revenge. Therefore, at your dear girl's urging, we've decided to pay them a visit tonight to sort things out.'

'*Yeah, she would be in favour of that approach, but I agree that in these circumstances, it's the best thing to do. Can we help?*'

'Not directly at this stage. I want to keep the boat well secure, so you and Alex stay on full alert and tonight, turn the hot rail system on. I don't know if the Foley's have made the connection to the boat yet, but just in case they do, be ready. What I would like you to do is to run Jasper ashore as soon as you can, and I'll meet you at the boat ramp with the Ute. We've got guns, but Jasper is a force multiplier without the noise of a gun.'

'*No problem. I'll be on my way in a few minutes. See you then.*'

By the time I'd told the ladies about the partial change of plan, found the keys in the ignition and drove the short distance to the deserted boat ramp, Dave was waiting with my beautiful, big black cat. I copped a loud 'Merowl' and a severe licking when I cuddled him, before slipping him into the Ute in case anyone turned up.

Dave scooted back to *Firebird* while Jasper and I returned to the house, where he joyfully greeted the ladies, then inspected the house again for strange people.

'Two bad men might come here today, boy. But only attack when I say, to make sure we get the bad guys.'

As usual, he looked carefully at me while I spoke, then huffed gently when I finished, which usually indicates that he understood. I've never figured out the process by which he understood human speech, or if perhaps he did it purely at a mental level, but either way, it worked and he generally followed our instructions, even when they were quite complex.

After a late breakfast, I asked Corrine to check in with Kelly and Sandy to see what the situation was with them and Darryl.

'*All good here, so far,*' Sandy reported, '*he was a bit slow last night since we got him pissed when he got back from trying to find out what the C-130 was doing, landing on his airfield late in the day. He was very put out when the Crew Chief told him that they were part of a Combined Services security exercise and therefore he couldn't and wouldn't say any more. He was also very pissed at the sight of several armed Airforce security guards surrounding the aircraft.*'

Corrine laughed, 'That really must have upset him! Particularly being told 'No' by a Flight Sergeant! No wonder he got stuck into the booze.'

'*He hates not knowing what's going on, but he was fairly quiet during the night. The Herkie-bird's departure this morning started him ranting again, but so far, he hasn't taken his frustration out on us.*'

'Thanks Sandy. Harry and Dell had some problems with the Foley brothers in the wee small hours and we're currently planning a strike back before they decide to hit us properly. They seem to think we might have nicked their smuggled reptiles and are a bit upset.'

'Good one. That would upset them, but do be careful. Kelly says they like to act like simple fishermen, but they are much smarter than that and Jack is actually the mastermind, although he lets Will do most of the talking.'

'Yep. Harry's already across that and he said when they came here early this morning, they didn't try to pretend any longer. We'll be careful and you too.'

'Thanks Girlfriend. We'll be in touch. Cheers.'

Relieved that our second major problem on the island, the part-time serial rapist, killer, and full-time policeman, Darryl, was quiet at the moment, we tried to work out a plan for taking the fight to the Foley's.

'Why not a repeat of the info raid we made before the great reptile rescue?' Dell suggested. 'We wait until they're asleep, then Corrine does her stuff to knock them down? Then arrest them or whatever is necessary.'

I nodded. 'Yep. That's probably the easiest plan. What do you think, Mouse?'

'Yeah. So long as the buggers get to sleep at a reasonable time, that'll work.'

'Good. Then the next thing to decide is whether we terminate them or call for an aircraft to come and collect them as prisoners.'

Dell once again looked distressed at the thought of killing in cold blood. 'If we're going to knock them out, why not keep them alive to hand them over to the ACP?'

Corrine looked like she didn't care either way, so I said, 'If we can take them down without danger to ourselves, then we'll keep them sedated and call for transport off the island. But if they become too difficult, they go down.'

She accepted that and Corrine agreed with a shrug, so I mentally locked it in.

Corrine briefly went back to her unit to get the first-aid kit, while

I sat at the kitchen table and started to strip down the three guns we were taking, to clean and check them.

Jasper did as he was asked and stayed out of sight unless he had to go pee or poop, a rare luxury for him to be able to do so in real dirt, and he had a lovely time scratching and digging far more than was necessary.

We had a quiet day with no alarms or incidents, but as evening crawled over the island on schedule, dragging the shroud of darkness behind it, the Foleys decided to take action. We'd been keeping the doors locked, so the first indication of trouble was when Jasper gave a series of soft growls, which were more like deep rumbles from his belly.

'Kill the kitchen light,' I said to Dell, as Corrine grabbed the PMR 30 that had the barrel threaded for the suppressor, and scooted out of sight, 'but leave the lounge room light on. Just walk through there as though you were getting something, then come back and wait in the guest bathroom. If they try to come through the window there, shoot the first one you see.'

She nodded grimly, checked the magazine load, then tucked the other PMR 30 in the waistband of her shorts in the small of her back where her shirttails could hide it. She flicked the kitchen light off as she headed down the hallway to the lounge room at the front of the house.

Softly, I called Jasper and said, 'Bad men, boy. Let them come in the back door and then you can attack the second one in, but watch out for guns or knives. OK?'

He stopped rumbling long enough to huff quietly, as I went to the back door and silently unlocked it. I picked up the Glock 32, softly told Corrine about Jasper and where I would be, before retreating behind the refrigerator in the corner of the room, diagonally opposite the back door. I didn't expect a response and didn't get one.

Unless really necessary, I also had no intention of firing the compact Glock, with its loud .357 SIG rounds, since the sound of the powerful loads would echo over half the island. For several minutes after we were positioned, all was quiet, including Jasper who seemed to appreciate the situation. Then there was a soft squeaking as the ancient brass doorknob slowly twisted until with a loud 'click', the door sprang free.

For nearly a minute, nothing happened, which suggested the Foleys had an unexpected level of patience, but finally the door eased open to admit a dim, bulky figure. He paused just inside the door, his head scanning the room for any threat, before slowly stepping into the room, a second figure close behind.

The pair paused again, waiting to see if there would be any response, only moving further into the room when all remained quiet. I was looking as best I could for any indication of weapons being held and finally saw a glint of something in the hand of the first man. The second figure eased the door partly closed behind him, then as they stepped further into the room, I clicked my tongue off the roof of my mouth. The loud thud of Corrine's suppressed .22 magnum was almost drowned by the spine-chilling yowl of Jasper as he launched like a missile at the back of the second figure. The lead man screamed in pain and fright, dropping the object in his right hand as he clutched at his right shoulder with his left hand.

An ear shattering 'bang', apparently from the dropped gun, was followed by another shriek of pain from the first man as his own bullet hit him somewhere painful. By contrast, the second man made only a distressed groan as his right arm was crunched into pieces by Jasper's powerful jaws, and the long-bladed knife he'd held clattered to the floor. Corrine flicked the room light on, then we waited silently as Jasper released the man's arm, dodged his swinging left fist, then leapt for his throat.

There was a sickening crunching sound, a disgusting gurgling, before he dropped to the floor like a sack of garbage, Jasper's black form springing clear of the spray of red that re-decorated the kitchen table and floor.

The light also revealed that it was Jack who lay in a spreading puddle of blood, with brother Will staring horrified at the sight of what looked like a small black panther snarling loudly at him, his open mouth displaying an impressive collection of very sharp, red-stained teeth. Will was also bleeding heavily from the right shoulder and from a large chunk of muscle torn from his right calf, presumably by the errant shot from his own dropped gun.

I stepped out from behind the fridge, Corrine appeared from the pantry on the other side of the room and Dell stepped into the room from the hall; making three guns levelled at the hapless remaining Foley.

I kicked a chair in Will's direction, 'Take a seat, old mate,' I said cheerfully, 'this hasn't exactly been your best day, now has it?'

To give him his due, he managed to glare at me, before slumping painfully into the chair.

'You arsehole! Why did you have to shoot me and sic that... thing, onto Jack.'

I laughed mirthlessly, 'So are you trying to say the gun you stupidly shot yourself with, and that rather dramatic knife your dear brother was carrying, were only going to be part of a show and tell session?'

He wisely decided to shut up at that point, realising his protest was futile as well as dumb. I retrieved the gun he'd dropped, finding it was a 9mm Glock 17 with one round fired, and the knife the late Jack had dropped was a US Military KA-BAR with a razor-sharp edge. Not exactly the type of gifts one takes on a friendly visit to friends!

Corrine sat across the table from him, the suppressed PMR 30 held in a rock-steady grip and trained on his right eye.

Will eyed her off carefully, cleared his throat and in a strained voice, asked, 'And who the hell are you, Girlie?'

I was about to warn him never to call Corrine, 'Girlie', when she shot the top off his right ear.

When his screams subsided, he cried out, 'What the fuck was that for?'

She glared at him, and in a steely voice said very slowly and clearly, 'Don't ever call me Girlie!'

'Ahhh.... fuck it! What's wrong with that?'

Mildly, she said, 'it shows disrespect and I don't hold with that.'

He was silent for a few minutes, then asked plaintively, 'Any chance of someone binding up my leg, shoulder and ear?'

Dell spoke up, 'Yeah. I'll do it.'

While she was very roughly bandaging his three wounds, he asked, 'How about Jack?'

I shook my head. 'Nothing to fix I'm afraid. The pair of you should have stuck to fishing. Playing in the big leagues has been a bit beyond you both.'

He hung his head and said nothing until Dell had finished, then obviously in great pain, said, 'So what's gunna happen to me? I suppose you're gunna hand me over to that prick Xavier?'

I looked at Corrine who smiled and nodded, so I told him.

'There is no Xavier anymore! The last we saw of him was about six weeks ago, being eaten alive, slowly, piece by bloody piece, by four very large Komodo Dragons on the beach of an island in the East Indonesian Archipelago.'

A look of intense confusion momentarily chased the pain lines off his face. 'But.... Who's been messing with our bank accounts; our reptile stock and us? That had to be Xavier! He's the only one who knew about everything!'

I gave him my very best smart-arse grin and pointed to Corrine, who bowed her head, then to Dell who stopped to give a little curtsey, then at my chest.

He eyes bulged, a vein stood out on his forehead and he went bright red in the face.

'You three? Arse-holes! But how could you get all those boxes out of the shed? And where did you put them all? There were nearly 200 of the little buggers!'

'Actually, there were 185 boxes, old chap and all I can say is that they are safely off the island.'

'But… but how? I checked the manifest of the Island Trader and very little went out this time. Certainly not 185 boxes! Was there another boat I didn't see?'

'Don't worry your tiny brain about it dear chap,' I said, bunging on my British accent. 'Where you're going, that'll be the least of your problems.'

'Who are you people?' he finally got around to asking.

I smiled, but it wasn't a very nice one. 'Possibly your worst nightmare, William! Now be a good chap and behave yourself, or my associate will have to make yet another hole in your very unworthy hide.'

'But what's gunna happen to me?' he asked, panic in his voice as his brother lay almost at his feet in a pool of congealing blood.

I looked carefully at him. 'At best, you're facing a long prison sentence. At worst; you can join Jack down there on the floor. Either way, it doesn't matter to us at all. In fact option #2 is by far the easiest and cheapest for everyone except you.'

I almost grinned at the change of expression he displayed. 'No, no. Option 1 is by far the best. I'll go along with that one. Don't you worry about that! I'll be very, very good! You won't even have to lock me up!'

Corrine gave a short bark of a laugh. 'OK Boss, we've heard enough bullshit from this mutt. How about I just pop him one and we have a dual disposal trip to the outer reef after dark? Like, two for the price of one?'

At that little piece of logic, Will let go an enormous fart and very nearly crapped himself.

'Oh no… No! You don't want to do that, dear Sir. I could be very useful to you. Oh yes I can! Particularly as you don't seem to know much about the island. I can help with whatever it is that you want to do.' I pretended to carefully consider his passionate request, looked at Corrine, then Dell.

'What do you think ladies? Is it worth keeping this sack of dogshit around or shall we just be rid of him?'

Will seemed to be finally getting the message that his life was literally hanging by a thread and none of us cared whether he lived or died right now.

The acrid smell of urine filled the air as he looked pleadingly at each lady in turn.

'Oh, please dear ladies. I know I've been very bad, but I don't want to die like this! Do what you want; tie me up or whatever! I don't care what you do; just don't shoot me like this!'

Corrine finally turned away in disgust. 'Oh for God's sake. Tie him and gag him, Harry, then chuck him out the back where I can't see or hear him. What a worthless piece of snivelling shit! Maybe I'll shoot him in the morning just to get the day off to a good start, but get him out of my sight for now!'

I almost spoiled it by grinning at Corrine's superb play-acting, something she was very good at, having refined the art in the desert with some professional bad guys, let alone an amateur clown like Will Foley.

'Okay. Hands behind you, dickhead, and stand up.'

The smell of urine was almost overpowering as I slipped a set of cable ties around his ankles and another around his wrists, making sure they weren't too tight. For good measure, I tied a length of cord between his wrists and ankles, frog-marched him to the back door and pushed him out onto the grass; a softer landing than he deserved.

A quiet word in Jasper's ear ensured that his own urine wouldn't be the only smell he would be experiencing that night.

I placed a quick call to Dave to inform him that his and Alex's expired body collection services would be required yet again immediately. Then it was back into the kitchen to find the girls had done a great job of cleaning up the mess left by both brothers. Jack's remains were wrapped in several garbage bags and the floor mopped and disinfected, while all trace of Will's various leakages had been removed. The 9mm hole in the cupboard frame under the sink could be passed off as accidental damage of some description, so long as nobody went digging.

We humped Jack out to the Ute and Dell volunteered to make the run down to the jetty to meet the dinghy, while I placed another call to 'M'.

'*Good evening Harry. You've been a very busy boy today. How can I help you this time?*'

'Hi, 'M'. Yes, it has been rather busy. I have another prisoner for you in the shape of a William Foley. He has a few puncture wounds, but is not in any immediate danger of falling off the perch, should you wish to arrange transportation. I'm afraid his brother didn't fare so well and won't be available.'

'*You have been busy! I can safely say we would be delighted to have a lengthy chat with Mr Foley, so if you'd care to hold for just a few moments, I'll arrange a taxi for him.*'

'*............ Sorry for the delay, but if convenient to you, a Beech King Air 250 will arrive on Lord Howe Island at dawn to collect your prisoner. There will be an armed escort and a paramedic aboard in case further treatment is required. May I ask the nature of Mr Foley's injuries?*'

'That sounds fine, thanks 'M'. Mr Foley has a .22 magnum bullet wound in his right shoulder with the fragmented bullet still embedded, a missing top to his right ear, and a through and through right calf wound caused by a 9mm bullet. That one was accidentally self-inflicted. He's had rudimentary first-aid, but that's our limit when it comes to gunshot wounds. By morning, he'll need some decent medical attention.'

'*Oh dear. In that case, I'll add a doctor with the appropriate repair kit and supplies to the crew. Anything further?*'

'Negative, thanks 'M'. We'll talk again soon.'

SUNDAY/MONDAY, THE ISLAND

Dell returned fifteen minutes later to report the transfer had been made without curious locals wondering what was being transferred from ute to dinghy.

'Bozo out the back is having a whinge through his gag, again,' she reported with a giggle, 'and it smells like Jasper has peed on him as well. Are we going to leave him out there all night?'

I thought a moment. 'Nah! Better not. Even with Jasper there, the risk is a bit high that someone might wander in and spot him. I mean, there's no fences anywhere. We can hose him off shortly and bung him in the guest bathroom for the night with Jasper at the door.'

Both Corrine and Dell liked that idea, so after I finished my meal of toasted sandwiches with a mug of tea, I went out back. Will Foley immediately tried hard to communicate something through the gag, so after warning him about the penalty for making a noise, I called Jasper in close and removed the bundle of dirty, smelly cloth that Dell had found under the sink. It looked like it had been last used to clean the toilet!

The smell of the cloth was nearly as bad as the smell of Will in general, as Jasper had indeed drained his bladder as instructed. The first job, therefore, was to fetch the hose and rinse Will off very thoroughly. Strangely, that didn't seem to improve his mood very much, which just proves how some people can be very ungrateful!

'Bloody hell! Enough with the water. I'm nearly drowned! Please don't put that gag back in. I will be quiet, I promise.'

I stared at him for a while without saying anything. 'Maybe you will, and maybe you won't, Mr Foley, but to keep you honest, my lovely cat, Jasper, will be keeping you company all night. I can assure you that he doesn't like you one little bit!'

I had to admit that at that moment, Jasper looked anything but lovely, with Jack's blood drying around his muzzle, matting his fur and staining his fangs. Some of Will's terror might have been due to the way Jasper chose to keep his fangs on display all the time, backed up by an almost continuous rumble of displeasure issuing from deep in his chest.

I whipped my survival knife from its belt pouch, noting how he cringed as I bent over his legs. With one light stroke, the tough nylon cable tie binding his ankles parted before the razor-sharp blade.

'OK. Get up. The good news is, you can spend the night inside. The bad news is, you'll be tied to the toilet and Jasper will be sharing the room with you. You know what he can do when he's unhappy with someone, so it will be in your interest to behave.'

'What happens to me after that?'

I gave a grim smile, 'Tomorrow, you get to take an aeroplane ride. That'll be fun!'

He looked sour. 'I hate flying!'

I laughed, 'Tough! Suck it up princess, because you don't have a choice! There are some people who want to have a lengthy chat with you about all those poor reptiles you were trying to export.'

His head sagged, then lifted, 'Look. Can we do a deal? I don't want to go to jail. Jack and I had some good money in bank accounts, but I suppose you were the one who cleaned those out?'

When I nodded, he went on, 'Slick job that. Anyway, how about if I tell you where Xavier has hidden his main stash.'

I shook my head. 'I think we already found it in the safe, I'm afraid. You'll have to try a lot harder.'

He gave a mirthless laugh. 'Do you mean that hidden built-in locker? That was only a small part of it. He was a cunning bastard, was Xavier. Never did believe in keeping all his treasure in one place.'

He had my attention this time. 'How come you know so much about it, if he was so cunning?'

'Jack and I set this whole thing up; the jewels, the reptiles, all of it. We played the part of dumb fishermen to keep the peace here on the island. When we talked Xavier into using his money and contacts to get it happening, we set up a couple of different hiding places for all three of us. This house always had a variety of house-keepers, therefore Xavier didn't want to leave his main stash here, so there's another one at our place.

How about I tell you where it is, if you let me go? It'll be well worth your while, I can promise you.'

'How about you tell me anyway, and maybe I won't turn Jasper loose on you,' was my counter-offer.

He shook his head, 'No way sport. I figure I'm fucked either way, so cut me loose or no deal!'

I pretended to think, then said, 'Let me think about that. In the meantime, you stay inside under guard. I'll let you know soon.'

'Ok, but you think hard, because there's a shitload of stuff been tucked away there. It was always meant to be Xavier's retirement fund.'

At that, I dragged him upright and helped him shuffle inside where he made a dripping mess of the floors on the way to the bathroom, his faithful, furry guard close behind. I made hobbles for his ankles like I'd done with Gerry, then closed them both inside, after fetching a thick blanket for Jasper to rest on. I wasn't concerned that Will would try to pinch it off him.

By the time I got out, the girls had cleaned the floors again, so I bunged the kettle on and told them what Will had said.

'Is he telling the truth, or is it just a last-minute hope you'll let him go?' Dell wanted to know.

'I think he's telling the truth, even though the gem stash we found in the safe here is stunning, it's quite feasible he had more.'

I looked at Corrine. 'There's no way we're going to let him go, so we need to extract the location of the stash from him. How about you use your spray; we might still have some left; to knock him down, then shoot him up with that lovely Scopolamine cocktail your chemist mate brewed up?'

She grinned, pleased as usual at the chance to get one back at the bad guys. And anybody who treated innocent creatures like he and his deceased, scumbag brother deserved what they got.

'No problem, Boss. We can do that anytime.'

'Ok. Let's finish this cuppa, then do it.'

Corrine got up and fetched her kit. 'I'm done anyway, so I'll go knock him down while you relax. I'll inject him then, but it'll be some ten minutes before he's fully receptive.'

She shooed Jasper out of the room, then we heard Will make a brief exclamation. A few minutes later, she was back.

'Job's done. I propped him up on the toilet and tied a couple of towels around him so he doesn't fall off. Give it a few more minutes and we can go in and ask what you want.'

'There was a faint lingering odour of the knockout spray, but Corrine assured me it wouldn't affect us. Will was slumped in a very uncomfortable pose on the closed toilet seat, his eyes flickering open occasionally.

Corrine slapped him across the face two or three times until his eyes opened some more and partially focussed on me.

'Hi Will. Can you hear me alright?'

'Yeah. I can hear,' he mumbled, 'who are you?'

"A good friend who can help you out of a very tight spot that you're in.'

'Tight spot. Yeah, I'm in one aren't I?'

'You sure are, sport. But to help you, I need to know where Xavier has his safe at your house.'

'Ah! You mean the one in the back shed in the far corner? Cagey bugger never would tell me the combination. Said there were only some papers in it, but I'm smarter than he is. He put all the really choice stuff in there.'

'But he had some really good stuff in this house safe. What about that?'

'Yeah. It was good stuff, but the stuff in the shed he collected in the early days when we could get a lot of really rare stuff from Sri Lanka, Myanmar and Tanzania. That dried up really quickly. He hasn't added anything to that stash for years! He really loved a pretty gem I must say. Had a good eye for the best stones in the rough, too! It was a real talent he had, did Xavier. Then he went and dudded us. Big time! Rotten bastard, pinching our stuff and money like that.'

'Good man. That should let us help you. Now my lovely assistant will fix things for you.'

Corrine stepped forward, expertly slid a fine needle into the crook of his elbow, then watched as he dozed off. Between us, we untied the towels and awkwardly lowered him to the floor, where he stretched out in a sleeping posture.

'He won't remember a thing when he wakes,' she said, 'so if you want, you can knock back his offer by saying that the police want to speak to him anyway and you don't believe there is another stash.'

'Great work, Mouse. Now we have to try to find the fool thing and then crack the combination.'

'You find it, boss. I'll work out the combination.'

She had her small backpack with her, so we left Dell and Jasper to mind the sleeping prisoner and walked to the Foley house, looking just like a couple out for a stroll after a late dinner. The town was very quiet and we saw no one anyway, but there still may have been eyes on us so we played it cool. We turned in at the Foley place and went straight around the back to the recently emptied shed and turned the lights on.

The crews had done a good job and even the floor had been swept clean. There was a small workbench along the back wall with a couple of old, rusty steel lockers standing at odd angles beside it. One locker was secured with a heavily rusted padlock that gave way with just two blows from a 2-kilo engineer's hammer, allowing the doors to squeal reluctantly open. The stupidity of otherwise bright people never ceases to amaze me, for sitting in the bottom of this rusty old locker, was a small and very dusty safe, with three equally dusty cardboard cartons stacked on top.

While the safe grabbed my attention, Corrine became very excited by the three cartons. All four items had ancient cobwebs festooned across them, suggesting as Will thought, nothing had been touched in years.

With hindsight, we should have looked at these lockers when we first inspected the reptiles, but I suppose we were too pre-occupied with the creatures at the time, thereby proving the concept of 'hiding in plain sight!'

'What do you think, Mouse? Hard to crack?'

Ignoring my question, she flicked a look at me. 'Harry. Do you know what that is?'

'What's this? Trick question time? It's a fucking safe! Just what we're looking for!'

'No, no, not that! The cartons, you dill!'

I was having trouble working out her fixation on the ratty-looking cartons, covered in years of dust and mouse crap. 'Okay, I'll bite, what about the cartons?'

I think she got just a little bit exasperated with me when she said very slowly, 'Read the fuckin' label, Boss!'

I peered at the very dusty side of the top box, more or less at eye level, where there were a series of barely-readable stencilled letters and numbers that seemed vaguely familiar as I ran my eye along them.

Then a faded name leapt out at me...! 'Shit! That's Semtex!'

Corrine grinned that I finally saw what she'd picked up in the first two seconds, 'Yeah! That's what it says it is!'

She awkwardly wrestled the top carton out of the locker and dumped it on the sagging workbench. Producing a folding pocketknife, she carefully opened the top flaps, revealing a layer of orange-red, rectangular bricks, wrapped in wax-paper and stacked four to a layer. She prised one brick out, hefted it, smelled it, dug a bit further to see that there were four layers and put it back.

'Yep! A one-kilo brick of standard Semtex 1A or 10. Yummy! It's old stock; definitely produced pre-1990! We'll take all 48 kilos with us. Way too dangerous to leave it lying around; kids could start playing with it. Besides, I used some of the stuff we had. Gotta keep the stocks up; never know when we might need it.'

'Hang on, how do you know when it was made? There's no date on the packaging.'

'A couple of things. Exports of Semtex in the 1990's were pretty much uncontrolled and anyone who had the money could get some. Then there's the lack of smell. Since 1990, explosives had to have a chemical tag added which lets sniffer dogs and machines pick up the presence of the stuff. Semtex has a chemical known as EGDN added, but before 1990, they didn't have to add a tag and therefore didn't. The good thing is that this will be very hard to detect when you take it all the way to South Africa and back to Australia.'

I spent a few moments contemplating the pleasure of sailing all that way with enough high explosive sitting in the bilges to blow the arse off an ocean liner! 'OK, I'll accept that. But what about the safe? Will that be a problem?'

'You're kidding! You could open it. It's designed to look far more impressive than to be secure.'

She opened her backpack and took out a soft bag that held a small box with a pair of wires coming out of it on one side that terminated in earbuds. The other side had a magnet that she clamped to the door beside the combination lock dial. She had to wipe the dust off the dial to see the numbers before she could start.

Five minutes later, she turned the handle with great difficulty and the door creaked open. While I looked inside, she detached her gear and packed it away. Inside were what looked like two large, old-fashioned cigar boxes. With the dust wiped off the lids, they turned out to actually be cigar boxes, one slightly smaller than the other, displaying the beautiful woodworking that went with the fine cigars normally inside. The labels proclaimed the original contents to be of Cuban variety and the tiny brass latches were still in functional condition.

The smaller one held a variety of pencil detonators, as well as some of the pyrotechnic-fuse type. A bag in the bottom of the safe held a roll of safety fuse, and another of det cord. A quick look inside the larger box showed the velvet-lined interior was divided into slots where the cigars had rested, but were now filled with a varied collection of dull-looking stones of different sizes. Most were around large marble size, but I didn't take the time to look more closely as the light was poor and I didn't want to attract the notice of a wandering citizen who dropped might have in for a late beer with the Foleys.

After carting the three cartons of Semtex to the front yard, we cleared up as best we could and left, the bag and cigar boxes carefully stowed in Corrine's backpack as we made the reverse stroll back to the house. We returned in the ute, stopping only long enough for Corrine to heave the cartons into the tray, before returning to the house.

Dell let us in and reported all quiet with the prisoner. As he was restrained as well as being unconscious, we left the bathroom door open and Jasper on the folded blanket watching him.

It seemed, therefore, a good time to have a look in the big cigar box under decent light.

The first thing we noticed was that the contents were once again a selection of uncut stones, generally two of each type. For instance, there were two crystal-shaped stones the size of the top joint of my thumb, in a very pretty, deep blue colour.

Then there were two lumps of a deep purple stone that looked like rather nice quartz or amethyst. Next to them were two nicely shaped, long hexagonal crystals of a transparent, bright red stone, each as long as my thumb and looked like they'd already been cut and polished.

Two more looked like large lumps of a greenish-red stone which also looked like quartz, and strangely, seemed to change colour as I turned it in the light. Next were two lumps of a black or charcoal-coloured translucent stone which looked like nothing of any value.

Then were two lumps of a milky blue/green stone looking like badly-coloured, poor quality quartz.

Three crystalline lumps of a semi-clear, pale blue/mauve stone were the second last type, with the last two stones having a quartz-look and were a pretty, deep red with a slight brown tinge in colour.

As I placed the last two back in the box and laid the velvet cloth over the top, Dell effectively summed up our thoughts with a snort.

'What a load of rubbish! There are a couple of pretty bits of quartz in there which might look good in a display cabinet, but the value would be all of ten dollars. Maybe this is a decoy set of rocks and the good ones are somewhere else again.'

I shrugged, 'Maybe, but as far as I'm concerned, we got the good stuff last time, so this collection of rocks can be a talking point for when this is all over. I'm not chasing any more of Xavier's red, green or blue herrings! I think this is his revenge rather than his legacy!'

'Here, here,' approved Corrine, 'so we might as well get some sleep if we have to be up early to meet the aircraft.'

'Yeah. It's supposed to be here at first light, so we should be out at the airport at 05:15 or so,' I said.

'OK. It's just after 22:00 now, so I'll do the first watch until 02:00, then I'll go back to my unit. You two can handle things from there and you've got Jasper to help.'

'Yeah, that'll be good, thanks Mouse. We'll be right. We might all get back to a quiet couple of weeks before the next shipment is due.'

'Fat chance,' she and Dell laughed.

I was gently shaken awake at 02:00 by a shadowy Corrine who

reported all was well, Will was awake, but very drowsy and hurting from his various wounds. I made a mug of tea when I got up and checked on him.

He was very drowsy like Corrine said and had trouble keeping his eyes open, so I left him under Jasper's watchful eyes and sat in the kitchen poking at our new find of gems or what-ever they were, but still not making much sense out of them.

They looked more like a kid's collection of pretty rocks than anything valuable, so I put the box aside and turned my mind to the other main problem we had; namely, a policeman masquerading as a serial rapist and murderer!

CHAPTER 33

MONDAY, THE ISLAND, AM

Whichever way I planned it, my old idea of trying to catch Darryl in the act of raping and/or strangling a victim was stupid, since he could strike anywhere or anytime. I don't know how I could have possibly have even thought of such a stupid scheme!

We'd need a huge team following him 24/7 to be able to catch him about to do the dirty on some young, unsuspecting maiden, so that plan fell apart like soggy newspaper left out in a downpour.

In fact, my original weird plan for catching the rogue copper, was based on the premise that he should be taken to face legal prosecution. But now with more information flowing in, we couldn't count on anything as Darryl proved to be a cunning and evasive target.

I decided to have a talk with Corrine later that morning after we'd handed our prisoner over.

With that decision made and postponed for later action, I made an early breakfast for Jasper and myself, leafing through an old National Geographic magazine as I ate. I had decided to let Dell sleep through, so I woke her at 04:45, figuring that she'd need extra time to wake up and get ready. While that was happening, I went out and removed the three cartons of Semtex from the ute, stacking them in the carport.

Dell surprised me by getting herself abluted and dressed in about five minutes, so I had her take a look at Will and his wounds. He woke more completely this time and suffered having his dressings changed in relative silence.

'What about my offer?' he asked. 'My freedom in exchange for Xavier's stash!'

I shook my head, 'Sorry. The police say they want to talk to you about the reptile smuggling operation. So far, I haven't mentioned the gem smuggling side of things, but that will come out in due course.'

That started him off on a rant, so I tightened the hobbles and had Jasper growl at him a few times. We gagged him for the trip to the airport, just in case some locals were up and about, but the roads were deserted. We hadn't been parked long when with a soft roar, a sleek Beechcraft King Air 250 touched down lightly on the strip and stopped well before the wet end.

I drove through the gates onto the main tarmac, then let the aircraft taxi up to park close by. The pilot stayed aboard, with the right engine still running with a muted whine, but two ACP officers in uniform came down the air stair to greet me. They both called me Commander, which was a bit unfortunate as it blew my cover with Will who took in the whole exchange.

'Thanks gentlemen, but I am supposed to be undercover, in case you weren't told.'

'Oh, yes Sir. Sorry Sir,' the Sergeant said.

'OK Sergeant. Change of plan on account of your most unfortunate slip. Now the prisoner is to be kept in total isolation from this point on. Apart from the pilot, I can see two more faces peering through the windows, who I assume are the medical team. The prisoner is therefore to remain gagged, and not allowed to communicate in any way with anybody, except the ACP handlers who meet this aircraft. Definitely not the medical team, so keep him gagged. If they object to that, you have my authority to tell them to back off. In fact, I'll tell them before the prisoner is loaded.

Additionally, there will not be any obligatory phone call to lawyers or anybody else. He's in total lockdown and isolation from this point on. Is that clear?'

They both looked ashamed, 'Yessir. Sorry Sir. It will be as you say.'

To reinforce the point, I called 'M' on the spot and explained the situation.

'No problem, dear man. We're getting good at keeping your prisoners in isolation. Speaking of which, I've been asked to pass on a reminder that your Protective Custody witness will be required to be available for court appearances in about three weeks. If you can make that happen, a lot of people will be very relieved'

'Yeah, can do. No trouble with that one, but how is the situation for her? Any contracts out?'

'No contracts that we know of, although we hear that several persons are still looking. That was a stroke of genius to keep her aboard your boat.'

'Thanks 'M'. I'll be in touch and good luck with Mr Foley.'

After shutting down the connection, I climbed the air-stairs and called the medical team to me. Both doctor and nurse were young and female.

'For reasons involving an on-going criminal investigation, your patient, who is currently my prisoner, is now to be kept totally incommunicado. He is currently gagged and will remain so until after he has been passed into the custody of an ACP crew at Sydney Airport. You may treat his wounds, but administer nothing by mouth and you will not remove the gag.......'

The young lady who looked too young to have even left home, burred up, 'I don't know who you are, or think you are, but I'm the doctor and that is my patient. He'll receive the best care my nurse and I can provide. You don't have the right to tell us what to do, so get off this aircraft and let us do our job properly without amateur interference.'

I took a deep breath, thought a moment, then mentally shrugged.

Addressing the nurse, I said sternly, 'Please go forward to the cockpit and close the door. You can tell the pilot he'll be able to depart in a few minutes, although the persons-on-board numbers might be lower, not higher.'

With a frightened glance at the doctor, she complied.

'What's that bit of nonsense about?' the doctor demanded. 'You can't order my staff about like that!'

Wearily told her to shut up and listen, and as she opened her mouth to let fly again, I said in my very best pissed-off Major-Commander voice.

'One more word from you, just one, and you and your nurse will be immediately placed under arrest for obstructing a Commonwealth investigation. You will both be restrained and off-loaded into my custody, to be transported back to the mainland at some future date. The holding facilities on the island are rather primitive, I'm afraid, but 'them's the breaks' as is said in the classics. You will serve jail time for your transgressions, although your nurse may get off with severe fines.

This aircraft will depart with the prisoner and the two ACP guards, his wounds untreated, apart from the basic first-aid my colleague administered.

Now... You have ten seconds to decide if this little performance will be done exactly as I say, or you will insist on taking the high moral ground. In which case, you will be placed under immediate arrest and can watch your career sail out the window of my guest bathroom which will be your cell for the next few days or so.'

Her face had lost all colour while I'd been speaking, but she rallied briefly as she eyed me up and down, taking in the ragged shorts, stained T-shirt and bare feet.

'You can't speak to me like that and you certainly can't do anything like what you've said!'

By way of answer, I stuck my head out the door and called the Sergeant over.

'The doctor has refused to accept my orders regarding the prisoner remaining gagged. As I cannot take the risk that she will disobey you in flight and talk to the prisoner, I have no choice but to arrest her for obstruction and interference in a Commonwealth investigation, and remove her from this aircraft.

I'd be obliged if you would handcuff the prisoner and escort her off the aircraft. I'm going to see if the nurse is willing to be more co-operative. If necessary, I'll arrest the blasted pilot as well and ground the aircraft.'

The Sergeant blanched and muttered, 'Terribly sorry, Commander. All my fault.'

'Yes, it was Sergeant, but an easy slip to make. Just don't do it again. Anyway, please get on with it and get this woman off the aircraft before I really get annoyed.'

'Aye, Sir. Please come this way, madam.'

The doctor was shocked into silence as the Sergeant mumbled through her rights, then rather more expertly 'cuffed her. She tried to speak several times, but all I did was raise one finger each time and she subsided.

I knocked on the cockpit door and opened it, beckoning the nurse out and closing the door behind her. She looked around the cabin for the doctor, so I jumped straight in.

'The doctor has decided to take the high moral ground and refused to comply with my instructions. Therefore, she won't be returning to Sydney for some time.

My question to you is; are you prepared to follow my instructions regarding the treatment of the prisoner to the letter, or would you also like a no-expenses-paid holiday on Lord Howe Island?'

She looked alarmed and puzzled.

'I'm sorry. I don't understand. What's the problem and where is Dr. Turner?'

My answer was to point out at the apron, where the diminutive form of Dr. Turner stood dejectedly between the two large, uniformed ACP gents, her hands out of sight behind her back. For the first time, I noticed she was wearing hospital scrubs.

The nurse looked back at me with wide eyes.

'Is she really staying on the island?'

I nodded. 'Yep. You can stay as well, or you can do exactly as I say and return with the aircraft to the mainland. You can give the prisoner what treatment you're able to, but must not attempt to talk to him or remove his gag. Those are the terms. Yes or no? Your call.'

'What are his injuries?' she sensibly asked.

'A through-and-through gunshot wound to his calf, a piece of his ear missing due to another gunshot and a fragmented .22 bullet wound to his shoulder. Rudimentary first aid only has been administered. Can you cope with that?'

She nodded briskly, 'Sure. But I won't attempt to remove the bullet fragments. That's a job for a surgeon anyway. I'll take care of the rest. Can I give him pain-killers?'

'Injection only. Nil by mouth. Can you live with those restrictions? The ACP gents will be peering over your shoulder the whole time.'

Confidently, she replied, 'No problem, Sir. It will be as you say.'

'Excellent nurse...Bell,' I peered at her shapely left breast where a small, brass nametag dangled, 'I'll leave you to your job and thanks for your co-operation.'

To forestall any further questions, I left the aircraft, spoke briefly to the Sergeant and Constable, and as they escorted a bemused Will Foley up the steps, I gave the pilot the universal wind-up signal. The Sergeant had officiously passed over a receipt for "one male person, carrying three fresh wounds". I thought I might frame it and stick it on one of the fridges on-board!

We waited until the King Air spooled up, taxied and took off, relieved that one more little Lord Howe puzzle was out of the way, except I'd landed myself with one more. Still, that was a minor one compared to the storm brewing with dear Darryl.

I placed a call to 'M', and passed on the good and bad news. She was both pleased and dismayed about the doctor, but conceded I had little choice of action.

'She's a contract medico, so should have known the rules about sensitive prisoners. However, arresting her might have been a bit extreme, but perhaps it was the only way to get the message across. Anyway, what are you going to do with her?'

'I thought I might give her the 'in custody' bit for a few days, then send her back on a commercial flight after a severe talking to. If necessary, if she won't co-operate, I'll have to keep her here until we at least wrap up the Darryl mess, if not the last gem drop.'

'*Bloody hell, Harry. That'll mean keeping her another couple of weeks.*'

'Yeah, I know. It'll be a real pain in the bum, but what else can we do? Your solitary confinement cells must be getting a bit full by now.'

She gave her deep, throaty chuckle. '*I must say you've contributed a lot to that state, but we'll manage. If you can hold her there, or get her agreement to be quiet, that'll be better. If not, I'll send another aircraft.*'

'Thank, M. It might come to that. I'll let you know. Bye.'

MONDAY AM

All this waffle had taken time, and owners of the light aircraft who'd flown in for the weekend, were starting to turn up to check their aircraft, and looking curiously at the strange trio standing beside the battered old ute parked on the apron. To forestall any further curiosity, I bundled Dr Turner unceremoniously into the back seat, still handcuffed, but with a small backpack which the Sergeant must have grabbed off the aircraft, and headed for the house.

Naturally, she arced up as soon as we were rolling.

'What the fuck do you think you're doing? You can't hold me like this. I'm a doctor.'

I adjusted the mirror to catch her eyes.

'Please understand, that by refusing to comply with my legitimate request for secrecy, you crossed the line to being obstructive in a delicate, on-going ACP operation. Therefore, I have all the power necessary to do whatever is necessary to keep you quiet until such time as we think it safe to release you.

You brought this on yourself by being such a smart-arse and

refusing to listen. Time was running out, and you backed me into a corner. I gave you a choice of action; you chose the wrong one, so now you get to live with it, and unfortunately, so do we.'

'But.....'

'Quiet! No more until we get to the house and have a round-table to sort out what to do with you. You've become a real pain in the arse, so don't push your luck any further. For now, just shut up!'

Now we just had to wait out the next two weeks, make the gem-stone pickup, then work out what to do with our rogue cop and a stroppy doctor!

CHAPTER 34

Sometimes I think Corrine is psychic, since she was waiting for us, the kettle on and mugs laid out when we got back. Her eyes widened as Dr Turner, still handcuffed, was led in by Dell.

'Good timing, Mouse,' I said wearily, 'I needed a cuppa and we need to have a round-table chat.'

She grinned, 'I thought you might, seeing as you've been so long. And turned up with a young lady in handcuffs. I'm starting to believe Sandy's assessment is correct; you shouldn't be allowed out unless you're on a lead. I guess you need to talk about this medical-type person you've arrested and what to do about Mr Serial Rapist?'

'Yuck, yuck! Very funny. But you've got the drift. Just give me a minute to park Dr Turner in our holding cell until we can work a few things out.'

I led the doctor into the guest bathroom.

'I'm going to remove these handcuffs, but I urge you to keep quiet and don't try to break out. The window is nailed shut and the door will be locked. You have water, a toilet and are still technically under arrest. Any further resistance from you will just make things a great deal worse. You truly have created a giant problem for us and we have to find a way out of the mess without blowing everything we've worked so hard for.'

For once, she was subdued, and said, 'I don't understand what's going on, but I'm not stupid enough to realise that I've stepped into something a lot bigger than my ruffled feelings. So, I'm willing to co-operate or even help if that's any consolation. You go have your round-table, whatever that means, and I'll be a good little doctor...

for a while. But I co-operate best when I'm kept in the loop. Please bear that in mind.'

We exchanged looks, until I backed out, closing and loudly locking the door behind me.

Back in the kitchen, I called the boat and asked Dave, Alex and Bree to come ashore and walk up to the house. 'We need to have a round-table. There's an additional complication.' Dave didn't waste time asking questions, and less than ten minutes later, everyone was seated.

I brought them up to date on the morning's happenings.

'The first thing is the problem of making sure Dr Turner doesn't run away or shoot her mouth off to anybody, although as I left her, she did say that if kept informed as to what was going on, she'd co-operate or even help.'

Corrine's input was predictable. 'I guess since your mob know you've got her, we can't just dispose of her?'

Grinning, I replied, 'No, dear Mouse. That's off the agenda.'

Dell, of lightning-fast mind fame offered, 'I'd be taking her up on her offer. Let her in on the Darryl problem only. We can't afford the time to guard her for the next couple of weeks, even with Jasper's help. We've got more than enough to worry about.'

'Good point, Dell. It is a tempting option.'

Corrine spoke again, 'Ahhh...Boss. When you hear my suggestion about Darryl, you might not want an outsider present. Let's talk about that first, then discuss when to bring Dr T into the circle.'

I nodded, 'Okay, Mouse. That makes sense so let's hear it.'

She sipped her coffee. 'It's the eternal dilemma of every law-enforcer, isn't it, Harry? Waiting to get enough evidence, without waiting too long.'

Dell jumped in with, 'From the sound of that, I'd have to say the only real option left was, in military terms, a pre-emptive strike!'

Both Corrine and I beamed at her. 'Well said that lady!' I

praised. 'You've got it in one! That is the only option left, except it then becomes a vigilante assassination.'

Dell smiled back, with a tinge of sadness. 'I must be getting hardened by all this violence around me, but I tend to think that it's a case of the greatest good for the greatest number. I mean, he's the one who crossed over the line; big time. And we know what will happen when he gets into the legal system.'

Corrine chipped in, 'Yeah! Some smart-arse solicitor either gets him off on a technicality, or the Judge has an attack of the criminal rights and tells him he's been a very naughty boy. Then he's sent forth to sin no more...until next time! I, for one, have had quite enough of Mr Fitzgibbon....literally. So, no more! And don't forget both Kelly and Sandy are on the receiving end of his rages.'

I nodded soberly, 'Yes, I hadn't forgotten, and I really don't want to leave it too late. So, is everyone in favour of acting first?'

There were grim nods around the table, until Dell spoke again, 'So the real decision is when and how, isn't it?'

Corrine and I nodded, but she spoke. 'Yes, that is the decision. The 'how' is my job, but we all need to decide on the 'when', keeping in mind what Harry said about waiting too long.'

'Well said, Mouse. Dare I ask about the 'how'? Do you have something diabolical in mind? I hope!'

She grinned, 'Of course. Remember when we were in Sumbawa Besar and went to the markets while we were waiting for the police to turn up and arrest Xavier's crew?'

I looked puzzled, 'Yes. You and Jill bought those very pretty scarves. I suppose that you could take all those lovely new rocks we found, and tie them in one scarf. Then if you whacked him over the head 20 or 30 times, you might knock him out.'

She got that pained look on her face that Sandy seemed to get every time I acted the smart-arse. 'Yes Boss. Very droll, I'm sure. Anyway, if you've been paying attention, I stopped at another little stall and bought some other items, namely, two blowpipes, a supply of darts and two varieties of lethal poison.'

Dell's eyebrows crawled up into her hairline, while the memory of the market trip came flooding back to me. 'I remember now. One pipe was quite short and the other was in three-pieces, but they fitted tightly together.'

'Very good, Big Dog. Anyway, I brought the short one and some darts with me, as well as the poisons.'

I felt a manic grin start to form. 'Outstanding, Mouse! That could be the perfect answer! I've been racking my brains trying to find the best way to take him out without creating a situation which invites a heap of awkward questions. What's the poison?'

'Choice of two, Boss,' came the brisk reply. 'BTX is the short name of one, and comes from the beautiful, but deadly Poison Dart Frog. A couple of New Guinea birds also carry the venom. In very small doses, if delivered by injection, it is lethal by causing muscle paralysis and heart failure.

The other is called TTX in short and comes from Puffer fish and the Blue-Ringed octopus. Tiny amounts are lethal and after some very nasty symptoms, death is by asphyxiation and/or heart failure!'

'Oh, I love the sound of the second one, TTX is it? A bunch of nasty symptoms on the way out would suit this diabolical arsehole perfectly!'

Suffering an amateur's usual attack of conscience, Dell started looking a bit upset. 'Ahh...Guys. We're talking about taking out Kelly's husband and a serving NSW Police Officer. Suddenly I'm not so sure!'

'He didn't bother to think of the lives of the two young girls he strangled after raping and beating them badly first,' I quietly pointed out.

'Yes, but... Aren't we lowering ourselves to his level by going this way?'

'Bad argument, Girlfriend,' Corrine added. 'Try thinking of the alternative situation where he gets taken into custody and eventually stands trial. Evidence is only circumstantial, so a clever Barrister will either get him off completely, or have the charges reduced to aggravated assault. Then he'll get time off for time served and good behaviour. He could be out in as little as 5 years. Do you think a spell in prison is going to rehabilitate a psychopath like Darryl? And don't you think he's going to be looking for the people who tried to shut him down?'

Dell looked confused. 'No. I mean, I know what you're saying, but he's terribly well-connected. There'll be an investigation and an autopsy.'

Corrine shook her head, spilling masses of her beautiful, red-gold hair around her shoulders.

'His death can be investigated until the cows come home, but they won't find anything. TTX breaks down very quickly after it's done its job, so the only real danger is some do-gooder actually trying to revive the prick. Humans can survive this toxin if they receive constant CPR for many hours. It takes 12 hours or more for the bulk of the toxin to be flushed from the system and as the victim is totally paralysed all that time, CPR has to be continuous.'

'OK. That raises a couple of points for discussion. Firstly, do we clue Kelly in on what we're going to do to take him down? Because if we do, she may well disagree with killing him outright. On the other hand, if we don't tell her, she may play the part of the do-gooder and jump in trying to save him.'

The girls thought for a minute or so, then Corrine said, 'Leave that for the moment. What's your second point for discussion?'

I looked at Corrine, 'Simply this; when do we pull the pin on him? He's had three shots at you, and heaps more at Sandy and Kelly. We've got about 10 days to go before we grab the last stone drop and then our official work here is done. I believe it would be preferable to knock him off sooner, rather than just before we're due to leave. Might look a bit too suspicious since we're supposed to be keeping a low profile.'

The group nodded as they assimilated those thoughts.

Dave offered the thought that Sandy should be asked about question number one, since she was closest to Kelly and should know how she'd feel about a final solution to her misery.

'It's still only early', Corrine said, 'let's give it an hour, then I'll drop around to see if she feels like a walk around the block. You and I can meet her outside the supermarket where those tables and seats are and talk it over in peace. We can see if Darryl is coming in case he's out and about.'

Shortly after that, Corrine left for her unit, but left her bag of tricks at the house. I stowed the cigar box in the safe which still held the $2.6 million in cash and would have to be cleared through our bank in Vanuatu. That started a train of thought concerning the aftermath of this operation and I remembered to tell Dell about her appointment in three weeks in Sydney for the preliminary hearings.

She was very philosophical about the need to return to the mainland.

'Oh well. It had to come sooner or later, but I'll miss being part of your team.'

'Do you know what you want to do after all the fuss has settled?' I asked. 'Because you can join back up with us if you want. You are part of the team.'

She teared up immediately, but gave a considered answer. 'Thanks Harry, that's a kind and generous offer, but I might try to make a new life if I can. I don't know where though.' She looked around appraisingly, 'This isn't a bad part of the world for a fairly wealthy lady to settle and I don't have to worry about a job. What's going to happen to this house? We found the title papers in Xavier's name when we first came here, didn't we?'

'Yeah, we did. There's no one else to lay claim to the house, so if you really want to stay on the island, I reckon Corrine could arrange the sale paperwork transferring it to you. That way you can do as you wish and you'll always have a home on Lord Howe.'

She thought about that one, then said, 'I'll sleep on that thought, but it does sound like a plan.'

We left the subject alone after that and when the hour was up, wandered off toward the supermarket and the chat with Sandy.

They were there as promised, but a mantle of icy rage slid over me when I saw my lovely lady looking terribly tired and knocked around with bruises peeping out from under her shirt sleeves and the hem of her shorts. She didn't normally wear dark glasses, a scarf around her throat and a wide-brim sun-hat, but I knew that they traditionally provided bruise camouflage.

I hugged her gently, noticing the little winces and the way she stiffly held herself. With a supreme effort, I held my temper in check.

'We were wondering why Darryl had been fairly quiet lately, so I guess this is the reason.'

Even Sandy's voice sounded strained as she said, 'Yes, although Kelly is probably worse. He's been almost out of control the last week. He takes those Viagra pills daily and both Kelly and I can vouch for how well they work. It's twice per day for each of us! But the last few days, he's worked himself up into a state of barely-controlled rage and has to take it out on someone, and as we were closest...we copped it. Sex isn't enough for him anymore though; it has to be violence as well. He's burning himself out, so this is the end of it!

I've left Kelly in bed; she can hardly move, but he's said that he'll be back in about an hour for another round and expects us both to be ready.'

Very quietly I asked, 'What are Kelly's feelings at the moment? I didn't think you'd let it go this far!'

Sandy tried to shake her head, 'It's hard to describe his mood; it's frightening and like trying to put the pin back in a live hand grenade. I was trying to support Kelly by providing some distraction, otherwise I think he'd have killed her by now. But to answer your question, she's like me. She knows he's totally lost it, so she's had enough too!'

'OK. So, if he were to have an accident, would Kelly be too upset?'

She gave a strained laugh, 'Hell, no! She reckons any crap which lands on him, he deserves! What have you planned?'

I told her that we had a plan, but hadn't been sure when to launch it.

She gave the first genuine smile that morning, 'Now would be a really good time to launch it, please, my darling man?'

CHAPTER 35

SATURDAY, THE DEMISE

While Corrine went to her unit to get a few items, Dell and I helped Sandy walk the short distance to the house. I let Dell help her get comfortable in bed, while I visited Janine in the bathroom.

She was sitting on the toilet, lid down, when I went in. 'What's happening, and I don't even know your name. What do I call you? I'm Janine Turner.'

I regarded her for a moment. 'I'm Harry Stevens, so call me Harry. You said earlier you were willing to co-operate and even help. Well, here's your chance. As things have escalated rapidly, I can now tell you that we've been investigating a criminal case involving wife-bashing, rape, attempted murder and murder. I'll give you more details later, but for now, we have one assault victim in need of treatment, and another one coming here shortly. The one here now happens to be my partner, and a Queensland Police Officer. Any assistance you can provide will be appreciated.'

To her credit, Janine didn't ask any more questions, but pointed out the door. 'Okay, Harry. Lead on. Where is she?'

I lead the way to the bedroom where Dell had helped Sandy stretch out.

'Sandy, this is Janine Turner and she's a doctor. She doesn't have much in the way of stuff with her, but she'll do what she can. Over to you Janine.'

Ten minutes later, Corrine and I left Janine and Dell to look after Sandy at our house. Jasper was in hiding with a strange person around and I told him I'd introduce him when I returned. We headed for Kelly's house, and the few people we passed on the way didn't seem to take any notice of us, apart from the usual 'Hello' and it was only a short distance to the house on the large block with the small Police Station office in front.

Corrine knew the layout of the place, and led the way as we carefully made sure Darryl hadn't returned ahead of us. Inside, the house looked fairly normal, although beds were unmade and the kitchen a bit messy, so we headed for the master bedroom where Kelly should be. She was still in bed as Sandy had said, and momentarily cringed when we entered, but then cranked up a smile from her bruised face when she recognised us.

It was distressing to see how relieved she was that it wasn't Darryl back early.

'Oh, Corrine and Harry. I'm so sorry you're seeing me like this. I suppose Sandy has told you what's been going on?'

I nodded, 'Yes. We just left her at our house with Dell and a doctor we picked up, looking after her. We've come to get you out as well.'

'Oh Harry. I can't leave. He'll be back soon and expects us both to be here. He's taking Viagra all the time now, and the rage is eating him up inside. I've never seen him this bad. He's tipped over the edge and is almost out of control. Sandy and I talked it over and thought if we could keep him just a little bit satisfied, he mightn't lash out at anybody else, which is what he really wants to do.'

'Well, he won't be lashing out at anybody else again, because we've going to try to help. However, it might be best if you weren't here. Can you walk?'

'Yes, sure. It's just painful to move at all, but nothing's broken, just bruised.'

'OK. Can you get to our place without going out the front?'

'Easy. There's access through the neighbour's yard. He's away for a few weeks.'

'Good. I'd like you to go there immediately and wait with Dell, Janine and Sandy. My cat Jasper is there and he'll look after you as well.'

A faint trace of amusement crossed her face at my last statement, but then she flicked the covers aside and swung her legs out of bed. Normally, my attention would have been drawn to the fact that she wasn't wearing any pants, just a T-shirt, and normally she would have looked terrific like that, but this wasn't normal.

Her legs were covered with bruises, some old and fading, but many others fresh and multi-hued. Most were above her knees and were right up to her hips, and when she stood, we saw they wrapped right around her bum as well.

She smiled grimly, noting where we were looking, but not minding. 'Pretty, aren't they? All the colours of the rainbow.'

She pulled her T-shirt up to show the mass of bruises across her flat stomach, with more up around her breasts. Neither her arms, nor her back had been spared, as she held the T-shirt up around her neck and turned a slow 360°.

No wonder she moved like an old lady!

I looked at Corrine. 'Have you got any Green Gold with you?'

She nodded and swung her backpack off her shoulders. Handing the small jar over, she said, 'I'll go out front and stand watch, Boss.' She then asked Kelly, 'When Darryl comes home, does he come in the front door or the kitchen?'

She looked up from the small green, glass jar in my hand, 'Oh. Normally the back door into the kitchen. Why?'

Corrine just gave her an enigmatic smile and silently disappeared.

'She's a strange girl, that one,' Kelly commented, 'but I feel a sort of bond with her, for some reason.'

'Yeah. She's good value, so long as she's on your side. She was one of my troopers in the desert.'

Enlightenment dawned. 'Oh! So, she's the one you rescued when you got shot up. What you got the award for?'

'Yeah. That's the one,' I said lightly, unscrewing the cap on the little jar.

'Sandy told me about all it. Said you don't like to talk about it for some reason. What are you going to do with that green goop?'

I grinned, 'Spread it on your sore bits, but maybe you should put most of it on. I'll do the bits you can't reach.'

She shook her head in exasperation, 'Oh, stop fucking around, Harry. That stuff is going to help; rub it in. I don't mind you seeing me like this.'

Like this was with her T-shirt still bunched up around her neck, and I must admit that even though being covered in bruises wasn't presenting her at her best, she was still a very attractive lady. So, I started at the top and worked my way down, front and back and before I even got to her belly, she was squirming a bit and I guessed that it wasn't just because I was hurting her.

'It hurts like hell when you rub it on, then the pain just seems to melt away. The bits you haven't got to yet still hurt heaps, but the rest is pain-free!'

She poked herself in a few spots which should have been agonising, without a reaction.

'It's not numb, either. That stuff's magic!'

By now I was starting to work down from her hips which was very distracting for me, particularly as Kelly was obviously starting to feel the other fun side-effect of the magical pain-reliever. Normally, when used as an analgesic, the other effect was masked by the pain, but I was putting a lot on, so some side effect was inevitable.

'Ah...Harry? I feel a bit strange. Pleasantly strange, which I certainly shouldn't under the circumstances, I might add. Is that normal with this stuff?'

I grinned and looked up from rubbing green gel onto her thighs, 'Yeah, I'm afraid so. Didn't Sandy tell you? It's a special herbal treatment we picked up in West Indonesia, which is unique to one island. It has two main effects and for you, the pain relief and healing side is the main one, but there is the other. Try to stay still while I finish down here.'

'It still feels very pleasant.'

I grinned again, and with some difficulty, kept my eyes on the job. 'You can try some once all the pain and bruising has gone, if you want. The side effect is much stronger without any pain to remove, but for now, you'll find the bruises will fade very quickly and the pain should stay away. Feeling a bit strange is the price to pay for being restored to normal.'

'Oh, no complaints either way, thank you dear Harry. To be rid of the bruises quickly, pain gone and to be feeling very pleasant as well, is like three bonuses in one!'

Finally, I was done and carefully stood up, my appearance making her giggle. 'My goodness! I hate to think how you'd react if I wasn't covered in bruises! But it does feel so much better, thank you.'

'You're welcome, but I'd like you to put some clothes on and get over to my place as quickly as you can. And don't forget to stay off the roads and out of sight as much as possible!'

She nodded, turning back to serious after a brief, light-hearted interlude. 'I will, Harry. Anyway, I just wanted to say that you should do what you have to do. This business has gone on too long and he's hurt too many people, including our lovely Sandy who has been such incredible support for me. Finish it the best and quickest way you can! Please?'

I smacked her lightly on the bare bum. 'Thanks for that. Now go!'

She pulled on loose shorts and tugged the T-shirt down, not bothering with underwear, and clutching the precious jar of green goop for Sandy, scooted out the back door and down the garden, moving almost normally.

I found Corrine in the front lounge room, keeping watch on the driveway from deep in the room where she wouldn't be visible.

'All quiet?' I asked.

She flashed a grin, 'Yeah, boss. All good here so far, and it sounded like it was good for Kelly in there with the green goop.'

'Yes, it helped a lot! Really, the perfect use for it. But getting back to business, how were you thinking of handling this?'

'As soon as we see him coming past the front office, we go to the kitchen and I'll wait in the corner behind him. Let him see you to draw his attention.'

She dug in her backpack and produced a PMR-30 pistol from *Firebird's* growing arsenal and screwed the tubular suppressor onto the muzzle which doubled the length of the gun, but more than halved the sound of a shot.

Handing it over, she said, 'Remember, he'll need to see the gun to stop him charging you. This stuff isn't instantaneous, even with the double or triple dose I'll be giving him, so it'll need at least a few minutes before paralysis sets in enough to keep him quiet. But please don't shoot him! That's very important since we can't disguise a gunshot wound afterwards! If you must fire, aim for the ceiling or something.'

When it came to the fine art of assassination, Corrine was the best I'd worked with, so I nodded dutifully and sat myself at the kitchen table, the PMR-30 close by my hand. Corrine resumed her lookout perch, passing the time by dipping the tip of the selected dart into a tiny glass vial of a thin grey paste, to apply even more of the incredibly potent TTX toxin to its tip.

'Bloody hell, Mouse. Be careful with that stuff! If it's as potent as you say, that much should drop him in his tracks!'

She shrugged, nonchalantly waving the lethal sliver of bamboo back and forth to speed the drying of the paste. 'I hope it does, so you don't have to fire a shot to stop him!'

'Yes dear, I'll be a good boy and try not to perforate the victim.'

It was another 30 minutes after that exchange when she quietly announced, 'We have ourselves a target.'

Being deep in the room, with the window shutters partly closed, allowed her to slip unseen out of the armchair and into the kitchen, where she tucked into in a corner along from the door, out of direct line of sight.

We heard humming, then the crunching of his boots in the

gravel of the carport, before the door was pushed open hard and rebounded off the cabinets with a loud crash and Darryl's stocky body filled the doorway.

As he came through the door, he called out, 'Get ready my love-lies, Daddy's home! I'm.....Who the fuck are you?' He apparently didn't recognise me, and took another couple of steps into the room.

As he paused again, Corrine seized the moment and with just a muted puffing sound, shot him in the neck with the blow dart. Darryl's head jerked with the sting, then he slapped his hand up to feel what it was, but the dart had already fallen from his neck and dropped down inside his left boot. It seemed to prick him again, for he slapped at the side of his left boot before spinning around, searching for the cause of the two stings.

'What the fuck's going on?' he bellowed, not immediately spotting Corrine who had crouched down in the corner.

He spun back to look at me, lurching to a stop when he saw a pistol with a long suppressor was pointing steadily at his right eye. That didn't stop him grabbing for his Service Glock 22 in its belt holster.

'Don't be silly, old mate,' I said calmly, but he was determined to fumble his gun out, presumably because it was bigger than mine!

So, I fired first, the ISIS suppressor muting the sound of the .22 magnum round to a loud thud. Knowing that Corrine would kick my bum if I hit him, I aimed a touch high and right, a large ceramic bowl on a shelf over his left shoulder exploding like a small bomb and showering the room with fragments.

That slowed him down enough for him to feel for the side of his neck again, looking confused, to see what had stung him, but he seemed to have trouble finding his neck and swiped at his nose instead. His mouth opened and closed a few times like a fish out of water, and it looked like he was trying to talk, but no sound came out. Then, his legs folded and quite gently, he fell in a heap on the floor.

Corrine came out from her corner, carefully dug the dart out of his boot top, and stowed it in a clear plastic tube.

'That was a bit faster than I expected,' she said, poking Darryl's slumped body with her runner.

'Maybe the extra four doses of TTX you put on the dart had something to do with it,' I commented, playing the smart-arse as usual.

'Yeah. That second prick on the ankle he got accidentally would have boosted the dose a lot! Anyway, do we leave him here? He'll stay paralysed right to the end.'

I looked at the tangle of limbs that was the ex-rapist and murderer of Lord Howe. 'Someone is going to have to discover the body and I don't want it to be Kelly. Sandy probably should because she is officially staying here.'

'Will she be alright with that?' Corrine asked.

'Yes, she should be. If not, you could come calling, but Sandy finding him would be perfect.'

She shrugged, 'Sure. Whatever works.'

'How long has he got?' I asked as we very carefully dragged Darryl's totally un-responsive body so it was laid out on the lounge room floor, partly propped up against the phone table where one of the few house phones on the island resided.

She looked at her watch, 'He seemed to react very strongly to the dose, so maybe it was very big. In that case, the expected minimum time of 4 hours could be well undercut. By the look of him and how he reacted, I reckon he won't last another hour.

He might get a bit messy shortly, on account of losing muscle control of bladder and bowels and since he's already been through the sweat stage, he's well on the way.'

Disconcertingly, Darryl looked and was fully awake, although the only sign was the awareness in his eyes, and a slight movement of his chest, so I felt obliged to tell him why this was happening. Squatting down beside him. I looked into his eyes and he looked right back.

'You've been a very bad boy, Darryl, and you've really pissed off a lot of people. You might have thought it was fun to rape, beat-up and kill all those young girls over the years, but you went a bit too far when you beat up your wife, who happens to be the sister of the Prime Minister of Australia and one of our mates. Did you really think you were going to get away with that?

Your next big mistake was to beat up her guest, Sandy. She happens to be my partner, as well as a serving Queensland Police Inspector, and I take grave exception to anybody doing harm to someone who is so near and dear to me!

Oh, yes. You've been watched for quite a while. No doubt you're wondering who I am? I'm Commander Stevens, Australian Commonwealth Police, sent here officially to sort you out.'

'Now! Getting to the how part; you've been given an injection of Blue-Ringed octopus venom by the young lady you've been forcing your unwelcome attention on these past few days. Unfortunately, she also happens to be an ex-SAS sniper and was our squad assassin. The only other thing I can tell you is that there's no antidote for this very nasty toxin. It's a pity you were such a bad boy; you had it all going for you. But you had to go and destroy all those young lives and even kill two beautiful young ladies! Goodbye Darryl.'

We left him and Corrine and I methodically cleared up the broken bowl, then wiped every surface we had touched. We left Darryl where he lay and followed the back pathway Kelly had taken, leaving the doors unlocked. Four minutes later, we walked into the kitchen of the ex-Xavier house where Dell, Janine, Sandy and Kelly were sitting around the table, with Jasper watching over them in the corner. While we were gone, Kelly and Dell had introduced Janine to the Green Gold paste, and spread it on Sandy, so both ladies were gently fizzing with lovely feelings, without an aching bruise between them for now.

They were very glad to see Corrine and me, and Sandy had introduced Jasper to Janine who was surprisingly calm about my lovely big cat.

With Janine sitting with them, marvelling at the miraculous

effects of the green goop, Kelly didn't mention anything about what had happened. Sandy, on the other hand, was busting to find out.

'I have to go out in half an hour or so to check something,' I said vaguely to Sandy, 'why don't you walk with me then?'

'OK, I will.'

While we waited, Dell and I brought the ladies up to speed on the latest developments with the Foleys, leaving out the details of the two operations, but including Dell having to attend preliminary court hearings in three weeks and her decision to take-over the Xavier house if Corrine could fudge a sale agreement. We largely ignored Janine, who alternated between looking stunned and looking puzzled, letting her try to work stuff out for herself, although I did address her briefly.

'I'll explain some of this stuff later, but I can't tell all, I'm afraid.'

She gave a rare grin. 'From what I've already worked out, I don't want to hear too much more. But just one question. Will the cause of the damage to these ladies be looking to continue his work?'

I looked at her carefully, before shaking my head. 'No, he won't.'

She smiled and held up one hand. 'Enough. But unofficially, I'm glad. I see too much of this sort of thing to feel any remorse for the psychopaths who do this to innocents.'

When it came to the house transfer, Corrine didn't think that a bit of back-dating of documentation would be a serious issue.

'Dell's going to become a Lord Howe lady of leisure,' I remarked with a grin, 'and a very wealthy one at that!'

Choosing her words carefully, Kelly said, 'I wasn't aware of either of the two operations and had no idea they were so big. As his wife, if Darry knew what was going on, I would have heard something,' she said, 'so he must not have known either.'

'Quite possible,' I said, 'both Xavier and the Foleys kept under the radar as much as they could and wouldn't share information or profits if they could avoid it.'

Finally, I judged sufficient time had elapsed, and led Sandy via a few tracks and overgrown back yards to the path onto the rear of the Police Station block. On the way I gave her a brief update on what had happened.

'You don't have to see him if you don't want to,' I said, 'but we can't do anything until he's discovered officially.'

'Well, why can't I do that? I mean, I am staying here, so it would be natural for me to come back from a walk and find him. Wouldn't it?'

'Yes, it would. But wouldn't you then be tied up in the investigation? Because there will be some sort of investigation.'

'Dear Harry...you aren't thinking this through properly. From what you've told me, he's died of heart failure. You said that TTX breaks down very quickly in the body, so unless there's an autopsy immediately, there won't be anything left to see. I imagine the doctor at the hospital here is a basic MD and not a forensic pathologist, so what's there to find? Overwork, stress, heart failure, dead!

We'll go inside through the kitchen and I'll discover his body in the lounge room where he was trying to reach the telephone. Don't you touch anything and I'll phone the hospital. I can reveal that I'm a serving Queensland copper which will make things even more official and above-board. Everyone knows Kelly got knocked around occasionally, but thanks to the green goop, I can pretend I'm fine. Before the troops arrive, I'll change into something which covers the bruises better, but they'll fade quickly now with the goop.'

I gave in gracefully since she was right. 'OK. I'll just go and make sure he really is dead, then you can make the call. I'll bail out before then because I've got no official reason to be here.'

She gave me a quick kiss before I went into the lounge room, where the smell of voided bowels and bladder was very strong. A careful check for a pulse at wrist and neck revealed nothing, although to be sure, I braced my senses against the smell, knelt down and put an ear to his chest. A deathly silence was my reward, so I called Sandy to come and make the call.

I waited until she made contact with the hospital who promised to get the doctor on his way when he could. Like there wasn't any real hurry, was there? Like, are you sure he's dead?

'I'm not a doctor,' Sandy said a trifle indignantly, 'just a serving Queensland Police Inspector, and to my untrained eye, he looks dead! But what if he is still alive...just! Isn't the doctor the one to make that assessment? I think you or someone should get here ASAP!'

Apparently the mention of her official rank stirred someone into action as help was promised almost immediately.

'Are you going to be okay with all this bullshit?' I asked.

She kissed me again, 'Of course. That's what I'm trained for! Personally, I'm very glad this arsehole is gone for Kelly's sake, as well as all the young girls he won't be assaulting in the future. I just have to stick to the very simple story we talked about earlier. When you get back to the house, prime Kelly on the story and let her come back in about an hour. She's just been visiting and the shortage of phones on the island can be blamed for not being able to find her. Maybe I'll tell them where she was going to visit. That might speed things up, but remind her she'd better do a good job of acting the part of the grieving widow! But not too much, since he did beat her, so her alibi is that she was with you, Dell, Janine and Corrine all morning.'

I smiled, 'Got the message dear lady. Anyway, I'd better go before the troops arrive. I wonder who'll take over police duties seeing as the victim was the only law-enforcement official?'

'Good question. Now bugger off.'

So, I did and none too soon as before I'd even cleared the back fence, I heard doors slamming out front. Back at the Xavier house, I passed on the news firstly to Kelly, not sure how she'd take it, but she burst into a flood of tears of relief that the years of abuse and doubt were over.

'I should feel some sadness, but I don't!' she said defiantly. 'Actually, I feel free for the first time since before I married him! I don't know how to thank you, Sandy and Corrine enough.'

I passed on Sandy's advice and was reassured she would act upset, but not too much.

Janine looked puzzled again, and slightly alarmed at mention of a deceased person.

'Please hold questions for now, thanks Janine. I'll explain some more later, but for now, you'd better change out of those hospital scrubs into normal clothing. Have you got anything in that backpack?'

She nodded, 'We always carry a change of underwear and other clothes in case we get stuck by bad weather or mechanical problems. Should I change now?'

'Yes. Immediately, please. There'll be a doctor or somebody coming around to officially inform Kelly of her husband's demise. You can just be part of our crew, so please don't mention you are a doctor.'

Her eyes had a twinkle of excitement as she replied, 'OK, I can do that. Although I must say that apart from a deceased person, this is all quite exciting.'

I smiled and steered her into the adjacent bedroom to change, and approved when she returned moments later in shorts and a loose top, much like the others.

'Nearly everyone in town knew that Darryl beat me,' Kelly was saying, 'so it's expected that I won't be totally shattered by the news. Darryl's boss will send another officer out here very soon, I imagine.'

Janine asked, 'Is it correct that your ex-husband was the serving Police Officer on the island?'

Kelly nodded.

'And he's the one who bashed you and Sandy?'

'Yes again,' Kelly replied, 'which is why we need your help and silence, as it is a very complicated situation.'

Janine looked troubled, thoughts tumbling through her mind. 'May I ask how your husband died?'

I took over. 'It appears to be a heart-attack, although the island doctor will confirm that. He should be here quite soon.'

Dell was concerned about Kelly's future. 'But what happens to you when they send another officer to take over?' Dell asked. 'I mean, that's been your home!'

She shook her head, 'I don't want to go back in that house, for any reason. I certainly couldn't stay there, even overnight, but the Service will arrange to ship all my belongings back somewhere, I don't know where. I'll book into one of the guest lodges for the next few nights until all the fuss has settled and I work out what I'm going to do and where I'll go.'

I smiled at her, 'Well, for starters my dear young lady, you'll stay right here for now. We have our next....ahh, operation in less than ten days, then after that, we'll be back on the boat. After her court appearances on the mainland, Dell will be here full-time.'

Kelly smiled her lovely smile, 'Thanks Harry for that offer and I'll accept gratefully. I'd love to stay with you guys for a little while, but after that, I don't want to stay here. I'm not close to anybody here at all and there are way too many bad memories!'

I nodded understanding, 'OK. After you've received the news, you can just stay here until we leave in ten days. Tell Corrine what bits and pieces you need and she'll go around and help Sandy round up stuff. Sandy will be back here tonight as well so you'll have plenty of support.'

A wild thought popped into my head and without thinking it through, I blurted out, 'Do you like boats?'

Kelly looked surprised by my odd question. 'Boats? Sure. I love being on the water. Why?'

'Oh, just a random thought. I'll work on it.'

CHAPTER 36

MONDAY, THE ISLAND

The rest of the day was a whirl of activity and officialdom at its worst. A harried-looking doctor arrived to treat the grief-stricken widow and was quite put out to find Kelly wasn't howling her eyes out. He wasn't quite so incompetent, however, that he missed the bruises on her neck, arms and thighs which she'd deliberately left as uncovered as possible.

'I'll leave you with a few sedatives, just in case, Mrs Fitzgibbon. And ah...in case there is more information required, will you be remaining on the island for a while?'

'Thank you, Doctor. Yes, I will be staying here with my friends for about 10 days. I don't want to go back into the house, and they will clear all my gear out tomorrow. I presume the Port Macquarie LAC will be sending a replacement officer out here very soon. My husband's belongings can be sent to his sister in Brisbane. The police will have her address. I don't want any of it. The house came fully furnished, so they can have the few additional things I bought.'

The hospital clerical person who came with the doctor was busy scribbling down the last of these instructions when the doctor said, 'Very well. My condolences and please call if you have any problems.'

'Thanks for all your help, Doctor. Goodbye for now.'

As we took up our seats around the kitchen table again, I asked Kelly, 'You'll let big brother know what's happened? Not the gory details; just the fact that Darryl has died of an apparent heart attack.'

She nodded, 'Yes, but could you talk to him first? Then I can say a few words after. Would you mind?'

'Of course, I don't mind. It might work out better. But won't he expect you to go and stay with him?'

Kelly smiled, 'He might, but he also knows I'd rather walk over broken bottles than to be anywhere near that rotten, corrupt political scene. Andy seems to thrive on it, somehow.'

Out of the corner of my eye, I could see Janine filing bits of information, and figured that I would need to have a D & M session with her very shortly.

'Do you have any rello's to go and stay with for a while until you find your feet?'

'No. No one. And very few friends that I knew well enough to barge in on for an extended stay.'

'If you don't mind me asking, how are you off for money?'

She smiled grimly, 'Frankly? Bugger all! Darryl insisted on looking after all the finances, even though I've got an MBA from before I married him, he still wouldn't trust me with the books. There'll be his superannuation and a small pension, and maybe some life insurance which I think the Department takes out for all employees. It's hard to work out how much it'd be, without knowing the rest of our finances, but I know Darryl refused to take out any extra cover. He always said he had better things to spend his money on.'

'OK. Got that. But remember it will be some time before anything flows to you from the insurance companies. In the meantime, you'll stay here with us until you decide what you want to do with your life. If you want, you can even come with us when we leave. We've got quite a bit of travelling to do for a while and you might find it interesting.'

She perked up a lot when I said that. 'Do you mean, go on your boat with you? Is there room? I mean, yes! I'd love to! That sounds wonderful; what a way to forget about all this crap!'

I laughed at her barrage of questions. 'Yes, on our boat with us and yes, there's room; just. But I'm buying a bigger one and with luck, it'll be ready soon. We have to go pick it up, so that'll be a bit of a trip.'

There was a new light in her eyes that was a delight to see.

'Where is the new boat; Sydney, Brisbane,...?

I grinned, 'St Francis Bay. It's in South Africa. But we have to go to Vanuatu first and visit our bank.'

She stared, momentarily dumbfounded, 'Vanuatu to visit your bank! Then South Africa to pick up the new boat! Really...all this in your boat? Why don't you fly? Surely it'd be much quicker?'

'Yes, it would be, but circumstances dictate that we go by boat. Secondly, we're going to trade-in my existing boat. Anyway, I've not been to South Africa before, so it should be fun.'

She looked thoughtful for a few moments, then smiled. 'You're right! It would be a very interesting trip.'

Dell looked a bit glum. 'I'd love to be there too, but life rolls on. Take the offer, Kelly. I love the boating life and I'm sure that you will too!'

'Well, if you're really serious about taking me along, then yes, great! But Sandy said there are others on the boat already.'

'That's alright. There's Dave, he's Corrine's partner. They have their own boat back on the Gold Coast and came on this trip to help us out. Then there's Bree and Alex. They came to us from an operation a few months ago over in Western Australia. But don't worry about room. Everyone does jobs and fits in on *Firebird*. I just hope you don't get seasick.'

'No, I don't. Or should I say that I haven't so far.'

I smiled, 'That's a better way to put it. Oh, and I should introduce you to Jasper. He normally stays aboard with his little furry mate, but has been helping us out here.'

As I went through the introductory routine, I could see Kelly puzzling over my words as was Janine with all this extra information, but now wasn't the time to go into those sorts of explanations, so I was just happy Jasper seemed to have taken to Kelly very well.

With that all done, I asked Corrine to come back to Kelly's house with me in the ute, to get their gear. She was keen to check out of the rented unit and re-join Dave on *Firebird*, so we went to Kelly's first, where Sandy had just got rid of the last of officialdom for the day. Thankfully, a clean-up detail from the hospital had been in and removed any traces of Darryl, so the house looked and smelled quite normal.

Sandy was very pleased to see us, since some reaction was setting in, now the effects of the green goop was wearing off and some pain was sneaking back. She had kept herself busy however, by getting all her stuff together out on the patio, then selecting as much of Kelly's as she thought necessary.

While we loaded everything, Corrine called Dave on the Sat-Phone and brought him up to date, something we should have done earlier. He enthusiastically said he'd meet us at the boat ramp in 30 minutes. Next stop was back to the house to unload Sandy and both lots of gear. Then Corrine and I went to her unit block, and while she went to pack, I made peace with George and Jill Slade, the owners, by paying them an extra month's rental in cash from Xavier's safe to cover Corrine's early check-out. They quickly stopped frowning and started beaming when I flashed the bundle of Aussie notes.

Then it was straight to the boat ramp where Dave was waiting to collect his lady. Corrine didn't have much gear and they were soon motoring back to the boat. I'd decided to keep Jasper with us for now, even though we seem to have identified and dealt with all the current crop of bad guys. Then it was back to the ranch to see if the ladies were settling in, and make some urgent phone calls.

Dell had been busy and had made up the other two bedrooms and diplomatically shifted her gear into the twin-bed one, with Kelly in the other double. Until I decided what to do with Janine, she'd have to bunk in with Dell. Surprisingly, given the events of the day, the atmosphere was very relaxed and cheerful, although a judicious application of green goop had a lot to do with that.

They had planned a simple dinner of steaks on the BBQ and a

fresh salad, but I had Dell, the chief cook, hold off for a short time while I made the phone calls.

Andy was the first call, so I went through Charlie.

'Harry!' came a delighted squeal. 'How's my lovely man? Where are you? Is everything alright?'

'Slow down, Charlie. You'll get a cramp in your tongue talking like that. All is well, we're on Lord Howe and I've got Kelly here with me. I would like to talk to Andy if that's possible.'

'Well, you're in luck! He just happens to be right here in the office with me. Hang on and I'll put him on. Can I listen in too?'

I knew she would anyway, but it was polite of her to ask. 'Yeah, sure Charlie.' There were some clicks, then Andy's deep melodious voice sounded in my ear.

'Hello Harry. It's been a while. How are things with you?'

'Good, thanks Andy. But I won't keep you long. I just wanted to let you know that Kelly's problem has been resolved and there should be no additional fallout. We uncovered a lot of nasties, but that's all been put to rest and shouldn't pop up again.'

'Oh, man! That's great news. Thanks for doing that for Kelly. And if there's no chance of repercussions, that's even better! Brilliant job and I'm even further in your debt!'

I laughed, 'That's fine Andy. I'm glad to help, and to see that Kelly is going to be okay makes it worthwhile. It may take a while for her to fully get over everything, but I've prescribed a sea cruise to start the healing process, but she'll tell you about that. I just wanted to tell you the good news myself first, so I'll hand you over to little sister and we'll talk again soon.'

He laughed, 'I can certainly vouch for how effective your cruises are for relaxing! Good luck, Harry, and I'll make mention of your excellent work to your people. Cheers, my good friend.'

With that, I passed the phone to Kelly who was in tears again, but she assured Andy she was fine, they were just tears of relief it was finally over, and that she would get better. I left them to talk for a while, then ducked back into the office to give her the wrap-up signal as I needed to tell my Control, the enigmatic lady 'M', how things were going.

When Kelly was finished, I made a quick call to base, reported the latest happenings and reassured them that no fall-out was expected from Darryl's demise. I added, dryly, that it was expected there would be a marked drop in assaults on young females on Lord Howe Island.

It raised a chuckle from 'M', before I also had to reassure her we were on track to make the final gemstone pickup in just over a week, but would be bailing out straight afterwards for a genuine holiday with my crew. I even believed it myself. I mean, how could 'M' find work for us in Vanuatu or South Africa? Anyway, I terminated the call to the sound of fulsome praises ringing in my ears and the delightful smell of BBQ'd steaks in my nostrils.

I was suspicious, however, because 'M' actually promised to leave us alone for the next few months!

After the lovely meal, I asked Janine to join me in the office, leaving the others to clean up.

I started the ball rolling by saying, 'There are a lot of things you've heard which may not make a lot of sense, so rather than let you speculate too much, I'm going to tell you some of what's been going on.'

'That would be very good, thanks Harry. Many aspects of this situation sound quite alarming to my uninformed ears.'

I smiled, 'Yes. I can appreciate how it would sound, so here's what you need to know, but first, I must remind you that I've checked with the ACP and learned you've already signed the Official Secret's Act. Do you recall the ramifications of that piece of paper?'

She nodded, 'Sure. Hard to forget being threatened with up to 20 years imprisonment for flapping my gums to the wrong people.'

'Good. In that case, I shan't wave it at you any further, and can tell you what's been going on.'

I told her everything, except for the cash and gems we'd retained. Her eyes widened at the talk of precious gems, but she looked disgusted to hear of the reptile smuggling operation.

'It's hard to believe so much has been going on in such a small and beautiful place. And to find out the Prime Minister's sister was the subject of such severe domestic violence is a big surprise. I can appreciate why you couldn't tell me earlier, and I apologise for my crass rudeness yesterday. Sometimes we get so wrapped up in our own little existences, we forget there's a much bigger picture with so many others worse off than we are.'

'Thanks Janine. I appreciate that. So, based on you being bound by the Official Secrets Act, I'm quite happy for you to fly back to Sydney on the first available commercial flight. However, I must ask that you don't even tell colleagues what's happened here. Your cover story will be that there was a minor emergency which needed your immediate attention, but that's been resolved and you've returned. I hope you'll be happy to support that?'

She smiled, 'Of course, Harry. Now I know what you've been facing, I'm happy to do anything to help.'

'Great. In that case, I'll get Dell to book a seat on tomorrow's aircraft, if there's space.

TUESDAY

The next day, Sandy and I went to collect the rest of Kelly's belongings, just getting in ahead of a cleaning service organised by the Police Dept, who moved in to do a total clean of the house, including packing up all Darryl's stuff. Kelly stacked her stuff in her room at our house and seemed to settle in better with that final job done.

In the afternoon, I ran Janine out to the airport where she bid me a surprisingly affectionate farewell and wished us all luck with the remainder of the operation.

<h1 style="text-align:center">CHAPTER 37</h1>

On Wednesday, a new Senior Constable, his wife and three kids arrived on the Qantas Dash 8 service, with the bulk of their gear coming by the Island Trader supply boat next week.

The next day, Thursday, he paid a courtesy call to say hi to Kelly, and seemed a very nice guy, with a temperament well-suited to the laid-back island lifestyle. He graciously expressed his condolences, and enquired about Dell, Sandy and me. I explained that we had been looking after the house on behalf of an old friend, but as it had been sold to Dell, who was a former business associate of the previous owner, Kelly, Sandy and I were going to be leaving on the boat next week.

While I held back from presenting my official credentials, Sandy presented hers, but emphasised she was on holiday with me and not on a work assignment. That went a long way to easing any concerns he might still have had about strange goings-on, as well as satisfying his official curiosity about the house and the boat at the same time. I kept Jasper out of sight, but let Dell tell him she would be becoming a permanent resident. I managed to get across that she was very wealthy, didn't need to work to support herself and would be coming and going frequently.

I caught a few strange looks from him which showed he might suspect we knew more about some of the strange doings lately, but being officially before his time, it was past history. Provided none of it revived itself!

Then things genuinely relaxed for a while, and to give them a break from boat life, Sandy, Kelly and I moved back onto *Firebird* that afternoon, so that Bree, Alex, Dave and Corrine could stay at the house. We took Jasper with us and installed Kelly in the small cabin forward of our main one. I thought it would be a good trial to see if she had any problems with sleeping there and being on the boat in general, but she loved everything about the boat, including the irrepressible bundle of black fur called Krazy.

Jasper's little companion was delighted to have him back aboard and pestered him and Kelly endlessly to play.

'Darryl would never have animals around,' she commented, the small cat chewing busily on her finger, wincing when the needle-sharp teeth were applied a bit too vigorously.

'He always said they were a waste of time and money.'

'Perhaps that was a reflection of his attitude toward people, and why he behaved the way he did,' I ventured cautiously, still not sure how fragile her psyche was.

She gave a wan smile, 'You're probably right, Harry.'

At tea time, Sandy looked thoughtful, then said, 'Remember when we talked about the video of Jasper and the Croc that Tracy put together?'

'Yeeesss?'

She must have taken that to be encouragement. 'Well, I had the thought that while we're waiting until the next rock drop, we could get those veterinarian friends of Roger's to come and take a look at Jasper. We'd be here to make sure they behave properly.'

I gave it a few moments thought. 'Yes. That would be okay if they can come over almost straight away. Do you want to call him?'

She did so immediately and managed to catch him between consults at the hugely successful Pain Relief clinic which he and his fiancée Jill, who was an RN and his former theatre nurse, had set up on the Gold Coast. The centre was based around using the magic pain-relieving properties of the Green Gold or 'Green Goop' as many liked to call it.

It was Roger who had said he had colleagues who were animal behavioural experts and would love to study Jasper. They had been shown the video of the first croc encounter and had been pestering

Roger to chase me up for a time and place to get together with my big pussy. Sandy passed the phone across to me and we exchanged pleasantries for a few moments.

'Well, you know my terms for any inspection, Roger. Absolutely nothing invasive and no taking blood samples. They can analyse his pee and poop all they want, but that's it. I'll allow a basic physical exam and an ultrasound, but no X-rays or MRIs.'

'Ok Harry. Understood and I'll pass that on to Beth and Georgia. They are both qualified vets as well. I'll call them now and let you know when they can be there. Is next Monday the last day they can have with Jasper?'

'Absolutely the last day, mate. If they can't get here by then, they shouldn't bother because we'll be gone.'

'No problem, thanks. I'll pass it on and get back soonest. Cheers, Harry.'

I looked at Sandy and Kelly, 'Well, that's done it. It sounds like we might get two frowsy, old female professors checking Jasper over. It'll probably take them a week just to work out their schedule, let alone get here, so I don't think we'll be bothered by them. But at least we made the motions.'

Sandy shrugged, 'Yes, we tried. That'll do.'

I forgot about the calls as we spent a pleasantly quiet night, with both Sandy and Kelly in need of small applications of Green Goop on the most painful bruises, before they went to bed early.

THURSDAY

Likewise, the next day nothing was planned so the ladies could sleep in or do as much or as little as they saw fit. In fact, they both took to the foredeck trampolines to let the sun provide some natural healing, while I acted as waiter and cook. Things were quiet to the point of being boring, when the SatPhone rang at around 14:45 that afternoon. An unknown, but very pleasantly-husky female voice announced she was Georgia and in company with her colleague Beth, had just landed on the island, were at the airport, and would be obliged if I could advise when it would be convenient to visit Jasper.

Giving them ten points for their rapid response, and another ten for Georgia sounding like she was 30 instead of 70, I replied, 'If you care to wait a little bit longer, I'll come and pick you up.'

'Thank you, Mr Stevens, that would be very kind of you.'

Calling out to the girls that I was just going to pick up the two old dears, I stayed like I was in my usual boat rig of tattered shorts and multi-holed T-shirt, the one held together with blobs of paint and patches of diesel sump oil. Unfortunately, by the time I'd puttered ashore, walked up to the house, told the others I was pinching the ute for a while, some 20-minutes had elapsed.

Trotting into the terminal, the last stragglers were just heading out to the Qantaslink Dash 8 for the return flight to the chaos of Sydney. Looking around, I couldn't see any old dears at first glance, just two gorgeous young ladies in shorts and tight T-shirts sitting on a couple of Pelikan cases, with two backpacks beside them.

One of the check-in girls was still doing paperwork at the counter nearby, so I wandered over.

'Excuse me, but are there any elderly passengers from the incoming flight still here?'

'No. No elderly ones I'm afraid. Do you have their names?'

I shook my head, slightly annoyed that I hadn't got their full names and that I didn't really expect them to get here at all, let alone so quickly. 'Not their full names. Just Georgia and Beth.'

The clerk smiled pityingly at me, then glanced pointedly over my shoulder as a husky female voice spoke behind me in an amused tone, 'Mr Stevens, I presume. I think we might be your 'elderly passengers', if that's all right with you?'

It's not often that I get so totally blindsided, but this was all due to my own stupid assumptions, as I turned to face one of the girls, a tall blonde with a cheeky grin on her pretty face. Her companion stood nearly as tall, a cascade of gleaming red hair reaching down past her broad shoulders. Both were very nicely proportioned and barely in their 30s, let alone qualifying for a pension card.

The blonde stuck out her hand and still grinning, shook mine vigorously with a very firm grip. 'I'm Octogenarian Georgia Wesley and this is my slightly less elderly colleague, Beth Tremaine.

CHAPTER 38

THURSDAY, THE ISLAND

To the continued amusement of the three ladies, I gathered up my scattered wits, extracted my foot from my mouth and tried to behave like a sophisticated ACP undercover operative, and owner of the mystical cat, Jasper, perhaps should.

'Oh, fuckit! I really blew that one! So sorry ladies, welcome to Lord Howe Island and please call me Harry.'

Beth stepped around Georgia and shook hands with an equally strong grip, 'Nice save, Harry. You're almost there. Nothing like a sincere apology to make two old ladies feel welcome.'

'Yeah, fair cop. Anyway, let's get you out of here.'

Apparently, they hadn't thought to book accommodation in the rush to get to the island, but when I suggested they might like to find a place and dump their gear, they waved that sensible suggestion away and asked to see Jasper first up.

'Okay. If that's what you want. When do you fly out?'

'On Saturday afternoon,' Beth replied, 'so that's not a lot of time to try to nut out what your remarkable cat is doing. We've seen the first video, of course, but Roger mentioned that there might be several more.'

'Yes, there are more. There's one more of the same giant croc, one of a pair of Orcas and a brief one of an albatross.'

That got them very excited, so I had to remind them of the ground rules with Jasper.

'Yeah, yeah! Roger told us and we said we'd be good, but there's a whole heap of tests we'd love to do! It's such a brilliant opportunity.'

I turned on my stern Major look and stated, 'No way! Either strictly by my rules or be content with the videos. I can drop you at a lodge and let you fly out tomorrow'

It was Georgia's turn to play nice Professor. 'Sorry Harry. I'm sure Beth didn't mean to imply that we would break any of your rules, so there's no need to dump us. We're cool with whatever conditions you want to impose and are just happy we can get to see him at all.'

That sounded a lot like she was blowing smoke up my arse and I wasn't happy with their attitude, so I resolved to make sure they weren't alone with Jasper for a minute.

'On second thoughts, I'm going to take you to a lodge where you can get rooms and a top feed, but I'll wait to take you to Jasper.'

That earned me a slight frosty look from Beth. 'That sounds like you don't trust us!'

I shrugged, and said as we turned off the lagoon road for the short run up to the lodge, 'Maybe, maybe not! But I think it would be better to have you not staying with Jasper 24/7. You can have a short visit now, then more time tomorrow.'

I was inwardly amused to see Georgia elbow Beth in the ribs as the pair fell silent until I pulled up at the lodge reception, pointedly leaving the engine running.

Still looking unhappy, Beth asked, 'How far is it to where Jasper is? Like, can we walk?'

I smiled at her and pointed straight back down the road that led to the lagoon, 'Sure thing. Two hundred metres to the beach and the jetty. Head down there when you're ready.'

Beth fumed silently as she climbed out and retrieved their gear, while Georgia made one last effort to redress the situation.

'Look, Harry. We all seem to have started out badly, even though we both thought the 'elderly lady' bit was funny. We get it all the time because of the 'Professor' thing. But I can see where Beth might have given you the wrong impression about our intentions. We are serious researchers...this is our job.

We have decent grants to study animal to animal interactions, as well as animal to human interactions with particular emphasis on mental communications.

We suspect some animals communicate telepathically, but there's been no way to prove or quantify it. Until Roger told us about Jasper, that is. And the fact that it is inter-species is totally unique!

That's why we might seem rather keen to get what information we can. We've been to the States studying tame gorillas, but they've been raised to use sign language, which is great, but not our thing.'

I let her have her say, which was unusual for me, but at least she wasn't trying to bullshit me. 'Look Georgia. I understand what you want to do, but I'm really am only concerned with Jasper's well-being. He has done some remarkable things which prove beyond doubt he can communicate complex information across different species, but I cannot allow him to be put on show on a lecture tour, for instance, or to have his brain wired to see if there's something that shows on an EEG trace. Absolutely isn't going to happen.

I'll give you copies of the videos and if Jasper is willing and able to put on some sort of demonstration, that's fine. Plus, a basic, external physical examination only.

I ask you to consider the scenario where you write up articles that create intense interest in Jasper's abilities from the scientific community and the greater unwashed pubic in general.

What sort of life would Jasper or I, for that matter, have being hounded by every crackpot who thinks Jasper can cure his kid's cancer or something like that?'

She nodded, 'I understand. But it was never going to be like that! Beth gets a bit pushy and very focussed on our work, so she tends to overlook the personalities involved. I have an agreement to show you which will guarantee anonymity for you and Jasper.'

'It's alright, Georgia. To be honest, I'm regretting ever agreeing to Roger's request, but I will honour my word and allow you all the time you want with him.

But I warn you now, that it won't be me who pulls you up if you try to beak my rules. I've already spoken to Jasper about having a visit from two researchers and I've told him not to allow anything other than a basic physical examination. You do **not** want to piss him off! He can get very defensive and I don't mind telling you that on several occasions, he has attacked people who were trying to hurt me or our friends.'

She gave me a strange look, 'Are you trying to scare me, Harry? Because we've been bitten and scratched by cats before. We are vets you know.'

'No matter! I'm trying to protect you. And Beth, for that matter. Did Roger happen to mention that Jasper has killed seven men?'

She went a bit pale under her lovely tan.

'No....no! He didn't mention that. Did they get a bad infection from a claw wound?'

I barked a short, mirthless laugh, 'No they didn't get a bad infection. They died from severe blood loss caused by having their throats ripped out. It's his favourite way to off someone who's threatening me.'

That thought faded her tan completely. 'But he's totally domesticated. He shouldn't be able to do that!'

'He might be domesticated, but I've discovered that he's 90% Indonesian Jungle Cat and only 10% Chausie. Not the other way around!'

'Oh!' was the best comment she could think of at the time.

Beth returned, a sour look still on her pretty face, wearing a backpack and twirling a key on one finger.

'Okay. We have a room. Any chance of meeting the beast we've come all this way to see?'

Georgia stated making flapping motions with her hands that I took to be addressed to Beth and saying that she should belt up and lay off the sarcasm.

'What's up with you, sister? Drying your fingernails again?'

'Harry has just told me that Jasper is 90% Indonesian Jungle Cat and has a record of directed violence against anyone who threatens Harry or his family.'

Beth rudely shrugged, 'So? What's that got to do with things?'

'Because, dopey, if Jasper thinks we're pushing to hard and Harry gets upset, Jasper could turn his attention on us! That has heaps to do with us, wouldn't you agree?'

'Maybe. We've handled angry cats before.'

'Jeez! You just don't get it! But I give up. Harry, do you mind taking me to see Jasper? We can leave my bucket-mouthed colleague right here. She can spend the afternoon getting pissed.'

'Oh no you don't, Miss smart-arse Professor! 'Wither thou goest, so goest I', and all that crap!'

So Georgia scooted over almost into my lap to let Beth climb in. Of course, it's entirely possible that I let the clutch out a bit too sharply before she got the door closed, but as I was in bare feet, I found that the pedals were slippery little suckers. Anyway, the Green Goop would take care of her bruises in a day or two. Unfortunately, the small group of genuinely elderly persons just passing, didn't seem to appreciate the spray of choice University language!

The general mood of our visitors hardly improved when I parked the ute, hopped out and wandered down the beach to the jetty. By the time I'd reached the dinghy, the girls had just caught up.

'Wait up, please Harry!' Georgia panted, 'Where the hell are we going? I can't see a cat on the jetty.'

Deadpan, I replied, 'That's because he lives on my boat where I live with my lady Sandy and three other crew.'

They scanned the bobbing fleet of mostly small or open fishing boats moored across the lagoon, until Beth said, 'I suppose it's that little white catamaran way out there. It doesn't look like there'd be room for that many people plus the cat.'

Despite bristling at her sarcastic tone, I calmly replied, 'Well, of course there isn't. And there's two cats, if you recall. But with only three bunks, the other two crew have to sit up waiting their turn. But we do at least have separate buckets for male and female toilets! A bit awkward when it's rough or wet, but that's half the fun of the boating life!'

By now Beth was screwing her nose up in disgust, while Georgia was getting the feeling that I was taking the piss, big time. As we came closer to *Firebird* even Beth began to realise that the 'little white catamaran' was a bloody big, white catamaran and promptly shut up.

My yell of, 'Visitors!' brought Sandy and Kelly to the stern, with little Krazy cat prancing around on the huge daybed, chasing her short tail, excited to have fresh bodies to pounce on.

Sandy tied up the dinghy and helped the ladies onto the boarding platform, introducing herself and Kelly at the same time. I chased them up the steps, admiring Georgia's bum just ahead at my eye level.

'These ladies don't look much like those elderly Professors who you told us you were picking up, my dear,' Sandy announced sweetly, dumping me in the poo all over again. 'Are you sure you found the right ones at the airport? You do have a habit of collecting attractive ladies from the strangest places.'

'Highly amusing and thanks, sweetheart, for reminding me of that attack of foot-in-mouth disease, but we've been there and are well past it.'

She grinned and settled the girls around the cockpit table where a late afternoon tea was laid out. I noticed Georgia was doing all the talking for the pair, while Beth's eyes were wide open and roaming over what she could see of the boat from where she was sitting.

Sandy noticed it too and smoothly said, 'Forgive my manners, ladies. Please come with me and I'll give you a quick tour of *Firebird*.'

She dragged them away, prattling on like a tour guide doing the rounds. Ten minutes later, they returned, Beth looking a lot more subdued. She looked at me and said, 'I would seem to owe you an apology, Harry. I've been a bit of a bitch about this whole thing and I'm truly sorry. I know we can't start afresh, but perhaps we could at least move on from where we were.'

I shrugged, 'Okay. But my conditions still stand for all the reasons I discussed with Georgia earlier.'

'Yeah. She told me and that's cool. But where is Jasper. That small female cat bouncing around on that huge bed isn't him, although she has the most amazing set of white or silver speckles in her fur. I've never seen markings like it before.'

By way of reply, I pointed up overhead and when she looked up at the roof which covered most of the cockpit, I whistled. Immediately, the sleek, black form of my beautiful large cat, performed a perfect drop-cat on Krazy in the middle of the daybed, then spun around to look at the two strangers. He stayed sitting on the daybed where he was at the same height or better, regarding them gravely with his, 'I'm not sure if I like you' stare.

In turn I said, 'Jasper. These ladies are the ones I told you about. They want to observe you and do some very basic tests and I'd like you to behave and not bite them too much. But if they try to do something they shouldn't, you can do what you want!'

Jasper actually seemed to grin, then gave a huge yawn, very effectively displaying his gleaming white set of large fangs.

Georgia looked at me in alarm. "But Harry, you can't say that! Not if it's true what you told me earlier, and by the look of that set of very healthy teeth, it probably is.'

They both got a flat stare. 'I can and did say it, and I can assure you that Jasper knows exactly what you are allowed to do, so he'll be the judge and executioner if you go too far. It's out of my hands.'

They both looked wildly at me, then at Jasper who chose that moment to give a huge 'huff' through his nose.

'Is he sick?' asked Beth, not a trace of her former arrogance to be seen.

Sandy and I laughed, 'No way! That's his way of agreeing with me. He seems to understand my words very well.'

Georgia jumped on that statement as a way to move forward. 'I agree it does seem true, but is there any way you can prove or demonstrate it?'

'Easy. What's in your backpack?'

'Recorder, notebook, spare pens, stethoscope, small, portable ultra-sound unit and a jersey in case it gets cool later.'

'OK. Leave it undone and place it on the floor with Beth's, also undone, beside it.'

They complied, so I addressed Jasper. 'This is one of the approved tests, boy. I'd like you to find Georgia's backpack, bring out the stethoscope, then put it on the table in front of her.'

He huffed neutrally, then jumped lightly down.

'Ladies, just sit quietly and don't try to pat him.'

As my big cat stepped forward, I noticed Beth stiffen as she saw how big he really was up close. He sniffed her legs, then Georgia's, sniffed both backpacks which looked the same, then burrowed into Georgia's, coming out with her stethoscope clenched lightly in his jaws. He then reared up beside her, forepaws on the table which was an intimidating sight as he's very long, and gently placed the instrument in front of her. He then returned to his perch up on the daybed, his bright green eyes fixed unwaveringly on the ladies.

I looked at Georgia. 'Does that prove anything to you?'

Both were busy scribbling notes and muttering into voice recorders, but Georgia nodded and mumbled a most emphatic 'Yes!' Following a few quiet words from me, the next hour was taken up with a routine physical, the stethoscope being used for its intended purpose. Beth used her very compact ultra-sound scanner which displayed the signal on her iPad. Georgia took an endless series of photos of Jasper, including a very detailed series of close-ups.

Tea-time came around and Sandy invited them to stay for a feed which she and Kelly had put together, although the questioning didn't stop. They reminded me I had promised to make copies of all the other mystical encounters we had videoed, so after tea, I did just that.

Finally, well after dark, they temporarily ran dry of questions, so I ran them ashore. They wanted to walk up to the Lodge to settle down the lovely roast pork dinner, so I let Jasper have a run on the beach, Krazy cat having her smaller version by staying close to me.

I told him he'd been a good boy with the ladies and he huffed good-naturedly and nuzzled my hand. 'Just one more full day, then they fly away on Saturday', I told him, 'and we'll be leaving here soon and going on a long sea journey.'

CHAPTER 39

The girls were back bright and early in the morning in a much more relaxed mood. Sandy must have spoken to them at some stage since they already had their bikinis on and were happy to try to blend in with Sandy and Kelly who hit the foredeck trampoline early. For my part, I only had to encourage Jasper to hang with the ladies for the day, something he and Krazy would have done anyway.

I was sharing morning tea break with them on the foredeck, which was visually very pleasant, when Beth asked, 'Is there any chance Jasper might find a wild marine creature to befriend? We love the videos you copied for us, but to see an encounter live would be icing on the cake.'

I considered, 'Good question and the answer is I don't know. He hasn't come across anything of size while we've been here, which is a couple of months so far. Anyway, the way it's been happening, they find him, not the other way around.'

The day passed lazily and although our two visitors took plenty of notes, there were no wild creature encounters for them to witness. I still kept a close eye on Beth who I reckoned was itching to draw a blood sample from Jasper, but we made sure she wasn't left alone.

They said their goodbyes that night, saying they'd have a look around the island in the morning before catching the afternoon flight back to Sydney.

I don't know about the others, but I was relieved when they left the next day.

On Saturday, when we went to the house to catch up on things, we found Corrine had received an urgent email from the Mumbai contact. He'd told her the drop was re-scheduled for tomorrow night, Sunday, and hoped we could be ready. There had been some suspicious police activity along the pipeline, so the suppliers were nervous and wanted to get rid of the latest lot of gems as quickly as possible.

During the afternoon, Dave, Alex and I picked up the Foley's boat from their front yard and brought it to Dell's house. I had Corrine produce a very convincing piece of paper that transferred the ownership of the boat to me. We also applied, officially, to the NSW Roads & Maritime Services for a registration transfer.

At the house, we checked the boat over carefully, especially the twin outboards and their fuel systems. A full flush of the fuel tanks and lines, as well as a change of spark plugs went a long way to easing my concerns about going offshore at night in an unfamiliar boat. We then launched it in the lagoon and went out to become more familiar with the treacherous North Passage entrance. It wasn't lit at night, but we found that the Foley's had fitted their boat with a very good chart plotter, radar and a 3D forward-looking sonar unit.

This equipment made the night passage much safer and also helped pin-point the drop site. Back at the ramp, we were satisfied the boat was reliable and we would be able to find the target ship in the dark.

Two fishermen were launching their own fishing boat as we pulled in, and one called out, 'Isn't that Will's boat?'

'Yeah, mate. It was. But he and Jack are buying a new one over on the mainland, so they sold me this one. They'll be back in a couple of weeks.'

'Well, bugger me!' exclaimed one. 'I never thought they'd sell that boat. They had it set up just the way they wanted it.'

I shrugged, 'I don't know about that, but it certainly is well setup. Anyway, Will said they were getting a new one with all the bells and whistles fitted and the old one had to go.'

'That's a turnup too! Will's too bloody tight to spend if he doesn't have to. Must've been Jack pushing for a new one!'

We parted amicably and took our newly-tested boat, firstly to the Foley house where there was a 200-litre drum of fuel with a hand pump to top the tanks, then back to the house. Corrine had been on-line again to the transport facilitator in Mumbai, answered with the correct codes, and been given co-ordinates and an RV time for tonight's drop.

We took the chart from the boat inside and went over it carefully, finding the Foleys had meticulously marked each RV point, and they were all clustered closely together.

Trip time therefore, from our previous surveillance of their operation, would be about 40 minutes from boat ramp to the RV point.

'Let's allow a full hour,' Dave suggested, 'even though the sea's quite calm.'

'Good idea. In that case, we'll leave the ramp at 21:00.'

The girls had made a roast lamb dinner with veggies and real lumpy gravy, so it was good to have everyone together again in one place, and the general mood was very happy. This in turn, helped Kelly lift her own mood and start to fit in with the crew.

We didn't have to rush, so at 21:00, we fired the motors and headed for open water.

Dave drove at a comfortable pace and it was a lovely night to be out on the water, with a half-moon hanging high overhead, casting its pale light over the gently heaving sea. Halfway there, Dave called out, 'Hey! Look at this blip on the radar near Ball's Pyramid. It seems to be moving.'

I carefully went from handhold to handhold, and peered closely at the screen of the digital pulse radar, but all I could see was the bright shape of the famous rock standing up like a giant tooth. 'Crap, Dave. There's nothing there except the rock and it hasn't moved in a few million years!'

'Very funny! Well, I know there was one and it was big. It must have gone behind the Pyramid.'

'Yeah, and maybe it was a whale breeching.'

Ball's Pyramid, the impressive tooth of bare rock which thrust up out of the sea, 16 miles SSE of Lord Howe Island, now lay directly to our south, while our course to the RV point was 10 miles due east of the north tip of the Island.

We were early to the RV, and waited with the two Yamaha 115's idling quietly. Right on schedule, a blip appeared on the radar and crawled rapidly straight toward us. The autopilot must have been turned off, since the ship adjusted course to pass within 50 metres of our tiny scrap of formed aluminium. It didn't slow down, and the three men at the stern gave a brief wave as they dropped a rectangular package overboard, a float with a pole attached to it with a rope. I fired off a series of photos with the hand-held IR camera from the *Firebird*, before we steered into the large wake left behind, then Dave turned and ran right beside the floating marker, making it easy to grab and haul everything aboard.

Our parcel was the size of two shoeboxes and was heavily wrapped in plastic, bound with copious amounts of gaffer tape. We left the area and 40 minutes later, were loading the boat on its trailer. We took the boat back to the house, figuring Dell might have need for it in the future. Will Foley certainly wouldn't!

Once again, the kitchen table did good service, as everyone wanted to see what Santa had sent to us. Kelly was especially curious, even though I'd told her what had been going on. She couldn't grasp the scope of the operation that had been happening for years under the nose of the resident police officer.

'C'mon, Harry. Stop fucking around and open the bloody thing,' my dear Sandy said, handing me the sharp carving knife. As a serving police officer, she probably should have seized the package as evidence, but in this case, my mob, the ACP, only wanted the pipeline to keep functioning this last time so they could grab the last of those involved in its operation. The Sydney end of the operation was already wrapped up, so no delivery there was needed.

Therefore, my lovely lady swapped hats to become the gemstone-loving, millionairess lady of leisure.

I slashed open the heavy wrapping to reveal, like last time, two parcels inside; one larger and one smaller. I let Sandy cut open the big one, while I operated on the smaller.

Her parcel produced a double handful of pigeon egg-shaped and sized, uncut gems, most apparently colourless, although three were a deep red. Having learned now that red diamonds were by far the rarest, I surmised that these red stones were probably fine rubies.

My smaller package contained a piece of soft cloth which was wrapped around eight smaller uncut stones, also roughly egg-shaped, but this time were a range of deep, intense colours. There was one each of blue, green, amber, purple, a steely-grey, a pale red/orange, a beautiful yellow/orange and a stunning blue/green or teal colour.

Kelly, in particular, started at the collection with a mix of wonder and disbelief.

'What happens with these, Harry? They become evidence, don't they?'

I shook my head with a smile, 'Actually, no. All previous shipments went through to the Sydney receiver and he's been rounded up with enough rocks in his safe to provide all the evidence needed. We get to keep these to swell our retirement fund.'

Her eyes widened. 'Is that for real? Surely you can't just keep these. They belong to somebody!'

I thought back to the same discussion I'd had several times, and pretty well trotted out the same answer. 'When I took the last batch of these smuggled, stolen gems in to be valued, the expert said that while he could sometimes trace each type to a region of origin, there was no way to trace any of them to a particular mine, so therefore, an actual owner cannot be identified.

Because individual miners smuggled the stones out of the

workings, there is no record of the stones anywhere. So, the question becomes; who would you turn the stones over to? Would you just pick a mine at random and hand them a stone or two?'

She thought about it for a few moments. 'So, there really is no way to trace which mine any stone came from?'

'That's right,' I replied patiently.

'Oh. Well in that case, it must be alright. Although as an ex-copper's wife, I have a final question on the subject.'

I grinned at her, having a fair idea of what she was going to say.

'As a serving ACP officer, aren't you obliged to hand over all and any stuff you acquire or confiscate?'

'As a normal ACP officer, yes. But I'm on permanent undercover assignment and tasked with maintaining a highly decadent and extravagant lifestyle as cover. There's no way the Department could afford to fund my boat and all this swanning around we do, including drinking too much! It was my boat and lifestyle which made them recruit me in the first place. Therefore, part of my deal is that I get to keep any loot I gain along the way to be used to support appearances. This new boat, for instance is going to cost over $10 mil. And that's with this one traded in! All I draw from the Department is a basic salary as a Commander. Plus, my disability pension which wouldn't feed this hungry mob for a day!'

Several raspberries were rudely blown my way, giving Kelly time to think. But then she said. 'OK. That all sounds good to me.'

'Oh, I nearly forgot,' I said in mock annoyance, 'because you officially joined the crew yesterday morning, you're entitled to a share in this haul. We usually just divide it equally amongst all persons involved in a particular operation; it's easier to work out that way, and you certainly were involved in this one.'

'But...but I didn't do anything!' she protested. 'I sat around the house all day.'

'Some of the others did too,' I said, waving around the table, 'but you were available to do something if necessary, so that's all that matters.'

She still looked unconvinced. 'You really mean that? I've got a share of all of these?' She gently poked her finger in amongst the pile of unexciting-looking rocks, but fondly touched the pretty blue/green one. 'Any idea of what they are worth?'

I shrugged, 'Not really. To realise their full worth, they need to be cut, and that costs money up front. There's also a risk the cutter will stuff up and ruin a stone. But because they are probably all exceptional stones even in the rough, and based on what has been suggested for the last collection, I'd reckon, in cut condition, you're looking at $40 to $50 million.'

Kelly was quiet for a moment then looked around the table, where everyone was smiling at her surprise. 'Oh, bullshit! You're just yanking my chain. There's no way they're worth that much! But even if they were, you wouldn't be giving away......'

'Six million, two hundred and fifty thousand dollars! Was that what you were going to say?' Dell chipped in.

'Yes...yes, exactly! You can't just give someone that sort of money!'

I drew a deep breath then smiled gently, 'What if I said that we already have ten times that amount in the bank and possibly 20 times that amount pending at auction very soon. And that's not including a stash we found a few days ago, nor including these lovely rocks in front of us. So, of course, dear lady, we can afford to give a worthy person like yourself a paltry $6.25 million.'

'You're serious, that after cutting and going to auction, I could receive up to $6.25 mil? Are there any caveats, strings, only if's or buts?'

'Nope. I discovered early on that it helps to be financially independent. Because if you can afford to do almost anything you want, you tend to do only the things that really matter to you, and not what other people say you have to, or you think you should.'

Sandy looked sideways at me. 'Back up the bus, Harry! Way too deep!' She looked at Kelly, 'Let's just call it an early Christmas present and leave it at that. Thanks mostly to Harry and several bunches of dumb bad guys, we have all made crazy amounts of money out of our last few operations. If you're going to cruise with us for a little while, it's less awkward for everyone if you've got money in the bank, so you don't feel like you're being looked after. Like we're a charity or something.'

Reality finally sank in and she broke down crying.

'I hope they're happy tears,' I commented, 'because I'd hate to see what you'd do if you scored some really decent money.'

She had to laugh through the tears, 'No, you idiot! It's just that no one has ever given me financial independence before, nor have I ever been a multi-millionaire before. For a simple ex-housewife, it's very liberating and scary at the same time. But thank you all and I'll try to pull my weight where I can.'

'Can't ask more than that,' I said.

CHAPTER 40

After the drop the night before, Bree and Alex, Sandy, Kelly and I had returned to *Firebird* since we were planning on heading for Vanuatu within a day or two. Dell had already cleared all her gear off the boat and had taken up residence in her house ashore, while Corrine and Dave decided to spend the last couple of days ashore keeping her company.

With all the tensions of the past few weeks resolved successfully, we had consumed a few too many NQ teas in celebration. I was enjoying a rare lie-in, snuggled up to my dear Sandy, with little Krazy cat kneading my back and purring loudly, when there was a loud knocking on the side of the hull across from our bed.

An equally loud, authoritative voice called out, 'Ahoy, *Firebird!* Are any of you landlubbers awake on that gin-palace? C'mon, rise and shine, motley crew! The sun's up and so should you!'

Cursing, I rolled out of bed, pulled on a pair of shorts and stumbled up top to be greeted by the sight of a large RIB with five or six uniformed sailors aboard, all grinning and amongst them three officers, two with two and a half gold stripes on their epaulettes.

It took me a moment to focus in the bright sunlight, but then I recognised Lieutenant Commander Paul Davy, skipper of the *Glenelg* patrol boat, along with the very attractive female Lieutenant Commander named Barbara Peters, his Executive Officer or simply called XO. The third officer was a Lieutenant, Clare Stahall, the boat's Weapons Officer.

I hadn't had any contact with them since the op in the Pilbara, so it was the work of moments to get them tied up and all aboard for a very happy reunion. I'd just made the rounds of everyone, when I looked out over the lagoon to see the unmistakable silhouette of the lean, grey patrol boat, HMAS *Glenelg*, anchored just out past the reef.

To my further surprise, anchored close by her was a large container ship!

When our Navy friends had met the rest of the crew, finally stirred into action by the noise, I said to Paul, 'What's with the ship? And what are you doing here?'

He laughed and let Barbara explain. 'It's all your fault again, Harry. You probably wouldn't recognise it, but that's the ship that dropped a package overboard last night. The package was picked up by two men in a 22-foot tinnie and brought back to the island. Sound familiar?'

'You mongrels! That was you hiding behind Ball's Pyramid! We saw you briefly on the radar, but then you went out of sight.'

Paul and Barbara smacked palms. 'Yep. That was us!' Paul said. 'We picked up your radar very briefly, although those new digital pulse compression units are difficult to detect. I made a bet with Barbara that you'd pick us up. Anyway, our job was to intercept the ship and sort out the bad boys in the crew. Thanks to some hi-res photos and video we'd been sent of three Asian guys tossing a package overboard, we were able to find the three and arrest them. Everyone else is screaming innocence.'

'Well, that's excellent work, Paul, but as for everyone else being innocent, that's crap! If you hadn't been lurking behind that bloody great rock, you might have seen the ship alter course to pass close beside our boat. He was just trying to make the drop as close as possible, but damn-near ran us down, so it was a manual steering job and needed at least the captain to be aware of what they were doing.'

'Ahh. That's good information, Harry. Thanks. We'll grab the skipper as well, in that case. Then we have to let the ship go. The owners are screaming already, but Interpol is settling them down with talk of massive fines or confiscation of the ship if they don't co-operate. I don't suppose you can tell me what's going on? Admiral Stallman just gave us the bare orders, although it was a very pleasant change of routine for an in-shore patrol boat to come way out here.'

I thought a moment, decided there were no security concerns with Paul, Barbara and Clare knowing the story, but I took them into the saloon, leaving the boat handlers in the cockpit to be fed fresh muffins, tea and coffee by Bree, Sandy and Kelly.

With the full attention of the Navy officers, I ran through the setup of the two smuggling operations, drawing expressions of disgust when they heard about the reptiles, and fascination to hear the details of the gem smuggling which had involved them.

'That's why we had to shadow the ship,' Barbara said, 'and that drop happened every month?'

I smiled, 'Yep! Fairly regular, usually the first Thursday and it'd been going on for several years. There were always two parcels in the one package. The big one with the select uncut stones to go to the mainland for disbursement, and the small one to stay on the island for collection by the backer of the scheme. The two fishermen who conceived the scheme in the first place and made the collections, got a percentage of the main package. Their bank accounts were bulging!'

Sharp as always, Barbara asked, 'What about the small bag contents? What happened to them?'

'Ahhh...The financier, Xavier Johnson, now deceased by the way, took the stock occasionally, but when we got to it, it had built up again.'

Clare chimed in with, 'But what are we actually talking about here Harry? I mean, I can't really get a handle on what all this fuss is about! I know precious jewels are lovely, but this seems a lot of fuss just for a few little emeralds or something.'

I looked at my dear friends thoughtfully, then went to the chart table drawer and took out the two bags from the last drop. One large and weighty; the other smaller and lighter. I resumed my seat across the dining table from them and sat the bags in front of Clare.

I poked the large bag with my finger. 'Go on. Open that one and see if it tells you what all the fuss is about.'

Suddenly nervous, she untied the white silken cord at the neck and upended the bag, spilling a clattering stream of large, but dull, crystalline rocks across the table. I could see the initial excitement fade from her eyes as she took in the lumps of pure carbon.

'Not very exciting, are they?' I asked.

Cautiously, Clare shook her head and picked up one of the larger lumps. 'No. They aren't much to look at.'

'Well, maybe it would make a difference if I told you, from what I've learned, that the one you're holding should cut to about 50 carats plus some smaller stones, and would be worth at least $9 million.'

She stared, then reverently placed the dull lump back on the table.

'Nine million! Is that Aussie or US?'

'Oh, US, of course. Which would make it about $13.5 mil Aussie.'

She recoiled in shock at the thought that she'd been handling a piece of rock so valuable, so I pushed the smaller bag at Barbara who was equally enthralled, diamonds definitely being a female thing.

Since being exposed to uncut gemstones, I had come to realise that males only think of the purchasing power of the rock, whereas females see it in cut form adorning their finger!

'Go on,' I gently urged, 'your turn. Open that one.'

She went through the motions and gingerly spilled the contents in a multi-coloured stream across the polished wood. The eight smaller, uncut and roughly egg-shaped stones were much more exciting to look at than the plain white diamonds, as they displayed a range of deep, intense colour.

Lying beside the white diamonds, the contrast was remarkable!

The coloured stones were much brighter, many with natural facets already, and without the dull, matt finish of the white diamonds, allowed the intense colour to shine through.

'I've heard that coloured diamonds are much less in value compared to whites,' she said, stirring them with a finger, 'but these certainly look beautiful.'

I chuckled, 'Perhaps they might look even better, when I say that these days, because of their rarity, the value of intense-coloured diamonds has climbed past whites and these will fetch maybe 20% more than an equivalent size white.'

Barbara picked up the unusual teal-coloured one, plus a similar size diamond from the original pile. 'Therefore, if this diamond could be worth around $13.5 mil, then this bluey green one could be worth about AU$15 mil?'

'I'd say at least that. Apparently, that is a most unusual colour, plus with the colour being so intense, it's even more valuable. They are very rare!'

The three officers sat back, bemused, but at least with some understanding of what was behind the orders sending them so far off-shore to intercept a container ship. And once again, the trigger for those orders sat grinning in front of them!

'Bloody hell, Harry!' Paul exclaimed, shaking his head in wonder. 'You really keep walking into situations, don't you?'

I was saved from making a suitable answer, when Clare made the idle comment, 'It's going to be hard to turn these lovely stones in. I know I'd find it nearly impossible.'

Being with people who'd risked their lives to help me, made it easier to say, 'Actually dear Clare, I'm not going to turn them in. Part of my deal with the ACP says that, unless needed as evidence, I get to keep any bounty I acquire, so I can support myself and the boat without drawing on ACP resources. I also need to maintain my cover.'

All three stared, but Paul spoke, 'I hope that's in writing, Harry. I'd hate to see you get caught out.'

'It's in writing, don't you worry about that!'

Barbara thoughtfully said, 'So you actually own all the rocks here, is that right?'

'Yep, that's right! Which means that if I want to, I could do this.' Reaching out, I gently pushed one of the diamonds across the table until it nudged gently up against Barbara's tanned forearm.'

She watched in silence, then said, 'What are you doing?'

'Call it a present from the team to you.'

'But....but. We aren't allowed to accept gifts from anybody.'

Paul reluctantly shook his head, 'Barbara's right, Harry. We can't take anything off confiscated boats, nor accept anything from you!'

I held up a finger. 'Wait one moment.'

I left the table and plucked the SatPhone from its cradle, dialling a number from the list sitting in the chart drawer.

'Hi Hillary, it's Harry Stevens. How are things with you?'

...'Excellent! Yes, really good, thanks. Look, is the Boss available for an update on a current operation?'

...'Good work. I know almost everything. Thanks Hillary, I'm sure he'll tell you.'

...'Good Morning, Admiral, and thanks for your time. I'll keep it brief. I'm currently on my boat at Lord Howe Island and I've got three of your best crew in front of me.'

...'Yes, they're the ones. I'm afraid I'm the one who sent those photos and video of the fellas on the container ship tossing some smuggled stolen gems over board.'

...'Yessir, sorry about that, but it's worked out very well and Commander Davy and crew have done another exemplary job and wrapped up this end of the smuggling pipeline.'

...'Oh, sorry. That's a shame they didn't tell you.'

...'Yes, I know. Orders are orders and all that. But I have brought Commander Davy, his XO and Weapons Officer up to speed on the background and I'd be happy to do the same for you, Admiral.'

...'Sure, I understand. Would tonight be a better time?'

...'Excellent! But just two quick things before you go; I want to make a small gift to Commander Davy and his crew, but he's being very official and proper about accepting lollies from strange men.'

...'Thank you. I knew you would. Now can you wave your magic wand and let him accept a very small token of our esteem for the work he did to help the cause in Western Australia all those months ago and again last night?'

...'Yes, the container ship is still anchored here. I had some further intel for the Commander which implicates the Captain, so he's going to arrest him shortly.'

...'Oh, that's wonderful, Admiral. May I tell him so?'

...'Brilliant! He'll be relieved. And just a quick final thing; I'm buying a new boat.'

...'More details tonight, Sir, but she's 80 feet long and very fast.'

...'20:00 tonight Admiral. Thank you Sir.'

I disconnected and turned to Paul with a cheesy grin on my face.

He just shook his head in disbelief. 'Oh, Harry! Only you could have twisted the Fleet Commander Australia around your little finger! You don't just call the Admiral asking for favours like that!'

I shrugged, 'Why not? We get on very well and it appears someone forgot to tell him what your operation was about, so I get to do that tonight, as well as talk sailing boats, which he loves. I think he's on the phone to our semi-secret intelligence organisation right now chewing someone's arse off. Now. About the gift thing; he's happy to waive the rule in this case given our history and the fact that it is a gift and you aren't stealing it or just helping yourselves. He only asks that you don't spread the news too widely.'

'I don't know, Harry. I'm still not comfortable with the idea, but I guess if the Admiral has okayed it, I'll go along. What did you have in mind?'

I beamed at him and called Sandy in from the cockpit where she, Bree and Kelly were being heavily chatted up by the randy boat crew.

She raised her eyebrows in query. 'Yes, dear?'

'I've just spoken with Admiral Stallman and he has given permission for Paul to accept some gifts from us in appreciation of sterling work done.'

'Excellent idea! You should have done it so much sooner.'

I turned back to Paul, 'How long are you staying?'

'Several days at least, now that you've implicated the Captain and possibly the First Officer. Probably more like a week. Why?'

'First present! The island's quiet at the moment, so we want to book a bunch of rooms at the best resort for you to rotate the crew ashore, if that suits? Say ten at a time, all expenses paid, including food and bar bills. All activities as well, whatever they want! Is that doable?'

Paul looked at Barbara, who in turn looked at Clare, and they all smiled.

'Yeah, that's doable,' Barbara said, 'but I hope the resort is prepared for a bit of mayhem. The lads and ladies are keen to let off a bit of steam after a long voyage!'

Paul took over, 'OK, thanks Harry, and you too Sandy. It'll be greatly appreciated by everybody. Now, you said this was the first present. Is this a 'but wait, there's more' moment?'

'I know the wages for sailors aren't overly generous, so we'd like to make a contribution to help. How about $5,000 per person as a bonus for jobs well done.'

Paul looked a bit uncomfortable, 'That's a very generous offer, but there's 25 crew onboard the *Glenelg* at the moment. That's a lot of cash.'

'Like $125K' said Clare, with the lightning-fast mind.

I looked at Sandy, 'Is that all? Seems like we're being too cheap!'

'Yeah, I did tell you. Bloody miser. Go on. Let the moths out!'

Paul got a bit agitated. 'No, no. Harry! Slow down! I'm not having my crew swamped with cash. Most won't know what to do with it. Half of them will just piss it up against the wall, anyway!'

'Look, Paul. We've come into legal possession of an embarrassing amount of cash. Your boss has given permission for a handout.

It's just up to you guys and us to work out how much is reasonable. Now because $10K is the limit for a single transaction in Australia without raising a red flag, I suggest the handout should be that amount. And if you want to be totally fair, everybody gets the same.'

The three officers looked at each other again.

'I won't say no, Skipper,' Clare said, 'nor will my troops.'

Reluctantly, Paul nodded. 'Alright Harry. $10K each. But that's $250,000. Are you sure that's alright?'

Sandy laughed as I pointed to a stack of cardboard cartons piled up under the chart table and more of the same were under the dining table where we sat.

'You've had your feet jammed up against cartons of cash for the last hour. Each one has $250,000 in it. To avoid embarrassing questions in Australia, we're sailing to Vanuatu soon to make a deposit in our bank. You're just helping with our ballast and space problem!'

The trio looked a bit stunned; the precious gems on the table and all the cash stacked around the cabin just a little bit overwhelming.

Paul stuck his fingers in his ears and cried out, 'La, la, la, la, la, la... I don't really want to know, Harry, but I thank you on behalf of the crew. We'll get them to thank you individually after we make the handout. That is really stunningly generous of you!'

Sandy and I smiled at them, 'Entirely our pleasure, Paul. You guys came to help us when we really needed it. This is something we can do in return.'

'Talk amongst yourselves a moment while I organise the resort.' I went back to the SatPhone, but whispered in Sandy's ear a moment. She nodded enthusiastically and went below.

'Hi. My name is Harry Stevens and I'd like to know how many rooms you would have available immediately?'

...'Yes, that's right. As of 14:00 today, shall we say. Can you have ten rooms available?'

...'No, not exactly. They are already here in fact. They're on a boat and would like to spend some time ashore in your lovely resort.'

...You're still checking? That's OK. Take your time. Oh, I forgot to say this will be an all-expenses-paid deal and will be in cash if that's alright with you?'

......Perhaps it might be best if I do just that. But you do have the rooms, is that correct?'

.....Wonderful! No problem. I'm sure we can work this out to everyone's advantage. I'll be there in twenty minutes. Cheers.'

I smiled at the Navy. 'Rooms are available at the Kentia Resort. It has an excellent restaurant, three bars, day spa and massage facilities and all the other stuff which resorts like to offer guests. I'm just going to head up there shortly to square things away with them, but you can send the first group of ten ashore just after lunch. It'll be three days per watch, if that suits your schedule, but you can have longer if you want.'

Barbara spoke for them as they stood, 'That's fantastic, Harry. You've done way too much, but thanks. The kids will love it! We will too!'

Sandy came back up, bearing three small pieces of paper, folded and taped, and handed one to each. 'Here's a small thing to remember us by. Don't lose it!'

While she did that, I pulled one of the cartons of cash out from under the chart table and carried it out to the cockpit. It was securely taped on all seams, and I gave it to the biggest of the seamen still chatting with Bree who looked slightly dazzled by the constant attention of three professional chat-up merchants!

They jumped to their feet when their officers came out, Paul's eyes bugging when he saw one sailor awkwardly holding the very heavy cash carton.

'Please be very careful with that, Mr Edwards,' he said to the puzzled sailor, 'it would be really good if it arrived back aboard in exactly the same condition as it is now. I assign it to your personal care for the duration and don't want it to leave your sight for a single second, until you deliver it to me in my cabin.'

'Aye, Sir. I can make sure of that!'

They all left, promising to come back for lunch, then Sandy and

I made ready to go ashore.

The Kentia Resort wasn't far from the boat ramp and as the name suggested, was set in grounds covered with the ubiquitous Kentia Palm. The resort itself was a sprawling arrangement where the rooms were individual huts, slightly separated from each other, linked by a covered walkway for wet weather. The central reception, dining and bar area were very open plan and cooled by sea breezes through large windows which could be folded up completely out of the way. We were greeted by the manager, Mrs Bowman, who was still trying to organise 10 rooms at very short notice.

'I hope you understand, Commander Stevens, that we are more accustomed to receiving plenty of notice of guests wanting to stay with us. I mean, they have to travel here and don't just drop in out of nowhere!'

'Of course, Mrs Bowman. We understand perfectly and are very grateful you are able to accommodate our young Naval people. They will be very grateful to have shore leave in such a lovely setting.'

Sandy dug me in the ribs, which usually means that I'm bunging it on a bit much.

Nevertheless, I carried on, 'Naturally, I would expect to pay a premium for the inconvenience and would be greatly obliged if I may leave a sum which should cover all costs involved with having one group of twelve and the other of thirteen. Each group will be staying just three nights and I wish to cover all costs incurred by the entire party of 25. That includes food and whatever drinks are consumed by the group. Oh, and add on any massage or other treatment facilities you have.

To that end, I would like to deposit the sum of $70,000 in cash to cover the account, but should more be required, you have only to call this number and I will make up the difference.'

Her eyes bugged as Sandy hefted a shopping bag onto the counter and started stacking seven bundles of banded $100 notes in front of her. She called her assistant to come and help count, but when I apologised for the inconvenience of cash, she nearly fell over herself reassuring me it was no problem at all.

And it certainly shouldn't be, I thought, already expecting to be touched up big time over the booze bill. *And I bet none of this gets written up in the books! Perhaps I should ruin her day by asking to sign the registration book!*

Finally, the cash was counted and whisked out of sight so fast, the ink nearly ran, so with exchanges of well-wishes, Sandy and I departed, confident the first watch would have beds to sleep in by 13:00, if not earlier.

Paul and Barbara were dropped off by the duty RIB at midday and were a lot more casually dressed than this morning, in shorts and colourful loose shirts. Barbara looked very attractive and full of thanks for her little 'present'. They told me Clare had drawn the short straw for Duty Officer.

'You really have done enough with the money and the resort,' Paul said, 'but thanks anyway. How big are those diamonds?'

I grinned, 'If you get them valued, you'll find they're about 5 to 6 carats and are classed as Fl or flawless, which is the highest grade possible. As such they are very rare and quite valuable.'

He gave me a funny look before asking, 'I suppose I shouldn't ask what you call 'quite valuable'?'

I shrugged. 'Ask Sandy. She hung onto a handful of the smaller ones when we turned the last lot in to be auctioned. She knows all the prices.'

Paul sidled up to Sandy who was bringing plates of tasty finger food which Bree and Kelly had whipped up. I didn't hear her answer, but Paul looked shocked and waggled his finger at me, so I smiled back. 'Enjoy, my friend. May it bring you happiness.'

'Bloody hell, Harry! That little rock will buy a very decent house; anywhere!'

'So, just do it. Or wipe out your mortgage if want to stay where you are. Just enjoy it like I do. I'm buying a new boat and I'm sure I'll enjoy that. These are opportunities, Paul, and you can either seize them with both hands, or let them float on past. Not everyone gets opportunities like these coming at them, so you aren't actually helping anybody else by letting them go! You're only hurting yourself.'

'Here. Have one of these little rolls. They're fantastic! I think Kelly's an even better cook than Bree!'

The afternoon was a great success, once Paul thought about my words and finally accepted what the sparkling little rock could do to make his life a bit easier or pleasant. He relaxed enough to have a couple of my NQ Teas, but they were wary of the hidden sting in the tail and Barbara stayed dry as a good XO should.

CHAPTER 41

MONDAY, THE ISLAND

Before we knew about the patrol boat's presence, I had planned to leave in the next day or two for our run to Vanuatu, but after discussion with the crew, we decided to delay our sailing until Thursday. I also arranged to refuel at the jetty on Tuesday.

On Sunday evening, Dave and Corrine had said they had decided not to do the run to Vanuatu as they wanted to spend some time back on their boat *Seeker*, on the Gold Coast. Accordingly, they made bookings to fly out today, Monday. For safety, Corrine left her blowpipe and darts aboard, as they planned to re-join us on our run back past Australia for the rest of the trip to South Africa.

That same night, I brought Admiral Stallman completely up to speed on the two smuggling operations, and mentioned, without giving too many details, the situation concerning Darryl. He got the message that much was left unsaid, but as it was all officially sanctioned at the highest level, he was happy.

We spent a lot more time talking about the new boat purchase and he was very keen to find out more, even looking it up on the internet.

'*Damn it, Harry! When can I get a decent trip on your boat? You promised me a cruise when we were in Western Australia.*'

I chuckled, 'I did, as I remember.' I thought quickly, then said, 'Can you take about ten days leave?'

'*Certainly, I can. No one's shooting at us at the moment, so the office is quiet. Moreover, that's why I've got the best XO in the Navy. When do I need to start and what have you got in mind?*'

'Two of our crew, Corrine and Dave, have had to go back to the mainland to sort out some business, but they'll re-join us on our way back across the top end of Aussie on the way to South Africa. They flew out this afternoon, so that leaves beds available for the run to Vanuatu and back. We'd planned to leave here Thursday. Can you make it? You can do the reverse change-over with them at Darwin.'

'Damn, that's tempting! I'd have to bring Hillary, if that's possible. Since she organises me so I can run the Navy, you can draw your own conclusions as to who actually runs the Navy! I suppose you've still got all those terribly complicated communication devices, haven't you?'

'Yessir, we have. I remember you saying you had to be available 24/7, so I can provide that. And Hillary would be very welcome. We got on very well the last time we met.'

'Yes. She always speaks highly of you. Anyway, I think she's indicating we can do it! Excellent! This is going to be a rush, but she just scribbled me a note to say we can be there tomorrow afternoon if that suits you?'

I laughed at the impetuous Rear Admiral, in charge of the entire Royal Australian Navy, but little-kid excited about taking a cruise on a sailing catamaran.

'No problem here, sir. We might have to shuffle cabins around since we have one new crew member, the ex-wife of the deceased policeman. We might put Hillary and Kelly in the stern cabin together if they don't mind, and you get your own small cabin in the bow ahead of mine. Alex and Bree already have the other queen forward cabin.'

'That's no problem for Hillary or me, thank you Commander. We'll just be happy to be aboard. And thank you again for making this happen, we'll see you tomorrow at the airport.'

TUESDAY

Starting from first thing this morning, we enjoyed the company of the whole crew of *Glenelg* who dropped by in rotation to say thanks for the resort stay and the cash, but usually ended up staying for drinks and food. Somehow, in all the excitement, I forgot to tell Paul and Barbara that their Boss was flying in.

The daily Qantas Dash 8 service arrived at 14:25 and left 30 minutes later, so I shuttled Dave and Corrine out to the airport in the ute and let them check in while I waited for the Admiral's aircraft to arrive.

There was no mistaking the muscular, stocky figure who marched down the steps, with the neat and trim figure of Hillary, daughter and secretary, close on his heels, toting two bulging briefcases.

True to form, they had minimal luggage and the Admiral had a cheerful smile as he spotted me waiting with Dave and Corrine. He and Hillary were already dressed in standard island fashion of shorts, joggers and loose shirts, although the outfit looked a lot better on Hillary than the Admiral. She'd let her hair grow a bit and it suited her pretty face.

'Hello Commander,' he said, beaming, 'great to see you again!'

'You too, Sir. And hi to you, Hillary. You're looking well.'

'Hi Harry. You too. This life seems to suit you.'

They remembered Corrine and Dave, who then had to board, so we said our goodbyes and left.

'How is the *Glenelg* tribe behaving, Commander?' the Admiral asked.

I laughed, 'As part of their care package, I took over most of a resort and Commander Davy is rotating them through one watch at a time for three days. All food and drink included and so far, all has been quiet.'

He laughed, 'Would I be correct in saying, and knowing your sense of humour, that you haven't told the Commander that I'm coming?'

I coughed, 'Ahh...I must confess Sir, in all the excitement, I did overlook that important piece of protocol!'

'Excellent! Just like a surprise inspection.'

Hillary spoke up, 'Be nice now, Dad. You are on leave.'

He chuckled, 'Yes dear daughter. I'll try to be good, but you must admit, this is fun!'

I left Dell's ute at the boat ramp for now and we motored out to *Firebird* without encountering any of the *Glenelg* crew. As the Admiral and Hillary were already familiar with the boat, they met the crew again and I showed them their quarters.

'Sorry to give you the small cabin, Admiral, but it was either here or bunk on the dining table. I think you'll agree that here is definitely more comfortable.'

'No problem. And now we're aboard, how about we drop the formality. I'm Alan and you're Harry. We can fall back to the formal stuff when other Navy personnel are around.'

'Sounds good to me, Alan. And don't worry about passing through our cabin at any time. As you probably know, modesty has to get suspended when on a boat in close company.'

'Yep. Familiar with that and no problem.'

'Now Hillary. I'm afraid you'll have to share a double bed with Kelly for the duration. She's staying with us for a while to recover from a dose of husband abuse and his death just a week ago. I won't say anymore, and leave it to her to tell you whatever she wants or needs to. We've found she's a lovely person, good crew and very well grounded. I hope you'll get on well, especially as you're sharing a bed!'

Hillary laughed, 'It'll be fine, Harry. Dad and I have had to bunk in some pretty strange places in the course of our travels. It's not always 5-star hotels, you know.'

I smiled at them both, 'Thanks Hillary. It really is good to have you both aboard and I hope you can relax for the next ten days or so.'

Alan clapped me on the back, 'We will, Harry. Count on it.'

Back up in the cockpit, I was delighted to see Paul and Clare, in very casual civvies, had dropped in and were comfortably sprawled in seats, mugs of tea and coffee on the table and both getting stuck into a large platter of Bree's fresh scones with strawberry jam and cream.

It was a real giggle to see their faces when the Rear-Admiral, Fleet Commander Australia, appeared from *Firebird's* saloon, greeting them jovially.

The pair jumped to their feet and being out of uniform, settled for coming rigidly to attention!

'Good afternoon Commander Davy and Lieutenant Stahall. Be at ease if you would. I see you've embraced the holiday atmosphere as well, and I believe you know my daughter, Hillary?'

In unison, they echoed, 'Good afternoon sir. And to you too, Hillary.'

Paul added, 'I'm afraid we weren't expecting you, sir. It would appear that Commander Stevens, with his somewhat warped sense of humour, had forgotten to pass on that bit of information!'

I made the effort to look sufficiently guilty for a few moments, before Alan said, 'Oh for heavens sake, Paul. Sit and resume eating those lovely-smelling scones. Just leave me a couple.'

'Yessir! Sitting and resuming eating. Lieutenant! Leave some for the Admiral!'

'Aye, skipper. Leaving some for the Admiral as requested.'

Alan had a good chuckle at the irreverence shown by two of his best officers.

'May I ask, sir,' Paul ventured, 'the purpose of your visit?'

He chuckled, 'No, you may not! But I'll tell you anyway. Hillary and I are on leave and about to go for a sailing cruise to Vanuatu, then to Darwin on board this lovely boat; courtesy of Harry and his crew. We flew in on the afternoon commercial flight.'

'Well, apart from being a surprise, I'm delighted to see you here, sir. It just happens that Lieutenant Stahall and I had dropped in to invite Harry and his crew ashore to the resort where Blue watch is staying, and have organised a fish BBQ for everyone. You and Hillary are more than welcome to attend. The drinks are already being served and the meal is served whenever it's ready. The boys and girls have invited all the resort staff as well, so relations with management are very cordial. So, if you'll excuse us, Admiral, we'll continue on our way and hope to see you there very soon.'

'You will, my lad, you will. I'll just get a mug of tea into me first, then we'll join you.'

'Thank you, Sir. And thank you, Harry! You got us that time!'

Their RIB boat crew fired the outboards as soon as they saw their Skipper moving and promptly whizzed them to shore.

'That was funny, Harry. However, knowing Paul, I fear that he'll pay you back one day!'

I grinned, 'Yeah, you're right there, Alan. But it was a rare moment!'

Soon after, we all headed for shore, leaving a forlorn Jasper and a perky Krazy cat in charge of the boat. I didn't feel too sorry for Jasper since he'd been busy all morning, meeting all his old friends as they dropped in to say hi and thanks.

By the time we got up the hill, the party was starting to roar, and it was obvious by her absence, that Barbara was duty officer on watch. Someone had to be the designated driver!

Determined the presence of their ultimate Boss wasn't going to dampen the party mood, Paul pressed a cocktail into the Admiral's hand and smiled with satisfaction when he downed it quite smartly, before calling for another. After a while, it was Hillary who put the brakes on the Admiral's boozing, but not until Alan had a decidedly cheery glow about him and had to be rescued from a very animated and raucous discussion with a group of younger sailors. Finally, after an excellent feed, we took a slightly wobbly Admiral back to the boat and got him settled into his small cabin. He was snoring within minutes, so Hillary and I joined the others in the cockpit for a re-introduction for her to a nightcap of a NQ tea; something she hadn't experienced for a fairly long time, but seemed to still like very much.

I was glad to see she and Kelly seemed to be very much at ease with each other, which would help make the unusual sleeping arrangements work.

The next couple of days went quickly with refuelling the boat and trips to the Co-Op store to re-stock what we could. When Alan offered to pay something to cover himself and Hillary, I pointed to the stacks of cartons under both the chart table and the saloon dining table.

'There's one under the chart table that's open, Alan. Take a look.'

He found it, then stood up, several bundles of green notes in his hands and his bushy eyebrows raised. 'How legit is this, Harry?'

'Legal spoils of war, Alan. It's written in my ACP contract. Unless it's evidence, it goes toward keeping this boat and my lifestyle intact for all to see so I can maintain my expensive cover.'

'Ahhh...' he nodded wisely, 'now I understand. Well done Harry!'

The other pleasant surprise was a lengthy phone call from Le Tromp in Amsterdam, the Netherlands, to the effect that my new boat was almost ready in the boatyard in St Francis Bay, South Africa, and was I still going to trade in the existing boat as they had several very keen potential buyers. They also wanted to know if I was still intending to sail the new one home myself. We sorted out a few other details, the most expensive of which involved changes I wanted made to the propulsion system, and ended with me agreeing to transfer another couple of million into their bank account.

At least under this drip-feed method, there wouldn't be much of a bill at the end!

Shortly after dawn, we dropped the mooring buoy and quietly motored out of the shallow lagoon via North Passage. Once clear of the hard and sharp bits, we hoisted sail, and with the Admiral on the wheel, a manic grin stitched to his face, made a very close-in speed run past the stern of *Glenelg*, letting loose with a blast of our triple trumpet airhorns.

Naturally, *Glenelg* responded with a blast of her horns that woke the town! Minutes later, we rounded Gower Island at South Head and took up a course of 043° for the southern tip of New Caledonia, 695 nautical miles away. I decided because there were some time constraints, we would maintain a cruise speed of 14 knots, regardless of conditions.

EPILOGUE

- The Captain, First Mate and three crew members of the Panama-registered container ship were arrested by Paul Davy and kept in the secure holding area aboard *Glenelg*, pending transfer to the mainland. They faced a series of charges relating to the smuggling of stolen gemstones. Harry was able to give video evidence at the trial of the five men, along with aerial UAV video of the drop itself.
- A second video of the drop was deemed too shaky and amateurish for effective use.
- Dell Petrie applied for permanent residency status on Lord Howe Island and based on various agreements and a Bill of Sale, her claim to the house formerly owned by Terry Xavier Johnson was accepted by the Lord Howe Island Administration Board. She attended preliminary Court hearings concerning the attempts to assassinate the Prime Minister. She also gave evidence against the senior administrators of the huge Union Superannuation funds, who were charged with conspiracy and misuse of public funds.

  Shortly after her evidence was given, and despite death threats being issued, Dell sought refuge back on Lord Howe Island. Several of her emails to Harry suggested that she thought life on the boat might be the only way to really stay safe, but in the meantime, she was under the protection of the close-knit community of Lord Howe.
- The body of Darryl Fitzgibbon was taken back to the mainland and cremated. His ashes were sent to his brother in Queensland. The Death Certificate listed cause of death as 'Accidental-Cardiac Arrest.'
- The various persons involved in the stolen, gemstone racket,

from the miners who found the outstanding stones in the first place, to bent supervisors and/or security guards and the various co-ordinators who sent the stones to the central dispatch point in Mumbai, India, were all rounded up and charged. The police forces of all involved countries, were encouraged to take strong action by the mine owners, who in turn were told to tighten security. The mine owners had the most to lose by not benefiting from the most valuable gems going through their own bank accounts.

- *Firebird* finally sailed from the beautiful Lord Howe Island, its crew having resolved all the problems they were originally tasked with, and a few more besides. There were few complaints though, as the liberated loot ensured that the coffers continued to swell, while they looked forward to a real holiday. With the Admiral and Hillary aboard as very welcome guests, talk tended to ignore the up-coming gem and pirate treasure auction back home. Their attention and discussion mainly focussed on the new boat, and the very long voyage from Vanuatu, across the top of Australia, the northern Indian Ocean, then down to St Francis Bay, South Africa. Naturally, the Admiral was busting to do that part of the voyage as well, so Harry simply said 'Let's wait and see how this first part works out.'

THE END

Harry Stevens, a Middle Eastern war hero, thought that recovering in Eden with his huge and mystical cat, Jasper, after his catamaran is bashed around by a storm, would be a delightful break from his sailing voyage around Australia. However, the finger of fate in the very pleasant form of an abused, runaway wife and her two lively, wilful and beautiful teenage daughters lands Harry in more trouble than he could ever imagine.

Harry's hopes for a quiet time in this beautiful and peaceful town are shattered as he learns that the psychotic, vengeful husband is pulling out all stops in an effort to locate, not just his wife, but even more so the girls for his own, much darker purposes. Suddenly on the run, Harry is forced to fall back on his natural inventiveness and SAS training to combat an increasingly resourceful foe who shows that there is truly no limit to human lust, greed, depravity and treachery.

Barely staying one step ahead of his pursuers, Harry forms some most unlikely alliances to try to defeat his many opponents with their limitless resources.

Harry Stevens, the Middle-Eastern war hero from Hitch-Hikers, the first book in the *Firebird* series, thought that having dinner at the pub and chatting up the waitress was a safe and pleasant way to pass an evening, but circumstances conspire to dump the delivery of a new super-drug as well as a large bag of bikie gang cash in his lap. Assumptions are made, confusions are leapt to, shots are fired, people are dead and Harry finds himself in the middle of a bikie gang war with both sides looking to take him out. And that's not to dinner!

Being on the hit lists of all the Outlaw Motorcycle Clubs in SE Queensland, Harry is forced to run for his life, but not before stocking up on lovely girls, rum and a few select close friends. Harry's mystical giant cat, Jasper once again proves that he's more than worth any two humans in a fight.

Harry, the floating trouble magnet, discovers that being shot in Afghanistan was nothing like being the focus of attention of all the OMC's in South East Queensland. His inventiveness gets the workout of a lifetime as he tries to stay one jump ahead of the bad guys as they form strange alliances to find him.

"This is Book 2 in the Firebird Series, and *Backpackers* leads us on another adventure with a maritime background. All the drama and action we have come to expect from Ian, we are left with just one question... when can we expect book three?"
—Alison Lewis, author of "Missing"

Praise for *Hitchhikers* (Book 1 of the Firebird Series)

"The hero, Harry, when asked what he has been doing lately, answers "Boats, bad guys, bullets and old friends." What he fails to add is — beautiful women, sex, a bad-ass black cat, and Bond type cunning to overcome the bad guys. Piqued your interest? This is a great fast paced read and I am looking forward to the next phase of Harry's life as promised by the author.
—Judith Flitcroft, Author of *Walk Back in Time*.

ALSO BY THE AUTHOR
IN THE FIREBIRD SERIES

An Eco-terrorist organisation formed with lofty ideals...a ratbag wealthy industrialist egomaniac...a plot to overturn the entire Australian political process...a major natural gas processing plant at risk...a giant crocodile...RAN patrol boats...an assassination contract targeting the PM. All the ingredients for a Firebird cocktail...definitely shaken, not stirred!

Book 3 in the *Firebird* series sees the Special Marine Strike Force (SMSF) head for the Pilbara to deliver their own special brand of mayhem and retribution on the bad guys.

ALSO BY THE AUTHOR
IN THE FIREBIRD SERIES

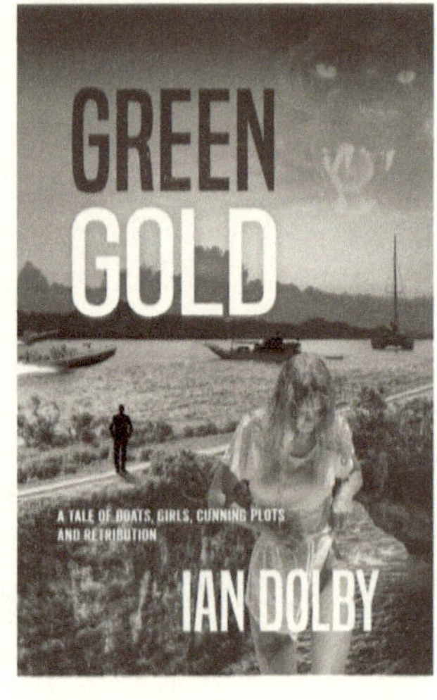

Driven by intense personal interest, including a shoulder with a bullet hole in it, Harry takes the Special Marine Strike Force across the Timor Sea to Indonesia in pursuit of the escaping Earth Care principals. Retribution and reward follow in the best Harry Stevens tradition, before the Strike Force take some well-deserved R&R and head for West Indonesia to keep their promise to their friends, Roger and Jill, in the search for the highly elusive and remarkable Green Gold.

Greedy islanders and pirates plying their age-old trade, do their best to complicate the process, but more treasure, along with the body count, keep piling up for the crews of the two boats, before some seized papers reveals details of an assassination plot against the Aussie PM and names the shadowy figures who were financing the EarthCare debacle!

Harry's not the only one with cunning plans - the special envoy who arrives to collect the papers comes up with a hare-brained scheme to safeguard the PM, but more strange alliances are formed as an old adversary unexpectedly re-surfaces.

A final round of havoc brews up that attracts Harry's particular brand of retribution, but who wins...who loses, and is the job really finished?